THE HOUSE OF MOURNING AND OTHER STORIES

The Urbana Free Library

To renew: call 217-367-4057
or go to *"urbanafreelibrary.org"*
and select "Renew/Request Items"

THE HOUSE OF MOURNING
MOURNING
AND OTHER
STORIES

DESMOND HOGAN

DALKEY ARCHIVE PRESS
CHAMPAIGN / LONDON / DUBLIN

First edition, 2013

"The Last Time," "The Mourning Thief," "Memories of Swinging London," "A Marriage in the Country," "Ties," "Miles," "Martyrs," "Winter Swimmers," "Caravans," "Pictures," and "Lark's Eggs" were first collected in *Lark's Eggs: New and Selected Stories*, published by the Lilliput Press, Dublin, 2005.

"Shelter," "Iowa," "Belle," "Little Friends," "Red Tide," "Sweet Majoram," "The Hare's Purse," "The House of Mourning," "Essex Skipper," and "Old Swords" were first collected in *Old Swords and Other Stories* published by the Lilliput Press, Dublin, 2009.

"Wooden Horse" originally appeared in *The Stinging Fly* 2:22, summer 2012.

Library of Congress Cataloging-in-Publication Data

Hogan, Desmond, 1951-
[Short stories. Selections]
The house of mourning and other stories / Desmond Hogan. -- First edition.
    pages ; cm.
ISBN 978-1-56478-855-9 (pbk. : acid-free paper)
I. Hogan, Desmond, 1951- Last time. II. Title.
PR6058.O346H68 2013
823'.914--dc23
2013005546

Partially funded by a grant from the Illinois Arts Council, a state agency

www.dalkeyarchive.com
Cover: design and composition by Mikhail Iliatov
Printed on permanent/durable acid-free paper

CONTENTS

The Last Time

The last time I saw him was in Ballinasloe station, 1953, his long figure hugged into a coat too big for him. Autumn was imminent; the sky grey, baleful. A few trees had become grey too; God, my heart ached. The tennis court beyond, silent now, the river close, half-shrouded in fog. And there he was, Jamesy, tired, knotted, the doctor's son who took me out to the pictures once, courted me in the narrow timber seats as horns played in a melodramatic forties film.

Jamesy had half the look of a mongol, half the look of an autistic child, blond hair parted like waves of water reeds, face salmon-colour, long, the shade and colour of autumnal drought. His father had a big white house on the perimeter of town—doors and windows painted as fresh as crocuses and lawns gloomy and yet blanched with perpetually new-mown grass.

In my girlhood I observed Jamesy as I walked with nuns and other orphans by his garden. I was an orphan in the local convent, our play-fields stretching by the river at the back of elegant houses where we watched the nice children of town, bankers' children, doctors' children, playing. Maria Mulcahy was my name. My mother, I was told in later years, was a Jean Harlow-type prostitute from the local terraces. 1, however, had hair of red which I admired in the mirror in the empty, virginal-smelling bathroom of the convent hall where we sat with children of doctors and bankers who had to pay three pence into the convent film show to watch people like Joan Crawford marry in bliss.

Jamesy was my first love, a distant love.

In his garden he'd be cutting hedges or reading books, a face on him like an interested hedgehog. The books were big and solemn looking—like himself. Books like *War and Peace,* I later discovered.

Jamesy was the bright boy though his father wanted him to do dentistry.

He was a problem child, it was well known. When I was seventeen I was sent to a draper's house to be a maid, and there I gathered information about Jamesy. The day he began singing 'Bye Bye Blackbird' in the church, saying afterwards he was singing it about his grandmother who'd taken a boat one day, sailed down the river until the boat crashed over a weir and the woman drowned. Another day he was found having run away, sleeping on a red bench by the river where later we wrote our names, sleeping with a pet fox, for foxes were abundant that year.

Jamesy and I met first in the fair green. I was wheeling a child and in a check shirt he was holding a rabbit. The green was spacious, like a desert. *Duel in the Sun* was showing in town and the feeling between us was one of summer and space, the grass rich and twisted like an old nun's hair.

He smiled crookedly.

I addressed him.

'I know you!' l was blatant, tough. He laughed.

'You're from the convent.'

'I'm working now!'

'Have a sweet!'

'I don't eat them. I'm watching my figure!'

'Hold the child!'

I lifted the baby out, rested her in his arms, took out a rug and sat down. Together we watched the day slip, the sun steadying. I talked about the convent and he spoke about *War and Peace* and an uncle who'd died in the Civil War, torn apart by horses, his arms tied to their hooves.

'He was buried with the poppies,' Jamesy said. And as though to remind us, there were sprays of poppies on the fair green, distant, distrustful.

'What age are you?'

'Seventeen! Do you see my rabbit?'

He gave it to me to hold. Dumb-bells, he called it. There was a fall of hair over his forehead and by bold impulse I took it and shook it fast.

There was a smile on his face like a pleased sheep. 'I'll meet you again,' I said as I left, pushing off the pram as though it held billy-cans rather than a baby.

There he was that summer, standing on the bridge by the prom, sitting on a park bench or pawing a jaded copy of Turgenev's *Fathers and Sons*.

He began lending me books and under the pillow I'd read Zola's *Nana* or a novel by Marie Corelli, or maybe poetry by Tennyson. There was always a moon that summer—or a very red sunset. Yet I rarely met him, just saw him. Our relationship was blindly educational, little else. There at the bridge, a central point, beside which both of us paused, at different times, peripherally. There was me, the pram, and he in a shirt that hung like a king's cloak, or on cold days—as such there often were—in a jumper which made him look like a polar bear.

'I hear you've got a good voice,' he told me one day.

'Who told you?'

'I heard.'

'Well, I'll sing you a song.' I sang 'Somewhere over the Rainbow,' which I'd learnt at the convent.

Again we were in the green. In the middle of singing the song I realized my brashness and also my years of loneliness, destitution, at the hands of nuns who barked and crowded about the statue of the Infant Jesus of Prague in the convent courtyard like seals on a rock. They hadn't been bad, the nuns. Neither had the other children been so bad. But God, what loneliness there'd been. There'd been one particular tree there, open like a complaint, where I spent a lot of time surveying the river and the reeds, waiting for pirates or for some beautiful lady straight out of a Veronica Lake movie to come sailing up the river. I began weeping in the green that day, weeping loudly. There was his face which I'll never forget. Jamesy's face changed from blank idiocy, local precociousness, to a sort of wild understanding.

He took my hand.

I leaned against his jumper; it was a fawn colour.

I clumsily clung to the fawn and he took me and I was aware of strands of hair, bleached by sun.

The Protestant church chimed five and I reckoned I should move, pushing the child ahead of me. The face of Jamesy Murphy became more intense that summer, his pink colour changing to brown. He looked like a pirate in one of the convent film shows, tanned, ravaged.

Yet our meetings were just as few and as autumn denuded the last of the cherry-coloured leaves from a particular house-front on the other side of town, Jamesy and I would meet by the river, in the park—briefly, each day, touching a new part of one another. An ankle, a finger, an ear lobe, something as ridiculous as that. I always had a child with me so it made things difficult.

Always too I had to hurry, often racing past closing shops.

There were Christmas trees outside a shop one day I noticed, so I decided Christmas was coming. Christmas was so unreal now, an event remembered from convent school, huge Christmas pudding and nuns crying. Always on Christmas Day nuns broke down crying, recalling perhaps a lost love or some broken-hearted mother in an Irish kitchen.

Jamesy was spending a year between finishing at school and his father goading him to do dentistry, reading books by Joyce now and Chekhov, and quoting to me one day—overlooking a garden of withered dahlias—Nijinsky's diaries. I took books from him about writers in exile from their countries, holding under my pillow novels by obscure Americans.

There were high clouds against a low sky that winter and the grotesque shapes of the Virgin in the alcove of the church, but against that monstrosity the romance was complete I reckon, an occasional mad moon, "Lili Marlene" on radio—memories of a war that had only grazed childhood—a peacock feather on an Ascendancy-type lady's hat.

'Do you see the way that woman's looking at us?' Jamesy said one day. Yes, she was looking at him as though he were a monster. His reputation was complete: a boy who was spoilt, daft, and an embarrassment to his parents. And there was I, a servant girl, talking to him. When she'd passed we embraced—lightly—and I went home, arranging to see him at the pictures the following night.

Always our meetings had occurred when I brushed past Jamesy with the pram. This was our first night out, seeing that Christmas was coming and that bells were tinkling on radio; we'd decided we'd be bold. I'd sneak out at eight o'clock, having pretended to go to bed. What really enticed me to ask Jamesy to bring me to the pictures was the fact that he was wearing a new Aran sweater and that I heard the film was partly set in Marrakesh, a place that had haunted me ever since I had read a book about where a heroine and two heroes met their fatal end in that city.

So things went as planned until the moment when Jamesy and I were in one another's arms when the woman for whom I worked came in, hauled me off. Next day I was brought before Sister Ignatius. She sat like a robot in the Spanish Inquisition. I was removed from the house in town and told I had to stay in the convent.

In time a job washing floors was found for me in Athlone, a neighbouring town to which I got a train every morning. The town was a drab one, replete with spires.

I scrubbed floors, my head wedged under heavy tables: sometimes I wept. There were Sacred Heart pictures to throw light on my predicament but even they were of no avail to me; religion was gone in a convent hush. Jamesy now was lost, looking out of a window I'd think of him but like the music of Glenn Miller he was past. His hair, his face, his madness I'd hardly touched, merely fondled like a floating ballerina.

It had been a mute performance—like a circus clown. There'd been something I wanted of Jamesy which I'd never reached; I couldn't put words or emotions to it but now from a desk in London, staring into a Battersea dawn, I see it was a womanly feeling. I wanted love.

'Maria, you haven't cleaned the lavatory.' So with a martyred air I cleaned the lavatory and my mind dwelt on Jamesy's pimples, ones he had for a week in September.

The mornings were drab and grey. I'd been working a year in Athlone, mind disconnected from body, when I learned Jamesy was studying dentistry in Dublin. There was a world of difference between us, a partition as deep as war and peace. Then one morning I saw him. I had a scarf on and a slight breeze was blowing and it was the aftermath of a sullen summer and he was returning to Dublin. He didn't look behind. He stared—almost at the tracks— like a fisherman at the sea.

I wanted to say something but my clothes were too drab; not the nice dresses of two years before, dresses I'd resurrected from nowhere with patterns of sea lions or some such thing on them.

'Jamesy Murphy, you're dead,' I said—my head reeled.

'Jamesy Murphy, you're dead.'

I travelled on the same train with him as far as Athlone. He went on to Dublin. We were in different carriages.

I suppose I decided that morning to take my things and move, so in a boat full of fat women bent on paradise I left Ireland.

I was nineteen and in love. In London through the auspices of the Sisters of Mercy in Camden Town I found work in a hotel where my red hair looked ravishing, sported over a blue uniform.

In time I met my mate, a handsome handy building contractor from Tipperary, whom I married—in the pleased absence of relatives—and with whom I lived in Clapham, raising children, he getting a hundred pounds a week, working seven days a week. My hair I carefully tended and wore heavy check shirts. We never went back to Ireland. In fact, we've never gone back to Ireland since I left, but occasionally, wheeling a child into the Battersea funfair, I was reminded of Jamesy, a particular strand of hair blowing across his face. Where was he? Where was the hurt and that face and the sensitivity? London was flooding with dark people and there at the beginning of the sixties I'd cross Chelsea bridge, walk my children up by Cheyne Walk, sometimes waiting to watch a candle lighting. Gradually it became more real to me that I loved him, that we were active within a certain sacrifice. Both of us had been bare and destitute when we met. The two of us had warded off total calamity, total loss. 'Jamesy!' His picture swooned; he was like a ravaged corpse in my head and the area between us opened; in Chelsea library I began reading books by Russian authors. I began loving him again. A snatch of Glenn Miller fell across the faded memory of colours in the rain, lights of the October fair week in Ballinasloe, Ireland.

The world was exploding with young people—protests against nuclear bombs were daily reported—but in me the nuclear area of the town where I'd worked returned to me.

Jamesy and I had been the marchers, Jamesy and I had been the protest! 'I like your face,' Jamesy once said to me. 'It looks like you could blow it away with a puff.'

In Chelsea library I smoked cigarettes though I wasn't supposed to. I read Chekhov's biography and Turgenev's biography—my husband minding the children—and tried to decipher an area of loss, a morning by the station, summer gone.

I never reached him; I just entertained him like as a child in an orphanage in the West of Ireland I had held a picture of Claudette Colbert under my pillow to remind me of glamour. The gulf between me and Jamesy narrows daily. I address him in a page of a novel, in a chip shop alone at night or here now, writing to you, I say something I never said before, something I've never written before.

I touch upon truth.

The Mourning Thief

Coming, through the black night he wondered what lay before him, a father lying dying. Christmas, midnight ceremonies in a church stood up like a gravestone, floods about his home.

With him were his wife and his friend Gerard. They needn't have come by boat but something purgatorial demanded it of Liam, the gulls that shot over like stars, the roxy music in the jukebox, the occasional Irish ballad rising in cherished defiance of the sea.

The night was soft, breezes intruded, plucking hair, thread living loose in many-coloured jerseys. Susan fell asleep once while Liam looked at Gerard. It was Gerard's first time in Ireland. Gerard's eyes were chestnut, his dark hair cropped like a monk's on a bottle of English brandy.

With his wife sleeping Liam could acknowledge the physical relationship that lay between them. It wasn't that Susan didn't know, but despite the truism of promiscuity in the school where they worked there still abided laws like the Old Testament God's, reserving carnality for smiles after dark.

A train to Galway, the Midlands frozen in.

Susan looked out like a Botticelli Venus, a little worried, often just vacuous. She was a music teacher, thus her mind was penetrated by the vibrations of Bach even if the place was a public lavatory or a Lyons café.

The red house at the end of the street; it looked cold, pushed away from the other houses. A river in flood lay behind. A woman, his mother, greeted him. He an only child, she soon to be a widow. But something disturbed Liam with excitement. Christmas candles still burned in this town.

His father lay in bed, still magically alive, white hair smeared on him like a dummy, that hard face that never forgave an enemy in the police force still on him. He was delighted to see Liam. At eighty-three he was a most ancient father, marrying late, begetting late, his wife fifteen years younger than him.

A train brushed the distance outside. Adolescence returned with a sudden start, the cold flurry of snow as the train in which he was travelling sped towards Dublin, the films about Russian winters.

Irish winters became Russian winters in turn and half of Liam's memories of adolescence were of the fantasized presence of Russia. Ikons, candles, streets agleam with snow.

'Still painting?'

'Still painting.' As though he could ever give it up. His father smiled as though he were about to grin. 'Well, we never made a policeman out of you.'

At ten, the day before he would have been inaugurated as a boy scout, Liam handed in his uniform. He always hated the colours of the Irish flag, mixing like the yolk in a bad egg.

It hadn't disappointed his father that he hadn't turned into a military man but his father preferred to hold on to a shred of prejudice against Liam's chosen profession, leaving momentarily aside one of his most cherished memories, visiting the National Gallery in Dublin once with his son, encountering the curator by accident and having the curator show them around, an old man who'd since died, leaving behind a batch of poems and a highly publicized relationship with an international writer.

But the sorest point, the point now neither would mention, was arguments about violence. At seventeen Liam walked the local hurling pitch with petitions against the war in Vietnam.

Liam's father's fame, apart from being a police inspector of note, was fighting in the GPO in 1916 and subsequently being arrested on the republican side in the Civil War. Liam was against violence, pure and simple. Nothing could convince him that 1916 was right. Nothing could convince him it was different from now, old women, young children, being blown to bits in Belfast.

Statues abounded in this house; in every nook and cranny was a statue, a statue of Mary, a statue of Joseph, an emblem perhaps of some saint Mrs Fogarthy had sweetly long forgotten.

This was the first thing Gerard noticed, and Susan who had seen this menagerie before was still surprised. 'It's like a holy statue farm.'

Gerard said it was like a holy statue museum. They were sitting by the fire, two days before Christmas. Mrs Fogarthy had gone to bed.

'It is a museum,' Liam said, 'all kinds of memories, curious sensations here, ghosts. The ghosts of Irish republicans, of policemen, military men, priests, the ghosts of Ireland.'

'Why ghosts?' Gerard asked.

'Because Ireland is dying,' Liam said.

Just then they heard his father cough.

Mr Fogarthy was slowly dying, cancer welling up in him. He was dying painfully and yet peacefully because he had a dedicated wife to look after him and a river in flood around, somehow calling Christ to mind, calling penance to mind, instilling a sense of winter in him that went back a long time, a river in flood around a limestone town.

Liam offered to cook the Christmas dinner but his mother scoffed him. He was a good cook, Susan vouched. Once Liam had cooked and his father had said he wouldn't give it to the dogs.

They walked, Liam, Susan, Gerard, in a town where women were hugged into coats like brown paper accidentally blown about them. They walked in the grounds of Liam's former school, once a Georgian estate, now beautiful, elegant still in the East Galway winter solstice.

There were Tinkers to be seen in the town, and English hippies behaving like Tinkers. Many turkeys were displayed, fatter than ever, festooned by holly.

Altogether one would notice prosperity everywhere, cars, shining clothes, modern fronts replacing the antique ones Liam recalled and pieced together from childhood.

But he would not forfeit England for his dull patch of Ireland, Southern England where he'd lived since he was twenty-two, Sussex, the trees plump as ripe pears, the rolling verdure, the odd delight of an Elizabethan cottage. He taught with Susan, with Gerard, in a free school. He taught children to paint. Susan taught them to play musical instruments. Gerard looked after younger children though he himself played a musical instrument, a cello.

Once Liam and Susan had journeyed to London to hear him play at St Martin-in-the-Fields, entertaining ladies who wore poppies in their lapels, as his recital coincided with Remembrance Day and paper poppies generated an explosion of remembrance.

Susan went to bed early now, complaining of fatigue, and Gerard and Liam were left with one another.

Though both were obviously male they were lovers, lovers in a tentative kind of way, occasionally sleeping with one another. It was still an experiment but for Liam held a matrix of adolescent fantasy. Though he married at twenty-two, his sexual fantasy from adolescence was always homosexual.

Susan could not complain. In fact it rather charmed her. She'd had more lovers since they'd married than fingers could count; Liam would always accost her with questions about their physicality; were they more satisfying than him?

But he knew he could count on her; tenderness between them had lasted six years now.

She was English, very much English. Gerard was English. Liam was left with this odd quarrel of Irishness. Memories of adolescence at boarding school, waking from horrific dreams nightly when he went to the window to throw himself out but couldn't because window sills were jammed.

His father had placed him at boarding school, to toughen him like meat.

Liam had not been toughened, chastened, ran away twice. At eighteen he left altogether, went to England, worked on a building site, put himself through college. He ended up in Sussex, losing a major part of his Irishness but retaining this, a knowledge when the weather was going to change, a premonition of all kinds of disasters and ironically an acceptance of the worst disasters of all, death, estrangement.

Now that his father was near death, old teachers, soldiers, policemen called, downing sherries, laughing rhetorically, sitting beside the bed covered by a quilt that looked like twenty inflated balloons.

Sometimes Liam, Susan, Gerard sat with these people, exchanging remarks about the weather, the fringe of politics or the world economic state generally.

Mrs Fogarthy swept up a lot. She dusted and danced around with a cloth as though she'd been doing this all her life, fretting and fiddling with the house.

Cars went by. Geese went by, clanking terribly. Rain came and church bells sounded from a disparate steeple.

Liam's father reminisced about 1916, recalling little incidents, fights with British soldiers, comrades dying in his arms, ladies fainting from hunger, escape to Mayo, later imprisonment in the Curragh during the Civil War. Liam said: 'Do you ever connect it with now, men, women, children being blown up, the La Mon Hotel bombing, Bessbrook killings, Birmingham, Bloody Friday? Do you ever think that the legends and the brilliance built from your revolution created this, death justified for death's sake, the stories in the classroom, the priests' stories, this language, this celebration of blood?'

Although Liam's father fought himself once, he belonged to those who deplored the present violence, seeing no connection. Liam saw the connection but disavowed both.

'Hooligans! Murderers!' Liam's father said,

Liam said, 'You were once a hooligan then.'

'We fought to set a majority free.'

'And created the spirit of violence in the new state. We were weaned on violence, me and others of my age. Not actual violence but always with a reference to violence. Violence was right, we were told in class. How can one blame those now who go out and plant bombs to kill old women when they were once told this was right?'

The dying man became angry. He didn't look at Liam, looked beyond him to the street.

'The men who fought in 1916 were heroes. Those who lay bombs in cafés are scum.'

Betrayed he was silent then, silent because his son accused him on his deathbed of unjustifiably resorting to bloodshed once. Now guns went off daily, in the far-off North. Where was the line between right and wrong? Who could say? An old man on his deathbed prayed that the guns he'd fired in 1916 had been for a right cause and in the words of his leader Patrick Pearse had not caused undue bloodshed.

On Christmas Eve the three young people and Mrs Fogarthy went to midnight mass in the local church. In fact it wasn't to the main church but a smaller one, situated on the outskirts of the town, protruding like a headstone.

A bald middle-aged priest greeted a packed congregation. The cemetery lay nearby, but one was unaware of it. Christmas candles and Christmas trees glowed in bungalows.

'O Come All Ye Faithful,' a choir of matchstick boys sang. Their dress was scarlet, scarlet of joy.

Afterwards Mrs Fogarthy penetrated the crib with a whisper of prayer.

Christmas morning, clean, spare, Liam was aware of estrangement from his father, that his father was ruminating on his words about violence, wondering were he and his ilk, the teachers, police, clergy of Ireland responsible for what was happening now, in the first place by nurturing the cult of violence, contributing to the actuality of it as expressed by young men in Belfast and London.

Sitting up on Christmas morning Mr Fogarthy stared ahead. There was a curiosity about his forehead. Was he guilty? Were those in high places guilty like his son said?

Christmas dinner; Gerard joked, Susan smiled, Mrs Fogarthy had a sheaf of joy. Liam tidied and somehow sherry elicited a chuckle and a song from Mrs Fogarthy. 'l Have Seen the Lark Soar High at Morn.' The song rose to the bedroom where her husband who'd had dinner in bed heard it.

The street outside was bare.

Gerard fetched a guitar and brought all to completion, Christmas, birth, festive eating, by a rendition of Bach's 'Jesu, Joy of Man's Desiring.'

Liam brought tea to his father. His father looked at him. ''Twas lovely music,' his father said with a sudden brogue, 'there was a Miss Hanratty who lived here before you were born who studied music at Heidelberg and could play Schumann in such a way as to bring tears to the cat's eyes. Poor soul, she died young, a member of the ladies' confraternity. Schumann was her favourite and Mendelssohn came after that. She played at our wedding, your mother's and mine. She played Mozart and afterwards in the hotel sang a song, what was it, oh yes, "The Star of the County Down".

'Such a sweetness she had in her voice too.

'But she was a bit of a loner and a bit lost here. Never too well really. She died maybe when you were a young lad.'

Reminiscences, names from the past. Catholic names, Protestant names, the names of boys in the rugby club, in the golf club. Protestant girls he'd danced with, nights at the October fair.

They came easily now, a simple jargon. Sometimes though the old man visibly stopped to consider his child's rebuke.

Liam gauged the sadness, wished he hadn't said anything, wanted to simplify it but knew it possessed all the simplicity it could have, a man on his deathbed in dreadful doubt.

Christmas night they visited the convent crib, Liam, Susan, Gerard, Mrs Fogtrthy, a place glowing with a red lamp.

Outside trees stood in silence, a mist thinking of enveloping them. The town lay in silence. At odd intervals one heard the gurgle of television but otherwise it could have been childhood, the fair green, space, emptiness, the rhythm, the dance of one's childhood dreams.

Liam spoke to his father that evening.

'Where I work we try to educate children differently from other places, teach them to develop and grow from within, try to direct them from the most natural point within them. There are many such schools now but ours, ours I think is special, run as a cooperative; we try to take children from all class backgrounds and begin at the beginning to redefine education.'

'And do you honestly think they'll be better educated children than you were, that the way we educated you was wrong?"

Liam paused.

'Well, it's an alternative.'

His father didn't respond, thinking of nationalistic, comradely Irish schoolteachers long ago. Nothing could convince him that the discipline of the old style of education wasn't better, grounding children in basic skills.

Silence somehow interrupted a conversation, darkness deep around them, the water of the floods shining, reflecting stars.

Liam said goodnight. Liam's father grunted. Susan already lay in bed. Liam got in beside her. They heard a bird let out a scream in the sky like a baby and they went asleep.

Gerard woke them in the morning, strumming a guitar.

St Stephen's Day, mummers stalked the street, children with blackened faces and a regalia of rags collecting for the wren. Music of a tin whistle came from a pub, the town coming to life. The river shone with sun.

Susan divined a child dressed like old King Cole, a crown on her head and her face blackened. Gerard was intrigued. They walked the town. Mrs Fogarthy had lunch ready. But Liam was worried, deeply worried. His father lay above, immersed in the past.

Liam had his past, too, always anxious in adolescence, running away to Dublin, eventually running away to England. The first times home had been odd; he noticed the solitariness of his parents. They'd needed him like they needed an ill-tended dog.

Susan and he had married in the local church. There'd been a contagion of aunts and uncles at the wedding. Mrs Fogarthy had prepared a meal. Salad and cake. The river had not been in flood then. In England he worked hard. Ireland could so easily be forgotten with the imprint of things creative, children's drawings, oak trees in blossom. Tudor cottages where young women in pinafores served tea and cakes home made and juiced with icing.

He'd had no children. But Gerard now was both a twin, a child, a lover to him. There were all kinds of possibility. Experiment was only beginning. Yet Ireland, Christmas, returned him to something, least of all the presence of death, more a proximity to the prom, empty laburnum pods and hawthorn trees naked and crouched with winter. Here he was at home with thoughts, thoughts of himself, of adolescence.

Here he made his own being like a doll on a miniature globe. He knew whence he came and if he wasn't sure where he was going, at least he wasn't distraught about it.

They walked with his mother that afternoon. Later an aunt came, preened for Christmas and the imminence of death. She enjoyed the tea, the knowledgeable silences, looked at Susan as though she was not from England but a far-off country, an Eastern country hidden in the mountains. Liam's father spoke to her not of 1916 but of policemen they'd known, irascible characters, forgetting that he had been the most irascible of all, a domineering man with a wizened face ordering his inferiors around.

He'd brought law. He'd brought order to the town. But he'd failed to bring trust. Maybe that's why his son had left.

Maybe that's why he was pondering the fate of the Irish revolution now, men with high foreheads who'd shaped the fate of the Irish Republic.

His thoughts brought him to killings now being done in the name of Ireland. There his thoughts floundered. From where arose this language of violence for the sake and convenience of violence?

Liam strode by the prom alone that evening, locked in a donkey jacket.

There were rings of light around distant electric poles.

He knew his father to be sitting up in bed; the policeman he'd been talking about earlier gone from his mind and his thoughts on 1916, on guns, and blazes, and rumination in prison cells long ago.

And long after that thoughts on the glorification of acts of violence, the minds of children caressed with the deeds of violence.

He'd be thinking of his son who fled and left the country.

His son now was thinking of the times he'd run away to Dublin, to the neon lights slitting the night, of the time he went to the river to throw himself in and didn't, of his final flight from Ireland.

He wanted to say something, urge a statement to birth that would unite father and son but couldn't think of anything to say. He stopped by a tree and looked to the river. An odd car went by towards Dublin.

Why this need to run? Even as he was thinking that, a saying of his father returned: 'Idleness is the thief of time.' That statement had been flayed upon him as a child but with time as he lived in England among fields of oak trees that statement had changed; time itself had become the culprit, the thief.

And the image of time as a thief was forever embroiled in a particular ikon of his father's, that of a pacifist who ran through Dublin helping the wounded in 1916, was arrested, was shot dead with a deaf and dumb youth. And that man, more than anybody, was Liam's hero, an Irish pacifist, a pacifist born of his father's revolution, a pacifist born of his father's state.

He returned home quickly, drew the door on his father. He sat down.

'Remember, Daddy, the story you told me about the pacifist shot dead in 1916 with a deaf and dumb youth, the man whose wife was a feminist?'

'Yes.'

'Well, I was just thinking that he's the sort of man we need now, one who comes from a revolution but understands it in a different way, a creative way, who understands that change isn't born from violence but intense and self-sacrificing acts.'

His father understood what he was saying, that there was a remnant of 1916 that was relevant and urgent now, that there had been at least one man among the men of 1916 who could speak to the present generation and show them that guns were not diamonds, that blood was precious, that birth most poignantly issues from restraint.

Liam went to bed. In the middle of the night he woke muttering to himself, 'May God have mercy on your soul,' although his father was not yet dead, but he wasn't asking God to have mercy on his father's soul but on the soul of Ireland, the many souls born out of his father's statelet, the women never pregnant, the cruel and violent priests, the young exiles, the old exiles, those who would never come back.

He got up, walked down the stairs, opened the door of his father's room. Inside his father lay. He wanted to see this with his own eyes, hope even in the persuasion of death.

He returned to bed.

His wife turned away from him but curiously that did not hurt him because he was thinking of the water rising, the moon on the water, and as he thought of these things the geese clanked over, throwing their reflections into the water grazed with moon which rimmed this town, the church towers, the slate roofs, those that slept now, those who didn't remember.

Memories of Swinging London

Why he went there he did not know, an instinctive feel for a dull
façade, an intuition borne out of time of a country unbeknownst to
him now but ten years ago one of excessive rain, old stone damaged
by time, and trees too green, too full.

He was drunk, of course, the night he stumbled in there at ten
o'clock. It had been three weeks since Marion had left him, three
weeks of drink, of moronic depression, three weeks of titillating
jokes with the boys at work.

Besides it had been raining that night and he'd needed shelter.

She was tired after a night's drama class when he met her, a small
nun making tea with a brown kettle.

Her garb was grey and short and she spoke with a distinctive
Kerry accent but yet a polish at variance with her accent.

She'd obviously been to an elocution class or two, Liam thought
cynically, until he perceived her face, weary, alone, a makeshift
expression of pain on it.

She'd filled that evening with her lesson, she said. Nothing had
happened, a half-dozen boys from Roscommon and Leitrim had left
the hall uninspired.

Then she looked at Liam as though wondering who she was
speaking to anyway, an Irish drunk, albeit a well-dressed one. In fact
he was particularly well dressed this evening, wearing a neatly cut
grey suit and a white shirt, spotless but for some dots of Guinness.

They talked with some reassurance when he was less drunk. He
sat back as she poured tea.

She was from Kerry she said, West Kerry. She'd been a few months
in Africa and a few months in the United States but this was her first
real assignment, other than a while as domestic science teacher in a
Kerry convent. Here she was all of nurse, domestic and teacher. She
taught young men from Mayo and Roscommon how to move; she
had become keen on drama while going to college in Dublin. She'd
pursued this interest while teaching domestic science in Kerry, an
occupation she was ill-qualified for, having studied English literature
in Dublin.

'I'm a kind of social worker,' she said, 'I'm given these lads to work with. They come here looking for something. I give them drama.'

She'd directed Eugene O'Neill in West Kerry, she'd directed Arthur Miller in West Kerry. She'd moulded young men there but a different kind of young men, bank clerks. Here she was landed with labourers, drunks.

'How did you come by this job?' Liam asked.

She looked at him, puzzled by his directness.

'They were looking for a suitable spot to put an ardent Sister of Mercy,' she said.

There was a lemon iced cake in a corner of the room and she caught his eye spying it and she asked him if he'd like some, apologizing for not offering him some earlier. She made quite a ceremony of cutting it, dishing it up on a blue-rimmed plate.

He picked at it.

'And you,' she said, 'what part of Ireland do you come from?'

He had to think about it for a moment. It had been so long. How could he tell her about limestone streets and dank trees? How could he convince her he wasn't lying when he spun yarns about an adolescence long gone?

'I come from Galway,' he said, 'from Ballinasloe.'

'My father used to go to the horse fair there,' she said. And then she was off again about Kerry and farms, until suddenly she realized it should be him that should be speaking.

She looked at him but he said nothing.

'Ten years.'

He was unforthcoming with answers.

The aftermath of drink had left his body and he was sitting as he had not sat for weeks, consuming tea, peaceful. In fact, when he thought of it, he hadn't been like this for years, sitting quietly, untortured by memories of Ireland but easy with them, memories of green and limestone grey.

She invited him back and he didn't come back for days. But as always in the case of two people who meet and genuinely like one another they were destined to meet again.

He saw her in Camden Town one evening, knew that his proclivity for Keats and Byron at school was somehow justified. She was

25

unrushed, carrying vegetables, asked him why he had not come. He told her he'd been intending to come, that he was going to come. She smiled. She had to go she said. She was firm.

Afterwards he drank, one pint of Guinness. He would go back, he told himself.

In fact it was as though he was led by some force of persuasion, easiness of language that existed between him and Sister Sarah, a lack of embarrassment at silence.

He took a bus from his part of Shepherd's Bush to Camden Town. Rain slashed, knifing the evening with black. The first instinct he had was to get a return bus but unnerved he went on.

Entering the centre the atmosphere was suddenly appropriated by music, Tchaikovsky, Swan Lake. He entered the hall to see a half -dozen young men in black jerseys, blue trousers, dying, quite genuinely like swans.

She saw him. He saw her. She didn't stop the procedure, merely acknowledged him and went on, her voice reverberating in the hall, to talk of movement, of the necessity to identify the real lines in one's body and flow with them.

Yes, he'd always recall that, 'the real lines in one's body.' When she had stopped talking she approached him. He stood there, aware that he was a stranger, not in a black jersey.

Then she wound up the night's procedure with more music, this time Beethoven, and the young men from Roscommon and Mayo behaved like constrained ballerinas as they simulated dusk.

Afterwards they spoke again. In the little kitchen.

'Dusk is a word for balance between night and day,' she said. 'I asked them to be relaxed, to be aware of time flowing through them.'

The little nun had an errand to make.

Alone, there, Liam smoked a cigarette. He thought of Marion, his wife gone north to Leeds, fatigued with him, with marriage, with the odd affair. She had worked as a receptionist in a theatre.

She'd given up her job, gone home to Mummy, left the big city for the northern smoke. In short her marriage had ended.

Looking at the litter bin Liam realized how much closer to accepting this fact he'd come. Somehow he'd once thought marriage to be for life but here it was, one marriage dissolved and nights to fill, a body to shelter, a life to lead.

A young man with curly blond hair entered. He was looking for Sister Sarah. He stopped when he saw Liam, taken aback. These boys were like a special battalion of guards in their black jerseys. He was an intruder, cool, English almost, his face, his features relaxed, not rough or ruddy. The young man said he was from Roscommon. That was near Liam's home.

He spoke of farms, of pigs, said he'd had to leave, come to the city, search for neon. Now he'd found it. He'd never go back to the country. He was happy here, big city, many people, a dirty river and a population of people that included all races.

'I miss the dances though,' the boy said, 'the dances of Sunday nights. There's nothing like them in London, the cars all pulled up and the ballroom jiving with music by Big Tom and the Mainliners. You miss them in London but there are other things that compensate.'

When asked by Liam what compensated most for the loss of fresh Sunday night dancehalls amid green fields the boy said, 'The freedom.'

Sister Sarah entered, smiled at the boy, sat down with Liam. The boy questioned her about a play they were intending to do and left, turning around to smile at Liam.

Sarah—her name came to him without the prefix now—spoke about the necessity of drama in schools, in education.

'It is a liberating force,' she said. 'It brings out—' she paused '—the swallow in people.'

And they both laughed, amused and gratified at the absurdity of the description.

Afterwards he perceived her in a hallway alone, a nun in a short outfit, considering the after-effects of her words that evening, pausing before plunging the place into darkness.

He told her he would return and this time he did, sitting among boys from Roscommon and Tipperary, improvising situations. She called on him to be a soldier returning from war and this he did, embarrassedly, recalling that he too was a soldier once, a boy outside a barracks in Ireland, beside a bed of crocuses. People sintled at his shattered innocence, at this attempt at improvisation. Sister Sarah reserved a smile. In the middle of a simulated march he stopped.

'I can't. I can't,' he said.

People smiled, let him be.

He walked to the bus stop, alone. Rain was edging him in, winter was coming. It hurt with its severity tonight. He passed a sex shop, neon light dancing over the instruments in the window. The pornographic smile of a British comedian looked out from a newsagent's.

He got his bus.

Sleep took him in Shepherd's Bush. He dreamt of a school long ago in County Galway which he attended for a few years, urns standing about the remains of a Georgian past.

At work people noticed he was changing. They noticed a greater serenity. An easiness about the way he was holding a cup. They virtually chastised him for it.

Martha McPherson looked at him, said sarcastically, 'You look hopeful.'

He was thinking of Keats in the canteen when she spoke to him, of words long ago, phrases from mouldering books at school at the beginning of autumn.

His flat was tidier now; there was a space for books that had not hitherto been there. He began a letter home, stopped, couldn't envisage his mother, old woman by a sea of bog.

Sister Sarah announced plans for a play they would perform at Christmas. The play would be improvised, bit by bit, and she asked for suggestions about the content.

One boy from Leitrim said, 'Let's have a play about the Tinkers.'

Liam was cast for a part as Tinker king and bit by bit over the weeks he tried, tried to push off shyness, act out little scenes.

People laughed at him. He felt humiliated, twisted inside. Yet he went on.

His face was moulding, clearer than before, and in his eyes was a piercing darkness. He made speeches, trying to recall the way the Tinkers spoke at home, long lines of them on winter evenings, camps in country lanes, smoke rising as a sun set over distant steeples.

He spoke less to colleagues, more to himself, phrasing and rephrasing old questions, wondering why he had left Ireland in the first place, a boy, sixteen, lonely, very lonely on a boat making its way through a winter night.

'I suppose I left Ireland,' he told Sister Sarah one night, 'because I felt ineffectual, totally ineffectual. The priests at school despised my independence. My mother worked as a char. My father was dead. I was a mature youngster who liked women, had one friend at school, a boy who wrote poetry.

'I came to England seeking reasons for living. I stayed with my older brother who worked in a factory.

'My first week in England a Greek homosexual who lived upstairs asked me to sleep with him. That ended my innocence. I grew up somewhere around then, became adult very, very young.'

1966, the year he left Ireland.

Sonny and Cher sang 'I Got You, Babe.'

London was readying itself for blossoming, the Swinging Sixties had attuned themselves to Carnaby Street, to discotheques, to parks. Ties looked like huge flowers, young hippies sat in parks. And in 1967, the year *Sergeant Pepper's Lonely Hearts Club Band* appeared, a generation of young men and horned-rimmed glasses looking like John Lennon. 'It was like a party,' Liam said, 'a continual party. I ate, drank at this feast.

'Then I met Marion. We married in 1969, the year Brian Jones died. I suppose we spent our honeymoon at his funeral. Or at least in Hyde Park where Mick Jagger read a poem in commemoration of him. "Peace, peace! he is not dead, he doth not sleep!"'

Sister Sarah smiled. She obviously liked romantic poetry too, she didn't say anything, just looked at him, with a long slow smile. 'I understand,' she said, though what she was referring to he didn't know.

Images came clearer now, Ireland, the forty steps at school, remnants of a Georgian past, early mistresses, most of all the poems of Keats and Shelley.

Apart from the priests, there had been things about school he'd enjoyed, the images in poems, the celebration of love and laughter by Keats and Shelley, the excitement at finding a new poem in a book.

She didn't say much to him these days, just looked at him. He was beginning to fall into place, to be whole in this environment of rough and ready young men.

Somehow she had seduced him.

He wore clean, cool, casual white shirts now, looked faraway at work, hair drifting over his forehead as in adolescence. Someone noticed his clear blue eyes and remarked on them, Irish eyes, and he knew this identification as Irish had not been so absolute for years.

' "They came like swallows and like swallows went," ' Sister Sarah quoted one evening. It was a fragment from a poem by Yeats, referring to Coole Park, a place not far from Liam's home, where the legendary Irish writers convened, Yeats, Synge, Lady Gregory, O'Casey, a host of others, leaving their mark in a place of growth, of bark, of spindly virgin trees. And in a way now Liam associated himself with this horde of shadowy and evasive figures; he was Irish. For that reason alone he had strength now. He came from a country vilified in England but one which, generation after generation, had produced genius, and observation of an extraordinary kind.

Sister Sarah made people do extraordinary things, dance, sing, boys dress as girls, grown men jump over one another like children. She had Liam festoon himself in old clothes, with paper flowers in his hat.

The story of the play ran like this:

Two Tinker families are warring. A boy from one falls in love with a girl from the other. They run away and are pursued by Liam who plays King of the Tinkers. He eventually finds them but they kill themselves rather than part and are buried with the King of the Tinkers making a speech about man's greed and folly.

No one questioned that it was too mournful a play for Christmas; there were many funny scenes, wakes, fights, horse-stealing and the final speech, words of which flowed from Liam's mouth, had a beauty, an elegance which made young men from Roscommon who were accustomed to hefty Irish showband singers stop and be amazed at the beauty of language.

Towards the night the play was to run Sister Sarah became a little irritated, a little tired. She'd been working too hard, teaching during the day. She didn't talk to Liam much and he felt hurt and disorganized. He didn't turn up for rehearsal for two nights running. He rang and said he was ill.

He threw a party. All his former friends arrived and Marion's friends. The flat churned with people. Records smashed against the night. People danced. Liam wore an open-neck collarless white shirt. A silver cross was dangling, one picked up from a craft shop in Cornwall.

In the course of the party a girl became very, very drunk and began weeping about an abortion she'd had. She sat in the middle of the floor, crying uproariously, awaiting the arrival of someone.

Eventually, Liam moved towards her, took her in his arms, offered her a cup of tea. She quietened. 'Thank you,' she said simply.

The crowds went home. Bottles were left everywhere. Liam took his coat, walked to an all-night café and, as he didn't have to work, watched the dawn come.

She didn't chastise him. Things went on as normal. He played his part, dressed in ridiculous clothes. Sister Sarah was in a lighter mood. She drank a sherry with Liam one evening, one cold December evening. As it was coming near Christmas she spoke of festivity in Kerry. Crossroad dances in Dún Caoin, the mirth of Kerry that had never died. She told Liam how her father would take her by car to church on Easter Sunday, how they'd watch the waters being blessed and later dance at the crossroads, melodious playing and the Irish fiddle.

There had been nothing like that in Liam's youth. He'd come from the Midlands, dull green, statues of Mary outside factories. He'd been privileged to know defeat from an early age.

'You should go to Kerry some time,' Sister Sarah said.

'I'd like to,' Liam said, 'I'd like to. But it's too late now.'

Yet when the musicians came to rehearse the music Liam knew it was not too late. He may have missed the West of Ireland in his youth, the simplicity of a Gaelic people but here now in London, melodious exploding, he was in an Ireland he'd never known, the extreme west, gullies, caves, peninsulas, roads winding into desecrated hills and clouds always coming in. Imagine, he thought, I've never even seen the sea.

He told her one night about the fiftieth anniversary of the 1916 revolution, which had occurred before he left, old priests at school fumbling with words about dead heroes, bedraggled tricolours flying over the school and young priests, beautiful in the extreme, reciting the poetry of Patrick Pearse.

'When the bombs came in England,' Liam said, 'and we were blamed, the ordinary Irish working people, I knew they were to blame, those priests, the people who lied about glorious deeds. Violence is never, ever glorious.'

He met her in a café for coffee one day and she laughed and said it was almost like having an affair. She said she'd once fancied a boy in Kerry, a boy she was directing in *All My Sons*. He had bushy blond hair, kept Renoir reproductions on his wall, was a bank clerk. 'But he went off with another girl,' she said, 'and broke my heart.'

He met her in Soho Square Gardens one day and they walked together. She spoke of Africa and the States, travelling, the mission of the modern church, the redemption of souls lost in a mire of nonchalance. On Tottenham Court Road she said goodbye to him.

'See you next rehearsal,' she said.

He stood there when she left and wanted to tell her she'd awakened in him a desire for a country long forgotten, an awareness of another side of that country, music, drama, levity but there was no saying these things.

When the night of the play finally arrived he acted his part well. But all the time, all the time he kept an eye out for her.

Afterwards there were celebrations, balloons dancing, Irish bankers getting drunk. He sat and waited for her to come to him and when she didn't, rose and looked for her.

She was speaking to an elderly Irish labourer.

He stood there, patiently, for a moment. He wanted her to tell him about Christmas lights in Ireland long ago, about the music of Ó Riada and the southern-going whales. But she persevered in speaking to this old man about Christmas in Kerry.

Eventually he danced with her. She held his arm softly. He knew now he was in love with her and didn't know how to put it to her. She left him and talked to some other people.

Later she danced again with him. It was as though she saw something in his eyes, something forbidding.

'I have to go now,' she said as the music still played. She touched his arm gently, moved away. His eyes searched for her afterwards but couldn't find her. Young men he'd acted with came up and started clapping him on the back. They joked and they laughed. Suddenly Liam found he was getting sick. He didn't make for the lavatory. He went instead to the street. There he vomited. It was raining. He got very wet going home.

At Christmas he went to midnight mass in Westminster Cathedral, a thing he had never done before. He stood with women in mink coats and Irish charwomen as the choir sang 'Come All Ye Faithful.' He had Christmas with an old aunt and at midday rang Marion. They didn't say much to one another that day but after Christmas she came to see him.

One evening they slept together. They made love as they had not for years, he entering her deeply, resonantly, thinking of Galway long ago, a river where they swam as children.

She stayed after Christmas. They were more subdued with one another. Marion was pregnant. She worked for a while and when her pregnancy became too obvious she ceased working.

She walked a lot. He wondered at a woman, his wife, how he hadn't noticed before how beautiful she looked. They were passing Camden Town one day when he recalled a nun he'd once known. He told Marion about her, asked her to enter with him, went in a door, asked for Sister Sarah.

Someone he didn't recognize told him she'd gone to Nigeria, that she'd chosen the African sun to boys in black jerseys. He wanted to follow her for one blind moment, to tell her that people like her were too rare to be lost but knew no words of his would convince her. He took his wife's hand and went about his life, quieter than he had been before.

A Marriage in the Country

She burned down half her house early that summer and killed her husband. He'd been caught upstairs. It was something she'd often threatened to do, burn the house down, and when she did it she did it quietly, in a moment of silent, reflective despair. She had not known he'd been upstairs. She'd put a broom in the stove and then tarred the walls with the fire. The flames had quickly explored the narrow stairway. A man, twenty years older than her, had been burned alive, caught when snoozing. Magella at his funeral seemed charred herself, her black hair, her pale, almost sucrose skin. She'd stooped, in numbed penitence. There was a nebulous, almost incandesced way her black curls took form from her forehead as there was about all the Scully girls. They made an odd band of women there, all the Scully girls, most of them respectably married. Magella was the one who'd married a dozy publican whose passion in life had been genealogy and whose ambition seemed incapacitated by this passion. She'd had a daughter by him. Gráinne. That girl was taken from her that summer and sent to relatives in Belfast. Magella was not interned in a mental hospital. The house was renovated. The pub reopened. People supposed that the shock of what she'd done had cured her and in a genuinely solicitous way they thought that working in the pub, chattering to the customers, would be better for her than an internment in a mental hospital. Anyway there was something very final about internment in a mental hospital at that time in Ireland. They gave her a reprieve. At the end of that summer Boris came to the village.

Stacks of hay were piled up in the fields near the newly opened garage outside the village which he came to manage, little juggling acts of hay in merrily rolling and intently bound fields. All was smallness and precision here. This was Laois. An Ascendancy demesne. The garage was on the top of a hill where the one, real, village street ended, and located at a point where the fields seemed about to deluge the road. The one loss of sobriety in the landscape and heaviness and a very minor one. Boris began his career as garage manager by, putting up flags outside the garage, and bunting, an

American, an Italian, a French, a Spanish, a German and an Irish flag. He was half-Russian and he'd been raised in an orphanage in County Wexford in the south-eastern tip of Ireland.

Boris Cleary was thin, nervously thin, black-haired, a blackness smoothing the parts of his face which he'd shaved and the very first thing Magella noticed about him, on coming close, under the bunting, was that there was a smell from the back of his neck, as from wild flowers lost in the deep woods which lay in the immediate surroundings of the village. A rancid, asking smell. A smell which asked you to investigate its bearer. Magella, drawn by the rancid smell from the back of a nervous, thin neck, sought further details. She asked Boris about his Russianness which was already, after a few weeks, a rampant legend, over her counter. His father had been a Russian sailor, his mother a Wexford prostitute; he'd been dumped on the Sisters of Mercy. They had christened him and one particular nun had reared him, cackling all the time at this international irony, calling him 'little Stalin.' Boris had emerged, his being, his presence in the world, had emerged from an inchoate night on a ship in the port of Wexford Town.

How a September night, the last light like neon on the gold of the cornfields, led so rapidly to the woods partly surrounding the village they later lost track of; winter conversations in the pub, glasses of whiskey, eventually glasses of whiskey shared, both their mouths going to a glass, like a competition—a series of reciprocal challenges. Eventually, all the customers gone one night as they tended to be gone when Magella and Boris got involved in conversation, their lips met. An older woman, ascribed a demon by some, began having an affair with a young, slackly put-together man.

The woods in early summer were the culminative platform for their affair. These woods that were in fact a kind of garden for bygone estates. Always in the woods, oases, you'd find a garden house—a piece of concrete—a Presbyterian, a Methodist, a Church of Ireland chapel. Much prayer had been done on these estates. Laois had particularly been a county in bondage. Now rhododendrons fulminated and frothed all over the place. And there were berries to admire, right from the beginning of the summer. They found a particular summer house where they made love on the cold, hard, almost penitential floor and soon this was the only place where they made love, their refuge.

In September, just over a year after Boris had come to the village, they got a taxi and visited Magella's daughter in Belfast. She lived off the Falls Road, in a house beside a huge advertisement on a railway bridge for the *Irish Independent*. Gráinne dressed in an odious brown convent uniform. She had long black hair. She looked at Boris. From the look in her eyes Magella afterwards realized she'd fallen in love with Boris at that meeting.

What were they flaunting an affair for? At first they were flaunting it so openly no one believed it was happening. Such things didn't happen in Laois in the 1950s. People presumed that the young Russian had taken a priestly interest in the older possessed woman. And when they brought their affair to Belfast, Boris in a very natty dark suit and in a tie of shining dark blue, a gaggle of relatives thought that there was something comic going on, that Magella had got a clown to chaperone her and prevent her from acts of murderous madness. They brought glasses of orange onto the street for the pair—it was a very sunny day—and oddly enough there was a spark of bunting on the street, the ordination of a local priest recently celebrated. A bulbous-cheeked, Amazon-breasted woman spluttered out a comment: 'Sure he reminds me of the King of England.' She was referring to the King who'd resigned, the only member of royalty respected in nationalist Belfast.

But behind the screen of all the presumptions—and it was a kind of smokescreen—something very intense, very carnal, very complex was going on. Magella was discovering her flesh for the first time and Boris was in a way discovering a mother. She'd always been the licentious one in her family but flailing her flesh around cornfields at night when she'd been young brought her no real pleasure. In the carnality, in love-making now, she'd found lost worlds of youth and lost—yes, inchoate—worlds of Russia. She was able to travel to Boris's origins and locate a very particular house. It was a house in a wood away from the dangers of the time. In this house she put Boris's forebears. In this house, in her sexual fantasies, she made love to Boris, his forebears gone and only they, random lovers, left in it, away from the dangers and the onslaught of the time. There was a tumultuous excitement about being lovers in a house in a wood with many dangers outside the borders of that wood. There was a titillation, a daring, and even a brusqueness about it. But those dangers eventually slipped their moorings in the world outside the wood.

Early in the second summer of their affair someone saw them making love in the summer house. A little boy. Tremulous though he later was about the event he was matter of fact enough to wait for a good view of Magella's heavy white thighs. He was the butcher's son. A picture was soon contrived all over the village, Magella and Boris in an act of love that had a Bolshevik ferocity. Killing your husband was one thing but making love to a young Russian was another. Within the month Magella was in a mental hospital.

The funny thing was that she'd had a premonition that all this was going to happen some weeks before the little boy saw them. Fondling some budding elderberries in the woods she remarked to Boris, looking back at the visible passage they'd made through the woods, that they, she and he, reminded her of the legendary Irish lovers, Diarmaid and Gráinne, who'd fled a king into the woods, feeding on berries. They'd invested Irish berries with a sense of doomed carnality, the berries which had sustained them, right down to the last morsels of late autumn. Here in these woods many of the berries had been sown as parts of gardens and it was difficult to distinguish the wild berries from the descendants of a Protestant bush—the loganberry, redcurrant, raspberry. These woods had been a testing ground for horticulture and parts of the woods had been cultivated at random, leaving a bed of mesmeric flowers, an apple tree among the wildness. Diarmaid and Gráinne would have had a ball here, Magella said. But for her and Boris the climate was already late autumn when the trees were withered of berries. Their days were up. She remembered the chill she'd felt at national school when the teacher had come to that part of the story of Diarmaid and Gráinne, reading it from a book which had an orange cover luminous as warm blood.

Boris tried to call on her in the mental hospital. He was wearing a suit. But there was a kind of consternation among nuns and nurses when they saw him—they weren't sure what to do—he stood, shouldering criminality, for a few minutes in the waiting room and then he turned on his heels and left. But there was a despatch from his childhood here. A statue of a frigid white Virgin as there'd been in the lounge of the orphanage. Magella had entered the house, all grey and fragmented with statues of Mary like falling crusts of snowflakes, of his childhood.

The years went by and the garage prospered. Gráinne came down from Belfast, having graduated from the convent. Her keen eye on Boris at their first meeting in Belfast led now, after all these years, to a romance. There'd been an unmitigated passion in between. Gráinne started walking out the roads with Boris, her hair cut short and the dresses of a middle-aged woman on her, dour, brown, her figure too becoming somewhat lumpy and, in a middle-aged way, becoming acquiescent. She was very soon linking Boris's arm. She and Boris went to see her mother who sat in a room in the mental hospital, a very quiet Rapunzel but without the long, golden hair of course. Boris, armed with Magella's daughter, was allowed in now. He approached Magella, who was seated, as if there'd been no carnality between them, as if he couldn't remember it, as though this woman was his mother and had been in a mother relationship with him. The affair with her, memory of it, had, in this Catholic village, evacuated his mind. Beside Gráinne he looked like a businessman, as someone who'd been operated on and had his aura of passion removed. He drooped, a lazily held puppet. There was a complete change in him, a complete reorganization of the state of his being, a change commensurate with collectivization in Stalinist Russia. Only very tiny shards of his former being remained, littered on the railway tracks of it, the thoroughfare of it. He didn't so much deny Magella as hurt her with an impotent perception of her. At the core of her love-making with him there'd been a child searching for his mother and now, the memory of passion gone, there was only the truth of his findings. A mother. The mother of a weedy son at that. The rancid smell at the back of his neck had turned to a sickly-sweet one. But Magella still ached for the person who would be revived as soon as she got her hands on Boris again. That person tremored somewhere inside Boris, at the terribleness of her abillty.

The romance between Boris and Gráinne lapsed and Gráinne went off to work in a beauty parlour in Bradford where relatives of her father lived. A few months after her departure, Boris—there'd been tiffs between them—repented of his irascibility in the weeks before her decision to leave and he went looking for her. He ended up beside a slime heap in Bradford, a house beside a slime heap, exiled Irish people. The beauty parlour was a few streets away. People in Bradford called Boris Paddy which further confused his sense of identity and he went home without resolving things with Gráinne to find Magella out of the mental hospital and having reopened the pub which Gráinne had tentatively opened for a while. Everything was ripe for a confrontation between them but Magella kept a quietness, even a dormancy in that pub for months until one night she raged out to the arage, wielding a broom, a like instrument to that of her husband's death. He met her at the door of his little house alongside the garage that was closed for the night. 'You scut,' she said, 'You took two dogs from me once and never gave them back.' True, Boris had taken two ginger-coloured, chalk cocker spaniels for his mantelpiece on the condition he'd return them when he found something suitable for the mantelpiece himself. 'I want them back,' she said. He let her in. The dogs were there. She stood in front of him, not looking at the dogs. Where there had been black hair there was now mainly a smoke of grey. She stood in front of him, silently, broom inoffensively by her side, as if to show him the wreck of her being, a wreck caused by involvement with him. 'Come down for a drink some night,' she said and quietly went off.

He did go down for a drink in her pub. He fiddled with drinks on the counter. Then Gráinne came back and Magella burned the whole house down, everything, leaving only a charred wreck of a house. She was put back into the mental hospital. There'd been no money left in the bank. Everything was squandered now and everything had been amiss anyway before Magella had burned the house down. Maybe that's why she'd burned the house down. But this wreck, this cavity in the street was her statement. It was her statement before Boris and Gráinne announced plans for marriage.

What Gráinne did not know when she was earnestly proposed marriage to was that Boris and Magella had slipped away together for a honeymoon of their own in Bray, County Wicklow, the previous June. They stayed in a cascade of a hotel by the sea. The mountains,

Bray Head, were frills on the sea. The days were very blue. Women walked dogs, desultory Russian émigrés in pinks, purples, with hats pushed down over their ears. You never saw their faces. Boris and Magella slept in the same room but in separate beds. There were rhododendrons on hills just over Bray and among the walks on those hills. Boris explained to Magella that she was the real woman in his life, at first a carnal one, then a purified, sublimated one. She'd been the one he'd been looking for. It was difficult for Magella to take this, that physical love was over in her life, but there was affirmation with the pain when she eventually burned down the house, on hearing of Boris's imminent marriage to Gráinne. She'd achieved something.

In Bray before they used to go to sleep Boris would light a candle in the room and sit up in bed thinking. 'What are you thinking of?' she asked. But he'd never answered. Nuns in Wexford, gulls streaming over an orphanage, poised to drop for crusts of bread on a grey playing area, sailors on the sea, migrations on foot by railroads in Russia, heavy sun on people in rags, a grandmother pulling a child by the hand, the only remaining member of her family.

'You've got to go through one thing to get to the other,' Boris said sagely as he sat up in bed one night, the lights still on, impeccable pyjamas of navy and white stripes on him which revealed a bush of the acrid black hair on his chest, he staring ahead, zombie-like.

In this statement he'd meant he'd gone through physical love with Magella to fish up a dolorous, muted ikon of a Virgin, of the untouchable but all-protecting woman. To get this holy protection from a woman you had to make her untouchable, sacred. For the rest of his life Magella would provide the source of sanity, of resolve, of belief in his life. She was the woman who'd rescued him from the inchoate Wexford night.

Magella was, of course, pleased to hear this but still restive. She did not sleep well that night. She longed, despite that statement, to have Boris, his nimble legs and arms, his pale well of a crotch, in her bed.

The marriage took place in July the following year. There was a crossroads dance the night before a mile or two outside the village. Rare enough in Ireland at that time, even in West Kerry and in Connemara, they still happened in this backwater of County Laois.

People stepped out beside a few items of a funfair, a few coloured lights strung up. An epic, a tumultous smell of corn came from the fields. A melodion played the tune 'Slievenamon.' 'My love, o my love, will I ne'er see you again, in the valley of Slievenamon?' Lovers sauntered through the corn. Magella was packing her things in the mental hospital to attend the wedding the following day.

On their second last day in Bray, by the sea, he'd suddenly hugged her and she saw all the mirth again in his face and all the dark in his hair. An old man nearby, his eye on them, quickly wound up a machine to play some music. There was a picture of Sorrento on a funfair caravan, pale blue lines on the yellow ochre caravan, cartoon Italian mountains, cartoon-packed Italian houses, cartoon operatic waves. Magella had looked to the sea, beyond the straggled funfair, and seen the blue in the sea which was tangible, which was ecstatic.

Magella danced with Boris at the wedding reception. She was wearing a brown suit and a brown hat lent to her by her sister in Tihelly, County Offaly. She looked like an alcoholic beverage, an Irish cream liqueur. Or so a little boy who'd come to the wedding thought. She danced with him in a room where ten-pound notes, twenty-pound notes and, of course, many five-pound notes were pinned on the walls as was the custom at weddings in Ireland. The little boy had come a long way that morning. His granny, on the other side of his family, whom he called on on the way, in her little house, had given him a box of chocolates that looked like a navy limousine. He still had it now as he watched Boris and Magella dance, the couple, a serenity between them, an understanding. They'd been looking for different things from one another, their paths had crossed, they'd gone different ways but in this moment they created a total communion, a total marriage, an understanding that only a child could intuit and carry away with him, enlightened, the notes on the walls becoming Russian notes with pictures of Tsars and dictators and people who'd changed epochs on them, the walls burning in a terrible fire in the child's mind until only a note or two was left, a face or two, sole reminders of an enraptured moment in history.

At such moments the imagination begins and someone else, someone who did not live through the events, remembers and, later, counts the pain.

A little boy walked away from the wedding, box of chocolates still under his arm, not wanting to look back at the point where a woman was dragged away, screaming, at a certain hour, to a solitary room in a mental hospital.

Years later he returned, long after Magella's death in the mental hospital, to the woods, at the time of year when rhododendrons spread there. He bent and picked up a decapitated tiara of rhododendron. There was a poster for Paris in the village, a Chinese restaurant run by a South Korean, a late night fish-and-chip takeaway. The garage was still open at the top of the village. The only change was that Boris had put up a Russian flag among the others. It was his showpiece. He'd gotten it from the Legion of Mary in Kilkenny who'd put on a show about imprisoned cardinals behind the Iron Curtain. But it was his pride. It demonstrated, apart from his roots, the true internationalism of the garage. There were no boundaries here. A bald man, lots of children scampering around him for years, would come out to fill your car and his face would tell you these things, a brown, anaemic work coat on him, a prosperous but also somewhat cowed grin on his face.

At her funeral in 1959 Boris had carried lilies, and there, in the graveyard, thought of his visit to Bradford, the exiled Irish there, a cowed, depressed people, the legacy of history, and of the woman who'd tried to overthrow that legacy, for a while. He'd put the lilies on the grave, Magella's lover, no one denying that day the exact place of the grief in his heart.

Everybody walked away except the boy and Boris and then Boris walked away, but first looking at the boy, almost in annoyance, as if to say, you have no right to intrude on these things, flashing back his black hair and throwing a boyish, almost a rival's look from his black eyes that were scarred and vinegary and blazingly alive from tears. In those eyes was the wound, the secret, and the boy looked at it, unreproached by it.

Years later he returned to find that there was no museum to that wound, only a few brightly painted houses, a ramshackle cramming of modernity. He took his car and drove out by the garage and the bunting and the flags to the fields where you could smell the first, premature coming of the epic, all-consuming, wound-oblivionizing harvest.

Our mad aunts, the young man thought, our mad selves.

Lady of Laois, ikon from this incumbent, serf-less, but none the less, I expect, totally Russian storybook blinding harvest, pray for the night-sea, neon spin-drift, jukebox-beacon café wanderer.

Ties

1

The Forty Steps led nowhere. They were grey and wide, shadowed at the sides by creeper and bush. In fact it was officially declared by Patsy Fogarthy that there were forty-four steps. These steps were erected by an English landlord in memorial to some doubtful subject. A greyhound, a wife? If you climbed them you had a view of the recesses of the woods and the places where Patsy Fogarthy practised with his trombone. Besides playing—in a navy uniform—in the brass band Patsy Fogarthy was my father's shop assistant. While the steps were dark grey the counter in my father's shop was dark and fathomless. We lived where the town men's Protestant society had once been and that was where our shop was too. And still is. Despite the fact my father is dead. My father bought the house, built the shop from nothing—after a row with a brother with whom he shared the traditional family grocery-cum-bar business. Patsy Fogartliy was my father's first shop assistant. They navigated waters together. They sold silk ties, demonstrating them carefully to country farmers.

Patsy Fogarthy was from the country, had a tremendous welter of tragedy in his family—which always was a point of distinction —deranged aunts, a paralysed mother. We knew that Patsy's house— cottage—was in the country. We never went there. It was just a picture. And in the cottage in turn in my mind were many pictures—paintings, embroideries by a prolific local artist who took to embroidery when she was told she was destined to die from leukaemia. Even my mother had one of her works. A bowl of flowers on a firescreen. From his inception as part of our household it seems that Patsy had allied himself towards me. In fact he'd been my father's assistant from before I was born. But he dragged me on walks, he described linnets to me, he indicated ragwort, he seated me on wooden benches in the hall outside town opposite a line of sycamores as he puffed into his trombone, as his fat stomach heaved into it. Patsy had not always been fat. That was obvious. He'd been corpulent, not fat. 'Look,' he said one day on the avenue leading to the Forty Steps—I was seven—'a blackbird about to burst into song.'

Patsy had burst into song once. At a St Patrick's night concert. He sang 'Patsy Fagan.' Beside a calendar photograph of a woman at the back of our shop he did not sing for me but recited poetry. 'The Ballad of Athlone.' The taking of the bridge of Athlone by the Williamites in 1691 had dire consequences for this area. It implanted it forevermore with Williamites. It directly caused the Irish defeat at Aughrim. Patsy lived in the shadow of the hills of Aughrim. Poppies were the consequence of battle. There were balloons of defeat in the air. Patsy Fogarthy brought me a gift of mushrooms once from the fields of Aughrim.

Patsy had a bedding of blackberry curls about his cherubic face; he had cherubic lips and smiled often; there was a snowy sparkle in his deep-blue eyes. Once he'd have been exceedingly good-looking. When I was nine his buttocks slouched obesely. Once he'd have been as the man in the cigarette advertisements. When I was nine on top of the Forty Steps he pulled down his jaded trousers as if to pee, opened up his knickers and exposed his gargantuan balls. Delicately I turned away. The same year he tried to put the same penis in the backside of a drummer in the brass band, or so trembling, thin members of the Legion of Mary vouched. Without a murmur of a court case Patsy was expelled from town. The boy hadn't complained. He'd been caught in the act by a postman who was one of the church's most faithful members in town. Patsy Fogarthy crossed the Irish Sea, leaving a trail of mucus after film.

2

I left Ireland for good and all 11 October 1977. There'd been many explanations for Patsy's behaviour: an aunt who used to have fits, throwing her arms about like seven snakes; the fact he might really have been of implanted Williamite stock. One way or the other he'd never been quite forgotten, unmentioned for a while, yes, but meanwhile the ecumenical movement had revived thoughts of him.

My mother attended a Protestant service in St Matthias's church in 1976. As I left home she pressed a white, skeletal piece of paper into my hands. The address of a hospital where Patsy Fogarthy was now incarcerated. The message was this: 'Visit him. We are now Christian (we go to Protestant services) and if not forgiven he can have some alms.' It was now one could go back that made people accept him a little. He'd sung so well once. He smiled so cheerily. And sure wasn't there the time he gave purple Michaelmas daisies to the dying and octogenarian and well-nigh crippled Mrs Connaughton (she whose husband left her and went to America in 1927).

I did not bring Patsy Fogarthy purple Michaelmas daisies. In the house I was staying in in Battersea there were marigolds. Brought there regularly by myself. Patsy was nearby in a Catholic hospital in Wandsworth. Old clay was dug up. Had my mother recently been speaking to a relative of his? A casual conversation on the street with a country woman. Anyway this was the task I was given. There was an amber, welcoming light in Battersea. Young deer talked to children in Battersea Park. I crept around Soho like an escaped prisoner. I knew there was something connecting then and now, yes, a piece of paper, connecting the far-off, starched days of childhood to an adulthood which was confused, desperate but determined to make a niche away from family and all friends that had ensued from a middle-class Irish upbringing. I tiptoed up bare wooden stairs at night, scared of waking those who'd given me lodging. I tried to write to my mother and then I remembered the guilty conscience on her face.

Gas works burgeoned into the honey-coloured sky, oblivious of the landscape inside me, the dirty avenue cascading on the Forty Steps.

'Why do you think they built it?'

'To hide something.'

'Why did they want to hide something?'

'Because people don't want to know about some things.'

'What things?'

Patsy had shrugged, a fawn coat draped on his shoulders that day.

'Patsy, I'll never hide anything.'

There'd been many things I'd hidden. A girlfriend's abortion. An image of a little boy inside myself, a blue and white striped T-shirt on him. The mortal end of a relationship with a girl. Desire for my own sex. Loneliness. I'd tried to hide the loneliness, but Dublin, city of my youth, had exposed loneliness like neon at evening. I'd hidden a whole part of my childhood, the 1950s, but hitting London took them out of the bag. Irish pubs in London, their Jukeboxes, united the 1950s with the 1970s with a kiss of a song. 'Patsy Fagan.' Murky waters wheezed under a mirror in a pub lavatory. A young man in an Italian-style duffle coat, standing erect, eddied into a little boy being tugged along by a small fat man.

'Patsy, what is beauty?'

'Beauty is in the eye of the beholder.'

'But what is it?'

He looked at me. 'Pretending we're father and son now.'

I brought Patsy Fogarthy white carnations. It was a sunny afternoon early in November. I'd followed instructions on a piece of paper. Walking into the demesne of the hospital I perceived light playing in a bush. He was not surprised to see me. He was a small, fat, bald man in pyjamas. His face and his baldness were a carnage of reds and purples. Little wriggles of grey hair stood out. He wore maroon and red striped pyjamas. He gorged me with a look. 'You're—' I did not want him to say my name. He took my hand. There was death in the intimacy. He was in a hospital for the mad. He made a fuss of being grateful for the flowers. 'How's Georgina?' He called my mother by her first name. 'And Bert?' My father was not yet dead. It was as if he was charging them with something. Patsy Fogarthy, our small-town Oscar Wilde, reclined in pyjamas on a chair against the shimmering citadels of Wandsworth. A white nun infrequently scurried in to see to some man in the corridor. 'You made a fine young man.' 'It was the band I missed most.' 'Them were the days.' In the middle of snippets of conversation—he sounded not unlike an Irish bank clerk, aged though and more graven-voiced—I imagined the tableau of love. Patsy with a young boy. 'It was a great old band. Sure you've been years out of the place now. What age are ye?' 'Twenty-six.' 'Do you have a girlfriend? The English girls will be out to grab you now!' A plane noisily slid over Wandsworth. We simultaneously looked at it. An old, swede-faced man bent over a bedside dresser. 'Do ya remember me? I used to bring you on walks.' Of course, I said. Of course. 'It's not true what they said about us. Not true. They're all mad. They're all lunatics. How's Bert?' Suddenly he started shouting at me. 'You never wrote back. You never wrote back to my letters.

And all the ones I sent you.' More easy-voiced he was about to return the flowers until he suddenly avowed. 'They'll be all right for Our Lady. They'll be all right for Our Lady.' Our Lady was a white statue, over bananas and pears, by his bed.

3

It is hot summer in London. Tiger lilies have come to my door. I'd never known Patsy had written to me. I'd never received his letters of course. They'd curdled in my mother's hand. All through my adolescence. I imagined them filing in, never to be answered. I was Patsy's boy. More than the drummer lad. He had betrothed himself to me. The week after seeing him, after being virtually chased out of the ward by him, with money I'd saved up in Dublin, I took a week's holiday in Italy. The trattorias of Florence in November illumined the face of a young man who'd been Patsy Fogarthy before I'd been born. It's now six years on and that face still puzzles me, the face I saw in Florence, a young man with black hair, and it makes a story, that solves a lot of mystery for me. There's a young man with black hair in a scarlet tie but it's not Patsy. It's a young man my father met in London in 1939, the year he came to study tailoring. Perhaps now it's the summer and the heat and the picture of my father on the wall—a red and yellow striped tie on him—and my illimitable estrangement from family but this city creates a series of ikons this summer. Patsy is one of them. But the sequence begins in the summer of 1939.

Bert ended up on the wide pavements of London in the early summer of 1939. He came from a town in the Western Midlands of Ireland whose wide river had scintillated at the back of town before he left and whose handsome façades radiated with sunshine. There were girls left behind that summer and cricket matches. Bert had decided on the tailoring course after a row with an older brother with whom he'd shared the family grocery-cum-bar business. The family house was one of the most sizeable on the street. Bert had his eyes on another house to buy now. He'd come to London to forge a little bit of independence from family for himself and in so doing he forwent some of the pleasures of the summer. Not only had he left the green cricket fields by the river but he had come to a city that exhaled news bulletins. He was not staying long.

He strolled into a cavern of death for behind the cheery faces of London that summer was death. Bert would do his course in Cheapside and not linger. Badges pressed against military lapels, old dishonours to Ireland. Once Bert had taken a Protestant girl out. They sailed in the bumpers at the October fair together. That was the height of his forgiveness for England. He did not consider playing cricket a leaning to England. Cricket was an Irish game, pure and simple, as could be seen from its popularity in his small, Protestant-built town.

Living was not easy for Bert in London; an Irish landlady—she was from Armagh, a mangy woman—had him. Otherwise the broth of his accent was rebuffed. He stooped a little under English disdain, but his hair was still orange and his face ruddy in fragments. By day Bert travailed; a dusty, dark cubicle. At evenings he walked. It was the midsummer that made him raise his head a little.

Twilight rushing over the tops of the trees at the edge of Hyde Park made him think of his dead parents, Galway people. He was suddenly both proud of and abstracted by his lineage. A hat was vaunted by his red hands on his waist. One evening, as perfumes and colours floated by, he thought of his mother, her tallness, her military posture, the black clothes she had always been stuffed into. In marrying her husband she declared she'd married a bucket. Her face looked a bit like a bucket itself.

Bert had recovered his poise. The width of his shoulders breathed again. His chest was out. It was that evening a young man wearing a scarlet tie stopped and talked to him under a particularly dusky tree by Hyde Park. 'You're Irish,' the young man had said. 'How do you know?' 'Those sparkling blue eyes.' The young man had worn a kind of perfume himself. 'You know,' he said—his accent was very posh—'there's going to be a war. You would be better off in Ireland.' Bert considered the information. 'I'm here on a course.' Between that remark and a London hotel there was an island of nothing. Masculine things for Bert had always been brothers pissing, the spray and the smell of their piss, smelly Protestants in the cricket changing rooms. That night Bert—how he became one he did not know—was a body. His youth was in the hands of an Englishman from Devon.

The creaminess of his skin and the red curls of his hair had attained a new state for one night, that of an angel at the side of the Gothic steeple at home. There was beauty in Bert's chest. His penis was in the fist of another young man.

Marriage, children, a drapery business in Ireland virtually eliminated it all but they could not quite eliminate the choice colours of sin, red of handkerchiefs in men's pockets in a smoky hotel lounge, red of claret wine, red of blood on sheets where love-making was too violent. In the morning there was a single thread of a red hair on a pillow autographed in pink.

When my father opened his drapery business he ran it by himself for a while but on his marriage he felt the need for an assistant and Patsy was the first person who presented himself for the job. It was Patsy's black hair, his child's lips, his Roman sky-blue eyes that struck a resonance in my father. Patsy came on in autumn day. My father was reminded of a night in London. His partnership with Patsy was a marital one. When I came along it was me over my brothers Patsy chose. He was passing on a night in London. The young man in London? He'd worn a scarlet tie. My father specialized in ties. Patsy wore blue and emerald ones to town dos. He was photographed for the Connaught Tribune in a broad, blue, black-speckled one. His shy smile hung over the tie. Long years ago my mother knew there was something missing from her marriage to my father—all the earnest hot-water jars in the world could not obliterate this knowledge. She was snidely suspicious of Patsy—she too had blackberry hair—and when Patsy's denouement came along it was she who expelled him from the shop, afraid for the part of her husband he had taken, afraid for the parcel of her child's emotions he would abduct now that adolescence was near. But the damage, the violation had been done. Patsy had twined my neck in a scarlet tie one sunny autumn afternoon in the shop, tied it decorously and smudged a patient, fat, wet kiss on my lips.

Miles

1

'Miles from here.' A phrase caught Miles's ear as he took the red bus to the North Wall. Someone was shouting at someone else, one loud passenger at an apparently half-deaf passenger, the man raising himself a little to shout. The last of Dublin's bright lights swam by. What took their place was the bleak area of dockland. Miles took his small case from the bus. He had a lonely and unusual journey to make.

Miles was seventeen. His hair was manically spliced on his head, a brown tuft of it. He was tall, lean; Miles was a model. He wore his body comfortably. He moved ahead to the boat, carrying his case: foisting his case in an onward movement.

Miles had grown up in the Liberties in Dublin. His mother had deserted him when he was very young. She was a red-haired legend tonight, a legend with a head of champion chestnut hair.

She had gone from Ireland and insinuated herself into England, leaving her illegitimate son with her married sister. The only thing known of her was that she turned up at the pilgrimage to Walsingham, Norfolk, each year. Miles, now that he was a spare-featured seventeen-year-old, a seventeen-year-old with a rather lunar face, was going looking for her. That lunar face was even paler now under the glare of lights from the boat.

The life Miles lived now was one of bright lights, of outlandish clothes, of acrobatic models wearing those clothes under the glare of acrobatic lights; more than anything it was a life of nightclubs, the later in the night the better, seats at lurid feasts of mosaic ice cream and of cocktails. Dublin for Miles was a kind of Pompeii now: on an edge. He was doing well, he was living a good life in a city smouldering with poverty. Ironically he'd come from want. But his good looks had brought him to magazines and to the omnipotent television screen. He was taking leave of all that for a few days for a pilgrimage of his own. There were few signs of garishness on him. The clothes he slipped out of Ireland in were black and grey. Only the articulate outline of his face and the erupting lava tuft of his hair would let you know he worked in the world of modelling.

The night-boat pulled him towards England and the world of his mother.

2

She'd come to Walsingham each year, Ellie, and this year there was a difference about her coming. She was dying. She came with her daughter Áine and with her son Lally. She walked, propped between them, on the pilgrimage, the procession of foot from slipper chapel to town of Walsingham. Áine was a teacher. Lally was a pop star.

3

Miles was in fact late for the procession. He arrived in the town when the crowds were jumbled together. He looked around. He looked through the crowd for his mother.

4

Afterwards you could almost say that Lally recognized him, rather than he recognized Lally. Lally was discomfited by lack of recognition here. Miles recognized him immediately. 'How are you? You're Lally.' A primrose and white religious banner made one or two demonstrative movements behind Miles.

'Yeah. And who are you?'

Who am I? Who am I? The question coming from Lally's lips, funnelled mesmerically into Miles's mind on that street in Walsingham.

5

Miles was an orphan, always an orphan, always made to feel like an orphan. He was, through childhood and adolescence, rejected by his cousins with whom he lived, both male and female, rejected for his beauty. Nancy-Boy they called him. Sop. Sissy. Pansy. Queer, Gay-Boy, Bum-Boy. The ultimate name—Snowdrop. His enemy cousins took to that name most, considering it particularly salacious and inventive. Miles was none of these things. He looked unusually pretty for a boy. The names for him and the brand of ostracization gave him a clue as to his direction in life though. He found an easy entrance into the world of modelling. He was hoisted gracefully into that world you could say. At seventeen Miles had his face right bang on the front of magazine covers. He'd become an aura, a national consciousness arrangement in his own right. This success allowed him to have a flat of his own and, supreme revenge, wear suits the colour of the undersides of mushrooms down the Liberties. Miles sometimes had the blank air of a drifting, unpiloted boat in these suits in the Liberties. There must be more to life than bright suits his mind was saying; there must be more things beyond this city where boys in pink suits wandered under slender cathedral steeples. There must be more to life than a geography that got its kicks from mixing ancient grey buildings with doses of alarmingly dressed and vacant-eyed young people. His mother, the idea of her, was something beyond this city and Miles broke with everything he was familiar with, everything that bolstered him, to go looking for her, to stretch his life: to endanger himself. He knew his equilibrium was frail, that his defences were thin, that he might inflict a terrible wound on himself by going, that he might remember what he'd been trying to forget all his life, what it was like as a little child to have your mother leave you, to have a red-haired woman disappear out the door, throwing a solitary backward glance at you, in a house not far from the slender cathedral steeple, and never coming back again.

6

Who am I? Ellie Tierney had asked herself as she walked on the procession. Who am I, she wondered, now that she was on the verge of dying, having cancer of the bone marrow. An immigrant. A mother of two children. A widow. A grocery store owner. A dweller of West London. A Catholic.

She'd come young to this country; from County Clare. Just before the War. Lived the first year in Ilford. Had shoals of local children pursue her and her brothers and sisters with stones because they were Irish. She'd been a maid in a vast hotel. Met Peader Tierney, a bus driver for London Transport, had a proposal from him at a Galway-men's ball in a West London hotel and married him. Had two children by him. Was independent of him in that she opened a grocery store of her own. He'd died in the early 1970s, long before he could see his son become famous.

7

Who am I? Lally had thought on the procession. The question boggled him now. He was very famous. Frequently on television. A spokesman for a new generation of the Irish in England. A wearer of nightgown-looking shirts. He felt odd, abashed here, among the nuns and priests, beside his mother. But he strangely belonged. He'd make a song from Walsingham.

8

Who am I? Áine had thought as she'd walked. A failure. A red-haired woman in a line of Clare women. Beside that young brother of hers nothing: a point of annihilation, no achievement.

9

It occurred to Lally that Miles had come here because he knew that he, Lally, would be here. Lally welcomed him as a particularly devoted fan.

'Where are you from?'

'Dublin.'

'Dublin?'

'Dublin.'

The hair over Miles's grin was askew. Miles waited a few minutes, grin fixed, for a further comment from Lally.

'We're driving to the sea. Will you come with us?'

10

The flat land of Norfolk: not unlike the sea. The onward

Volkswagen giving it almost an inconsequential, disconnected feel; a feel that brought dreams and memories to those sitting, as if dumb-struck, silently in the car. Mrs Tierney in front, her face searching the sky with the abstracted look of a saint who had his hands joined in prayer. Walsingham was left behind. But the spirit of Walsing-ham bound all the car together, this strangeness in a landscape that was otherwise yawning, and to Irish people, alien, unremarkable— important only in that it occasionally yielded an odd-looking bird and that the glowering sweep of it promised the maximum benefit of the sea.

That they all considered it flat and boundless like the sea never occurred to them as being ironic; a sea of land was something almost to be feared. Only by the sea, in landscape, they felt safe.

Or in a small town like Walsingbam which took full control over its surroundings and subjugated them.

The people of Britain had called the Milky Way the Walsingham Way once. They thought it had led to Walsingham. The Virgin Mary was reckoned to have made an appearance here in the Middle Ages. The young Henry VIII had walked on foot from the slipper chapel to her shrine to venerate her. Later he'd taken her image from the shrine and had it publicly burned in Chelsea to the jeers of a late-medieval crowd. Centuries had gone by and an English lady convert started the process of reconstruction, turning sheds back into chapels. To celebrate the reconsecration of the slipper chapel vast crowds had come from all over England on a Whit Monday in the 1930s. Ellie remembered the Whit Monday gathering here in 1946, the crowds on the procession, the prayers of thanksgiving to Mary, the nuns with head-dresses tall as German castles, pictures of Mary in win-dows in Walsingham and the flowers on doorsteps—a gaggle of nuns in black, but with palatial white headdresses, standing outside a cot-tage, nudging one another, waiting for the Virgin as if she was a military hero who'd won the war. The statue of Mary had come, bedecked with congratulatory pink roses. For Ellie the War had been a war with England, English children chasing her and brutally rain-ing stones on her.

Her head slumped in the car a little now: she was tired. Her son, Lally, the driver, looked sidelong at her, anxiously, protectively. Her memories were his this moment: the stuff of songs, geese setting out like rebel soldiers in a jade-green farm in County Clare.

11

Lally was the artist, the pop star, the maker of words. Words came out of him now, these days, like meteors; superhuman ignitions of energy. He was totally in command: he stood straight on television. He was a star. He was something of Ireland for a new generation of an English pop audience. He wheedled his songs about Ireland into a microphone, the other members of his group standing behind him. His face was well known in teenybop magazines, the alacrity of it, the uprightness of it.

How all this came about was a mystery to his mother; from a shambles in a shed, a pop group practising, to massive concerts—a song in the charts was what did it. But a song with a difference. It was a song about Ireland. Suddenly Ireland had value in the media. Lally had capitalized on that. His sore-throat-sounding songs had homed in on that new preoccupation. Without people realizing it he had turned a frivolous interest into an obsession. He remembered —through his parents. His most famous song was about his father, how his father, who'd fled Galway in his teens, had returned, middle aged, to find only stones where his parents were buried, no names on the stones. It had never occurred to him that without him, the son of the family, there'd been no one to bury his parents. He had a mad sister somewhere in England who talked to chickens. Lally's father had deserted the entire palette of Ireland for forty years, never once writing to his parents when they were alive, trying to obliterate the memory of them, doing so until he found his way home again in the late 1960s.

That song had been called 'Stones in a Flaxen Field.'

Words; Lally was loved for his words. They spun from him, all colours. They were sexual and male and young, his words. They were kaleidoscopic in colour. But they spoke, inversely, of things very ancient, of oppression. A new generation of young English people learnt from his songs.

And only ten years before, Ellie often thought, her grocery store was stoned, one night, just after bombs went off in Birmingham, the window all smashed.

Ah well; that was life. That was change. One day scum, the next stars. Stars . . . Ellie looked up from her dreams for the Milky Way or the Walsingham Way but it was still very much May late-afternoon light.

12

Her father told her how they used to play hurling in the fields outside his village in County Galway in May evening light, 'light you could cup in your hand it was so golden.' There are holes in every legend. There were two versions of her father. The man who ran away and who never went back until he was in his fifties. And the man who'd proposed to her mother at a Galwaymen's ball. 'But sure he was only there as a spy that day,' Áine's mother would always say. Even so it was contradictory. Áine resented the lyricism of Lally's version of her father; she resented the way he'd used family and put it into song, she resented this intrusion into the part of her psyche which was wrapped up in family. More than anything she resented the way Lally got away with it. But still she outwardly applauded him. But as he became more famous she became older, more wrecked looking. Still her hair was very red. That seemed to be her triumph—even at school. To have this almost obscenely lavish red hair. She got on well at school. She had many boyfriends. Too many. She was involved on women's committees. But wasn't there something she'd lost?

She did not believe in all this: God, pilgrimage. Coming to Walsingham almost irked her. She'd come as a duty. But it did remind her of another pilgrimage, another journey, almost holy.

13

It had been when Lally was a teenager. She'd gone for an abortion in Brighton. A clinic near the sea. In winter. He'd accompanied her. Waiting for the appointment she'd heard the crash of the winter sea. Lally beside her. He'd held her hand. She'd thought of Clare, of deaths, of wakes. She'd gone in for her appointment. Afterwards, in a strange way, she realized he'd become an artist that day. By using him as a solace when he'd been too young she'd traumatized him into becoming an artist. She'd wanted him to become part of a conspiracy with her, a narrow conspiracy: but instead she'd sent him out on seas of philosophizing, of wondering. He'd been generous in his interpretation of her from out on those seas. His purity not only had been reinforced but immeasurably extended. While hers was lost.

There'd been a distance between them ever since. Lally was the one whose life worked, Lally was the one with the pop star's miraculous sweep of dark hair over his face, Lally was the one with concise blue eyes that carried the Clare coast in them.

Toady she saw it exactly. Lally was the one who believed.

14

Miles was so chuffed at being in this company that he said nothing; he just grinned. He hid his head, slightly idiotically, in his coat. The countryside rolled by outside. All the time he was aware of the journey separating him from his quest for his mother. But he didn't mind. When it came to the point it had seemed futile, the idea of finding her in that crowd. And romantic. When he looked out from a porch, near a pump, at the sea of faces, it had seemed insane, deranged, dangerous, the point of his quest. There'd been a moment when he thought his sanity was giving way. But the apparition of Lally had saved him. Now he was being swept along on another odyssey. But where was this odyssey leading? And as he was on it, the car journey, it was immediately bringing him to thoughts, memories. The landscape of adolescence, the stretched-out skyline of Dublin, a naked black river bearing isolated white lights at night as it meandered drunkenly to the no-man's-land, the unclaimed territory of the Irish Sea. This was the territory along with the terrain of the black river as it neared the sea which infiltrated Miles's night-dreams as an adolescent, restive night-dreams, his body shaking frequently in response to the image of the Irish Sea at night, possibly knowing it had to enter that image so it could feel whole, Miles knowing, even in sleep, that the missing mechanisms of his being were out there and recoiling, in a few spasmodic movements, from the journey he knew he'd have to make someday. He was on that journey now. But he'd already left the focus of it, Walsingham. What had come in place of Walsingham was flat land, an unending succession of flat land which seemed to induce a mutual, binding memory to the inmates of the car. A memory which hypnotized everybody.

But the memory that was special to Miles was the memory of Dublin. This memory had a new intensity, a new aurora in the presence of Lally; the past was changed in the presence of Lally and newly negotiated. Miles had found, close to Lally, new fundamentals in his past; the past seemed levitated, random, creative now. Miles knew now that all the pain in his life had been going towards this moment. This was the reward. It was as if Miles, the fourteen, fifteen-year-old, had smashed out of his body and, like Superman, stormed the sky over a city. The city was a specific one. Dublin. And remembering a particular corner near his aunt's home where there was always the sculpture of some drunkard's piddle on the wall Miles was less euphoric. The world was made up of mean things after all, mornings after the night before. That's what Miles's young life was made up of, mornings after the night before. Maybe that's what his mother's life had been like too. Now that he was moving further and further away from the possibility of actually finding her he could conjure an image of her he hadn't dared conjure before. He could conjure an encounter with her which, in the presence of an artist, Lally, was a hair's breadth away from being real.

15

Rose Keating had set out that morning from her room in Shepherd's Bush. She was a maid in a Kensington hotel where most of the staff were Irish. Her hair, which was almost the colour of golden nasturtiums, was tied in a ponytail at the back. Her pale face looked earnest. She made this journey every year. She made it in a kind of reparation. She always felt early on this journey that her womb had been taken out, that there was a missing segment of her, an essential ion in her consciousness was lost. She'd almost forgotten, living in loneliness and semi-destitution, who she was and why she was here. All she knew, instinctively, all the time was that she'd had to move on. There had been a child she'd had once and she'd abandoned him because she didn't want to drag him down her road too. She felt, when she'd left Dublin, totally corrupt, totally spoilt. She'd wanted to cleanse herself and just ended up a maid, a dormant being, a piece of social trash.

There was a time when it was as if any man would do her but the more good-looking the better: at night a chorus of silent young men gathered balletically under lampposts in the Liberties. Then there was a play, movements, interchange. Which would she choose? She looked as though she'd been guided like a robot towards some of them. All this under lamplight. Her face slightly thrown back and frequently expressionless. There was something wrong with her, people said, she had a disease, 'down there,' and some matrons even pointed to the place. Rose loved the theatre of it. There was something mardi gras about picking up young men. My gondoliers, she called them mentally. Because sometimes she didn't in fact see young men from the Liberties under lampposts but Venetian gondoliers; the Liberties was often studded with Venetian gondoliers and jealous women, behind black masks, looked from windows. Rose had a mad appetite, its origins and its name inscrutable, for men. There was no point of reference for it so it became a language, fascinating in itself. Those with open minds wanted to study that language to see what new things they could learn from it. No one in Ireland was as sexually insatiable as Rose. This might have been fine if she'd been a prostitute but she didn't even get money for it very often; she just wanted to put coloured balloons all over a panoramic, decayed, Georgian ceiling that was in fact the imaginative ceiling of Irish society.

It was a phase. It hit her, like a moonbeam, in her late teens, and it lasted until her mid-twenties. She got a son out of it, Miles, and the son made her recondite, for a while, and then she went back to her old ways, the streets. But this time each man she had seemed tainted and diseased after her, a diseased, invisible mucus running off him and making him curl up with horror at the awareness of this effect. He had caught something incurable and he hated himself for it. He drifted away from her, trying to analyse what felt different and awful about him. Sex had turned sour, like the smell of Guinness sometimes in the Dublin air.

But Rose, even living with her sister, could not give it up; her whole body was continually infiltrated by sexual hunger and one day, feeling sick in herself, she left. The day she left Dublin she thought of a red-haired boy, the loveliest she had, who'd ended up spending a life sentence in Mountjoy, for a murder of a rural garda sergeant, having hit him over the head one night in the Liberties, with a mallet. He'd been half a Tinker and wore mousy freckles at the tip of his nose—like a tattoo.

London had ended all her sexual appetite: it took her dignity; it made her middle aged. But it never once made her want to return. She held her child in her head, a talisman, and she went to Walsingham once a year as a reparation, having sent a postcard from there once to her sister, saying: 'If you want to find me, find me in Walsingham.' That had been at a moment of piqued desperation. She'd written the postcard on a wall beside a damp telephone kiosk and the postcard itself became damp; people, happy people, sauntering, with chips, around her.

For a few years she found a companion for her trip to Walsingham, a Mr Coneelly, a bald man from the hotel, a hat on his head on the pilgrimage, a little earthenware leprechaun grin on his face under his hat. He had an amorous attachment to her. There was always a ten-pound note sticking from his pocket and a gold chain trailing to the watch in that pocket. But the romance ended when white rosary beads fell out of his trousers pocket as he was making love to her once on a shabby, once lustrous gold sofa, she doing it to be obliging, and he taking the falling rosary as a demonstration by his dead mother against the romance. In fact he found a much younger girl after that and he made sure no rosary fell from his pocket in the middle of making love. He had been company, for a while.

Rose had geared herself for a life of loneliness. Today in Walsingham it rained a little and she stood to the side, on a porch and watched.

16

Sometimes Áine's feelings towards her brother came to hatred. She never pretended it. She was always courteous, even decorous with him: the worst and the most false of her, 'schoolmistressy.' She resented his strident, bulbous shirts, the free movements of those shirts, the colours of them. She resented what he did with experience, turning it into an artifact. Artifacts weren't life and yet, for him, they created a life of their own: those Botticelli angels looking at him from an audience, full of adulation. Áine wanted reports on life to be factual, plain; Lally, the Irish artist, threw the facts into tumults of colour where they got distorted. Eventually the words took on a frenzy, a life of their own. They were able to change the miserable facts—rain over a desultory, praying horde at Walsingham, crouched in between Chinese takeaways—and turn themselves into something else, a miracle, a transcendence, an elevation and an obliviscence: wine turned into the blood of Christ at mass. A mergence with all the Irish artists of the centuries. Of course Lally was only a pop star and yet his words, she had to admit sometimes, were as truthful as any Irish writer's. His words exploded on concert stages, on television, and told of broken Irish lives, red-haired Irish women immigrants who worked in hotels in West London.

17

Miles had stood not very far away from his mother that day and Lally had noticed Miles's mother, when there was rain, as she stood talking to two men from Mayo. There was a hullabaloo of Irish accents between Rose and the two men from Mayo. Lally paused; a story. Then he went on. Miles didn't tell Lally in the car that he'd come in search of a red-haired woman. He said very little and was asked very little.

18

Rose, sheltering her body from the rain, got into a livid conversation with two men. They were bachelors and they were both looking for wives. They came to Walsingham, Norfolk, from Birmingham each Whit Monday looking for wives and they went to Lisdoonvarna, County Clare, in September looking for wives. So far they'd had no luck and their quest was telling on them: their hair and their teeth were falling out. One bandied a copy of the previous day's Sunday Press as if it was the portfolio of his life's work.

'And do you have a husband?' one of them asked.

'What do you think?'

'You've had your share of fellas,' the other one said grinning. 'A woman like you wouldn't have gone without a man for long.'

'What do you mean. A woman like me?'

'Well, you're not fat but you've loads of flesh on you. Like a Christmas goose. That's not derogatory. You look as firm as my grandmother's armchair.'

Rose screeched with laughter.

'And you both look as though the hinges are coming out of you.'

'Mentally or in the body?'

Rose laughed again.

'Whatever hope there is in Clare there's no hope here. Unless you want a Reverend Mother.'

'Oh, you'd be surprised.' A twinkle in the eye. 'Lots of randy women go on pilgrimages.'

19

Nearing the sea as though it was the Atlantic Ocean that blanketed the west coast of Ireland all kinds of words and images came into the head of Lally, the driver: sentences, half-heard at Irish venues—music festivals, Irish ballrooms—and elaborated on by him. So they could take their place in a narrative song. But more than words and images came now—an apotheosis came too. Lally was flying with the success and daring of his life. He was proud of himself. He'd turned something of the decrepitude and semi-stagnation of his parents' lives into art. More than that. Art for the young. He'd dolled his ancestry up in fancy dress.

20

How many days and months would she have to live? Ellie thought of Clare where she'd been born, the harvest fields there she'd walked before leaving Ireland, those blond, human fields, warm after days of summer sun. The imminence of death brought the friendliest images of her life.

21

The bastard, Áine thought, the bastard, he's taken everything that was of my creativity; he's used up my creativity. He's left me as nothing. There's no more to go around. He's a man, an exploiter, a rampant egotist. He doesn't see who he's trampled on to get where he's got, who he hurts. He doesn't see he's squashed my self-confidence out.

22

For Miles, as they neared the sea, it was a trip backwards: at least this journey, this expedition to Walsingham had allowed him to be solemn about his life, to see it: he sat back as though his life hitherto, as he could see it, was a state funeral.

There had been state funerals he'd seen in his life. De Valera's for instance, which he'd seen with his aunt, 'Ah, sure, look at his coffin.' All kinds of voices came back from Miles's life. Especially the voices of early adolescence. 'Ah, sure, look at the little eejit. The fool. Nitwit. Silly git.' All kinds of names were planted on Miles's always withdrawing figure with its gander legs in thin jeans. That figure was a continual epilogue, always disappearing around corners, always on the edge of getting out of the picture. But maybe that was because he knew there'd be an area where he could totally affirm himself, totally show himself—when the time came. Now there were ikons of Miles in fashion magazines, the young archangel in suave clothes. His tormentors in the Liberties would be bilious. But the young man in the picture was unmoved by this prospect. He seemed frigid of countenance. This loveliness was the product of pain. These secretive eyes in all the pictures looked back on tunnels of streets in the Liberties, streets where his mother had gathered men as if they'd been daisies.

As they neared Wells-next-the-Sea the sky, towards evening, had almost cleared and there were a few white clouds in it—like defeated daisies.

People in the car were mumbling, conversations were going on. Suddenly Miles wanted to go back to Walsingham.

'Mammy.'

23

Rose's shadow departed through the back door after her. Miles should have known there was something funny about her going that day. In fact he did know. Memory consolidated that fact. Rose's shadow writhed off a yellowy picture showing military-shouldered women in white, straw hats on their heads, holding bicycles, in some Edwardian wood of the Dublin mountains.

24

'And the queer thing is that Gabrielle knew Marty years before in Kiltimagh.'

Rose was in a Chinese restaurant in Walsingham with the two immigrants who were originally from Mayo. They'd discovered they had an acquaintance in common; a partisan in this tide of menial, immigrant Irish labour. Rose had encountered her in a hotel room once where the carpets had been rolled up after some VIP visitors had spent a lengthy stay. The room, grandiose in proportions, was being renovated. Rose did not know what to dwell on, the conversation with the two odd men or the drama of the encounter years before. Her concentration ultimately flitted between the figment of now and the thought of then. This caused an almost clownish agitation in her features.

'She had the devil of a temper.'

'Oh yes, she'd flare up at you like a snake.'

'There was cuddling in her though.'

'You dirty . . .'

Rose's mind had fled the banter between the two men. A woman in a hotel room in London years before, a blue workcoat on her, a conversation, commiseration, companionship then for a few months. But some family tragedy had brought the woman back to Ireland

and then Rose never saw her again; no more Friday evenings over a candle-lit, hard-as-a-horseshoe pizza in Hammersmith.

'Go on out of that. Don't be disparaging a woman's reputation. She's not around to defend herself.'

Rose's mind had drifted. She could see the sea, the grey sea such as it was piled up, a mute and undemonstrative statement, around Dublin and longed for it as though it had the confessional's power of absolution.

25
Miles stumbled by the sea. A few boats there, backs up. Now it was grey again, an overall grey. Walking done, the group went to a seaside café.

26
Words, they're my story, they're my life. Here by the sea, dusk, the jukebox going, Dusty Springfield, 'I Just Don't Know What to do with Myself,' no song of mine on the jukebox. Chips, a boy, already tanned, looking from behind the counter, mystically, a Spaniard's or a Greek's black moustache on him. I'll make another song, another story. Stories will get me by, words, won't they, won't they? The stage, the lights, the mammoth audience. Is this a Nazi dream of power?

27
Today the religion they tried to kill. My religion. Remember when Peader and I went to the Church of the English Martyrs in Tyburn and we, privately, consecrated our marriage there on the site where the head of Oliver Plunkett, the Irish martyr, was chopped off, the nuns all singing, white on them. What will it be like to be dead?— back in that dream of a hymn sung in unison by nuns in white where Irish bishops in the long ago met their deaths.

28

Lally went obsessively, again and again, to the jukebox, standing over it, putting on more songs as though lighting candles in a bed of church candles. Midsummer dusk was out there, the strangeness of it. A woman soon to die looked at it. Lally's backside was very blue.

29

Loneliest of all was Miles, the stranger here, the one picked up and talked to as if being picked up was favour enough or as if he was supposed to sit in silent wonderment. He was an oddity from the sea of fans. He was an orphan among these people who, in a strange, unknowing way, patronized him.

30

The strangeness, the awkwardness became more evident as the number of coffees coming to the table multiplied, each set of coffees being ushered in more frenetically than the last. No one told their story aloud or was asked to.

31

Rose, though, was telling her story very loudly indeed not many miles away. Sweet and sour chicken, a plate of it, went by as she got to the part about leaving Ireland. Her immediate listeners were enthralled but their wonderment was more at how gauche exiles very often hid the most amazing secrets, how they hid horror, terror and great magnitudes of sin—incest, homosexuality, lesbianism, prostitution, now, rare enough, nymphomania. England dusted off the sins and made people just foolish—just foolish Irish folk.

'The child? The little lad?'

'Sure he's grown now. He wouldn't want to see me.'

32

O Mother of God, Star of the Sea, pray for us, pray that we

find loved ones. Someone's limbs to get caught up with in a mildly comfortable bed.

Lally remembered, from childhood, a Sacred Heart picture over the bed of a dying, bald uncle, a gay uncle who had a festive chamber pot under his deathbed, a chamber pot with crocks of gold running around it. Before AIDS was invented, that uncle seemed to be dying of something like AIDS. Or maybe merely an overdose of failure, an overdose of incohesion. His version of Ireland didn't merge with England.

The harvest fields of Clare didn't get him by here: England scoured him. England debilitated him. England killed his spirit and then killed him. But not before he carried on a kind of maudlin homosexuality. The white hands of a corpse Lally saw, a rosary entwined in them, had been lain on his genitalia when he was a child, a St Stephen's Day Christmas tree behind the merry lecher, other people gone to bed.

Ireland kicked up such stories like sand in your feet on a beach: Ireland was so full of sadness. Ireland fed itself into Lally's songs now. They came out, these stories, renewed, revitalized, pop songs for a generation who swayed and sometimes jived to them and couldn't be unnerved by them.

Star of the Sea, pray for the wanderer, pray for me. Lally's blue-shirted wrist wrestled with a bottle of Coke now. He was on to Coke. And he being the pop star, everyone watched the movement of his wrist, everybody's attention had gone to his wrist in alarm, people realizing that they'd been neglecting Lally for a while and that his wrist was telling them so.

And despite resenting him a little maybe they were glad for the coherence he gave to something of their lives. Even to death.

'Beach at Brighton, Baby-death.' Áine was looking at her brother in stillness now, not in anger or resentment.

33

As stars came out they walked on the beach. Lally tried to identify the stars in the sky. The Walsingham Way? Next week he'd be in California. By the Pacific. Watching the sky of stars over the Pacific. But he'd take something from here. Pointers to his mother's life and death. Ellie too saw her life and death in the stars tonight. A constellation of stars like a constellation of wheat fields in County Clare. 'A time to plant and a time to pluck up that which is planted.' Áine saw London classrooms in the sky, children of many races, rivers of children's faces. Miles, away from the group, dissociated from it, didn't look at the stars but poked the sea with a stick.

34

'Goodbye to yis all now.' Drunk, unpilgrim-like, Rose tottered out of a pub near the Chinese restaurant in Walsingham, looking behind at a constellation of lights in the window of that pub that might have distinguished it as a brothel if it had been in a city. The lovers stood at the door, goodbyes in their eyes. They were bent on returning, getting *stociously* drunk and staying the night in Walsingham. A bus would take Rose home. Her hair down on her shoulders she was a manifestation of Irishness in her dowdy coat. Her back stooped a little: she was an aged pilgrim. The successive pilgrimages were gradations, demarcations of age. But there was a wicked youthfulness about the way she stepped on the bus and turned around, shouting back to the men who hadn't yet gone back into the pub. 'Up Mayo.' Bandy knees afar twitched in response to her salutation: two Mayo bachelors looked suddenly spectral, looked like a vision in a wash of white light from a turning car. Then they were gone, gone into the album.

35

In the middle of summer in Wells-next-the-Sea there would be boys with faces pugnaciously browned by sun, boys whose crotches would be held in by aerial blue jeans, battalions of these boys unleashed on the place and their eyes, the explosive look in their eyes, turning the nights into a turmoil. Boats would be lined up on the beach. Lanes would meander down to the beach as they did now. The jukeboxes would be more active. England would come here to be loved, ladies from Birmingham, factory boys, boys with backsides tight and fecund as plums. This is where England would take a few weeks off, the boring country of England becoming carnal, becoming daring, becoming poetic. Caution and pairs of cheap nylon stockings would be thrown to the nervy summer breezes. The grey would go for a few weeks, making room for a blue that visited the place from the deep Mediterranean.

Ellie would be dead in July. Her funeral would be in West London on a very hot day. Áine would cry more than anybody. Lally would be silent, a pop star in black and white, no tie, white *fin de siècle* shirt spaciously open in the cemetery. There'd be a red rose in his black lapel. The sun would be gruesomely hot. Áine would be crying for a country she never really knew, a country for which her red hair was an emblem.

Miles would start losing his soul that summer, if soul you could call it; his sensitivity, vulnerability, belief in something. Walsingham and Wells-next-the-Sea would have been the last stops for his openness. After that, though still in media terms outrageously beautiful, he'd start becoming hard, calculating, eyes, those brown eyes of his, focused on attainment. All he'd want to do would be to be a star and oblivionize, kill anything else in him. There'd be no sign of Rose in this Italian suit dolled-up boy.

36

Rose let herself in the hall door. 14 Bolingbroke Road, Shepherd's Bush, London. Inside the light wasn't working. The smell of urine came from the first-floor toilet. She was a little drunk still. Her drunken form merged with the darkness. The smell of urine was aquatic in the air the further she walked in. But the darkness was benign to her. It shrouded her unhappiness, the unhappiness which had suddenly come on her in the bus as she remembered what she'd been trying to forget for years, what she'd been successfully putting Walsingham between it and her for years. Now pilgrimages, trips to Walsingham, the cabbalistic charades of them and the inexact hope they gave off didn't work any more and all she could see, right in front of her, was the greyness, the no-hope, the lethargy land of *it*.

37

The lights of a motorway going back to London and the lights rearing up at you, daisy trails of them. Four silent people in the car, one sleeping, the strange boy, a phrase coming to Lally's head as he drove, a phrase he wouldn't use in a song, an unwelcome phrase even. It came from a prayer of his mother's he remembered from childhood.

'And after this our exile.'

Martyrs

Ella was an Italian woman whose one son had been maimed in a fight and was now permanently in a wheelchair, still sporting the char-black leather jacket he'd had on the night he'd been set upon. Ella's cream waitress outfit seemed to tremble with vindication when she spoke of her son's assailants. 'I'll get them. I'll get them. I'll shoot them through the brains.' The formica white walls listened. Chris's thoughts were set back that summer to Sister Honor.

The lake threw up an enduring desultory cloud that summer—it was particularly unbudging on Indiana Avenue—and Chris sidled quickly by the high-rise buildings which had attacked Mrs Pajalich's son. Sister Honor would have reproached Ella with admonitions of forgiveness but Chris saw—all too clearly—as she had in Sister Honor's lucid Kerry-coast-blue eyes the afternoon she informed her she was reneging on convent school for state high school that Sister Honor would never forgive her, the fêted pupil, for reneging on a Catholic education for the streams of state apostacy and capitalistic indifference. Chris had had to leave a Catholic environment before it plunged her into a lifetime of introspection. She, who was already in her strawberry and black check shirt, orientated to a delicate and literary kind of introspection. Sister Honor's last words to her, from behind that familiar desk, had been 'Your vocation in life is to be a martyr.'

The summer before university Chris worked hard—as a waitress—in a cream coat alongside Mrs Pajalich. Beyond the grey gravestone citadels of the city were the gold and ochre cornfields. At the end of summer Chris would head through them—in a Greyhound bus—for the university city. But first she had to affirm to herself, 'I have escaped Sister Honor and her many mandates.'

Ella Pajalich would sometimes nudge her, requesting a bit of Christian theology, but inevitably reject it. Ella had learnt that Chris could come out with lines of Christian assuagement. However, the catastrophe had been too great. But that did not stop Ella, over a jam pie, red slithering along the meringue edges, from pressing Chris for an eloquent line of heaven-respecting philosophy.

Rubbing a dun plate that was supposed to be white Chris wondered if heaven or any kind of Elysium could ever touch Ella's life; sure there were the cherry blossoms by the lake in a spring under which she pushed her son. But the idea of a miracle, of a renaissance, no. Mrs Pajalich was determined to stick the café bread knife through someone. If only the police officer who allowed his poodle to excrete outside her street-level apartment. Ella had picked up the sense of a father of stature from Chris and that arranged her attitude towards Chris; Chris had a bit of the Catholic aristocrat about her, her father an Irish-American building contractor who held his ground in windy weather outside St Grellan's on Sunday mornings, his granite suit flapping, a scarlet breast-pocket handkerchief leaping up like a fish, his black shoes scintillating with his youngest son's efforts on them and his boulder-like fingers going for another voluminous cigar. 'Chris, you have the face of fortune. You'll meet a nice man. You'll be another Grace Kelly. End up in a palace.' Chris saw Grace Kelly's face, the tight bun over it, the lipstick like an even scimitar. She saw the casinos. Yes she would end up living beside casinos in some mad, decadent country, but not Monaco, more likely some vestige of Central or South America.

'Chris, will you come and visit me at Hallowe'en?' The dreaming Chris's face was disturbed. 'Yes, Yes, I will.'

Summer was over without any great reckoning when Sister Honor and Chris slid south, through the corn, to a city which rose over the corn, its small roofs, its terracotta museums by the clouded river, its white Capitol building, a centrepiece like a Renaissance city.

Sister Honor had imbibed Chris from the beginning as she would a piece of revealing literature; Chris had been established in class as a reference point for questions about literary complexities. Sister Honor would raise her hand and usher Chris's attention as if she was a traffic warden stopping the traffic. 'Chris, what did Spenser mean by this?' Honor should have known. She'd done much work in a university in Virginia on the poet Edmund Spenser; her passion for Spenser had brought her to County Cork. She'd done a course in Anglo-Irish literature for a term in Cork University. Red Irish buses had brought her into a countryside, rich and thick now, rich and thick in the Middle Ages, but one incandesced by the British around Spenser's time. The British had come to wonder and then destroy. Honor had come here as a child of five with her father, had nearly forgotten, but could not forget the moment when her father, holding her hand, cigar smoke blowing into a jackdaw's mouth, had wondered aloud how they had survived, how his ancestry had been chosen to escape, to take flight, to settle in a town in the Midwest and go on to creating dove-coloured twentieth-century skyscrapers.

Perhaps it had been the closeness of their backgrounds that had brought Chris and Honor together—their fathers had straddled on the same pavement outside St Grellan's Catholic Church, they'd blasted the aged and lingering Father Duane with smoke from the same brand of cigars. But it had been their ever-probing interest in literature which had bound them more strongly than the aesthetic of their backgrounds—though it may have been the aesthetic of their backgrounds which drove them to words. 'Vocabularies were rich and flowing in our backgrounds,' Sister Honor had said. 'Rich and flowing.' And what did not flow in Sister Honor she made up for in words.

Many-shaped bottoms followed one another in shorts over the verdure around the white Capitol building. The atmosphere was one of heightened relaxation; smiles were 1950s-type smiles on girls in shorts. Chris found a place for herself in George's bar. She counted the lights in the constellation of lights in the jukebox and put on a song for Sister Honor. Buddy Holly. 'You Go Your Way and I'll Go Mine.' A long-distance truck driver touched her from behind and she realized it was two in the morning.

She had imagined Sister Honor's childhood so closely that sometimes it seemed that Sister Honor's childhood had been her childhood and in the first few weeks at the university—the verdure, the sunlight on white shorts and white Capitol building, the fall, many-coloured evening rays of sun evoking a primal gust in her—it was of Sister Honor's childhood she thought and not her own. The suburban house, hoary in colour like rotten bark, the Maryland farm she visited in summer—the swing, the Stars and Stripes on the verdant slope, the first- or second-edition Nathaniel Hawthorne books open, revealing mustard, fluttering pages like an evangelical announcement. In the suburbs of this small city Chris saw a little girl in a blue crinoline frock, mushrooming outwards, running towards the expectant arms of a father. Red apples bounced on this image. Why had she been thinking of Sister Honor so much in the last few months? Why had Sister Honor been entering her mind with such ease and with such unquestioning familiarity? What was the sudden cause of this tide in favour of the psyche of a person you had tried to dispose of two years beforehand? One afternoon on Larissa Street Chris decided it was time to put up barriers against Sister Honor. But a woman, no longer in a nun's veil, blonde-haired, hair the colour of dried honey, still tried to get in.

Chris was studying English literature in the university—in a purple-red, many-corridored building—and the inspection of works of eighteenth- and nineteenth-century literature again leisurely evoked the emotion of the roots of her interest in literature, her inclination to literature, and the way Sister Honor had seized on that interest and so thoughts of Sister Honor—in the context of her study of literature—began circulating again. Sister Honor, in her mind, had one of the acerbic faces of the Celtic saints on the front of St Grellan's, a question beginning on her lips, and her face lean, like a greyhound's, stopped in the act of barking.

'Hi, I'm Nick.'

'I'm Chris.'

A former chaperon of nuclear missiles on a naval ship, now studying Pascal, his broad shoulders cowering into a black leather jacket, accompanied Chris to George's bar one Saturday night. They collected others on the way, a girl just back from the People's Republic of China who said she'd been the first person from her country to do a thesis at Harvard—hers was on nineteenth-century feminist writers. George's bar enveloped the small group, its low red, funeral-parlour light—the lights in the window illuminating the bar name were both blue and red.

Autumn was optimistic and continuous, lots of sunshine; girls basked in shorts as though for summer; the physique of certain girls became sturdier and more ruddy and brown and sleek with sun. Chris found a tree to sit under and meditate on her background, Irish Catholic, its sins against her—big black aggressive limousines outside St Grellan's on Sunday mornings unsteadying her childhood devotions, the time they dressed her in emerald velvet, cut in triangles, and made her play a leprechaun, the time an Irish priest showed her his penis under his black soutane and she'd wondered if this was an initiation into a part of Catholicism—and her deliverance from it now. The autumn sun cupped the Victorian villas in this town in its hand, the wine-red, the blue, the dun villas, their gold coins of autumn petals.

Chris was reminded sometimes by baseball boys of her acne—boys eddying along the street on Saturday afternoons, in from the country for a baseball match—college boys generally gave her only one to two glances, the second glance always a curious one as she had her head down and did not seem interested in them. But here she was walking away from her family and sometimes even, on special occasions, she looked straight into someone's eyes.

What would Sister Honor have thought of her now? O God, what on earth was she thinking of Sister Honor for? That woman haunts me. Chris walked on, across the verdure, under the Capitol building beside which cowboys once tied their horses.

The Saturday-night George's bar group was deserted—Nick stood on Desmoines Street and cowered further into his black leather jacket, muttering in his incomprehensible Marlon Brando fashion of the duplicity of the American government and armed forces—Chris had fallen for a dance student who'd raised his right leg in leotards like a self-admiring pony in the dance studio. The plan to seduce him failed. The attempted seduction took place on a mattress on the floor of his room in an elephantine apartment block which housed a line of washing machines on the ground floor that insisted on shaking in unison in a lighted area late into the night, stopping sometimes as if to gauge the progress of Chris's and her friend's lovemaking. In the early stages of these efforts the boy remembered he was a homosexual and Chris remembered she was a virgin. They both turned from one another's bodies and looked at the ceiling. The boy said the roaches on the ceiling were cute. Chris made off about three in the morning in a drab anorak, blaming Catholicism and Sister Honor, the autumn river with its mild, off-shooting breeze leading her home. Yes, she was a sexual failure. Years at convent school had ensured a barrier between flowing sensuality and herself. Always the hesitation.

The mortification. Dialogue. 'Do you believe we qualify, in Martin Buber's terms, for an I-thou relationship, our bodies I mean?' 'For fuck's sake, my prick has gone jellified.'

Chris knew there was a hunch on her shoulders as she hurried home; at one stage, on a bend of the river near the road, late, home-going baseball fans pulled down the window of a car to holler lewdnesses at her. She's never been able to make love—'Our bodies have destinies in love,' Sister Honor rhetorically informed the class one day—and Chris had been saving her pennies for this destiny. But tonight she cursed Sister Honor, cursed her Catholicism, her Catholic-coated sense of literature and most of anything Sister Honor's virginity which seemed to have given rise to her cruelty. 'Chris, the acne on your face has intensified over Easter. It is like an ancient map of Ireland after a smattering of napalm.' 'Chris, your legs seem to dangle, not hold you.' 'Chris, walk straight, carry yourself straight. Bear in mind your great talent and your great intelligence. Be proud of it. Know yourself, Chris Gormley.' Chris knew herself tonight as a bombed, withered, defeated thing. But these Catholic-withered limbs still held out hope for sweetening by another person.

Yes, that was why she'd left convent school—because she perceived the sham in Sister Honor, that Sister Honor had really been fighting her own virginity and in a losing battle galled other people and clawed at other people's emotions. Chris had left to keep her much-attacked identity intact. But on leaving she'd abandoned Sister Honor to a class where she could not talk literature to another pupil.

Should I go back there sometime? Maybe? Find out what Honor is teaching. Who she is directing her attentions to. If anybody. See if she has a new love. Jealousy told Chris she had not. There could never have been a pair in that class to examine the Ecclesiastes like Honor and herself—'A time of war, and a time of peace.' Chris had a dream in which she saw Honor in a valley of vines, a biblical valley, and another night a dream in which they were both walking through Spenser's Cork, before destruction, by birches and alders, hand in hand, at home and at peace with Gaelic identity and Gaelic innocence or maybe, in another interpretation of the dream, with childhood bliss. Then Sister Honor faded—the nightmare and the mellifluous dream of her—the argument was over. Chris settled back, drank, had fun, prepared for autumn parties.

The Saturday-night George's bar group was resurrected—they dithered behind one another at the entrance to parties, one less sure than the other. Chablis was handed to them, poured out of cardboard boxes with taps. A woman in black, a shoal of black balloons over her head, their leash of twine in her hand, sat under a tree in the garden at a party one night. She was talking loudly about an Egyptian professor who had deserted her. A girl approached Chris and said she'd been to the same convent as Chris had been. Before the conversation could be pursued the room erupted into dancing—the girl was lost to the growing harvest moon. Chris walked into the garden and comforted the lady in black.

'Dear Sister Honor.' The encounter prompted Chris to begin a letter to Honor one evening. Outside, the San Francisco bus made its way up North Dubuque Street—San Francisco illuminated on the front—just about overtaking a fat negro lady shuffling by Victorian villas with their promise of flowers in avenues that dived off North Dubuque Street, heaving her unwieldy laundry. But the image of Sister Honor had faded too far and the letter was crumpled. But for some reason Chris saw Honor that night, a ghost in a veil behind a desk, telling a class of girls that Edmund Spenser would be important to their lives.

Juanito was a Venezuelan boy in a plum-red T-shirt, charcoal hair falling over an almost Indian face which was possessed of lustrous eyes and lips that seemed about to moult. He shared his secret with her at a party. He was possessed by demons. They emerged from him at night and fluttered about the white ceiling of Potomac apartments. At one party a young man, José from Puerto Rico, came naked, crossed his hairy legs in a debonair fashion and sipped vodka. So demented was he in the United States without a girlfriend that he forgot to put on clothes. Juanito from Venezuela recurred again and again. The demons were getting worse. They seemed to thrive on the season of Hallowe'en. There was a volcanic rush of them out of him now at night against the ceiling. But he still managed to play an Ella Fitzgerald number, 'Let's Fall in Love,' on a piano at a party. José from Puerto Rico found an American girlfriend for one night but she would not allow him to come inside her because she was afraid of disease, she told him, from his part of the world.

Chris held a party at her apartment just before the mid-term break. Juanito came and José. She'd been busy preparing for days. In a supermarket two days previously she'd noticed as she'd carried a paper sack of groceries at the bottom left-hand corner of the college newspaper, a report about the killing of some American nuns in a Central American country. The overwhelming feature of the page, however, had been a blown-up photograph of a bird who'd just arrived in town to nest for the winter. Anyway the sack of groceries had kept Chris from viewing the newspaper properly. The day had been very fine and Chris, crossing the green of the campus, had encountered the bird who'd come to town to nest for the winter or a similar bird. There was goulash for forty people at Chris's party— more soup than stew—and lots of pumpkin pie, apple pie and special little buns, speckled by chocolate, which Chris had learned to make from her grandmother. The party was just underway when five blond college boys in white T-shirts entered bearing candles in carved pumpkin shells flame coming through eyes and fierce little teeth. There were Japanese girls at Chris's party and a middle-aged man frequently tortured in Uruguay but who planned to return to that country after this term in the college. He was small, in a white T-shirt, and he smiled a lot. He could not speak English too well but he kept pointing at the college boys and saying 'nice.' At the end of the party Chris made love in the bath not to one of these boys who'd made their entrance bearing candles in pumpkin shells but to a friend of theirs who'd arrived later.

In the morning she was faced by many bottles and later, a few hours later, a ribboning journey through flat, often unpeopled land. The Greyhound bus was like her home. She sat back, chewed gum, and watched the array of worn humanity on the bus. One of the last highlights of the party had been José emptying a bottle of red wine down the mouth of the little man from Uruguay.

When she arrived at the Greyhound bus station in her city she understood that there was something different about the bus station. Fewer drunks around. No one was playing the jukebox in the café. Chris wandered into the street. Crowds had gathered on the pavement. The dusk was issuing a brittle, blue spray of rain. Chris recognized a negro lady who usually frequented the bus station. The woman looked at Chris. People were waiting for a funeral. Lights from high-rise blocks blossomed. The negro woman was about to say something to Chris but refrained. Chris strolled down the street, wanting to ignore this anticipated funeral. But a little boy in a football T-shirt told her 'The nuns are dead.' On a front page of a local newspaper, the newspaper vendor forgetting to take the money from her, holding the newspaper from her, Chris saw the news. Five nuns from this city had been killed in a Central American country. Four were being buried today. One was Honor.

When Chris Gormley had left the school Sister Honor suddenly realized now that her favourite and most emotionally involving pupil—with what Sister Honor had taken to be her relaxed and high sense of destiny—had gone, that all her life she had not been confronting something in herself and that she often put something in front of her, prize pupils, to hide the essential fact of self-evasion. She knew as a child she'd had a destiny and so some months after Chris had gone Honor flew—literally in one sense but Honor saw herself as a white migrating bird—to Central America with some nuns from her convent. The position of a teaching nun in a Central American convent belonging to their order had become vacant suddenly when a nun began having catatonic nightmares before going, heaving in her frail bed. With other sisters she changed from black to white and was seen off with red carnations. The local newspaper had photographed them. But the photograph appeared in a newspaper in Detroit. A plane landed in an airport by the ocean, miles from a city which was known to be at war but revealed itself to them in champagne and palm trees. A priest at the American Embassy gave them champagne and they were photographed again.

There was a rainbow over the city that night. Already in that photograph when it was developed Honor looked younger. Blonde hair reached down from under her white veil, those Shirley Temple curls her father had been proud of and sometimes pruned to send snippets to relatives. In a convent twenty miles from the city Honor found a TV and a gigantic fridge. The Reverend Mother looked down into the fridge. She was fond of cold squid. A nearby town was not a ramshackle place but an American suburb. Palm trees, banks, benevolent-faced American men in panama hats. An American zinc company nearby. The girls who came to be taught were chocolate-faced but still the children of the rich—the occasional chocolate-faced girl among them a young American with a tan. Honor that autumn found herself teaching Spenser to girls who watched the same TV programmes as the girls in the city she left. An American flag fluttered nearby and assured everyone, even the patrolling monkey-bodied teenage soldiers, that everything was all right. Such a dramatic geographical change, such a physical leap brought Honor in mind of Chris Gormley.

Chris Gormley had captivated her from the beginning, her long, layered blonde hair, her studious but easy manner. Honor was not in a position to publicly admire so she sometimes found herself insulting Chris. Only because she herself was bound and she was baulking at her own shackles. She cherished Chris though—Chris evoked the stolidity and generosity of her own background; she succeeded in suggesting an aesthetic from it and for this Honor was grateful—and when Chris went Honor knew she'd failed here, that she'd no longer have someone to banter with, to play word games with, and so left, hoping Chris one day would make a genius or a lover—for her sake—or both. Honor had been more than grateful to her though for participating in a debate with her and making one thing lucid to her—that occasionally you have to move on. So moving on for Honor meant travel, upheaval, and finding herself now beside a big Reverend Mother who as autumn progressed kept peering into a refrigerator bigger than herself.

A few months after she arrived in the convent however things had shifted emphasis; Honor was a regular sight in the afternoons after school throwing a final piece of cargo into a jeep and shooting —exploding—off in a cantankerous and erratic jeep with other nuns to a village thirty miles away. She'd become part of a cathectics corps. Beyond the American suburb was an American slum. Skeletal women with ink hair and big ink eyes with skeletal children lined the way. Honor understood why she'd always been drawn to Elizabethan Irish history. Because history recurs. For a moment in her mind these people were the victims of a British invasion. At first she was shy with the children. Unused to children. More used to teenage girls. But little boys graciously reached their hands to her and she relaxed, feeling better able to cope. The war was mainly in the mountains; sometimes it came near. But the children did not seem to mind. There was one child she became particularly fond of—Harry after Harry Belafonte—and he of her and one person she became drawn to, Brother Mark, a monk from Montana. He had blond hair, the colour of honey, balding in furrows. She wanted to put her fingers through it. Together they'd sit on a bench—the village was on an incline—on late afternoons that still looked like autumn, vineyards around, facing the Pacific which they could not see but knew was there from the Pacific sun hitting the clay of the vineyards, talking retrospectively of America. Did she miss America? No. She felt an abyss of contentment here among the little boys in white vests, with little brown arms already bulging with muscles. Brother Mark dressed in a white gown and one evening, intuiting her feelings for him—the fingers that wanted to touch the scorched blue and red parts of his head—his hand reached from it to hers. To refrain from a relationship she volunteered for the mountains.

What she was there would always be in her face, in her eyes. Hornet-like helicopters swooped on dark rivers of people in mountain-side forests and an American from San Francisco, Joseph Dinani, his long white hair like Moses' scrolls, hunched on the ground in an Indian poncho, reading the palms of refugees for money and food. He'd found his way through the forests of Central America in the early 1970s. There were bodies in a valley, many bodies, pregnant women, their stomachs rising out of the water like rhinoceroses bathing. Ever after that there'd be an alarm in her eyes and her right eyebrow was permanently estranged from her eye. She had to leave to tell someone but no one in authority for the moment wanted to know. The Americans were in charge and nothing too drastic could happen with the Americans around.

She threw herself into her work with the children. For some hours during the day she taught girls. The later hours, evening closing in in the hills, the mountains, she spent with the children. They became like her family. Little boys recognized the potential for comedy in her face and made her into a comedienne. In jeans and a blouse she jived with a boy as a fighter bomber went over. But the memory of what she'd seen in the mountains drove her on and made every movement swifter. With this memory was the realization, consolidating all she felt about herself before leaving the school in the Midwest, that all her life she'd been running away from something—boys clanking chains in a suburb of a night-time Midwest city, hosts of destroyers speeding through the beech shade of a fragment of Elizabethan Irish history—they now were catching up on her. They had recognized her challenge. They had singled her out. Her crime? To treat the poor like princes. She was just an ordinary person now with blonde curly hair, a pale pretty face, who happened to be American.

The Reverend Mother, a woman partly Venezuelan, partly Brazilian, partly American, took at last to the doctrine of liberation and a convent, always anarchistic, some nuns in white, some in black, some in jeans and blouses, became more anarchistic. She herself changed from black to white. She had the television removed and replaced by a rare plant from Peru. An American man in a white suit came to call on her and she asked him loudly what had made him join the CIA and offered him cooked octopus. Honor was producing a concert for harvest festivities in her village that autumn.

There was a deluge of rats and mice—no one seemed quite sure which—in the tobacco-coloured fields that autumn and an influx of soldiers, young rat-faced soldiers borne along, standing, on the fronts of jeeps. Rat eyes imperceptibly took in Honor. They had caught up with her. A little girl in a blue dress crossed the fields, tejacote apples upheld in the bottom of her dress. A little boy ran to Honor. They were close at hand. At night when her fears were most intense, sweat amassing on her face, she thought of Chris Gormley, a girl at a school in the Midwest with whom she'd shared a respite in her life, and if she said unkindnesses to her she could say sorry now but that out of frustration comes the tree of one's life. Honor's tree blossomed that autumn. Sometimes rain poured. Sometimes the sky cheerily brightened. Pieces moved on a chess table in a bar, almost of their own accord. In her mind Honor heard a young soldier sing a song from an American musical: 'Out of My Dreams and Into Your Arms.'

The night of the concert squashes gleamed like moons in the fields around the hall. In tight jeans, red check shirt, her curls almost peroxide, Honor tightly sang a song into the microphone. Buddy Holly. 'You go your way and I'll go mine, now and forever till the end of time.' A soldier at the back shouted an obscenity at her. A little boy in front, in a grey T-shirt from Chicago, smiled his pleasure. In her mind was her father, his grey suit, the peace promised once when they were photographed together on a broad pavement of a city in the Midwest, that peace overturned now because it inevitably referred back to the turbulence that gave it, Irish—America, birth. And she saw the girl who in a way had brought her here. There was no panic in her, just an Elysium of broad, grey pavements and a liner trekking to Cobh, in County Cork. 'Yea, though I walk through the valley of the shadow of death, I will fear no evil: for thou art with me; thy rod and staff they comfort me.' In the morning they found her body with that of other nuns among ribbons of blood in a rubbish dump by a meeting of four roads. No one knew why they killed her because after the concert a young, almost Chinese-skinned soldier had danced with her under a yellow lantern that threw out scarlet patterns.

Afterwards Chris would wonder why her parents had not contacted her; perhaps the party with its barrage of phone calls had put up a barrier. But here, now, on the pavement, as the hearses passed, loaded with chrysanthemums and dahlias and carnations, she, this blonde, long-haired protégée of Sister Honor, could only be engulfed by the light of pumpkins which lit like candles in suburban gardens with dusk, by the lights of windows in high-rise blocks, apertures in catacombs in ancient Rome, by the flames which were emitted from factory chimneys and by the knowledge that a woman, once often harsh and forbidding, had been raised to the status of martyr and saint by a church that had continued since ancient Rome. An elderly lady in a blue mackintosh knelt on the pavement and pawed at a rosary. A negro lady beside Chris wept. But generally the crowd was silent, knowing that it had been their empire which had put these women to death and that now this city was receiving the bodies back among the flames of pumpkins, of windows, of rhythmically issuing factory fires, which scorched at the heart, turning it into a wilderness in horror and in awe.

Winter Swimmers

Winter swimmers, you brave the cold, you know you've got to go on, you make a statement. A Tinker's batty horse, brown and white, neighs in startlement at the winter swim. A man rides a horse on Gort Hill, disappearing onto the highway. Tinkers' limbs, limbs that have to know the cold to be cleansed.

'The Tinkers fight with one another and kill one another. If someone does something wrong they beat the tar out of them. But they don't fight with anyone else. You never see a Tinker letting his trousers down,' a woman whispered in Connemara, sitting on a wicker pheasant chair. The flowering currant was in blossom outside the window.

A Traveller boy in a combat jacket with lead-coloured leaves on it stood outside his Roma Special, among washing machines, wire, pots, kettles, cassettes, tin buckets.

Some day later there were lightening streaks of white splinters across the road where the Travellers had been.

In early summer the bog cotton blew like patriarchs' beards, above a hide, the stems slanted, and distantly there were scattered beds of bog cotton on the varyingly floored landscape under the apparition-blue of the mountains.

I was skipping on Clifden Head when a little boy came along. The thrift was in the rocks. 'Nice and fit.' He wanted to go swimming. But he had no trunks. 'Go in the nude,' I said. 'Ah, skinny-dipping. Are you going again?' I was drying. 'No, I'll go elsewhere and paddle.'

'I used to pass him in the rain outside his caravan,' the woman in Connemara told a story before she went to mass, about a Tinker man who died young, standing in an accordion-pleated skirt, 'sitting by a fire against the wall. "Why don't you go inside?" I'd ask him. "Sure I have two jackets," he'd say. "I have another one inside. I can put on that one if this one gets wet."'

'Are you a buffer or a Traveller?' a Tinker boy asked me. On their journeys there are five-minute prayers at a place where you were born, where your grandmother died.

There was a Traveller's discarded Jersey in a bush. Buffer—settled—Travellers stood in front of a cottage with the strawberry tree—the white bell flower—outside.

A Traveller in a suit of Mosque blue came to the door one day to try to buy unwanted furniture, carpets. 'He had a suit blue as the tablecloth,' went the story after him. Part of his face was reflected in the mirror. It was as if a face was being put together, bit by bit.

A Traveller youth in a cap and slip-on boots which had a triangle of slatted elastic material held his bicycle in a rubbish dump against a rainbow. The poppy colours of the montbretia spread through the countryside in the hot summer. There were sea mallows between the roads and the sands.

You felt you were nuzzling for recovery against landscape.

The sides of the sea road towards fill were thronged with hemp agrimony. The seaweed was bursting, a rich harvest full of iodine. As I was leaving Galway the last fuschia flowers were like red bows on twigs the way yellow ribbons were sometimes tied around trees in the Southern States.

'Now therefore, I pray thee, take heed to thyself until the morning, and abide in a secret place, and hide thyself.'

You felt like a broken city, the one sung about in a song played on jukeboxes throughout Ireland. 'What's lost is lost and gone forever.' In May 1972 you heard a lone British soldier on duty sing 'Scarlet Ribbons' on a deserted sun-drenched street in that city.

Old man's beard grew among the winter blackthorns in West Limerick. Tall rushes with feathery tops lined the road to Limerick. Traveller women used to fashion flowers from these rush tops.

The bracket fungus in the woods behind my flat was gathered on logs like coins on a crown, stories.

On the street of this town the Teddyboy's face came back, brigand's moustache, funnel sidelocks, carmine shirts, the spit an emblem on the pavement. He had briar-rose white skin.

'They'd come in September and stay until Confirmation time,' a woman in a magenta blouse with puff sleeves whispered about the Travelling people. When I was a boy Travellers would draw in for the winter around our town.

A pool was created in the river behind the house in which I was staying and I swam there each morning, the river, just after a rocky waterfall, halted by a cement barrier. On this side of the town bridge the river is fresh water. On the other it is tidal. Swans often sat on the cement barrier when only a meagre current went over it.

On this side it is a spate river and the current, always strong at the side, after rain, is powerful, I did not gauge its power and one morning I was swept away by it, over the barrier, as if by a human force. I had no control. There was no use fighting. I was carried down the waterfall on the other side of the barrier to another tier of the river, drawn in a torrent. I saw pegwood in red berry on the bank. I got to the side, crawled out. In Ancient Ireland they used to eat bowls of rowan berries in the autumn.

One morning I tried the tidal part of the river at the pier called Gort. In Irish *gort* means field, field of corn. It is very close to the word for hunger, famine—*gorta*. The flour ships from Newcastle and Liverpool used to come here. People would carry hay, seaweed to the pier. A slate-blue warehouse shelters you from view.

When I was a boy they used to hold a rope across the river at the Red Bridge, someone on either side, swimmers clutching it and then the swimmers would be pulled up and down.

I remembered a man drying the hair of a boy in the fall of 1967.

I had a friend who used to swim naked when he found he had the place to himself. One day someone hid his clothes in the bushes and a group of girls came along. He hid behind a bush until they went.

He was writing what he called a pornographic novel for a while. As we passed some Travellers' caravans one autumn day he told me a story. A boy, a relation, a soldier in Germany, came from England, slept in the bed with him. At night they'd make love. The evenings during his visit were demure. They'd have cocoa as if nothing had happened. My friend had a modestly winged Beatle cut, wore vaguely American, plum or aubergine shirts with stripes of indigo blue or purple blue.

A Traveller in a stove-pipe hat called to the door one afternoon and offered five pounds for a copper tank that was lying behind the house, his hand ritualistically outstretched, the fiver in it. I said I couldn't give it to him. It was my landlady's. The copper tank disappeared in the middle of the night.

An English Gypsy boy with hair in smithereens on his face, his cheeks the sunset peach of a carousel horse's checks, in a frisbee, carnelian hearing aid in his left ear, on a bicycle, stopped me one day when I was cycling and asked me the way to Rathkeale. I was going there myself and pointed him on.

In Rathkeale rich Travellers have built an enclave of pueblo-type and hacienda-type houses. They were mostly shut up, the doors and the windows grilled, the inhabitants in Germany, the men tarmacadaming roads. A boy with a long scarf the lemon-yellow of the Vatican passed those houses on a piebald horse.

I moved down the river to swim in the mornings, nearer the house where I lived, and swam among the bushes, putting stones on the ground where there was broken glass. There'd been a factory opposite the pool.

When I was a boy it was an attitude, swim in rain, ice, snow, brave these things, topaz of sun often in the wet winter grass, topaz in the auburn hair of a boy swimmer.

A group of young people used to swim through the winter. Even when the grass was covered with frost and the blades capped with pomegranate or topaz gold. They'd pose for photographs in hail or snow. I was not among them but later I had no problem swimming in winter, in suddenly, after some months of not swimming, taking off a Napoleon coat in winter and swimming in winter in the Forty Foot in Dublin or on a beach in Donegal.

There was something benign about these young people. Mostly boys. But sometimes a few girls.

One day in Dublin I met one of the boys just after his mother died. It was winter. We didn't say much. But we got on the 8 bus to the Forty Foot and had a swim together. He went to the United States shortly after that.

Some English Gypsies were camped outside town and one day a boy on a Shetland pony, with copper crenellated mid-sixties hair and ocean-ultramarine irises, asked me, 'Did you ever ride a muir?'

'Look at the horse's gou,' he said referring to a second Shetland pony a boy with skirmished hair was holding, 'Would you like to feak her?'

It's like a bandage being removed I thought, plaster taken off, layer and layer, from a terrible wound—a war wound.

Christmas 1974, just before going back to Ireland from London, I slept in a bed with an English boy under a bedspread with diamond patterns, some of them nasturtium coloured. He had liquid ebony hair, a fringe beard. He wore his bewhiskered Afghan coat, spears of hair out of it. In bed his body was lily-pale—he had cherry-coloured nipples. On our farewell he gave me a book and I put the Irish Christmas stamp with a Madonna and Child against a mackcrel-blue sky in it.

All the journeys, hitch-hiking, train journeys overlap I thought, they are still going on, they are still intricating, a journey somewhere. It's a face you once saw and it brushes past the Mikado orange of Southern Switzerland in autumn, a face on a station platform. It is the face of a naked boy in an Edwardian mirror in a squat in London with reflections of mustard-coloured trees from the street.

When I returned to England in the autumn of 1977 I went on a daytrip to Oxford shortly before Christmas with some friends and we listened to a miserere in a church and afterwards sat behind a snob-screen in a pub where tomtits were back-painted on a mirror. It was another England. I was sexually haunted. By a girl I'd loved and who'd left me. By a boy I'd just slept with.

In Slussen in Central Stockholm I once met a boy with long blond centre-parted hair, in a blue denim suit, and he told me about the tree in Central Stockholm they were going to cut down and which they didn't, people protesting under it. I bought strawberries with him and he brought me in a slow, glamorous train to his home on the Archipelgo, a Second Empire-type home. There were Carl Larsson pictures on the wall. It was my first acquaintance with that artist. He sent me two Carl Larsson images later. Images of happiness.

Years later I met that boy in London. He was working in the Swedish army and leading soldiers on winter swims or winter dips.

At the Teddyboy's funeral there were little boys in almost identical white shirts and black cigarette trousers, like a uniform, girls with bouffant hairdos, shingles at ears, in near-party dresses, in A-line dresses, in platform shoes, in low high heels with T-straps, with double T-straps, carrying bunches of red carnations, carrying tulips. In Ancient Rome, after a victory, coming into Rome, the army would knock down part of the city. At the Teddyboy's funeral it was as if people were going to knock part of the town.

The Teddyboy wore a peach jacket in the weeks before he was drowned. He was laid out in a brown habit. My mother said it was that sight which made her forbid me to swim at the Red Bridge with the other young people of town. In the summer when I was sixteen I tried to commit suicide by taking an overdose of sleeping pills at dawn one morning. I just slept on the kitchen floor for a while. At the end of the summer a guard drew up on the street opposite our house in a Volkswagen, the solemn orange of *Time* magazine on the front of the car. He'd come to bring me to swim at the Red Bridge. Years later, retired, he swam in the Atlantic of Portugal in the winter.

At the end of the summer of 1967, when I was sixteen, I started swimming on my own volition.

In early February the wild celery and the hemlock and the hart's-tongue fern and the lords and ladies fern and the buttercup leaves and the celandine leaves and the alexanders and the eyebright and fool's watercress came to the riverbank or the river. There was the amber of a robin among the bushes who watched me almost each morning.

Here you are surrounded by the smells of your childhood, I thought, cow dung, country evening air, the smell the grass gives off with the first inkling of spring, cottages with covert smells—the musk of solitary highly articulate objects—and a mandatory photograph on the piano. My grandmother lived in a house like the one I lived in now. She had a long honed face, cheekbones more bridges, large eyes, Roman nose. She was a tall woman and spoke with the mottled flatness of the Midlands.

Here's to the storytellers. They made some sense from these lonely and driven lives of ours.

When I was a child in hospital with jaundice there'd been a traditional musician who'd been in a car accident in the bed beside me. There were cavalcades of farts, an overwhelming odour as he painfully tried to excrete into a bedpan behind the curtains but the insistent impression was, in spite of the pain, of the music in his voice, in his many courtesies.

You heard the curlew again. 'The cuckoo brings a hard week,' they said in Connemara. One year was grafted onto another. 'March borrows three days from April to skin an old cow,' they'd said a month earlier, meaning that the old cow thinks he's escaped come April. Two swans flew over the Deel and the woods through which golden frogs made pilgrimages among the confectioner's white of the ramson—wild garlic—flower, soldering stories.

On a roadside in County Sligo once I sat and had soup from a pot with legs on it with a Traveller couple. Now I knew what the ingredients were—nettles, dandelion leaves.

With May sunshine I started to go to Gort to swim each day. Traveller youths swam their horses in the spring tide, up and down with ropes, urging them on with long pliable horse goads with plastic gallon drums on the end. One of the Traveller youths had primrose-flecked hair. Another a floss of butter-chestnut hair. Another hair in cavalier style. 'You've a decent old tube,' said the boy with the primrose-flecked hair.

During the day I noticed his hair had copper in it.

One evening during spring tide I saw him stand in a rose-coloured shirt, not far from cottages, by the river where it was bordered by yellow rocket float down.

The first poppy was a bandana against the denim of the bogs of West Limerick.

In the evenings of spring tide when the Travellers came along and swam their horses I was reminded of St Maries which I'd visited twenty years before, when the Gypsies would come and lead their horses to the water on the edge of the Mediterranean. To Saintes Maries had come Mary, mother of James the Less, Mary Salome, mother of James and John, and Sarah, the Gypsy servant, all on a sculling boat. There were bumpers by the sea and in little dark kiosks jukeboxes with effects on them like costume jewellery. Lone young Gypsy men wandered on the beach, great dunes on the land side of the beach. A little inland, horsemen with bandanas around their noses rode horses through the Camargue.

Back briefly in the river pool one evening I found the Traveller youth with the cavalier hair shampooing himself after a swim. His underpants were sailor blue and white.

Later that week when I came to Gort the boy with the primrose-flecked hair was there alone with his horse, a Clydesdale, ruffs at his feet. A few days' growth on his face, he was naked waist up. There was the imprint outline of a tank top—the evidence of hot days, his nipples not pink—hazel, a quagmire of hair under his arms, freckles berried around his body. His body smelt of stout like the bodies of young men who gathered in my aunt's pub in a village in the Midlands when I was a child. A rallying, a summoning in the body to dignity.

I am in the West of Ireland, I thought. Illness prevents me from seeing, from looking. Like a soot on the mind. Sometimes I raise my head. Like Lazurus recover life—especially vision.

One Friday evening as I cycled home from Gort the youth with the primrose-flecked hair introduced himself 'Cummian.' And he introduced the other two youths. 'Gawalan. Colín.'

'You need a relationship,' he said.

When the tide came in in the evening again his horse had a wounded leg and he tied it to the ship rung on the pier and it would stand in the water for hours. Cummian stayed with it and he'd watch me swim and between swims he'd tell stories.

'There was a man who fucked his mares. He tied them to trees.'

'Someone sold a horse to a man who lived on Cavon Island off Clare and the horse swam back across the Shannon estuary to West Limerick.'

Two Traveller brothers troubled over a horse at Gort, their voices becoming muffled. They seemed to wager the tide. The river had a mirror-like quality after rain. Late one evening Cummian was sitting in the bushes to one side with some men, one of whom was holding up a skinned rabbit. Boys would often fish on the pier with the triple hook—the strokeall—for mullet. On the far side young men would hunt for ribbits with young greyhounds. On summer nights Travellers would draw up on the pier in old cars—Ford Populars, Sunbeams. In Scots Gaelic there's a word, *duthus*—commonage. That's what Gort was, people coming, using the place in common. The winter, the dark days were a quarter I thought, now I have to face people, I have to communicate. There was often a bed of crabs on the river edge as I walked in.

'If I wasn't married, I'd get lonely,' said Cummian one evening.

Water rats swam through the water with evening quiet, paddling with their forepaws. The tracks of the water rat made a V-shape.

Sometimes in the early evening there'd be a harem of Traveller boys on the pier in the maple red of Liverpool or the strawberry and cream of Arsenal or the red white of Charlton FC or the grey white of Millwall FC.

'Where are you from?' asked a boy in a T-shirt with Goofy playing basketball on it.

'You don't speak like a Galwayman but you've got the teeth.'

Cummian would tell stories of his forebears, the Travelling people—beet picking in Scotland, 'We lie down with manikins.' That ancestor used to write poems and publish them in *Moore's Almanac* for half a crown.

Sometimes he got four and six pence. 'Some of them were a mile long,' said Cummian.

'They used stuff saucepans with holes with the skins of old potatoes and they'd be clogged. They used milkcans especially. Take the bottoms out of milkcans. Put in new ones.'

With his talk of mending I thought, recovery is like a billycan in the hand, the frail, fragilely adjoined handle.

In the champagne spring tide of late July Cummian rode the horse in a bathing togs as it swam in the middle of the river.

One afternoon there was a group of small boys on the pier fishing. One had a Madonna-blue thread around his neck, his top naked, his hair the black of stamens of poppies.

'I'll swim with you,' he said, 'if you go naked.' I took off my togs. They had a good look and then they fled, one of them on a bicycle, in a formation like a runaway camel.

Sometimes, though rarely, Traveller girls would come with the boys to the pier, with apricot hair and strawberry lips, in sleeveless, picot-edged white blouses, in jeans, in dresses the white of white tulips. Cummian's wife came to the pier one evening in a white dress with the green leaves of the lily on it, carrying their child.

Cummian was a buffer, a settled Traveller and lived in one of the cottages near the river, incendiary houses—cherry, poppy or rosette coloured—with maple trees now like burning bushes outside them. There'd be horses outside the Travellers' cottages—a jeremiad for the days of travelling.

One night Travellers were having a row on the green by the river—there was a movement like the retreat of Napoleon from Moscow, hordes milling across the green. Cummian, holding his child, looked on pacifically. 'You're done,' someone shouted in the throng.

There was a rich crop of red hawthorn berries among the seaweed in early fall, at high tide gold leaves on the river edge. Reeds, borne by the cork in them, created a demi-pontoon effect.

A woman in white court high heels came around the corner one day as I stood in my bathing togs. 'This place used to be black with swimmers during high tide. Children used to swim on the slope.'

A swan and five cygnets pecked at the bladderwort by the side of the pier and the cob came flying low up on the river, back from a journey.

In berry the pegwood, the berberis, the rowan tree were fairy lights in the landscape. The pegwood threw a burgundy shadow onto the water. With flood the reflection was the cinnabar red of a Russian ikon.

One day in early November Cummian was on the pier with his horse alongside a man with a horse who had a sedate car and horse trailer. The grass was a troubled winter green. The other man, apart from Cummian, was the last to swim his horse.

'He likes winter swimming,' Cummian said of his. 'Like you. He'd stay there for an hour. And he's only a year.'

With the tides coming in and going out there was a metallurgy in the landscape, with the tidal rivers a metallurgical feel, something extracted, called forth. A sadness was extracted from the landscape, a feeling that must have been like Culloden after battle. On Culloden Moor the Redcoats with tricornes had confronted the Highlanders.

'Why do you swim in winter?' asked Gawalan who was with Cummian one evening.

'It's a tradition,' I said, 'I used to do it when I was a boy,' which was not true. Other people did it. I did it later, on and off in Dublin.

Jakob Böhme said the tree was the origin of the language. The winter swim sustains language I thought, because it is connected with something in your adolescence—the hyacinthine winter sunlight through the trees on the other side of the river. It is connected with a tradition of your country, odd people—apart from the sea swimmers—here and there all over Ireland who'd bathe in winter in rivers and streams.

A rowing boat went down the river one afternoon in late November, a lamp on the front of it, reflection of lamp in the water.

Gawalan and Colín went to England. They'd go to see female stripteasers first in the city and then male stripteasers.

With November floods there were often piles of rubbish left on the riverbank. A man in a trenchcoat, with rimless-looking spectacles, cycled up to the pier one evening. 'I hear them dumping it from the bridge at midnight. It kills the dolphins, the whales, the turtles. You see all kinds of things washed in farther down, pallets, dressers.' He pointed. 'There used to be a lane going down there for miles and people would play accordions on summer evenings. A boxer used to swim here with wings on his feet. There was a butcher, Killgalon, who swam in winter before you. He swam everyday up to his late eighties.'

The river's been persecuted, vandalized I thought, but continues in dignity.

Early December the horse swam in the middle of the river, up and down, and I swam across it. The water rubbed a pink into the horse.

Hounds, at practice, having appeared among the bladderwort on the other side, crossed the river, in a mass, urged on by hunting horns.

A tallow boy's underpants was left on the pier. Maybe someone else went for a winter swim. Maybe someone made love here and forgot his underpants. Maybe it was left the way the Travellers leave a rag, an old cardigan in a place where they've camped—a sign to show other Travellers they've been there—spoor they call it.

Towards Christmas I met Cummian near his cottage and he invited me in. 'Will you buy some holly?' a Traveller boy asked me as I approached it. Cummian's eyes were sapphirine breaks above a western shirt, his hair centre parted, a cowlick on either side.

There was a white iron work hallstand; an overall effect from the hall and parlour carpets and wallpaper and from the parlour draperies of fuschine colours and colours of whipped autumn leaves.

He sat under a photograph of a boxer with gleaming black hair, in cherry satin-looking shorts, white and blue striped socks. On a small round table was a statue of Our Lady of Fatima with gold leaves on her white gown, two rosaries hanging from her wrist, one white, one strawberry; on the wall near it a wedding photograph of Cummian with what seemed to be a pearl pin in his tie; a photograph of Cummian with a smock of hair, sideburns, Dom Bosco face, holding a baby with a patina of hair beside a young woman in an ankle-length plaid skirt outside a tent.

We had tea and lemon slices by Gateaux.

Christmas Eve at the river a moon rose sheer over the trees like a medallion.

Christmas Day frost suddenly came, the slope to the water half-covered in ice. In the afternoon sunshine the ice by the water was gold and flamingo coloured.

Sometimes on days of Christmas the winter sun seemed to have taken something from the breast, the emblem of a robin.

Cummian did not come those days with his Clydesdale. I was the only swimmer.

I was going to California after Christmas. I thought of Cummian's face and how it reminded me of that of a boy I knew at national school, with kindled saffron hair which travelled down, smote part of his neck, who wore tallow corded jackets. His hand used to reach to touch me sometimes. At Shallowhorseman's once I saw his poignant nudity, his back turned towards me. He went to England.

It also reminded me of a boy I knew later who smelled like a Roman urinal but whereas the smell of a Roman urinal would have been tinged with olive oil his was with acne ointment. One day after school I went with him to his little attic room and he sat without a shirt, his chest cupped. There was a sketch on the wall by a woman artist who'd died young. He often used to walk with his sister who wore a white dress with a shirred front and a gala ribbon to an aboriginal Gothic cottage in the woods.

He went to England in mid-adolescence.

He was in the FCA and would sit in the olive-green uniform of the Irish Army, his chest already manly, framed, beside a bed of peach crocuses on the slope outside the army barracks which used to be the Railway Hotel, a Gothic building of red and white brick, a script on top, hieroglyphics, the emblems of birds.

It snowed after Christmas. The trees around the river were ashen with their weight of snow. There were platters of ice on the water.

As I cycled back from swimming Cummian was standing with two Traveller youths in the snow. There was a druidic ebony greyhound in historic stance beside them. Their faces looked moonstone pale.

I knew immediately I'd said something wrong on my visit to Cummian's house. It didn't matter what I'd said, it was often that way in Ireland, having been away, feeling damaged, things often came out the way they weren't meant. Hands in the pockets of a monkey jacket, hurt, Cummian's eyes were the blue that squared school exercise books when I was a child.

There was a Canadian redwing in the woods behind my flat who'd come because of the cold weather in North America. Never again I thought, as I was driven to Shannon, the attic room of beech or walnut, a boy half-naked, military smell—musk—off him, a montage on the wall. Choose your decade and change the postcards. Somebody or something dug into one here.

I have put bodies together again here I thought, put the blond or strawberry terracotta bricks together.

In San Diego next day I boarded a scarlet tram and a few days later I'd found a beach, the ice plant falling by the side, plovers flying over, where I swam and watched the Pacific go from gentian to aquamarine to lapis lazuli until one day, when the Santa Anas were blowing, a young man and a young woman came and swam naked way out in the combers, then came in, dried, and went away.

The Red Bridge, a railway bridge, always porous, became lethally porous, uncrossable by foot. Cut off was an epoch, gatherings for swims.

People would trek over clattery boards who knew it was safe because so many people went there.

In the fall of 1967 trains would go over in the evening, aureoles of light, against an Indian red sun. You'd hear the corncrake.

A little man who worked in the railway would stand in the sorrel and watch the boys undress.

Shortly before he died of cancer he approached me, in a gaberdine coat, when I was sitting in the hotel, back on a visit. He spoke in little stories.

Of Doctor Aveline who wore pinstriped suits, a handkerchief of French-flag red in his breast pocket, and always seemed tipsy, wobbling a little.

Of Carmelcita Aspell whose hair went white in her twenties, who wore tangerine lipstick and would stand in pub porches, waiting to be picked up by young men.

Of Miss Husatine, a Protestant lady who went out with my father once, who didn't drink but loved chocolate liqueur sweets.

Of the bag of marzipan sweets my father always carried and scrummaged by the rugby pitch; squares of lime with lurid pink lines; yellow balls brushed with pink, dusted with sugar, with pink hearts; orbs of cocktail colours; sweets just flamingo.

And he spoke of the winter swim. 'It was an article of faith,' he said.

Caravans

The September river was a forget-me-not blue and the bushes on the other side were gold brocade. The old man who stood beside me as I got out of the river had glasses tied by a black strap around his head. He lived in a cream ochre ledgetop Yorkshire wagon with green dado, near the river.

'I've been here fourteen years but I'm moving tomorrow to a field near Horan's Cross,' he said, 'The children torment me. I hit some sometimes and I was up with the guards over it. We were blackguards too. They used to wash clothes on stones in streams. There was an old woman who used to wash her clothes and we'd throw stones at her.'

Looking at the river he said: 'A young butcher and a young guard used to swim to the other pier, practising for the swim across the estuary in the summer. I used to swim the breast stroke, the crawler. But then I'd put on swimming togs and go out and stand in the rain. It was as good as a swim.'

There'd been another caravan parked beside the old man when I first came to live in a caravan nearby and an Englishwoman lived in it sometimes dressed as a near punk—in an argyle mini skirt with a chain girdle—and sometimes as a traditional Gypsy with a nasturtium yellow shawl with sanguine dapples and a nasturtium yellow dress with sanguine dabs on it which had attennae.

In my first few weeks living in a caravan by a field there was the blood translucence of blackberries, the mastery of intricate webs, the petrified crimson of ladybirds on nettles.

On one of my first mornings the guards arrived in plain clothes. A guard with jeans tight on his crotch banged on the door. 'Mrs Monson has objected to you,' he said referring to a woman who lived in a cottage nearby.

In my first few weeks in a caravan I realized that living in a caravan there was always the laceration, the scalding of a nettle on you, the tear of a briar, the insult of a settled person. But you noticed the grafts in the weather, mild to cold in the night, fog to rain. You saw the pheasant rising from the grass. Close to the river you were close to the hunger of the heron, the twilight voyages of the swan, the traffic of water rats.

In the night there was a vulnerability, a caravan by a field near a main road, a few trees sheltering it from the road, the lights of cars flashing in the caravan, a sense of your caravan's frail walls protecting you.

Coming to live in a caravan by a field near a main road was part of a series of secessions.

A few weeks after I'd come to live in West Limerick I was gathering firewood in the wood behind my flat, yellow jelly algae on the logs, sycamore, maple, ash wings on the grass, when a little boy in a frisbee and a shirt with chickens wearing caps and flowers and suns on it, came up to me on a bicycle. His hair had the gold allotted to pictures of the Assumption of Mary in secretive places. The sky over the river was a brothel pink. 'Pleased to meet you.' When I raised my axe a little he dashed away.

Sometimes as I walked in the fields in the winter I'd see him, tatterdemalion against the trunk of a rainbow. Dogs were often digging for pigmy shrews in the fields.

One day he was in the fields with two greyhounds of a friend on leashes, one white with marigold mottles, the other fleecy cream and tar black with a quiff on the back.

In the spring he knocked on my door. 'I'm looking for haggard for my horse. I wonder can I put a horse behind your house?' He had a seed earring in his right ear now.

'If I be bereaved of my children, I am bereaved.' Sometimes on summer nights when I swam in the artificially created pool in the fresh water part of the river behind my house he'd be there. On one side of the town bridge the river was fresh water. On the other side it was tidal water. He'd be leaping from the high cement bank with other Traveller children. Ordinarily he looked boxer-like but in swimming togs I saw that his legs were twig-like—almost as if he was the victim of malnutrition.

'On your marks, ready, steady, go,' he'd command the other children. 'Did you ever tread the water?' he'd ask me. Meaning being almost still in near-standing position in the water.

In the early autumn when I'd go to swim on the pier in the tidal part of the river he'd often be there with his horse, shampooing his horse's tail. The horse was a brown horse with one foot bejewelled with white and with a buttermilk tail. The boy's features were hard as a beech nut or an apple corn now. He'd look at me with his blueberry and aqua-blue mix eyes. 'I can't swim her now. She's in foal.' The foal when it came was sanguine coloured. The boy left both of them in a meadow on the town side of the pier. The foal would sometimes go off on a little journey, a little adventure, and the mare, tied, would whinny until his return.

I went to the United States and after my return in the spring I found the flat I'd been living in had been given away. I moved into another flat in the same house. It was unsatisfactory. Cycling to the pier I'd watch and listen for the little boy. There was no sign of him. I wondered if his family had moved on, if he was in England. Then one day at the end of April he rode to the river on his horse. The time for swimming the horses had come again.

Up and down the Traveller men swam their horses. Steel greys— white horses with a hall of dark grey on them, Appaloosas—speckled Indian horses, skewbalds—batty horses, piebalds.

Handsome horses with sashes of hair on their foreheads. A man with round face, owl eyes, stout-coloured irises, hard-bargained-for features, in an opaque green check shirt, spat into the water as he swam his horse. On his forearm he had tattoos of a camel, a harp, a crown.

The boy when he brought his horse to the water had a new bridle on her, viridian and shell pink patterned. He told me of the things that happened while I was away. In February the otters had mated by the pier.

I found a cottage in the hills outside the town and the boy's father who had kettle-black eyebrows, piped locks, roach hairstyle, wore a Claddagh ring—two hands holding a gold crown—on his finger, drove me there.

I put a reproduction of Botticelli's *Our Lady of the Sea* over the fireplace, her jerkin studded with stars.

'Say a prayer to St Mary,' an English boy, the son of a painter, who cycled to a flat of mine in London in an apricot T-shirt, said to me.

The cottage was near a church but despite that fact I soon found that local people were knocking on the back windows at night, cars were driving up outside the house at night and hooting horns.

I'd cycle to the river everyday. There were roads like Roman roads off the road through the hills. 'Finbarr Slowey bought a house there and brought his wife and children,' a Traveller man with Indian-ink-black hair and Buddha-boy features who was at the river with his strawberry roan, told me, 'and they drove up outside his house at night and hooted horns. If they don't want someone to live in their village they hoot horns outside their houses at night.'

Many sumach trees grew in this area as in the Southern States and I kept thinking of the Southern States. The bunch of antebellum roses; the tartan dickie bow; the hanging tree beside a remote bungalow with a dogtrot. The brother of a friend of mine from a Civil Rights family was killed by the Ku Klux Klan on the Alabama-Georgia border. This area was very similar to the border country of Alabama and Georgia. Great sheaves of corn braided and left out for hurling victors; boys in green and white striped football jerseys dancing with girls at the Shannonside to the music of a platform band; the shadow of a man in a homburg hat at night.

'The IRA's up there,' said the Traveller boy, 'And vigilante groups. They tar and feather people.'

At night when I'd be trying to sleep people would stand behind the house and bang sticks. I didn't think there was any point going to the guards. A guard with black lambchop sidelocks and a small paste-looking moustache came by at about eleven o'clock one night and asked me if I was working.

I couldn't sleep at night. I didn't see the Traveller boy by the river so I sought him out. I always thought his family were settled Travellers but when I enquired in the cottages near the river they said: 'He lives in a caravan up by the waterpump.'

A long sleek caravan with gilt trimming, occasional vertical gilt lines, flamingo shadows in the cream. Behind it, on the other side of the road, was a flood-lit grotto. His mother was standing by the window—buttermilk blonde hair, mosaic face over a shirt with leg-of-mutton sleeves—above the layette, the celestial cleanliness of aluminium kettles and pots laid out for tasks. She wore a ring with a coin on it. There was a little blonde girl with yellow ducks on her dress and a little boy with cheeks the yellow and red of a cherry and eyes a turquoise that looked as if it had just escaped from a bottle. On the caravan wall was a framed colour photograph of a boxer with a gold girdle and on a cupboard a jar of Vaseline. I remembered an English girl whose father was a miner telling me that miners always put Vaseline in their hair before going down into the mines. The Traveller boy was wearing wellingtons the colour of sard.

'You've no choice,' said his father, 'but to buy a caravan and move into it.'

The boy's father got a little caravan for me and I moved into it.

The hazelnuts were on the trees by the river the day I moved into the caravan. In being moved from house to caravan I found out the boy's name, his father referring to him. Finnian. A hawk had brought St Finnian the hand of an enemy who had tried to slay him the previous day.

A middle-aged single woman who had connections with the Travelling people moved into the cottage in which I'd been living and they started banging on her window at night. She couldn't sleep. A room was found for her on Maiden Street in Newcastle West. I'd often see Traveller boys with piebald horses on Maiden Street in Newcastle West.

Shortly after I moved into the caravan a little boy with a Neopolitan black cowlick and onyx eyes knocked at the door. 'I heard you like books. I have murder stories. Will you buy some?'

'Do you want to buy a mint jacket?' asked Gobán, a Traveller boy with a sash of down growing on his lips who lived in a caravan near Finnian's. He was wearing a plenitudinous pair of army fatigue trousers. He went into his caravan and brought it out. It was malachite-cream, double-breasted, almost epaulette shouldered, with a wide lapel.

He and Finnian would often come to my caravan and I'd get them to read poems.

The nineteenth autumn has come upon me
Since I first made my count:
I saw, before I had well finished,
All suddenly mount . . .

Both Finnian and Gobán were in identical Kelly-green fleece

jerseys. 'Will I tell you a joke?' said Gobán as Finnian read. 'Stand up and be counted or lie down and be mounted.'

Finnian and Gobán and I would have tea, and half-moon cakes and coconut tarts I'd buy in Limerick.

Sometimes when Finnian would be out lamping for rabbits at night he'd knock at the caravan door and request Mikado biscuits.

The boys would come at night and tell stories; of the priest who used to go on pilgrimage to Lough Derg and bring a bottle of Bushmills around with him on the days of pilgrimage; of the local woman who dressed in religious blue, spring gentian blue, and broke into the priest's house one night and put on his clothes; of the single Traveller man with the handlebar moustache who lived in a caravan and had a bottle of Fairy Liquid for ten years; of Traveller ancestors who met up with other Travellers they knew from Ireland on Ellis Island before entering the United States; of a relative of Finnian's who went to America, joined the American navy and was drowned while swimming in Lough Foyle during the Second World War when his fleet was stationed there.

'Long ago in West Limerick,' said Finnian's father, 'they had rambling houses—went from house to house telling stories.'

Every year settled Travellers in Ireland—buffers—make a long walk to commemorate the days of travelling. One year it was Dublin to Downpatrick, County Down. Despite the insults, the contumelies heaped against Travelling people, you keep on walking.

On December twenty-first, the winter solstice, Finnian and Gobán and Gobán's smaller brother Touser brought a candle each and put them in the menorah in my caravan and lit them against the winter emerald of West Limerick. Touser had a fresh honey blond turf cut, a pugilist's vow of a body.

A rowing boat with a red sail had gone down the river that day.

Patrick—Patricius—had once lit the paschal flame in this country.

When he couldn't sleep Caesar Augustus would call in the story-tellers and as we had tea and Christmas cake they told stories and jokes and in the middle of stories and jokes came out with lines from Traveller songs—'I married a woman in Ballinasloe,' 'I have a lovely horse'—and, the lights of cars flashing in the caravan, it was as though all four of us were walking, were marching through the evening.

Shelter

They're seasonal. Like the laughing goose.

They come to the art-deco shelter on Sunday evenings in January.

Boys from Greenmount in the south of Cork city in Manchester United bobble hats, baseball caps with slogans like 'Whip Me' or 'Yankees,' Crusaders' headdresses from Dunnes Stores, cowls. Many of them with blotched faces like the spots on the woundwort flower.

They're typical of groups of boys you see in Cork or Limerick, who have no association with female company, and who are obsessed with soccer.

In January they have neophytes, sixteen-year-old boys, down over their lips like the teeth of the dog's-tooth violet, with faces like kittiwakes or guillemots and Damien Duff razor shaves, sea-anemone ear studs or maybe white plastic rosaries or pendants with gold knobs of Our Lords head around their necks under a Cristiano Ronaldo T-shirt or T-shirt with a 2Pac epitaph: 'Only God can judge me!'

In Greenmount in Cork they have sex games with one another in a shed.

But more often than not they play shadow games—they mime what each other is doing.

Or they might retell a legend learned at community college, like how Fionn MacChumhaill was the Hercules of Ireland and another Hercules, Cúchulainn—no one knew whether he was Scottish or Irish, Celtic or Rangers—came to fight with him.

Fionn MacChumhaill lay in a cradle, pretending he was a baby, bit off the middle finger of Cúchulainn's right hand—his strength— and then killed him.

In the shed is a poster of Mayfield's Roy Keane, of Cúchulainn -stature, in an Etruscan-red jersey, black knee-high stockings with scarlet tops, which have galloons of gold, beside a picture of Princess Diana in cream linen jeans holding a child in Bosnia; David Beckham with a topknot; Wayne Rooney just out of De La Salle in Croxteth kicking a ball; Keanu Reeves in a shirt of gold brocade patterned with blue-and-red blossom and green foliage, and codpiece, as Don John in *Much Ado About Nothing*.

'I had rather be a canker in a hedge than a rose in his grace.'

In the summer in cobweb-muscle T-shirts they pick potatoes near Bandon, which was settled with Somerset people in Shakespeare's day.

On summer evenings, in the hoops—emerald and white of Celtic—they congregate at the mallard sanctuary in the Lee Fields where elderly men lie way out on the Lee as if it was a jacuzzi.

On Saturdays they watch soccer at Turner's Cross, originally home of Evergreen United.

In the 1950s soccer was played at the Mardyke, home of Cork Athletic.

There were no toilet facilities at the Mardyke in the 1950s and men and boys urinated over the stiles. Soccer was a phallic tradition in Cork.

Black and Tans, called after a pack of hounds in south Tipperary, once played soccer on the greenswards of Cork in zebra-striped jerseys, jerseys with enlarged vertical stripes of black and white. Some of them did charity work with a boys' club in Greenmount.

Others of their number, using trench ladders, during a Gaelic football match in November 1920, stormed Croke Park and shot dead thirteen people, including three boys of ten, eleven, fourteen, and the Grangemockler cornerback Michael Hogan in white-and-gold Tipperary stripe.

Poinsettia red is the colour of the Cork Gaelic team and in O'Keefe Park in Black-and-Tan days it was customary to start matches with the singing, by a soloist in a bowler hat with a red carnation in his lapel, of 'My Dark Rosaleen':

> O my Dark Rosaleen
> Do not sigh, do not weep!
> The priests are on the ocean green,
> They march along the deep.
> There's wine from the royal Pope
> Upon the ocean green . . .

The Palace Theatre of Varieties opened in King Street, Cork, Easter 1897, with the overture to *Semiramide*, by Rossini, the Miller Girls in Gainsborough costumes singing 'By Shannon's Dancing Waters,' the good fairy Goldenstar doing a leg-show in front of a backdrop of Pope's Quay, and it didn't close before Fred Karno brought his Ladies' Soccer Team in blue-and-white Kilmarnock stripe.

'My Old man is one of the Boys and I am one of the Girls.'

Speedwell is one of the first flowers to come to the coast and one of the last to leave. Crimthann's eyes are speedwell blue. He is relatively small, like Tottenham Spurs' Robbie Keane. Hair cut Turkish style—slash at the side, slash in the brow.

The barber in Cork who cut his hair has a statuette in his shop of a clown-client in a barber's chair seizing the clippers from a bobby barber.

On a January Sunday evening, the pharos on Loop Head in County Clare signalling, Crimthann sits alone in the shelter.

His father buys antiques—a painting of Judith with the head of Holofernes, a statuette of Charlie Chaplin in pumps with white laces seated under a lamppost with a dog—and sells them.

'My grandparents are Pavvies in Kilmallock. My parents are Buffers in Greenmount. My cousins are Rathkealers.'

In the front garden of his Greenmount home is a nymph with outsized breasts on a petalled stone mound, two cherubs who look as if they'd done military service with the task of holding up the urn.

Many of the Buffer—settled—Traveller boys in Greenmount now play soccer whereas they once played hurling and Gaelic football. Their soccer team recently won against the guards' team. There used to be a notorious remand home in Greenmount near St Finbarr's Cathedral.

But the worst fate was to be sent to one in Daingean, County Offaly, in the midlands.

Some of Crimthann's group ventured to work in the meat factory in Charleville, in north-west Cork, where there were fights with slash hooks and pickaxe handles on Saturday nights. A few went to work in Pat Grace's Famous Fried Chicken in Dublin—Pat Grace had managed the Limerick soccer team for a while. Others went to Germany where they invested their earnings twice a month in the

Deutsche Bundesbank.

But when Steven Gerrard made his debut playing against Ukraine, Crimthann went to England.

David Beckham and Posh Spice being married, on the wall of a room in Dollis Hill, in angel-white Confederate tails and oyster satin antebellum dress, by the Protestant Bishop of Cork, in Luttrellstown Castle, County Dublin, which the Bishop blessed so the marriage could take place in it; David Beckham and Posh Spice in identical mulberry change of gear, cutting the cake, which looked, taking its theme from the castle grounds, as if it was adorned with marzipan honeysuckle and marzipan holly.

For the first few weeks Crimthann worked laying pipes for McNicholls in Thornton Heath. Originally two brothers from Bahoula, County Mayo—one brother with green trucks, the other brother with brown trucks.

He took a ride on a black Shetland pony on Weymouth Strand, sprouted with Union Jack sunscreens; sat under a London pub mirror decorated with eagles, phoenixes, sheaves of wheat in warm gold and cold silver, for a striptease to an Eminem song by a boy in an American football helmet, fishnet football Jersey, jocks; swam in Blackpool in October where a member of the Manchester United Youth Team had once famously walked out of a guesthouse in hi-waist swimming togs to avoid paying his bill to a Jayne Mansfield lookalike landlady and changed into bumfreezer jacket and tie with small knot and square ends, on the Golden Mile.

Union Jack bunting on the Golden Mile; women with dicky-bow earrings or fake-pearl ties linking arms with Morecambe-and-Wise husbands; illuminations of the tower, of a ferris wheel, of the dodgems reflected in the Irish Sea.

Crimthann's grandfather, who had a greyhound called Dinny and a shihtzu called Sheila, had once taken a cattle boat from Cobh and seen a flea circus in Blackpool and Dick Turpin's ride to York reenacted in a circus.

Wall's ice cream; Brylcreem; Durex—'Better for Both'; Movietone News; fish and chips on Friday nights; black shirts with white buttons.

Thick cotton soccer jerseys with stiff collars and billowing shorts—but Duncan Edwards, the Greek *kouros*, defied them by rolling the elastic on his waist to show his thighs.

Duncan Edwards' face in an Oxford frame—Cinestar quiff, laconic smile—a Greenmount family legend; Munich . . .

Crimthann's grandfather told him how, just after the Second World War, Moscow Dynamos, in blue, presented their opponents, Chelsea, in red then, not the gentian blue of now, with bunches of red carnations before a game at Stamford Bridge.

Ten years later, the Roman Catholic Church banned attendance at a match in Dalymount Park, Dublin, between Ireland and Yugoslavia, because Yugoslavia was a communist country, but 33,000 people turned up.

'My grandfather in the Seychelles cussed me for being light-skinned,' an elderly black woman in a coat fastened with loops and bone toggles, in the Royal Take Away on the South Pier, said to him.

'He was a communist. Nearly threw myself under a bus when he died. My dad went to America then. My mother left for England with me and my sister. We lived in Sunderland on the Wear, between the Tyne and the Tees, at first.

'It was just after the war. When the lights went on again, all over the world.

'My mother died. Then we moved to Blackpool. My sister was always telling me what to do. And I said, it's like locking the gate on an ass that's galloping in the fields.

'Met a boy on the Golden Mile. His name was Marshall. Marshall Gold. A coincidence. He had apple-blossom waves of hair. Parma violets in his lapel.

' "How does it feel to be handsome?" I said. "Is it alright?"

' "You' ve a nice body," he said. "It's your face that's the problem. I'm in the travel business," he said. "I take trips to Jamaica. Will you travel with me?"

'Went out with him for a few years. Watched Alf Ramsey and Stan Matthews play at Bloomfield Road with him.

'Walked with him by the lights of the Festival of Britain in London.

'The rock-and-roll cafés were springing up nineteen to a dozen in Blackpool.

'I cut my wrists. I was in love and all that. But the dead dwell in a land of no return.

'Where there's life there's hope. Now I'm satisfied with my life. Just as it is. I'm getting older bit by bit, day by day, and I don't notice. Lord have mercy.'

Crimthann knew of Salome's dance, but now there were male Salomes.

Boys in London pubs who dropped quilted workman's trousers to reveal Calvin Klein, Armani, Lonsdale, aussieBum underwear, and then dropped their underwear. Boys naked but for jungle-army fatigue caps held at their crotch. Apricot-coloured boiler-suit acts.

But the most popular were soccer and rugger acts. The difference was that the Will Carling or Daragh O'Shea lookalike rugger boys held balls for their acts.

A rugger stripper might be marigold hirsute; a soccer stripper a beetroot-coloured adolescent boy's penis.

At one of these shows the boy beside him, with shot-gold brindled hair, shot-gold goat's beard, told him the story of the Jacobean-featured David Scarboro who once played Mark Fowler, a confused teenager in *EastEnders* on television.

He felt trapped, typecast, and left the programme.

Even if he tried for ordinary jobs he was seen as Mark Fowler.

He became clinically depressed and was admitted to a mental hospital.

On his return home telephoto tenses were focussed on his bedroom by England's paparazzi.

The paparazzi claimed he was known in his village as Dracula because he was white as a sheet and emerged from his home only at night.

He became overwhelmed by this persecution and his body was found at the bottom of Beachy Head, near Eastbourne, East Sussex.

> Are you going to Scarborough Fair?
> Parsley, sage, rosemary and thyme,
> Remember me to one who lives there,
> For he once was a true love of mine.

Did ye ever travel twixt Berwick and Lyne?
Sober and grave grows merry in time
There ye'll meet wi' a handsome young man
Ance he was a true love o' mine.

Crimthann would trek Hampstead Heath late afternoons. The houses on the margin of the Heath lighted up. Wine doors, diamond-glass windows, floriated lace curtains, lozenge shapes in the transoms, Japanese red maple trees in the cobbled front yards, rock-rose bushes.

Other people's homes.

The crested grebe with their black-and-grey summer headdresses live on Hampstead Heath. Flocks of seven or eight pass over the Heath, diving into Highgate ponds, making sounds like a hawk swooping for prey. Frequently, crested grebe are drowned by fishermen's nets in the ponds, as are cygnets.

The coots build their nests in the lifebuoys on the ponds with stalk, leaves of bulrushes, flag, reed, mace reed.

Like the crested grebe they cover their eggs with weeds.

The continental fighting coot comes in winter to the Heath, passing over Beachy Head on the way, and when the ponds are frozen fight other birds on the ice, with their feet as well as their beaks.

'We sailed by Beachy, by Fairlight and Dover.'

In a dingle on the Heath a man with a walrus moustache, chinless face, tattoo of a woman in bondage gear on his belly, who said he was from Chingford, Essex, enticed Crimthann to use poppers.

He tried to force Crimthann to have sex with him.

'You've done the Paddy on me,' he shouted after Crimthann as Crimthann walked away.

In the all-night café at Victoria Station, fake rose in a Panda orangeade tin, Crimthann had tea in a mug with Princess Diana on it in a poppy dress, with a boy with filamented hair, mushroom ears and explosions of green eyes, who said he was a boxer.

'I've lived in Liverpool, Ringsend and Galway. I was a heavyweight. Now I'm a middleweight.'

Crimthann remembered a story from community college, where they were continually reminded that in Iraq soccer players who played badly were tortured; how in early May 1916, Countess Markievicz, who'd worn a slouch hat with cock feathers and a green tunic with silver buttons for the Rising, sentenced to death, each morning hearing the shots as her comrades were executed, heard a tap on the prison door.

The teenage British soldier with Mancunian accent, standing guard outside, unlocked the door, let himself in, offered her a shag cigarette and talked with her through the night.

He'd seen Liverpool play Burnley at Crystal Palace when King George V, who bathed the golden-haired, pink-skinned Prince Edward himself while Queen Mary looked on in a choker of uncut emeralds, was present.

He produced a cigarette-box picture from his pocket of Adonis-faced Steve Bloomer, then interned in Ruhleben in Germany, who'd played for Derby, in quartered cap, against a balustrade trussed with tea roses.

The reprieved Countess Markievicz was haunted by this young soccer fan for the rest of her life and thought to go searching for him, a face, but decided she might get him into trouble if she revealed what he'd done.

'I live in King's Cross,' the boxer said, 'dreadful place. Six-year-olds beat up a woman in a wheelchair.'

Jack Doyle, the boxer, a stevedore from Cobh, County Cork, home of the Cobh Ramblers, had drawn an audience of 90,000 in White City in the 1930s, starred in two films, married a Mexican film star, Movita, with Remembrance Day-red lips.

Toured England with her as a double singing act. Remarried her to national headlines in St Andrew's Church, Westland Row, Dublin.

She left him to wed Marlon Brando. Later in life Jack Doyle became a tramp with a red carnation in his buttonhole.

Crimthann's last days in England were spent sleeping in a shop-front near Victoria Station until 9.30, spending the day in the day centre in Carlisle Street, intermittently going to admire the portrait of Queen Sophia Charlotte, who wore a high white wig, in an out-spread gown studded with little bows, in the Queen's Gallery where the attendant, who wore a waistcoat with gold threaded stripes, coarse velvet knee breeches, buckled pumps, was from Crumlin,

Dublin—terraced or semi-detached 1930s house—where Niall Quinn was from.

Crimthann had been good at art at community college, which was taught through Gaelic.

There'd been a teacher at community college with a grin like a Cheshire cat who invited some of the boys home and showed them penitentiary pornographic films or naked soccer matches on Copacabana and Ipanema beaches in Brazil.

When Crimthann had been at community college, Ed O'Brien, a young IRA volunteer from the Irish Republic, accidentally blew himself up aboard a London double-decker bus while ferrying a bomb to its intended target, injuring several passengers.

Grief-stricken and deeply shamed parents greeted his body as it crossed into the Irish Republic.

In January 1957, 20,000 people had turned out in Limerick for the funeral of Seán South, a clerk at a Limerick timber firm and founder of a Limerick branch of Maria Duce, a right-wing Roman Catholic association, who was killed during an attack on Brookeborough RUC Barracks in County Fermanagh, including Crimthann's family, the Brogans, who watched it from the O'Connell Monument.

Men with black armlets and men in the olive-green Fianna Éireann uniforms flanked the motor hearse, which had difficulty passing through the streets, the crowds were so dense.

Lord mayors, county and urban councillors, city corporation members, Roman Catholic dignitaries, had all extended their sympathy to Seán South's widowed mother and his two brothers.

In Greenmount in Cork, beside a photograph of Duncan Edwards, was a photograph of Seán South—Maureen O'Hara-red hair, wire glasses like Pope Pius XII.

Crimthann's grandfather always burst into the same song at family weddings.

No more he'll hear a seagull cry o'er the murmuring Shannon tide . . .
A martyr for old Ireland, Seán South of Garryowen.

'Sit in the back and it will be a longer journey,' said a man in a flat cap on the bus going to Stranraer, 'Life is not easy. You make plans and there's a hitch. It never turns out the way you think it will.'

The bus broke down at Salford but there was a mechanic on board.

Later there was a pitched battle between some passengers at a transport café.

Crimthann crossed from Stranraer to Larne. There'd been some boys in the blue of Glasgow Rangers on the boat.

He'd always wanted to see Windsor Park, home of Linfield Football Club, who wore emerald green.

'Lillibulero' was sung by the Apprentice Boys after the Siege of Derry in 1689.

It was sung by the victors after the Battle of the Boyne in 1690.

In London, ladies had the tune printed on their fans.

It was still occasionally sung after soccer matches at Windsor Park, as it had been on the Cregagh estate, Belfast, where George Best, whose grandfather was a Protestant hurler in the Glens of Antrim, once kicked a plastic Frido ball, in a Davy Crockett cap.

'Lillibutero bullenala'

Near Cregagh estate Crimthann purchased fish and chips wrapped in the *Shankill Mirror*, a wall painting to the side of the fish-and-chip shop with King Billy in a Quaker collar, on a Hanoverian cream horse.

Crimthann's father had been a George Best lookalike when young.

George Best, taken from his home at fifteen to join a team that originated in Newton Heath, an Irish Catholic area of Manchester.

First, Irish Catholic players had to change half a mile from the soccer pitch in the Three Crowns public house.

George Best used to score with his head.

Would meet his Irish Catholic colleagues, Nobby Stiles and Paddy Crerand, outside a Roman Catholic church in Manchester on Sunday mornings.

Announced his retirement at twenty-six.

Sent off at Southampton a few years after his retirement for foul and abusive language.

Awarded a red card for obstreperousness.

Like Jack Doyle, he toured English provincial theatres, in his case telling soccer stories.

Crimthann's father had told Crimthann this soccer story: when Norman Whiteside, the Shankill Road skinhead, the youngest-ever player in the World Cup, kissed Kevin Moran, former Dublin Gaelic champion, after Manchester United's victory against Everton in the FA finals in 1985, his ikon was universally taken down on the Shankill Road.

Crimthann took a Goldliner bus to Dublin, a Lonsdale bag slung over his shoulder.

A poster of Coventry City's six-foot-one Gary Breen with Minnie Mouse side-hair was brought back from England.

Crimthann had seen a picture of Gary Breen in a McNicholls' hut in Thornton Heath, a postcard of Lifford, County Donegal, beside it, where Shay Given was from, who now played in Newcastle magpie.

Gary Breen's father was from County Kerry. Mother from southwest Clare where gannets make white flame against the sea.

Grandfather, Des, won an All-Ireland Gaelic football medal in 1913.

Himself a child of Kentish Town.

As a boy Gary Breen played centre forward for Westwood Boys in Camden Town.

Some boys from Camden Town used to make a pilgrimage to Walsingbam at the beginning of June each year in soccer shorts and Puma football boots, passing through Horsham St Faith where St Robert Southwell was from and after the pilgrimage play soccer on the beach by Wells-next-the-Sea.

Generations of Irish immigrants had knelt in despair before the image of Our Lady of Walsingbam in her pomegranate dress and three-pronged crown curled at the end like Arabian slippers.

Camden Town boys in their soccer shorts would present bunches of Spanish bluebells or red camplon or shining cranesbill or marsh orchids, picked along the way, to her.

As a Westwood Boys centre forward Gary Breen got a tumour in his lower spine. It was cut away in hospital. He was unable to walk properly for a year and had difficulty sleeping. The doctors told his parents he'd never play football again but within a few years he'd signed on with Gillingham.

His grandmother in Clare lit candles from Lourdes and candles blessed on St Brigid's Day when he was playing.

A week before the Second World War broke out, when men emigrated from Ireland with their belongings wrapped in brown paper under their arms, an IRA bomb killed five people in Coventry.

In February 1940, James McCormick and Peter Barnes were hanged in Winson Green Prison, Birmingham, for a bombing it was subsequently proved they didn't do.

> Plow the land with the horn of a lamb
> Parsley, sage, rosemary, and thyme,
> Then sow some seeds from north of the dam
> And then he'll be a true love of mine.

Crimthann's twenty-first birthday was the following summer.

Earlier in the summer, on Lapp's Quay, he and his friends witnessed a pod of orca whales—the Demon Dolphin, Wolf of the Sea, black, grey saddle—bull, cow, female, which had come as far as City Hall, doing spy-hops and tail-slaps there.

There was a ricepaper photograph in the middle of Crimthann's cake of Crimthann in the signal-red jersey with butterfly-cream sleeves of Arsenal.

Flahri, Afro hair—Irish mother, cuckoo Libyan father, father who ran away—with a miniature ArmaLite rifle on a chain around his neck, which he says was a gift, sang Phil Colclough's 'Song for Ireland.'

Daire, one of Crimthann's friends, on holiday from Germany, in a tank top that showed his tattoo—a leprechaun in tank top with the words 'Irish Power' beneath him—told a soccer story.

A donkey who was mistreated ran away and met a dog, a cat and a cockerel on the road in a similar predicament and they went together to Bayern—home of Bayern Leverkusen.

'They talk about the Birmingham Six or the Guildford Four,' Crimthann says as a lighted tanker passes from the Shannon estuary to the Atlantic, 'but there are other Irish incarcerations in England that are not known or heard of, people who had to leave, who feel they had to leave, who couldn't face home, who ended up in their own prisons in England, unwanted, outcast, barely tolerated, neglectful of themselves, holding on only to a few items—pictures on the wall of Gary Breen or Princess Di.

'There are so many prisons in England and the prisons are Irish people who live in loneliness and isolation and abandonment and even self-torture—knowing they can never go back, that there's been some crime, some unforgivable sin . . .'

Pictures

My father and I were looking at Veronese's *Saints Philip and James the Less* in the National Gallery in Dublin one summer's day when the curator approached us in a gameplumage tweed jacket and started explaining it to us.

The curator was from a part of the Shannon estuary where learned-looking goats ran wild and where bogland printed itself on sand. He'd been an officer in the Royal Field Artillary during the First World War, had twice been wounded at the Battle of the Somme in which men who gathered by the Lazy Wall in the Square in our town had fought.

The curator was renowned for his clothes.

Women would go to a church in Dublin to see him walking to Holy Communion in glen tweed suits, houndstooth cheviot jackets, rosewood flannel trousers, enlarge check trousers, Edelweiss jerseys, Boivin, batiste, taffeta shirts, black and tan shoes, button Oxford shoes.

A seated St Philip in a pearl-grey robe, sandals with diamond open-work, clutched a book as if he was afraid the contents might vanish, another book at his feet. St James the Less in a prawn pink robe, a melon cloak tucked into his belt, had a pepper-and-salt beard, carried a cross, and was talking to an angel with spun gold hair descending upon them both, perhaps asking the angel to help them save the contents of the books.

My father told the curator how I'd won first prize in a national art competition that spring.

I'd won it for a painting inspired by an episode of 'Lives of the Caesars' on radio that showed Julius Caesar, during a night battle off Alexandria, fireballs in the air, having jumped off a rowboat, swimming to the Caesarean ship, documents in his raised left hand, burgundy cloak clenched in his teeth to keep this trophy from the Egyptians.

I'd been presented the prize in a Dublin hotel by a minister's wife with a pitchfork beehive, a tawny fur on her shoulders that looked like bob-cat fur.

The hotel, I later learned, was one where young rugby players from the country spent weekends because the chambermaids had a loose reputation and they had hopes of sleeping with them.

My mother, usually silent, on the train back west, in a wisteria-blue turban hat with two flared wings at the back she'd had on for the day, spoke of the weeks after my birth when it snowed heavily and she used to walk me, past the gaunt workhouse, to the Ash Tree.

A beloved sister died and the Christmas cakes were wrapped up and not eaten until the Galway Races at the end of July when they were found to have retained their freshness.

After we left the gallery my father and I took the bus, past swan-neck lamp posts, to the sea.

In a little shop my father bought American hardgums for himself and jelly crocodiles for me.

We walked past houses covered in Australian vine, with pineapple broom hedges, to the sea at the Forty Foot.

In winter, when I was off school, sometimes I accompanied my father on his half day to Galway. We'd have tea and fancies in Lydon's Tea House with its lozenge floor mosaic at the door and afterwards go to Salthill where we'd watch a whole convent of nuns who swam in winter in black togs and black caps.

I was spending a few days now in Dublin with my father. The previous summer I'd gone by myself to stay with an aunt and uncle in County Limerick for my holidays.

I arrived at Limerick bus station, a land beside it of *Ireland's Own*, where I read of the Limerick tenor Joseph O'Mara and of the stigmatic Marie Julie Jaheny, and of Russian cakes—almond essence, sugar syrup, chocolate.

In my aunt and uncle's village there was a Pompeian red cinema called the Melody. Outside it a picture of Steve Reeves in his bathing togs, standing in hubris, his chest mushrooming from his waist. In the film, which I saw while there, a prostrate Sylva Koscina, with a frizzed top, a racoon tail of hair by her face, clutches Steve Reeve's foot, who, as Hercules, is about to leave on an inexorable journey. The audience stamped its feet while reels were being changed. Boys, some of whom were reputed to have been in Cork Jail, on the steps outside during the day, spoke with Montana accents like Steve Reeves.

My uncle was a garda sergeant and wore a hat big as a canopy. In the kitchen at night, a bunch of nettles behind a picture of St Brigid of Sweden to keep off flies, he'd tell ghost stories. Of boys who were drowned in the river and who came back. 'The river always takes someone,' he said.

On 'Céilidhe House' on radio one night we heard a girl sing:

> And when King James was on the run
> I packed my bags and took to sea
> And around the world I'll beg my bread
> *Go dtiocfaidh mavourneen slán.*

My uncle told us of the Wild Geese who sailed to Europe after the Treaty of Limerick in autumn 1691 on the nearby estuary, and of how at the beginning of that century Red Hugh O'Donnell had ended O'Donnell's overlordship of Donegal by casting O'Donnell pearls into a lake on Arranmore Island.

On one of my first days there I was driven to a lake by a castle where about a dozen people with easels were painting pictures of the castle.

At the end of my holiday I was taken to a seaside resort on the mouth of the Shannon.

My uncle wore sports shoes and sports socks for the occasion. My aunt a cameo brooch that showed a poodle jumping into an Edwardian lady's arms. My two older girl cousins, who'd covered the walls of my room with Beryl the Peril pictures, saddle shoes—black with white on top and then a little black again at the tip. My youngest cousin, who'd recently made her First Holy Communion, wore her Communion dress so she was a flood of Limerick lace. My aunt recalled being taken by car with my mother to the Eucharistic Congress in Dublin when Cardinal Lauri granted a partial indulgence to all who attended the big mass.

On the way we stopped at a house where a poet had lived, a mighty cedar of Lebanon on the sloping hill beside it. I'd had to learn by heart one of his poems at school, 'The Year of Sorrow—1849.'

Take back, O Earth, into thy breast,
The children whom thou wilt not feed.

The poem was taught by a teacher who'd told us about the boy who ferried the Eucharist in his mouth in Ancient Rome and, John McCormack's 'My Rosary' frequently played to us on a gramophone, how when Count John McCormack returned to give a concert by the Shannon in his native Athlone no one had turned up.

On arrival in the resort, in a soda fountain bar on the main street, we had coffee milkshakes and banana boats.

On the wall was a photograph, cut out of *Movie Story* or *Film Pictorial*, of the Olympic swimming champion Johnny Weismuller in his Tarzan costume.

Johnny Cash sang 'Forty Shades of Green' on a public loud-speaker in the town.

'It's a lovely song, "The Forty Shades of Green",' my uncle said, 'Johnny Cash wrote it. Went around Ireland in a helicopter. The song tells you about all the counties. He saw them from a helicopter.'

Near the beach, on a windowsill, was a swan with a shell on its back, an Armada ship with sails of shells.

Women with their toes painted tulip red sat on camp stools on the beach. Young men wore ruched bathing togs. Little boys like bantam hens marched on the sea and afterwards some of them stood in naked, even priapic defiance.

'I'm so hungry I could eat a nun's backside through a convent railing,' my uncle said after a few hours so we left.

There was a bachelor festival in the town and ten bachelors from different counties were lined up on a podium. They wore black, box, knee-length jackets with velvet-lined pockets, Roman-short jackets, banner-striped shirts, cowboy Slim Jim ties, crêpe-soled beetle-crusher shoes. Some had slicked-back Romeo hair, some Silver-Dollar crewcuts. We were told about one of the bachelors, that he'd been a barber in County Longford, his business motto being 'Very little waiting,' that he'd recently migrated to one of the north-eastern counties but he was missed in Longford. He had a flint quiff, flint cheekbones, an uncompromising chin like Steve Reeves. John Glenn sang 'Boys of the County Armagh' on the loudspeaker.

A man with the marcel waves of another era, who had been studying the bachelors, declaimed:

'I worked hard all my life. Training greyhounds. Can't sleep at night thinking about how hard I worked. Met a girl once. She liked going to dances and all that kind of thing. I liked greyhounds and greyhound races. So we stopped seeing one another. But it was a wonderful thing making love.'

On the way back my aunt sang 'The Last Rose of Summer' as she used to as a girl at ginger-ale parties in a room in my grandparents' house with a picture of a Victorian girl with the word 'Solitaria' underneath it.

> Oh! Who would inhabit
> This bleak world alone?

The fields of County Limerick were covered with yellow agrimony which was said to cure skin rashes and external wounds and yarrow which was said to cure the innards it looked like. Traveller boys called at the door selling dulse that they'd picked on the coast and dried themselves, popular with young guards because it was good for the physique.

Before I left my aunt and uncle gave me a large biscuit which was a walnut on a biscuit base buried under marshmallow sealed with twisted and peaked chocolate, and I clutched the canary's leg in a cage.

At Limerick bus station, where I wore a sleeveless jersey with a Shetland homespun pattern and mid-calf socks, a woman in a Basque beret said to me:

'Margaret Mitchell was a very small woman but she wrote a very big book.'

The Irish Sea was Persian blue.

My father and I had a swim and afterwards a man with a malacca cane, in a linen Mark Twain suit and a Manila straw hat, who had been watching us, told us the history of the Forty Foot.

Two boys listened intently to the lesson, one with a sluttish Jean Harlow face, the other with a Neptune belly and ant legs.

The Forty Foot was called after the Forty Foot Regiment stationed in the Martello tower built during the Napoleonic Wars. Twenty Men. Forty Feet.

At the beginning of the century Oliver St John Gogarty used to frequently swim between the Forty Foot and Bullock Harbour in Dalkey where monks had lived in the Middle Ages.

Oliver St John Gogarty had fox-blond hair then with an impertinent crescendo wave, eyebrows in askance, shoulders poised for riposte, Galwegian lips.

He was Arthur Griffith's white boy.

Arthur Griffith had founded the non-violent Sinn Féin movement in 1905 in order to set up an Irish republic. He had a brush moustache, wore wire glasses, a stand-up collar, neckcloth.

One day, in his tailored swimming costume, he decided to swim to Bullock Harbour with Oliver St John Gogarty. He expired a few yards out at sea.

A few years after that visit to the Forty Foot, when my father bought me a set of art books, there was a reproduction of Titian's *Flaying of Marsyas* in one of them in which Titian depicted the death of self.

The Flute Player Marsyas is flayed alive, upside down, to the accompaniment of violin music, watched by a little Maltese dog and by King Midas, with ass's ears, who is Titian himself who'd recently given the prize of gold chain to and publicly in Venice embraced Veronese, lavish with red lake like himself, as his successor. Titian —his arms still muscular in the painting, his honeyed and diamanté chest strung with a salmon-vermilion cloak—painted it with his fingers.

I thought of the story of Arthur Griffith when I got the books, that it must have been the death of some part of Arthur Griffith's self that day.

Gogarty, who'd rescued a suicide in the Liffey by knocking him out, brought the leader to shore.

In the evening my father and I stopped at a fish and chip shop near the Forty Foot. On a cyclamen, jay blue and lemon jukebox the Everley Brothers sang 'Lonely Street.' A boy, in a blue shirt with white, sovereign polka dots, stood eating chips. On his wrist was a tattoo; the name of a place—army barracks or jail—and a date.

In the fish and chip shop I thought of a story my uncle told me as he brought me to Limerick bus station the previous year.

'They get baked jam roll and baked custard in Cork Jail. Better than they get from their mothers. One fellow was given a month and said to the judge, "That's great. I get baked jam roll and baked custard there that I don't get from my mother." "All right," said the judge, "I'll give you three." '

Later, in a room in a house in North Dublin where there was a false pigment art deco light shade with tassels, a picture of St Dymphna, patron saint of people with nervous disorders, my father spoke, as he was laying out a handkerchief of robin's-egg blue and rose squares as he might have laid out a Chicago tie once after a date with a Protestant girl in a tango-orange dress from whose house Joseph Schmidt could often be heard on the street singing in Italian, about cycling with other young men, some with aviator hairstyles, when General O'Duffy was president of the National Athletic and Cycling Association, to swim in the Suck at Ballygar.

Larks' Eggs

There was a hotel on Tay Lane at the back of the town between river and canal, run by Pancake Ward, a little man in a spec cap with a Connemara weave who wore hobnail boots, where young, middle-class men hid out when their families were in dudgeon with them and my father had to stay there for a few days because of his relationship with a Protestant with bangs, Miss Husaline.

His hair still smelling from Amami shampoo after a trip to Dublin with Miss Husaline, in a tie with cedar-green and asparagus-green bars, flannel trousers, navy socks with jay-blue stripes; there was a chamber pot with purple peonies, pink anemones, fern under his bed, and by night a young English travelling player, with hair crescendo-curled to one side, who was staying there, would wander around in a Jaeger dressing gown, studying his part aloud:

> For valour, is not Love a Hercules,
> Still climbing trees in the Hesperides?
> Subtle as sphinx, as sweet and musical
> As bright Apollo's lute, strung with his hair;
> And, when Love speaks, the voice of all the gods
> Make heaven drowsy with the harmony.

In the mornings there was a view of the river, of Teampollín, an ancient church with surround houses where illegitimate and still-born children were buried. The monks who'd lived there wore iron chastity belts. Now there was an erotic air about the grass, the ruins.

In the summer women would wander on a monk's pass—a path leading from one monastery to another—by the Suck, collecting bur-marigolds for smallpox, measles, or to rub nipples during breast feeding, wild thyme for menstrual disorders, chest infections and sore throats, plantain—waybread—for dry coughs, haemorrholds, beestings.

It was the year 1934. The calves had been slaughtered in Ireland in February of that year because of surplus and the Land Annuities dispute with England, and in August the Tailteann Games, re-enacting funeral games in honour of Queen Tailte of Ireland, had been held in Dublin. In January of the previous year Hitler had become Führer and in June of that year General von Schleicher, his wife and others were dragged from their beds and slaughtered. The carillon of children's voices could be heard from the Protestant national school, with its Gothic, diainoiid-pane windows, with a recitation:

Far as the tree does fall, so lyes it ever low.

A short while before my father stayed there an American in hobo dungarees had stayed in the hotel. He ran out of money and stood in the Square with the spalpeens—roaming men looking for a day's work. The Lazy Wall was on one side of the Square. The spalpeens gathered on the other. The American was carrying his banjo. When they asked him what he could do he said: 'All I can do is play the banjo.'

The English travelling players came to the town every October after the fair when the green in which they pitched their marquee was like a sea, the colours like that of a late autumn blackberry bush penetrated by late afternoon sunshine.

In the entr'acte of *Love's Labour's Lost* that he attended while in the hotel, Phoebe Rabbitte, a Protestant lady, in a hat with a cockatoo feather, offered my father a cigarette from a chased cigarette case. Phoebe Rabbitte's black Daimler could frequently be seen parked outside the chrome-green Medical Hall, from whose roof snipers used to fire with Gatling machine guns during the War of Independence.

Pancake Ward, in a pearl-white waistcoat, held a party for the players. A man who sold football colours in crêpe paper at matches mimed to 'Champagne Charlie,' 'Not for Joseph,' 'I'll Send You Some Violets' on a horn gramophone and one of the players did a Highland dance on a table, lifting his royal tartan kilt to show his bare backside.

Bran Ahearne, a Jesse boy with a waxed moustache, could be heard telling an English player on a sofa with an antimacassar patterned with mice in friar robes: 'People on Tay Lane love taking opposite sides, during the Boer War some were Connaught Rangers and went into battle, only a couple coming back. Others were Boers and kissed the Tricolour by firelight on the Transvaal.'

On the canal side of Tay Lane lived a man with goat-whiskers who used his front garden as a lavatory and grabbed passing Rhode Island chicks as toilet paper.

Thomasine Solan and her mother, Tay Lane's courtesans, both in backless dresses, feathered boas and strings of bugle-beads, were present and were seated beside a flowering cactus in an Edward VII and Queen Alexandra coronation mug.

When she was a girl Thomasine's mother used to accompany the Connaught Rangers to the station in the evenings with a cresset lantern.

When wings were falling from the sycamore, maple and ash trees outside the Protestant church, my father and Miss Husaline had gone to Dublin to see Douglas Fairbanks in *Mark of Zorro* at the O'Connell Street Picture House and afterwards they did the foxtrot at Mitchel's Tea Rooms before getting the train home.

In Miss Husaline's house was a soapstone elephant from India on which she put a mouse. Beside it, in an oxidized frame, a photograph of a Protestant orphan, Hyacinth Connmee, with a pudding-bowl haircut, against sea pools with submerged bunches of thrift. Hyacinth Connmee had been sent to a Protestant orphanage in North Connemara. A hotel owner there converted to the Church of Ireland and the Protestant orphans came back from England, from their houses with Margaret Hartness roses outside, and stayed in the hotel.

Beside the photograph was a postcard, 'The Lark's Song' by Margaret W Tarrant, Hyacinth had sent from England.

My father and Miss Husaline had discovered larks' eggs on the Hill of Down by the Suck, pointed oval, greenish-white, mottled with pale lavender, with markings of rufous.

Miss Husaline's father, who wore a cricket shirt winter and summer, had been at a wedding in The Park as a child when there'd been a pyrotechnic display—a golden fuschia tree in blossom, snowdrops in bloom, rose blossoms in violet stars, immense sheafs of wheat downfalling on the East Galway country.

Miss Husaline always served an aurora borealis of white-iced queen cakes or Boston sponge she made herself on a powder-blue

Worcester plate that showed a Ho-Ho bird on a rock.

The bishop's palace used to be in the town but it moved to a town where a priest wrote a book which caused a great outcry, and the priest went to live in London where he was photographed in the English papers with women in flapper dresses who wore monocles. There was a doctor in town, who drove an Auto Carrier Aceca Six, who was a champion rugby player and one day, knocked out during a game on the mental hospital grounds, when some Campbeltown Malt Scotch whisky was poured down his throat, he leapt up, shouting: 'I am a teetotaller!'

There was rumoured to have been a homosexual orgy in the changing rooms in the mental hospital grounds that winter, men whose genitals smelt of young mushrooms—the blame put on a few bottles of Canada brandy bought by a cross-border team with carp-rugby features who wore cloth caps during the game—and the orgy went down in town lore but all the participants married, except Éanna Geraghty who worked in the London brick-orange bank, rolled his own cigarettes with Wills' Capstan tobacco, and wore an Inverness cape.

He had a rendezvous with one of the Northern players, a youth with nougat-coloured hair, sheepdog-fringe, butcher-lie eyes, who wore an old Portoran tie, in Lyon's Corner House in London just before the War, having sallyslung and coffee with him.

In his flat opposite the house with an ivy-coloured door where Theobald Wolfe Tone had stayed, where the town makes a parabola and then a glissade towards Galway City, there was a print of Antonio Pollaluolo's *Battle of Naked Men*. He attended dinner dances, however, at the Clonrickarde Arms Hotel with another bank employee, a woman with a bull fringe who on these occasions wore a lamp-black dress with a fishtail train or a rose-blue robe-de-style with a corsage of fritillaries.

The English players couldn't come to Ireland during the War so an amateur drama society was formed in the town and their first production was *Death's Jest-Book* by Thomas Lovell Beddoes, whose mother was from County Longford, about the Duke of Munsterberg in Silesia who was stabbed to death by his court fool. Éanna Geraghty played Isbrand the fool in Arabian slippers.

Phoebe Rabbitte cycled to performances in cavalry-cord trousers on a high nelly.

Life's a single pilgrim
Fighting, unarmed among a thousand soldiers.

For his holidays Éanna Geraghty would go to Bachelor's Walk in Dalkey. There was a swimming hole nearby where, before the War, he met a man from Plymouth whose only sport, because of spinal trouble, was swimming, who would swim out to Sorrento Point. When he was a boy Irish time and English time were different and when he got back to England from Irish visits, he told Éanna, he'd set his watch to Irish time because he loved swimming in the swimming hole in Dalkey so much.

In the evenings of his holidays, when V-2 rockets were falling on England, Éanna Geraghty would go to a hotel with mouldings of dolphins outside where a man in a grasshopper-green dickie bow, by a grand piano, incessantly played and crooned Jessie Matthews' 'Over My Shoulder Goes One Care, Over My Shoulder Goes Two Cares.'

At the end of the War he got a senior post in Aer Teoranta at Shannon Airport and when that closed in 1949 he went to Paris where he lived in an apartment block smelling of ammonia in the Faubourg outskirts and he'd attend rugby matches when the Irish team was playing and some of the Irish rugby players, young men with forelocks, came to his flat with a picture of Theobald Wolfe Tone's wife, Martha Witherington, in a sugarloaf cap on the wall and, on a bamboo-motif chair, by a Bauhaus lamp, he'd offer them Disque Bleu cigarettes and tell them how in Corfe Castle, Dorset, during the Middle Ages a football was accepted instead of a marriage shilling, by the local lord, from the most recently married young man, carried ceremoniously to him with a pound of pepper; how rugby was started at Rugby School in 1823 when a pupil, William Webb Ellis, picked up a ball and ran with it and in 1839 the Dowager Queen Adelaide, wife of William IV, visited the school to see the new game; how the Connaught Rangers marched through Alexandria at the beginning of the Dardanelles Campaign in July 1915 in khaki drill, playing 'Brian Boru,' 'Killaloe' and 'Brian O'Lynn,' led by the tallest of the company, an international rugby player who carried the Jingling Johnny with its red and black horse-hair plumes; of the scrummage in the winter of 1934 when there was yellow jelly algae on fallen logs in the mental hospital grounds, the ram's head push between other men's buttocks.

> Queenie, Queenie, who kicked the ball,
> Was he fat or was he small?

Queenie Waithmandle was a Protestant woman with Blanc de Madame de Courbet roses outside her house.

She always attended Sunday rugby games, in a trilby hat and a beaver-fur dickie front, or a jacket trimmed with monkey fur, or a pinstripe flannel jacket with boxy shoulders, stilettos with louis-type heels or monk-fronted shoes.

In the summer she'd go with relatives from Galway to North Connemara to catch up on the legations of ragged robin by the ocean and perhaps be awed by the dream of a nobby—a boat with red sail.

When she was in her early fifties she became pregnant and went to England to live with relatives and have her baby. 'Mind yourself in this town as they say,' she bid me before getting the Dublin bus, as a man in a black shirt with puff sleeves in a marquee tent, in a performance of *The Duchess of Malfi* by the travelling players, which Queenie and I attended the same night, advised the audience to be 'mindful of thy safety.'

In Webster's day the Shoemaker's Guild in Chester would present the Draper's Guild with the handful of a football on Shrove Tuesday. One year at a presentation a battle broke out between the two guilds which became known as the Battle of Chester.

My father was a draper.

In the eighteenth century in the East of Ireland football players wore white linen shirts.

A common prize for football winners was Holland linen caps with ribands.

Shortly after Queenie Waithmandle left, I held my father's hand at a Sunday rugby game.

The bulbous vein around the forehead, like a trajectory, the bald head, and yet still—the beauty.

One of the players that day was a young man with a roach like a duck's egg who'd been Queenie Waithmandle's lover.

When my father was a youth with cherry-auburn hair, field-green eyes, freckles big as birds' eggs, with a Shakespeare collar, a young British soldier was found shot dead by the River Suck where the otters run, with a picture of Marie Lloyd in his pocket, who once came out on the picket line on behalf of the most lowly of Music Hall workers.

The British soldiers used to play rugby and hack one another —kick one another's shins—in the mental hospital grounds, in tiger-striped jerseys, the sforzandos from the field heard by the riverbank.

Fathers and sons, it's a smell from the genitals, a smell from the earth.

Sons come from sexuality—homosexual or heterosexual or a mixture. So your sexuality, homosexual or heterosexual, has to be protected. Sometimes there are people who would destroy it. So this means leaving one country for another. Or leaving that country and going back to the other. On my return to Ireland, by the River Suck, in the place where the young British soldier was found shot dead, beside a clump of dandelion leaves—dandelion leaves cleansing for the liver and kidneys—I found some larks' eggs—olive-white, speckled with lavender grey, with markings of umber.

Iowa

At a booth table in a bar in Iowa, a nearby field of early Quaker graves, stones with no name on them, under snow, an exile from Clare, in an Eskimo parka, who teaches students, some of them as tall as Arthur Rimbaud, over a rainbow-rayed cocktail, told me, during a brief stopover on a Greyhound bus journey, about the colossus of a garda sergeant with earthed barley-sugar hair and eyes that were the grey-blue of his uniform—a goalkeeper who'd won six gold medals—who used to cycle a Darley Peterson of army green to a remote rocky swimming place in Clare during the Second World War and seduce the boys among the white thrift, the bird's-foot trefoil, the kidney vetch, the white rock roses, the *buachalán*—ragwort—the scarlet pimpernel, a brief Dionysian dispensation about this place—boys with lobster-coloured body hair holding broadcloth shorts or knit briefs or olive-drab briefs with V-notches to themselves in a moidered way, while a harem of lamenting seals looked on.

The man returned one winter from his university in Iowa, where he had a girlfriend, who wore glitter jodhpur boots, who'd lived in a monkey colony in the mountains before fleeing the Chinese Revolution, with whom he went to look at the Colombian sharp-tailed grouse and the whooping cranes, and revisited the swimming place—the boys in the nearby town in their laurel-green school jackets like the boys from Plato's *Symposium* now—a few cubicles newly built with a lifebuoy alongside them, a porpoise thrashing in the mica of sleet in the winter rain.

In a local speakeasy he'd been told the story of how the paediatrician widow of a Royal Irish Constabulary inspector, murdered in County Wexford in 1920, after his death presented a painting she'd purchased in Edinburgh to the Jesuit community in Dublin and that recently the painting was discovered to have been by Caravaggio who loved painting boys.

> If I take the wings of the morning, and dwell in the uttermost
> parts of the sea;

Even there shall thy hand lead me, and thy right hand shall hold me.

Frederick Rolfe, Baron Corvo, took photographs of naked Italian boys.

But the garda sergeant took photographs of naked Irish boys and had them developed by an accomplice in Ennis, where the Code of the Irish Constabulary had been printed in 1820.

Boys with rousse-auburn hair and cranberry pubic hair. Walnut hirsute. Heron's features or faces like young kangaroos. Some with hair the orange of the pheasant in ascent. Others with Creole curls. Many with identical passion-fruit lips.

Frequently a Woodbine cigarette in the mouth of a nude. A few of them reclining like lizards. One or two in yachting caps like the man on the Player's cigarette packet and nothing else.

There were nudes in sunglasses. Nudes with Lucania bicycles. Nudes with hurleys.

It was hurling in east Clare and football in west Clare and it was mainly footballers he photographed.

Very occasionally there were Falstaffian interlopers from Garryowen and St Mary's rugby teams in Limerick.

A man who teaches in the Gothic St Flannan's College in Ennis still has a photograph taken by the garda sergeant.

Boy with pompadour quiff, in belted scoutmaster shorts, standing against the rocks where frogs live in abundance, hands on the rocks, his chest thrown forward, Lana Turner-style.

It was not forgotten in County Clare that during the War of Independence, in Dublin, some boys shot British agents in their beds, some beside their wives.

Then, as they were being searched for in the city, they played a football match. A few of those boys later went mad and ended up in mental homes.

Michael Cusack himself, who'd founded the Gaelic Athletic Association in 1884, was from Carron in County Clare.

It had never been forgotten that shortly after the Irish defeat at the Battle of the Boyne in County Meath, where Gaelic football was particularly popular and used to be followed by wrestling, some Wexford men crossed to Cornwall, tied yellow ribbons around their waists to distinguish themselves, and trounced the Cornish men at hurling.

Nor was it forgotten that after the Battle of the Boyne the victors had sung 'The Protestant Boys,' composed by the Marquis of Wharton, frequently sung by Lord Byron's friend, the County Clare poet Thomas Dermody, as 'Lillibulero.'

The Gaelic Athletic Association spread like prairie fire in the years just after its foundation, Michael Cusack said.

One of the first football teams used flour bags as jerseys.

The Gaelic Athletic Association turned up en masse to Parnell's funeral in 1891, to which his widow in Brighton, Kitty O'Shea, was afraid to go.

On the day the Second World War broke out Kilkenny was playing Cork in hurling in Dublin, a day of thunder and lightning and rain, Kilkenny winning with a decisive point from a man from Castleshock.

Roscommon won the All-Ireland football final that month.

Often the Clare boys went to Ballinasloe to play games, where the football star Michael Knacker Walsh was from, staying in the workhouse, singing 'The West Clare Express' in the showers: 'It spends most of its time off the track.'

Connaught finals were played in St Coman's Park in Roscommon and these were a treat because the people of Roscommon town opened their houses as guesthouses for the occasions and served spice cake and butterfly buns at their hall doors.

People converged on the town in thousands on bicycles for these occasions.

At the end of September some of the Clare boys journeyed to Dublin, staying in the Grand Hotel, Malahide, to see the All-Ireland football final for a cup modelled on the Ardagh Chalice.

On these visits to Dublin it was mandatory, in suits with long jackets and padded chests, to call in on the all-day cartoon show in the rich-crimson, basement Grafton Cinema, which sold claret, port, rum and champagne gums in the foyer, and to admire the interlaced roundels and the floriated scrollwork of the Book of Kells in Trinity College.

A few of them went to a production of *The Duchess of Malfi* at the Gate Theatre in which all the actors wore hearse-cloth costumes.

> O, this gloomy world.
> In what a shadow, or deep pit of darkness,
> Doth womanish and fearful mankind live!

The garda sergeant was a great fan of John McCormack and in the barracks at night on a gramophone he'd play John McCormack singing Don Ottavio in *Don Giovanni*, Rachmaninoff's 'When Night Descends,' Handel's 'Tell Fair Irene,' Earl Bristol's 'Farewell,' 'The Short Cut to the Rosses,' 'The Snowy Breasted Pearl,' 'Green Grows the Laurel,' Villiers Stanford's 'Lament for Owen Roe O'Neill.'

He himself was known to sing the renowned ballad, 'The Peeler and the Goat,' about a drunken goat who was impounded by an Irish Constabulary officer in County Tipperary.

In the nineteen-thirties and -forties, while the rest of Ireland suffered, it was common to have garda sergeants who were libertine or even bohemian.

Garda Sergeant Clohessy was from Galway city and, in the extreme viridian of Galway before it changed to maroon and white and in snowflake-white calf stockings, used to play football with the Kilconierin team.

In the years just after independence, his hair Rudolph Valentino -style, he went to train as a guard in the Phoenix Park Depot, where sick members of the Royal Irish Constabulary used to wear bottle blue to distinguish themselves from the rifle green of their healthy colleagues, sleeping on a triple bedboard.

He began taking photographs of other garda recruits in woollen -bib swimming costumes with striped trim on the trousers of the trunks on Jameson's Beach in Howth with a Wollensak camera.

He was among two hundred and fifty pilgrim gardaí, whose organization had been founded in the Gresham Hotel, Dublin, shortly after the Treaty, who travelled to Rome in the autumn of 1928, met at the umber Rome Central by the staff and students of the Irish College, parading to lay a wreath on the Tomb of the Unknown Soldier, wearing medals with the cradle-blue ribbons of pilgrimage on their uniforms with buckram-stiffened high necks, addressed and lauded by Pius XI whose predecessor Pius X, on the occasion of his jubilee, had been entertained with bagpipes by the son of a County Galway Royal Irish Constabulary Officer, in full kilted uniform, shown the paintings of the Vatican Gallery by a priest from the Irish College; the carmines, the damasks, the loganberries, the coral reds, the cyclamen red, the rose reds of the *St Jerome of Francesco Mola*, the *St Jerome* of Girolamo Muziano, the *Deposition of Christ* by Caravaggio, *The Vision of St Helena* by Veronese, the *Martyrdom of St Erasmus* by Poussin.

But it was the statue of Caesar Augustus with his double forelock and parade armour, which attracted the most attention, who, the priest told them, put a serpent nearly ninety feet long in front of the Domitium and decreed crossroad gods should be crowned twice a year, with spring and summer flowers.

Back in Galway, stationed in Eglinton Street Barracks, he won his medals, playing in places like Parkmore, Tuam and Cusack Park, Mullingar, wearing a Basque beret on the field.

The Galway team had a trainer then, who used to cut pictures of Greek gods out of books and frame them, who'd take them to Tuam where they'd stay in Canavan's Hotel and eat lashings of boiled potatoes.

He'd have them run for miles as far as Greenfield where they'd jump into Lough Corrib.

In 1934 Garda Clohessy travelled with the Galway team on the Manhattan to the United States, sighted the petrel known to sailors as Mother Carey's chicken in the eastern Atlantic, heard Guido Ciccolini who'd sung at Rudolph Valentino's funeral.

The former commissioner of the guards, who'd been received by Benito Mussolini and a goose-stepping cohort during the pilgrimage of 1928, relieved of his post earlier that year by Mr de Valera, had become leader of the Irish Fascist Movement in 1933,

In November 1936 five hundred of the Irish fascists turned up in Galway to sail for Spain and fight for Franco.

Thirty-four of them had a last-minute change of mind and

turned back.

Two of the Irish fascists were shot on their arrival in Spain by Franco's men because of their strange uniform.

When a French actor in a greatcoat, known in Galway for his performance as a French revolutionary murdered in a bath, was giving street performances in Eyre Square in September 1937, Garda Clohessy was promoted to sergeant, given a uniform with chevrons of silver braid on the sleeve, and transferred to Clare.

Ned Hannaford's circus was playing on his arrival; an entrée act of a giraffe-necked woman in gold-leaf brassiere and trunks on a Suffolk Punch horse followed by United States cavalrymen; Poodles Hannaford in a leopard-skin loincloth driving six Rosinback horses of flea-bitten hue tandem, standing astride; a brief scene from Shakespeare's A *Midsummer Night's Dream* accompanied by Catherine wheels . . . 'kill me a red-hipped humble-bee on the top of a thistle'; pigmy African elephants waited upon by baboons in frock coats.

In Rome Garda Sergeant Clohessy had been told by the priest from the Irish College how Lucius Aemilius Paullus had deserters in the war against Perseus trampled to death by elephants in the Circus Flaminius.

An English fair used to come to the town, where some of the houses were painted Wallis Warfield Simpson blue, each year before the war and the gaff boys, many with the common features of Venetian-blonde hair—dark mottled with blonde—and dead-white lips, and wearing costume rings, used to swim in the swimming hole.

It was these that Garda Sergeant Clohessy started his nude photography on, with a Voigtlander Prominent.

Some of the local boys left with the fair and themselves stood around the dodgems and gondolas and ghost trains as gaff boys in places like St Briavels in Gloucestershire.

The Clare Champion featured one of the garda sergeant's earliest efforts, that of a football star from Fedamore in County Limerick, with auburn cockscomb, eyes the blue of the gentians that grew in places where wintering cattle had curtailed the hazel trees, after some triumph.

What *The Clare Champion* didn't know was that at the football game at Killarn the garda sergeant photographed the football star, with the chest of an Eros the Spartans used to sacrifice to before going to war, in shorts with gripper fasteners on Dunbeg beach, the youth's hands on his crotch, against the sea, which was the colour of shillings that magpies would steal, on a day the Irish leaders de Valera, Cosgrave and Norton took their seats at a pro-neutrality rally in Dublin, and afterwards, without his shorts, lying face down, among the purple saxifrage of the dunes.

To ease his reservations Garda Sergeant Clohessy cited the mature *Apollo Belvedere*, naked but with a *paludamentum*—cloak—the *Belvedere Torso* on panther skin that had inspired Michelangelo, the boy who combats naked with a goose, Bernini's near-naked *Daniel* with sideswept, cricket-boy hair, all in the Vatican Gallery.

A youth from South Hill in Limerick, ash-blond hair and barley-coloured freckles, his left nostril murdered, cut away in a pub brawl, was among those photographed.

Hands in the black bog rush, legs provocatively apart, head thrown back in abandon.

As the Allies were landing in Sicily and there were riots in Hollywood, some girls with braids like Pippi Longstocking arrived in the swimming hole but they were chased away with a stick by the garda sergeant.

People came to the sea on donkeys and carts then; crubeens—pigs' feet—were proffered for a penny. There was a café near the main beach run by an immense Italian man, which sold sea bass, soft cod's roe.

An American film about Charles Stewart Parnell starring Clark Gable and Myrna Loy was brought from Limerick in cans and shown in the parochial hall, where there were photographs of Pope Pius XII and of Cardinal Franz von Galen von Löwe of Münster, and afterwards the garda sergeant's boys mingled with the holiday-making girls from Limerick, many of them wearing flared linen trousers, and led some of them to the fields, which were a festival of orchids.

Tramming the hay, building cocks of hay it was called then, and Christian Brothers, on leave from schools around Ireland, were employed to tram the hay.

Garda Sergeant Clohessy even convinced a Christian Brother with cowslip-coloured hair and eyes the blue of the Peloponnesos where the two seas meet, to pose in the nude.

A boy with a sea-cow belly took a photograph of Garda Sergeant Clohessy and in it he looks like Caesar Augustus: Roman nose; accentuated, slightly feminine lips; pennon neck; cauliflower ears.

The previous June he'd been photographed leading the Corpus Christi procession through the town, women in coats with large collar-revers and boxy shoulders immediately behind him.

Someone had put a bunch of cornflowers in front of a nearby shrine that told: 'My name is Jeremiah Marriman. I built this shrine in thanksgiving for being cured. Also for my son Loughlin. Thanks be to God and Our Blessed Lady'—red, orange and white plastic flowers in front of a picture of Thérèse of Lisieux, a little statue of Christ beside a black snail with citron rings.

The Spanish Armada ship *San Esteban* had floundered in the vicinity and its crew did not suffer the fate of the Spanish Armada ship whose crew had been massacred by Dowdarra Roe O'Malley in County Mayo, but had married in the neighbourhood and sometimes when Garda Sergeant Clohessy took a photograph he was confronted by an ebony-haired boy from the land of El Greco who, if he wasn't painting portraits, was conducting lawsuits.

Cromwellian soldiers had chopped off the head of a monk in the uplands where the hen harrier preyed on young rabbits and young hares.

Sometimes when he photographed he was photographing boys with burnt-orange hair and Wedgwood-blue eyes who were descended from soldiers from the English midlands.

Goats came down the slope and looked as he was photographing some boys from Limerick city with Marlovian grins and lamp-black hair who would hang about the truck stop at Harvey's Quay in blanket trousers and seersucker shirts and stand under the trees in

Arthur's Quay Park at night or sit late at night in the Treaty Café.

In deference to the goats who were present the garda sergeant sang a bit of his song about the goat:

"'Oh, Mercy Sir,' the goat replied, 'and let me tell my story-o.'"

The Emperor Heliogabalus had been a teenager, he told them, wearing long purple Phoenician garments, embroidered in gold; linen shoes, necklaces, jewels, rouging his cheeks and painting his eyes, appointing actors to the most important posts in the Empire, murdered with his mother Soaemias, by his own soldiers and their bodies thrown into a sewer that ran into the Tiber.

But it was generally agreed that the garda sergeant's most beautiful model was a Jewish refugee from Prague with doe-like limbs who lived in the town for a few years during the war.

'This is what we fought and died for,' the naked garda sergeant greeted the boy on his first arrival at the swimming hole in riding breeches, golf stockings and a thistle dicky bow—a bow with flaps that opened out at both ends—when the comfrey was in white bloom on the sea slopes, before it turned blue.

Father Coughlin's broadcasts in the USA against the Jews were famous in Ireland.

The boy could talk to the garda sergeant about Boccherini, and about Mozart who'd sojourned in a Naples-yellow house in Prague.

The boy's family had brought a reproduction of a painting with them from Prague, which they put in the hall of their house where his mother, who wore culottes as she partook in table quizzes with the local women, made plaited challah bread; a little boy in grey and he had the same polo-pony features as the Jewish boy.

Black bow tie with white polka dots, Eton collar, double-breasted grey suit, straw hat in right hand, toy Pomeranian biting hat, a little greenery behind the boy, left hand in pocket, straw-blond Eton crop, forget-me-not-blue eyes, prince's apricot smirk.

The boy's hand accidentally touched a gull's egg, light olive with spots of umber, as he was being photographed.

A boy who had been used to a bathing establishment on the Elbe in an Irish summer; a towel slung over one shoulder like a Roman exomis.

The chough lived here—the crow with red legs—a raven lived near here, the natterjack toad—yellow stripe down his back—roamed here. Gannets frequently made passage by the swimming hole.

A light bib-top, which is usually joined with a zip to dark trunks but the trunks removed—fire-red body hair.

At night the boy would go to the garda station with cherry-and-sultana sponge cakes his mother had made and tea would be served on a tray with the Guinness pelican in the penetralia of the garda station, which was dominated by a framed picture of Venus with Adonis's naked leg wrapped around her and he and Garda Sergeant Clohessy would listen to 'Song of the Seats,' 'Farewell and Adieu to You,' 'Sweet Spanish Ladies,' 'So We'll Go No More A-Roving.'

As a trainee guard in Dublin, Garda Sergeant Clohessy had heard how a lock of Byron's hair in a locket had been lost in Kildare Street and he cut off a curl of the Czech boy's hair as a keepsake.

Lord Byron had loved John Edleston more than any human being.

The boy left with his family to live in a house with Virginia creeper on it, which was the red of splodges on a baby's bottom, in the autumn, when de Gaulle entered Paris, but not before he told a Jewish story to the gathering at the swimming hole, a torch of monbretia on the slope above, about a migratory bird with feathers so beautiful they were never seen before, who came for the winter and built his nest at the top of the tallest cedar, how the king ordered a human ladder to be built to the top of the tree so that the bird and his nest could be brought to him, but the people at the bottom of the ladder grew impatient because it was taking so long and broke away so that the ladder collapsed and the bird was never inspected.

On his arrival in Dublin the boy sent the garda sergeant a postcard of an Eros with flashing forget-me-not-blue eyes, in a wolfskin surcoat, playing a flute.

The parenthesis lasted until the end of the war when two nuns picking burnet roses for the Feast of St Colmcille saw a naked man with naked boys washing themselves with Pears' and Lifebuoy soap.

A stamp featuring Douglas Hyde, the first Protestant president of Ireland, was omnipresent at the time and Des Fretwell and his

Twelve Piece Orchestra played at the Queens Hotel in Ennis.

The nuns were stronger than the garda sergeant and swiftly got word to a superior and the garda sergeant was transferred to a border county, where the football team wore ox-blood red, when Lord Haw Haw who was from the Lough Corrib country of north Galway, who'd disparaged the naval vessel *Muirchu* on German radio in a nasal voice the result of a broken nose at school, was executed in Wandsworth Prison, and more or less never heard of again except for a sighting by some Claremen who'd accompanied Canon Hamilton of Clare at the Polo Grounds, home of a baseball team, when on the only occasion ever, for the centenary of the Great Famine of 1847, the All-Ireland football final was played outside Ireland.

He was also fleetingly seen at the Commodore Hotel afterwards among the swing dancers, in a hat with the crown flattened into pork-pie shape, with a young man who had a butch cut.

Others said he was sighted on Jones Beach, Long Island, where Walt Whitman used to go with an eighteen-year-old Irish boy, Peter Doyle, to look at the sea fowl, in 1949, which would lead one to believe he decided to settle in the United States.

A garda sergeant in Ennis, a vigilant agent for the Censorship of Publications Board, ambushed Garda Sergeant Clohessy's friend in Ennis, leaping out of hens' and chickens' shrubbery at him, and seized a major part of Garda Sergeant Clohessy's archives, which also included a picture of Johnny Weissmuller as Tarzan, Maureen O'Sullivan as Jane, a golden-haired boy-child and an ape seated on the branch of a tree, and they were never seen again.

From the end of the war people dared only swim in the swimming hole in full regalia, except for an English painter with a Vandyke beard, who'd sit on the rocks in nothing but a rag hat and who referred to the sea by the Greek word *thalassa*.

Young married Traveller boys, many with hair dyed sow-thistle yellow, meet in the town now the first week of August each year, parking their caravans by a football field or on a cliff head, swimming together last thing each evening in the swimming hole in mini-bikini briefs, or boxer shorts with Fiorentina players, or cerulean moons, or in cowboy-faded denim shorts, joining the elderly men who come here in safari shorts, ankle socks, baseball caps, before they move their English-registered caravans to the Killorglin Puck Fair.

Belle

I first made her acquaintance in the cabin the little man who worked on the railway lived in, when I was eleven.

On his wall was an advertisement for Y-fronts based on James Fenimore Cooper's *The Last of the Mohicans*—Hawkeye and Uncas with butch cuts, in Y-fronts, marching alongside one another, with a turkey in long johns bearing a mace on the front of them; a photograph of Cardinal Tien, Archbishop of Peking and exiled Primate of China; Margaret Mitchell in a black antebellum dress with an aigrette of gems at her neck; a photograph of a boy with sideburns in nothing but a peach waisted coat and brothel creepers; and his sterling possession—a postcard of Belle Brinklow, the London music-hall artiste who'd married the young earl of the local manor—red cinnamon hair, heliotrope eyes, mousseline Gibson girl dress with scarlet flannel belt, the words, 'To the Idol of My Heart,' underneath.

The manor was now a boys' school and when I started there boys had pudding-bowl Beatles' haircuts and wore dun-and-wine turtle-neck jerseys and Australian bush shoes with elasticated sides.

There were three mementoes of the Belle still in the school:

A lunette-shaped daguerreotype of her music-hall colleague, Maude Branscombe, clinging to the Cross of Christ.

A Worcester coffee pot with tulip trees and quail on it she and Bracebridge, the young earl, used to have their hot chocolate from.

A portrait Sarah Purser did of the Belle when she was working on the stained-glass windows of Loughrea Cathedral nearby—for which the Belle donned her music-hall apparel: shepherdess hat with a demi-wreath of cornflowers, ostrich-feather boa, seed-pearl choker, tea-rose pink dress with double puff sleeves, bouquet of lavender and asters from the autumn garden in her hand.

Belle Brinklow, who was from Bishop's Stortford, used to perform in theatres with names like the Globe, Royal Alfred, Britannia, Surrey, Creswick, Trocadero, Standard, and in sing-song halls of pubs like the Black Horse in Piccadilly and the Cider Cellars in Maiden Lane.

An orchestra in front with brass, woodwind, percussion, a bit of

Brussels carpet on the stage, a drop scene of Edinburgh Castle or a Tudor village.

In a Gainsborough hat or a Cossack hat, she'd do the cancan—the Carmagnole of the French Revolution—a handkerchief skirt dance, a barefoot Persian dance or a clog dance; in a Robin Hood jacket, knee breeches, silk stockings, in Pierrot costume, in bell-bottom trousers and coatee she'd sing songs like 'They Call Me the Belle of Dollis Hill' or 'Street Arab Song':

> Out at
> Dawn, nothing got to do.

Then a man in a bat cloak and viridian tights might come on and recite a bit of Shakespeare.

> Now for our Irish wars.
> We must supplant those rough rug-headed kerns,
> Which live like venom . . .

One Shakespearean actor who followed her died on stage, in biretta and medieval-cardinal red, reciting Cardinal Wolsey's farewell speech from *Henry VIII*.

Occasionally the Belle teamed up with her sister who was another Belle—who otherwise wore woodland hats—for the purpose of doing leg shows, both of them in winged Mercury hats, tight bodices and gossamer tulle basket skirts with foamy petticoats.

They did matinées at the Gaiety Theatre on the Strand where Ireland's leader Charles Stewart Parnell and the hoydenish Kitty O'Shea, who wore dresses fastened to the neck with acorn buttons, fell in love in a box during a performance in 1880.

The duettists were known to conclude performances with the singing of 'Shepherd of Souls' from *The Sign of the Cross*.

Bracebridge was one of the few men who were allowed backstage.

Others were Lord MacDuff, the Marquess of Anglesey, Sir George Wombwell and the notorious Posno brothers, both of whom were fond of turning up in deerstalkers.

In a Chinese-red waistcoat from Poole's Gentleman's Outfitters, Limerick gloves in hand, cornucopia of golden cockerel hair, eyes the blue of the woodland bugle flower, he came into her dressing room one night and escorted her to Jimmies—the St James Restaurant in Piccadilly.

Afterwards they'd go to the Adelaide Galleries—the Gatti's Restaurant in the Strand or Evan's Song and Supper Rooms where there was a madrigal choir.

She married him in a dragonfly-blue art-nouveau dress with a music-hall corsage of myrtle blossoms in St James's in Piccadilly.

At the end of the nineteenth century and at the beginning of the twentieth there was a craze for music-hall girls to marry into the peerage.

In 1884 Kate Vaughan, star of *Flowers and Words* by Gilbert Hastings McDermott, married Colonel Arthur Frederick Wellesley, son of the Earl of Cowley and nephew of the Duke of Wellington.

Three years after the Belle married Bracebridge, Connie Gilchrist married the Earl of Orkney.

Maud Hobson married a captain of the 11th Hussars and went to Samoa with him where she befriended Robert Louis Stevenson and sang 'Pop Me on the Pier at Brighton' to him while he was dying.

In the mid-nineties, Rosie Boote, the County Tipperary music-hall girl, who was fond of posing in doges' hats, married the Marquess of Headfort and became the Marchioness of Headfort.

At the beginning of the twentieth century Sylvia Lillian Storey became the Countess Poulett; Denise Orme, Baroness Churston; Olive 'Meatyard' May, Countess of Drogheda; Irene Richards married Lord Drumlanrig.

One music-hall girl was courted by an Italian count who bought her a silvered leopard-skin coat worth three thousand pounds; she ran away with him, he divested her of her coat and she came back to the stage door, begging for work, was sent to music halls in the north, where Jenny Hill used to polish pewter in pubs during the day and sang in the song halls at night before being acclaimed on the London stage.

As late as 1925, Beatrice Lillie married Robert Peel, great-grandson of the prime minister.

Before she left for Ireland, Bracebridge brought the Belle to a production of *The Colleen Bawn* at Her Majesty's in Haymarket, which was about a young lord in the west of Ireland who married a peasant girl, got tired of her and drowned her, the horses refused to cross the bridge to his place of execution and he got out and walked to his own execution.

In the foul-smelling Broadstone Station where they got the train to the west she wore a black riding hat with foxtail feathers and a bear muff, he a Hussar-blue covert coat with brandenbourgs—silk barrel-shaped buttons.

On the terrace of the manor he showed her how the pear and cherry blossom came first, then the apple, then the lilac, then the chestnut and laburnum, the oak last. He indicated the kitten caterpillar, the thrush snail, the speckled wood butterfly, which were abundant because the garden bordered on the woods, approached by the Long Walk.

A year after she arrived in Ireland the Irish clown Johnny Patterson, with whom she frequently appeared on the London stage, was killed during a riot at a circus in Castleisland, County Kerry.

Four years after she came to Ireland her friend, the Belle Daisy Hughes, after a performance at the Brighton Empire, threw herself from the balcony of the Grand Hotel, Brighton, to her death.

The Belle gave two performances in Ireland.

One at the Gaiety Theatre where, shortly after its opening in 1871, Emily Soldene rode a horse on stage in Renaissance pageboy leggings.

In a beefeater-red chiffon dress, trimmed with petals, against a drop scene of Sleepy Hollow in Wicklow, she sang 'When the Happy Time Shall Come' from H.J. Byron's *The Bohemian Girl*, 'The Belle of High Society,' 'Molly the Marchioness,' 'O, I Love Society,' 'Tommy Atkins,' 'The Butler Kissed the Housemaid,' 'The Footman Kissed the Cook,' 'It was a Year Ago,' 'Love,' 'In the Balmy Summer Time.'

She shared the bill with an underwater acrobatic couple in broadly striped bathing costumes who displayed in a tank, and Nat Emmett's performing goats.

The other was at the Leinster Hall in Hawkins Street where, shortly after it opened as the New Theatre Royal in 1821, a bottle was thrown at the Lord Lieutenant. In the old Theatre Royal in Smock Alley guns were used to clear the audience off the stage.

In a tartan dress and glengarry—a Scottish hat—against a drop scene of Galway docks with swans, she sang 'The Titsy Bitsy Girl,' 'Tip I Addy Ay,' 'Louisiana Lou,' 'Her Golden Hair,' 'I saw Esau Kissing Kate,' 'Our Lodger's Such a Nice Young Man,' 'Maisie is a Daisy,' and the oldest vaudeville song, 'Lillibulero,' sung by the victors after the Battle of the Boyne, sung in Dublin as part of an all-child cast production of *The Beggar's Opera* in 1729.

On the bill with her were dogs ridden by monkeys in jockey caps and Miss Hunt's possum-faced Ladies' Orchestra, all in bicorne hats and Hussar uniforms, who played Thomas Moore's 'Melodies' to a weeping audience.

Captain O'Shea, Kitty O'Shea's husband, whose mother was a papal countess, had been Member of Parliament for Bracebridge's area, Parnell having endorsed him with a speech in Galway in 1886, and the Bishop of Galway alleged it was a prostituted constituency, in return for Captain O'Shea's connivance in the Parnell-Kitty O'Shea liaison.

When Captain O'Shea finally decided to sue for divorce at the end of 1889, the year the Belle came to Ireland, by all accounts the London music-hall stage had a feast, and the hilarity was compounded by a maid's declaration at the divorce trial that Parnell had once escaped out the window by means of a rope fire escape.

Parnell was represented with a Quaker collar, frock coat, Shetland clown's trousers, hobnail boots. Comediennes wore whalebone corsetting to emphasize Kitty O'Shea's rotundities. Captain O'Shea was usually endowed with an enlarged curlicue moustachio like a Dion Boucicault sheriff.

'Notty Charlie Parnell!' Drop scene painters had a Hibernian spree. One Parnell production featured a Barbary ape in a bowler hat, sealskin waistcoat, trousers embroidered with salad-green shamrocks.

At the end of the 1890s the Belle heard how comedians came on stage in London dressed in prison uniform and their comedienne partners addressed them as 'Oscar' with a flip of the hand.

Lord Alfred Douglas wore a school straw or a domed, wide-brimmed child's hat, Eton jacket with white carnation, drawers, calf stockings, his cheeks the red of a carousel horse's cheeks.

The Prince of Wales, shortly to be Edward VII, an aficionado of the music halls, was said to have turned his back in his box when Lord Alfred Douglas was presented in black-and-pink striped drawers. But shocked ladies actually left the theatre when he appeared in Jaeger pyjamas with frogged breast buttons.

In 1900 the Belle was one of the ladies who helped serve bon-bonnières to fifteen thousand children in the Phoenix Park on the occasion of the visit by Queen Victoria, a return visit to the city where in 1849 she autographed the Book of Kells.

The Guards Band on the terrace of Windsor Castle were one day playing one of the music-hall songs the Belle used to sing, 'Come where the Booze is Cheap,' when Queen Victoria, who was taught singing by Mendelssohn, sent Lady Antrim to find out what the wonderful music was.

The Belle's colleague Kate Vaughan's marriage broke up with Colonel Arthur Frederick Wellesley and she went to Johannesburg where, in elbow gloves on bare arms and a corsage of wild gardenias, she became the Belle of the Gaiety Theatre there. Shortly after she wrote to the Belle about the mauve raintree and the coral tree with cockatoo flowers, she died on a night when Gertie Millar, who was to marry the Earl of Dudley, was playing in one of her roles in *Ali Baba* in London. The Belle had a photograph of her disembarking at Cape Town in a matinée hat.

The owl-like Catholic landlord in neighbouring Loughrea, renowned for promoting boys' choirs, decided to build a new cathedral and the Belle and Bracebridge would often take a brougham there and watch the stained-glass windows being put in, most often speedwell blues, and sometimes at evening the Belle would stand under windows depicting the Ascension and the Last Judgment and recall visits before shows with the French music-hall artiste, Madame Desclause, in her black Second Empire dress, to the Royal Bavarian Church in Piccadilly.

On late-autumn afternoons as they returned from Loughrea the beeches would be old gold and the bushes assaulted to misshape.

A music-hall poster, which depicted a chorus girl holding up a short dress edged in chinchilla-like material, caused clerical outrage in Cork but the clergy were appeased by the king's frequent visits to the music hall, very often in a kilt with a cockade on his stockings. A Dublin music hall caused all-round offence by featuring Admiral Nelson from Nelson's Pillar in Sackville Street with Lady Hamilton in a negligée. The king visited Galway, for the second time in his reign, in gaiters, the Queen in pillar-box red with a Spanish riding hat, a group of Connaught Rangers singing a music-hall song, 'Tara-ra-boom-de-ay,' as an anthem for them.

The Belle read *Jane Eyre* bound in red morocco, by Charlotte Brontë, who'd died while pregnant, married to a parson, Arthur Bell Nicholls, and was remembered for walking alone in a *barège* dress by the Shannon.

On the terrace the Belle and Bracebridge would incessantly play on a horn gramophone a Gramophone & Typewriter record of Joseph O'Mara singing 'Friend and Lover,' as they had their hot chocolate from a tray with the rose, the thistle, the shamrock. Bracebridge sometimes took an opera hat to Kilkee in the summer where they had listened to the German band on the boardwalk. The gilt and cranberry theatres of Dublin magneted with pantomimes—*Jack and the Beanstalk*, *Puss in Boots*, *Aladdin and Princess Badroulbadour*.

There was a brief visit to Belgium where they looked at a Rubens painting. Auburn moustachio. Watermelon-pink cleavage. Plumed hat. Boy with peach slashings on his arms. Cirrus horse. Despite the smiles the sky tells you that war is near.

The Belle was one of the ladies' committee who saw the Connaught Rangers off from the North Wall in August 1914, with chocolates and madeleines.

The swallows in the eaves had a second brood that year and didn't leave until October. When the alders were in white, pulpy berry on either side of the Forty Steps at the end of the Long Walk she'd go there, stand on top of the steps, sing her music-hall songs lest they be stamped out in her.

Soldiers camped in the demesne and at night sang 'It's a Long Way to Tipperary,' which the Melbourne music-hall girl, Florrie Forde, who ran away when she was fourteen, used to sing, the words printed an inch high at the footlights so thousands could join in.

A late Indian summer visit to Kilkee—dramatic mare's tails in the morning sky, a dense fruit of bindweed flowers on the bushes, ladybirds doing trapeze acts on withered fleabane, the late burnet roses becoming clusters of black berries, a dolphin thrashing in the horseshoe bay, a coloratura rendition of 'Take, Oh Take Those Lips Away' from *The Bohemian Girl* at an evening get-together by a man with a Vandyke beard when news came that the mail boat was sunk just after leaving Kingston Harbour, with the loss of five hundred lives.

During the War of Independence, from a window, over bonfires at night or under the ornamental crab-apple tree or the weeping-pear tree in the garden she could hear the soldiers sing songs from the music halls: 'On Monday I Walked Out with a Soldier,' 'The Girl the Soldiers Always Leave Behind Them,' 'All Through Sticking to a Soldier,' 'Aurelia was Always Fond of Soldiers,' 'Soldiers of the Queen,' but especially, 'Soldiers in the Park,' which was where they were, burning leaves.

When the Black and Tans raced up and down Sackville Street in vans covered in wire and there was a curfew, she was one of Dublin's few theatre-goers, taking the tram from a house in Dalkey to Harcourt Street Station, which replaced summer bivouacs in Morrison's Hotel in Dawson Street, in a taffeta hobble skirt tied near the ankle with sash lace, so that the horrible hobble of British taste made her less likely to be a target.

It was commonplace in those days to see Countess Markievicz, the minister for labour in the revolutionary government, cycling around Dublin on a battered bicycle, in a beehive bonnet from which cherries dangled. Her sister, Eva Gore Booth, had devoted part of her life in England to the rights of women music-hall artistes.

The need to perform overcame her because she sang 'Goo-Goo' from *The Earl and the Girl* at a concert in the Theatre Royal, Limerick, spring 1922, in aid of those made homeless by the War of Independence. She was photographed on that occasion outside Joseph O'Mara's house, Hartstonge House—Eton-crop hair now, pumps with Byzantine, diamanté buckles.

The Belle and Bracebridge were in St Nicholas's Cathedral in Galway in early summer 1922, to see the colours of the Connaught Rangers, the harp and crown on yellow, which dated back to 1793, being removed, on the first stage of their Journey to Windsor Castle.

At the beginning of 1923, during the Civil War, the Belle started out two days early, defying derailed trains and broken bridges, joining hordes from his native Athlone to hear John McCormack singing 'The Last Rose of Summer' in a black cloak lined with ruby silk, at a home-visit concert.

Near the Forty Steps that spring, with its bloody cranesbill and its blue cranesbill, she found an abandoned blackbird's nest, covered in moss.

There were ladybird roundabouts in the Fair Green when she and Bracebridge left, childless, to live in a Queen Anne revival lodge near the red-brick Victorian Gothic church of St Chad's in Birmingham, but not before she was received into the Roman Catholic Church, under a portrait of Cardinal Wiseman in garnet red, in the local church, joining the faith of a London music-hall Belle who claimed to be related to Father Prout the poet, a Cork priest who penned 'The Bells of Shandon,' rowed with his native city, was an associate of Charles Dickens and W.M. Thackeray, mixed his priestly duties with the bohemian life, travelled as far as Hungary and Asia Minor, with his Latin translations of the songs of Thomas Moore was a leading attraction at Mrs Jameson's Sunday evening parties in Rome and ended up with his rosary and psalm book in a mezzanine in Paris.

The manor was sold to priests; there were people cycling on the Suck that winter it was so cold, and the priests came and taught Thucydides.

One of the *inculabula* that survived the transaction, which instilled fear in the boys, especially at Lent, was one with an illustration of Caroline of Brunswick in a celestial blue dress, with matching jacket edged in swan's down, and a high-crowned Elizabethan gentleman's hat, banging on the doors of Westminster Cathedral during the coronation of George IV in 1820, demanding to be allowed in as the Queen of England, the doors barred against her.

It joined the books that the priests favoured, which were books with illustrations by Arthur Rackham so that boys going to the school got a vision of life with boys in bathing costumes and girls in dresses with sailor's trim by the tide's edge; New York streets crowded with pigs in derby hats or cloche hats; women in mob caps cherishing their babies in clapboard New England towns; couples enshrined in four-poster beds with rose-motif curtains; bare-footed girls carrying bundles wrapped in peacock-eye patterned cloth through fox-coloured forests; ancient Irish heroes in togas doing marathon runs; small boys in glove-fitting short trousers stomping on plethoric daisies; bare-breasted Rhine maidens in Heimkunst rites.

Just before I left England I visited a man in Bath who'd been a student in the school during the Second World War when a song the Belle sang, 'Maisie is a Daisy,' was revived and sung on radio by Maidie Andrews alongside Gracie Fields' 'So I'm Sending a Letter to Santa Claus to Bring Daddy Safely Home to Me.'

A Palladian square of the Adam style, façade breaking into towers.

A man with a Noah beard in the green, brown and off-white of the Epicurean Graigian sect on it.

A room with lyres, garlands, acanthus on the walls.

A man with mud-green eyes, hirsute brows, in a lap robe, reflected in a photograph of a Beau Brummell of the Irish midlands in a striped beach jacket and cricket shirt.

Christmas 1943, shortly after Churchill, Stalin and Roosevelt met in Teheran, he played Fifi, in Salvation Army fatigues, in *The Belle of New York* at the school, having played Prudence in *The Quaker Girl* the year before and Countess Angela in *The Count of Luxembourg.*

The production was directed by a priest who'd seen the new pope, Eugenio Pacelli, being hailed with the Nazi salute by German boy scouts, summer 1939. He'd caught a swim in the shock-cerulean Mediterranean in Portovenere, where Byron used to swim, on the day the German-Soviet Non-Aggression Pact was signed.

As Fifi, the man I visited had to sing 'Teach me How to Kiss, Dear,' a song that became popular in the rugby changing rooms.

The priest-director commented that he was an annual reminder that the Emperor Nero had married a boy.

Each night when Blinky Bill—who had a slight goat's moustache and was fond of quoting 'Tragedy is true Guise. Comedy lies,' from his schoolteacher father in Creggs, County Galway, where Parnell made his last rain-soaked speech—sang 'She is the Belle of New York,' the ghost of the Belle could be seen in the wings in a haremscarem skirt—a skirt with cuffed and buttoned ankles like Turkish pantaloons—summer sombrero, music-hall, droplet earrings under shingled hair.

Little Friends

Recently I came across a red Silvine exercise book with a sentence
of Eugène Delacroix's I jotted down when I was sixteen: 'To finish
demands a heart of steel . . .'

He has gone to the place
Where naught can delight him.
He may sit now and tell of the sights he has seen of,
While forlorn he does mourn on the Isle of St Helena.

Ailve Ó Cóileáin came from a place not far from where Daniel
O'Connell, the Liberator, was born, where leviathans could regularly
be sighted.

In the late-eighteenth century his family defied the Penal Laws,
sending their children to school in France, building handsome
houses from lime and cows' blood, storing the beeves in autumn for
winter and feasting far from London, from the nucleus of an Empire
that had hastily broken the terms of the Treaty of Limerick and, in
response to the War of the Spanish Succession, which brought the
aged Louis XIV to the gates of Amsterdam, intensified the Penal
Laws. Priests in the instinct-red vestments of the eighteenth century had continued to say Mass through the Penal Laws here where
the common puffin, the red puffin, the seal lived and iodine was
exported from here to Seville where Murillo had painted the pelota
players and the water-sellers when his wife died after twenty years of
marriage.

Ailve's family owned a Swiss castle-hotel with a bar to the side
with an advertisement outside for Turf Virginia Cigarettes with a
picture of a centaur on the packet.

Two of the customers in blue serge suits sent from the United
States would join their foreheads as they sang a song together about
Napoleon.

Framed in the bar was a cartoon from the *Empire News* of a local
butcher-businessman from whom Buckingham Palace had ordered
pork just after the Second World War and who had the pigs killed

on the mail boat in the middle of the Irish Sea so they'd be fresh for the royal feast.

St Gobnait, patron saint of bees, and in County Kerry usurping St Brigid as patron saint of blacksmiths, had lived near here. She had the power to carry live coals in her apron. Once she went to the forge for coals. Idlers were hanging around the forge. She put the coals in her apron, lifting her skirts to miniskirt level. 'Nice pair of legs,' a lecher declared. She was thrilled with the compliment and immediately the coals burned through her apron and she lost the power forever.

Starlings came from all over the British Isles here for the winter and had rallies. They were great mimickers and could mimic the lamentation of the herring gull.

'I'm an autumn person,' Ailve told me, over a mug with a ladybird—*une coccinelle*—on it, at the first French lesson.

Eyebright, with its lonely flame, grew on the cliffs in August.

Burnet moths, olive wings stippled with scarlet, on the cliff scabious in September.

The tree mallow still flourishing in October, where the butcher-businessman dispatched pigeons with gold to England after the Second World War when gold was scarce there.

The fly agaric mushroom, blood-luminous and yellow, in November, where the storyteller Seán Ó Conaill went from house to house.

In December necklaces of birds' footprints on the beaches, the cries of the winter birds like the full-time whistle at a Gaelic football match, tortoiseshell sunshine.

Ailve had a host of relatives who were nuns in France and at fifteen she was sent to a convent in Paris, where at the end of the war, thanks to the Irish Red Cross, which included some of Ailve's relatives, Tipperary cheese in a box with a picture of a cow on it had been in vogue.

Leaving Ireland she had to say goodbye to a Gaelic student who saved the hay with farmers where the kings of Kerry used to booley—leave their permanent residence and graze their cattle for the summer.

But she had a Kodak colour photograph with a white border, a boy with cranberry-auburn hair.

At school in Kerry she'd been taught the eighteenth-century Killarney poet, Aogán Ó Rathaille, who lamented he'd got no periwinkles as a child. He wrote of visions, the Beautiful Lady. Ailve found the Beautiful Lady again in a Russian church in Paris—Holy Sophia. After a few years she attended the Sorbonne.

Her beloved Proust saw Queen Alexandra with followers approach a Parisian buffet table in royal procession.

Ailve saw the Duke of Windsor in linen jacket and white buckskin shoes in the Bois de Boulogne.

I learnt from her at the first French lesson that Racine had written about the Duke and Duchess of Windsor situation centuries before in *Bérénice*.

I was sixteen when I met Ailve, autumn 1967.

She was teaching French for a year in a convent with a statue of St Rose of Lima, first saint of the Americas, outside it, in the town where I lived.

I started going to her for French lessons, bringing red Silvine exercise books.

'My little friends,' she told me Gauguin called the postcards on his wall and her postcards, in a room overlooking the river, were Proust's friend Robert de Montesquiou in Napoleonic-green coat by Lucien Doucet; Berthe Morisot's portrait of her sister in ultramarine dog collar and mother in black Second Empire gown; *Salome* by Delacroix; *Lot's Wife Turning to Salt* by Maître François.

A few years before my father had bought me a set of art books. Loose colour reproductions went with them and one of them had been Dürer's *Lot and his Daughters*: a loftily turbaned Lot leaving Sodom with wine slung over his shoulder, which he's later to drink and lie down with his daughters and have children by them; basket of eggs in hand; one daughter merrily with the family moneybox although her mother has visibly turned into a pillar of salt behind her. When Sodom was burned, Proust noted that a few of those sodomites had managed to escape, Ailve illuminated me.

She would play arias from *Iphigénie en Aulide*, which Pauline Viardot used to sing to Flaubert in his Turkish knitted waistcoat with brown-and-red stripes and green oriental slippers.

Pride of place on her shelf was the Penguin Classic edition of Flaubert's *Bouvard and Pécuchet* with *The Farmers of Flagey* returning from the fair by Courbet on the cover, and she called the fair that had just ended in the town a 'pardon.'

Many Travellers stayed in the countryside near the town for the winter after the fair.

The Traveller children could indicate the hazelnut and the wild plum for you. The heron was anthropoid for them, and the ferret.

What really brought Ailve here I never knew.

Her elfin face was distinctive above a black polo-neck sweater, her legs in lurex-thread stretch tights or ribbed orange tights under a mid-thigh miniskirt, her hair, brown-blonde, a little bucket of it, nearly unkempt, not quite, her eyes the green of the dado on the stairway. But it was her clown's mouth, her Toulouse-Lautrec Cirque Fernando mouth, that distinguished her most of all.

She told me about Paris: blue scooters, Brigitte Bardot ponytails, ankle-length ladies' pants, zip-fastened jackets, ski socks, scarlet armlets on First Holy Communicants, Chanel lipstick.

Her own lipstick was usually tiger-lily red.

In Paris she never stopped thinking of Daniel O'Connell, who witnessed the bloodbath of the Revolution and henceforth vowed himself to peaceful means, dying of heartbreak in Genoa, May 1847, on his way to Rome to pray for famine-stricken Ireland.

Bonfires had lit all over Ailve's peninsula in 1829 for Catholic Emancipation as bonfires were still lit in east Galway near Offaly, on Midsummer's Night, groups of young men, shirts off, holding hands, jumping over them in unison to airs on a squeezebox like 'Seán South of Garryowen.'

'For he fell beneath a Northern sky, brave Hanlon at his side.'

After two lessons Ailve told me about her affair with an Austrian novelist called David. He was inquisitive about her because so many of the Wild Geese—Irish soldiers who'd fled the Jacobite Wars—had gone to Austria.

Maria Theresa, who had Goldkette the rope dancer and bareback rider perform at her coronation ceremony and had emancipated Gypsies, appointed Count Browne of Limerick as commander-in-chief of her armies.

Ailve had a Polaroid photograph of David, taken at a terrace café in Italian sunglasses, jacket with a Persian-lamb collar.

She was adamant that theirs had not been primarily a sexual relationship but spiritual, an elevating of things into a vision.

Mutually looking at Rodin's sculpture *La Pensée*—a woman's head in deep thought—Ailve had been struck by its totality, the way it expressed the coming together of things, adolescence and adulthood, a moment when one was self-aware and self-welcoming.

Ailve and David touched, they briefed one another in their individual pain but he faded into the romanticism of other flesh—male as well as female.

She finished at the Sorbonne, returned to Kerry, but not before, like St Gobnait, she showed her legs, making love to American GIs with skin felted like the wild raspberry, hair blond as canary grass, who had the mock orange of Idaho or the flowering dogwood of North Carolina embroidered on their uniforms; Japanese tourists who wore Jean-Paul Sartre jackets; not to mention wealthy Parisian bachelors who wore glove-fitting jeans, in apartments on the boulevard des Italiens, avenue de l'Opéra, boulevard Montmartre.

Ailve and I had tea and tipsy cake—pink icing, sponge base with chocolate fondant, jam syrup and sherry.

'Oh God,' she cried. 'Where are they? The painters, the writers, the musicians, more than anything the young, the young in spirit?'

She began having an affair with Jerome Denmyr, an engineer with collar-length hair, who was from a town where an Irish revolutionary's handcuffs were kissed by his mother as he was taken away in 1918. On Sundays she went to the mental-hospital grounds to see him play rugby. Mental-hospital patients stared from behind iron bars. The heron was the totem of this town and there was always one making a journey along the nearby river. After the rugby marches Jerome always smelled of American Bay Rum.

People stood around the gallery during dances in the local ballroom they went to together—the artistes were Maisie McDaniels in bootlace tie, miniskirt, Edwardian pantomime-boy boots; Butch Moore with silver-dollar crew cut and polo-neck shirt; Joe Dolan in mauve jacket; Eileen Reid in air-hostess's outfit; Dickie Rock and the Miami Showband in plum-coloured blazers and trousers with knife-sharp creases—various laps to the evening until eventually lights lowered, red, girls' arms intricated around men's shoulders.

Alternatively they went in his Volkswagen Beetle to the Prince of Wales Hotel in Athlone, which I always imagined to be called after the Duke of Windsor, who, in his pancake cap and smoking a shag cigarette, on a visit to the United States in 1922, when asked by a hostess who he wanted on the guest list, picked the Dolly Sisters as his first choice, which gave enormous joy to the gossip columnist Cholly Knickerbocker.

Ailve wore a black silk brocade dress when she was with him, a cotton Watteau dairymaid dress, or a dress with multi-coloured paisley design.

Balzac, she said by way of explanation, had one of his heroines wear a different dress for every meeting with her lover.

On a sojourn back in Paris from Tatilti, on his walks home with his adolescent girlfriend Judith Molard, Gauguin nightly pissed in the courtyard.

Jerome would piss in the courtyard of Ailve's house at night on his way back from the pub with her.

Judith Molard bought flowers for Gauguin when he was leaving for Tahiti for the last time, but because the colours were too nondescript for one who was lavish with Veronese greens, she was ashamed and threw them away.

'And where are the flowers here, might I ask?' Ailve deplored.

She often quoted Maude Gonne McBride in old age when she was photographed by Horvath with a lioness-face brooch at her throat: 'My heart is for Ireland and my love for France.'

The floods grew higher and she was like one of those mental-hospital patients behind iron bars. Her face became thin and papier-mâché-like. Her eyes grew large, looming even, and her mouth grew longer, more tragic, an entrée clown's mouth.

I wanted to believe everything she told me about her life. Sometimes I doubted. But what one could not easily dispense with was an image, an inspiration, Rodin's *La Pensie*—'The Thought'—self-confrontation, the tentative approach to a work of art that for one moment objectifies our life, arrests its flow, creating something, wonder in the eyes, remorse in the heart, sublimation.

Ailve saw herself through that sculpture, a girl in Paris, in a short, black, plastic wrapover coat, and scarf with large geometric patterns.

Her stories about French literature became more prolific.

How Flaubert was inspired to write *Madame Bovary* by a woman's face he saw as a young man in a small town in Brittany. Her Penguin Classic edition featured *Madame de Calonne* by Gustave Ricard on the cover.

How George Sands used to jump into icy water to cure herself of illness. How one of the duchesses Proust wrote about died of starvation during the Occupation and was eaten by one of her own greyhounds.

And she might end with one about Vincent Van Gogh: how he had a print—a little friend—of Irish emigrants on his wall.

When I mentioned after Christmas I'd seen the pantomime *Cinderella* in Dublin she retold Charles Perrault's *Cinderella* as Seán Ó Conaill might tell a story; the pumpkin turned into a gilded coach; the mice turned into mouse-coloured horses; the rat turned into a coachman; the lizards turned into footmen.

When I was a child the mother in a family farther up the street had been from Warsaw where her house had been lit by gas lamps in childhood.

They had a book with an illustration of Charlotte, one of the ugly sisters, in an ultramarine-ash wig and ice-green ruffles.

They also had a book with illustrations of a fox in scarlet hunting jacket and a woman in a coal-skuttle hat, with peach cape, riding a goose.

I asked the Little Lord Fauntleroy son if he'd be my friend but he categorically said, 'No.'

I felt like Cinderella when addressed by Charlotte as 'Cinder-breech.'

Through Ailve's affair with Jerome Denmyr she was a daily Communicant at Mass, going to the altar in a Cossack hat, a straw boater with Hawaiian ribbon-band, or beret with brooch trim.

Spring came with bird-cherry blossom on the outskirts of town.

Ailve wrote a letter to Mr Brezhnev about women political prisoners in the small zone unit at Barashevo in Mordovia.

Solzhenitsyn got eight years, she reminded me, for referring to Stalin as 'the whiskered one.' 'Be careful what you say.'

She accompanied me to François Truffaut's *Fahrenheit 451* in the town hall.

I wore a cravat patterned with orange-coloured prints of a potato-cut done in art class. She wore a suit with polka-dotted Peter Pan collar and decorative polka-dotted handkerchief in breast pocket.

Literature is banned. Men in boiler suits seize books. Mechanical hounds with needles shoot transgressors. Helicopters drop bombs. People retire to the mountains, light fires, and, to keep them alive, recite aloud, individual people with the task of an individual author, *Wuthering Heights* by Emily Brontë, the stories of Matthew, Mark, Luke and John.

'As soon as they were come to land, they saw a fire of coals there . . .'

Ailve returned from a weekend in Kerry, where she'd gone to a country-and-western night at the Gleneagle Hotel, Killarney, and told me she was pregnant.

What would she do?

Have an abortion, she decided. Like any good Catholic Irish teacher.

I was due to go to France on a student-exchange scheme but I volunteered to run away and join her in London.

No, she said, Jerome was going with her.

'No use dragging you into it.'

She was wearing flared pants with spotted hyenas on them and large hoop earrings.

'I came back to be mediocre again, to re-establish that part of myself. Now look at me. Having an abortion with a man who sweats too much.'

I was moved by her and without warning she was in my arms, weeping, feeling the width and breadth of my shoulders as I conquered her waist, a little package in a blouse as white as an Arlésienne's Holy Communion dress.

'Do not forget to go to see Rodin's *La Pensée*,' she told me, as if making her last will and testament.

She gave me a gift of a bloater tie intended for Jerome, with a pattern of Camberwell butterflies, deep yellow with purple borders, telling me how Princess Mathilde, Napoleon's niece, gave Proust some silk from one of her dresses to make a cravat.

The sycamore blossomed and the oak, the chestnut trees that could have been planted, like Stendhal's in the days of the Sforzas, when, in a blue-and-white fleck suit, Miss Ó Cóileáin drove away in a cherry-red Renault, after a gala day in the convent—when an extract from Racine's *Bérénice* was enacted as it first had been by the young ladies of Madame de Maintenon's Academy attached to the court of Louis XIV—skedaddling off to Kerry, thence to London.

'A sad example of the Sleights of Love.'

For the performance I had worn a Sergeant Pepper shirt patterned with black-eyed Susans my mother had bought for me in Dublin.

Ailve wrote to me in Parts that summer.

16 Bolingbroke Road,
London W14,
23 August 1968

Desmond, a Chara,
It is the Feast of St Rose of Lima.
Had my abortion. It was like a butterfly slipping away,
I went to the Church of the Benedictine Adorers of the Sacred Heart of Montmartre in Marble Arch afterwards.

It's very hot here, scorching. The dustbins are overflowing. Stendhal said the soul goes down in price in England.

Jerome plays Radio Luxembourg late into the night.

I put a PG tips historical card of Mary Stuart, one-time Queen of France, on the mantelpiece.

Ronsard said her fingers were like the branch of a tree. He also wrote a poem about her opponent, Elizabeth I, who sent him a gold sovereign for his efforts.

I'm alone here, thinking of a Kerryman who was educated in France.

'The freedom of Ireland is not worth the shedding of a single drop of blood.'

I feel I've killed something for Ireland, the baby within me. There's a space within me they can't fill, the nuns, the schoolgirls, the statues of St Rose of Lima.

It will go on and on, gathering force like a huge wave. I wish you were here.

I know you'd understand but even you couldn't stop it.

I've murdered a part of myself and buried it under the floor of a classroom.

> *Lots of kisses,*
> *Ailve*

On Alive's recommendation I went to see Édouard Manet's portrait of his sister-in-law Berthe Morisot in the Musée d'Orsay but was dismayed to find the entire face was covered with a fan.

I also went to see Rodin's *La Pensée*.

In a wet and grey summer, staying in a suburb, nearby factories emitting flames that burned into the mind, it was the highlight, this wonder of marble.

Looking at it I confronted a fragment of myself, a boy in a white shirt with a peaked collar who had complimented a girl in a white blouse.

I wondered if it had been real, her affair in Paris, but knew that it didn't matter because we'd been real, we'd touched, my head had sunk into hers and our mutual tremor would shake our lives, going on and on when guns raged in another part of Ireland.

When I returned to Ireland that autumn she was nowhere to be seen. Jerome Denmyr was back, excelling himself on the rugby pitch.

In Buenos Aires Manchester United's Nobby Stiles was backheaded in the face by an Estudiantes player, and El Beatle, George Best, at the height of his pudding-bowl pompadour, took appropriate reprisals.

Peter Sarstedt sang 'Where Do You Go To (My Lovely)?' from Enzo's Café.

I wondered what had happened to her. Had she died from the after-effects of abortion?

Had she returned to Paris as she said she might?

In either case I was determined on going on, the shadow of a Rodin sculpture inside, the knowledge gained from art that life is worth holding on to, that if you keep fighting it will come, freedom.

Ailve had given me the first lesson in freedom.

It was up to me to go on, rung by rung, until I met someone or something that touched me again as deeply as Rodin's *La Pensée*.

I travelled. I saw the pearwood Virgin in Chartres Cathedral, the statuette of Philosophus outside it again; I visited Stes-Maries-de-la-Mer, to which the black Madonna was borne on a cloud of red sand, in a house or stone coffin, with the other two Maries. I saw a Spanish Mercheros Gypsies' encampment, just like a painting by Van Gogh, by a necropolis and young blonde German Jenisch Gypsies in wingtip shoes in cafés where the jukeboxes played *Schlagermusik* sung by Czech Vlachs Gypsies.

My little friends were Gauguin's naked *Breton Boy*, strong black lines separating his body from the grass he's lying on; Van Gogh's night-time café in Arles, which he painted with candles in his hat; Vermeer's *View of Delft*.

Ailve had told me the story.

Proust thought *View of Delft*, which he saw as a young man, the most beautiful painting in the world. A few years before he died there was a Vermeer exhibition at the Jeu de Paume. He temporarily collapsed before going to it. There he saw *View of Delft* again and still thought it the most beautiful painting in the world.

Another of her stories had been about the Liberator's poetess aunt Eibhlín Dhubh Ní Chonaill who married Art Ó Laoghaire, a young captain in the Hungarian Hussars and lived with him near Macroom, west Cork.

Art had a bitter quarrel with Abraham Morris, the high sheriff, and was shot dead by Morris's bodyguard.

When Art's sister arrived from Cork city for the wake she was outraged to find Eibhlín in bed, that she wasn't mourning sufficiently.

The accusation of not mourning enough was always being flung at me.

It was flung once more at me when most of the members of the Miami Showband, which Ailve regularly danced to, were murdered on their way back from a country-and-western night near Newry, County Down.

When Sandy Denny—wind-blown blonde hair, sunburst jellabas—who sang songs as old as Chaucer's 'Poor Person' or Blind

Mary's father John Bunyan, died as a result of falling down a stairs, I heard that Ailve, after a brief career as an actress in Dublin, had married a politician.

In her brief career as an actress in a cul-de-sac theatre, she'd played Beatrice in Stendhal's play *The Cenci*, about an Italian count who raped his daughter; she in turn tortured and murdered for her part in his murder. It was in this role, for which she won considerable acclaim, that Ailve caught the politician's attention.

Some years later I visited her in Galway.

A pathway led to a white house that was identical to the illimitable miles of white houses that swept around me.

In an exercise suit patterned with palm leaves, blue canvas beach shoes, hair with long fringe now, Ailve answered the door, half-fearfully, her face sunken in.

When Queen Elizabeth, who receives a sprig of thorn each Easter from Glastonbury where the Irish monks used to venerate Patrick, visited the dying Duke of Windsor in Paris, and there was a Georges de la Tour exhibition in the Orangerie des Tuileries, which did for de la Tour, not overlooked by Ailve's Proust, what an exhibition in Milan in 1951 did for Caravaggio, she had returned to Paris as she suggested she might but found the streets forever led back to a street in Kerry where there were Holy Communion dresses in full blossom in one shop window, which always had messages about lost keys.

When you see life through a maze of fifteen thousand novels, you must get a queer impression of things and see them from an odd angle, Flaubert's cousin Guy de Maupassant said.

The fifteen thousand novels had led us both to fifteen thousand suburban houses.

Ailve showed me in.

Black flags had been flying in County Mayo, which I'd just returned from, for the recent H-Block deaths, as they'd flown throughout Ireland early in 1957 for Seán South from Henry Street, Limerick, and Feargal O'Hanlon from Monaghan town, killed during an attack on a police barracks in County Fermanagh, and the country-and-western voice of Louise Corrigan, from Bansha, County Tipperary, where a girl was tortured to death as a witch at the end of the nineteenth century, sounded from every café.

On Ailve's Laura Ashley wallpaper was a reproduction of the Belfast artist Paul Henry's painting of the two Umhall mountains in County Mayo, with Knockmore on Clare Island to the west.

When the French landed in Killala in County Mayo in 1798, a County Mayo landlord's son was declared president of the republic of Connaught.

On a beanbag cushion was a book, *Cinderella*, a palace garden with trees in blossom on the cover.

Ailve's children were Segda, a girl, and Breffni, a boy.

My first impulse was to embrace her but I was restrained by the look on her face.

Ailve Ó Cóileáin looked at me and I saw myself, for the first time in years—rooms full of little friends, and suddenly as if the little friends went up in flames, having to move on—still trying as she tried, her face white and sunken now but her eyes still burning and alive, repeating themselves over and over in my mind just as the white houses of the republic of Connaught repeated themselves, over and over again, until they reached the sea.

Red Tide

Tonight is the night of the Red Tide—St Valentine's Day. Nutrients from inland, with the change of season, after rainy weather, light up the combers, blue and white.

For some days patisserie windows have been full of pralines—cakes composed of mousse, caramel and pecan nuts. Earlier there were boys on skateboards on the boardwalk, in Bermuda shorts with busbies or traveller's cheques on them, carrying bunches of Greek windflowers. Groups of old ladies in owl-eye glasses, in the ruby lake of Mickey Mouse or the lemon of Donald Duck, paraded by the ocean.

An elderly man in a Borsalino hat passed a shaven-headed Chinese boy, with a birthmark on his face like a great burn, who was staring at a flock of plovers, and I thought of shirts I'd worn in London as if they'd been women I'd known—a long-sleeved terracotta shirt with sepia roosters, a short butterfly-sleeved vermilion shirt with coral-grey swallows.

'How do you get to Amsterdam? You take a bus through Ranelagh.' I had this dream shortly before I went to Amsterdam for the first time.

I went with Rena. We were going to travel south from there. In London before setting off we went to an Andy Warhol double bill and all the beautiful, naked young men inspired a greater intensity in our love-making.

We stayed with a Dutch couple we'd met while hitchhiking that summer in north Connemara, on Gerard Doustraat. In the window of the corner café, despite the fact that it was late September, there was a Santa Claus with a hyacinthine beard with little acorns on it.

The couple gave us kipper soup for supper and the following morning we had breakfast cake. On our one full day in Amsterdam we purchased two dozen or so postcards of Jan Mankes paintings and drawings to send to friends. A few self-portraits of Mankes. One in a tiny Roman collar and smock, with a wing quiff, against a lemon landscape. Hair sometimes brown, sometimes amber. Eyes sometimes blue, sometimes brown. A woman in silhouette tending geese. A woman with head dipped in a gaslit room. Salmon-coloured roofs. An old person with a nose like a root vegetable. Birds in snow. An art-nouveau, besequined turkey. A landscape breaking into water. A bunch of honesty. A mouse in the snow. Geese with their beaks to heaven. Goats looking as if they're wearing clogs. A rattan chair. A nightingale. A kestrel. A thrush. An owlet. A reading boy. Birch trees.

It was as if these cards and their images by a painter who'd died young, held together, before being dispatched, on a day when cyclists held golf-sized umbrellas, composed our lives as they had been together.

In Paris we slept near the statue of Henry IV on Pont Neuf.

Then we hitchhiked south. We had an ugly row when we reached the warmth but then a truck took us and brought us as far as Marseille where we both had our first sight of the Mediterranean, cerulean-ash.

The grapes were translucent, hands reaching under them. The hills of Provence were vertigo at evening, little stone walls like the west of Ireland, Roman ruins.

A truck driver with a moustache took us to Monaco where he put us up for the night in an apartment looking to the sea, gave Rena a T-shirt with Gerd Müller of Bayer Leverkusen soccer team on it.

Our first day in Italy we had pasta in a workers' café in the suburbs of Milan, given to us by a blonde waitress in black.

In Venice Rena's face, with her silver-blonde hair and starling's egg-blue eyes, was reflected in glass just blown in a little canalside glass-making place. Her life, her anxieties were in those reflections; a French schoolboy's cape, autumn leaves in Dublin, mustard-coloured leaves lining the long avenue.

We did not stay in the Excelsior Hotel on the Lido. We slept in a large cement pipe but we took advantage of the cordoned-off beaches around the Excelsior. Last effigies of beauty on these beaches in the faltering sunshine of Fall—boys in hi-waist bathing togs.

On the way back we took a tram through the narrow streets of La Spezia, then walked by the apricot, papaya, yellow-ochre-coloured houses of Portovenere to the rocky place where the Harrow mutineer, Byron, used to swim.

Perhaps it was the light or the lack of sleep but I saw a child there, a little boy in a blue-and-white striped T-shirt.

Rena went back to Dublin from London. I stayed in a house in Hanwell with a reproduction of Arthur Rackham's young Fionn on the wall.

Later in the Fall I ventured to Italy again. Mustard-coloured leaves were reflected in the front mirror of a truck heading towards Florence.

In the Uffizi a Japanese girl with bobbed hair, in a long skirt and high heels with bevelled undersides paused in front of Botticelli's young man in a skullcap holding a honey-coloured medallion.

On a day trip to Siena I sent a postcard reproduction to Dublin of a self-portrait Dürer did at twenty-two, red tasselled cap, carrying field eryngo in his hand. *Mannstreu* in German meaning man's fidelity.

I saw the turbaned ancient Eygptian Hermes Trismegistus in a pavement mosaic at the entrance to the cathedral.

In Viareggio where the drowned Shelley was cremated with salt and frankincense in the flame, the sky was grey, there were tankers at sea, gold lace on the combers. I swam on the beach there. The grey lifted shortly after Viareggio.

In Rome the skies were cerulean. I paused in front of Pope John XXIII's pilgrim door, I saw the statue of a young, early Christian shepherd with corkscrew curls, I saw a mural Mussolini had commissioned depicting Odysseus embracing his son Telemachus, I sat in the sunshine near the persimmon throat of a fountain, I listened to Bob Dylan's 'A Satisfied Mind' under the statue of Giordano Bruno.

That statue spoke years later. I read somewhere that he'd said: 'Through the light which shines in the crocus, the daffodil, the sunflower, we ascend to the life that presides over them.'

One night when I slept in a train by Rome's pre-war brown station I was beaten up and everything I had robbed. I had to return to England with a document the Irish embassy gave me and some money my father sent me.

An English girl on the train gave me a jersey of kingfisher blue. The sea was harebell blue at Folkstone. I was stopped by the police.

The English girl stood with me.

Back in Dublin at Christmas I found Rena was having an affair with a boy with a Henry-VIII horseshoe beard.

I started teaching in the New Year in a school where a boy brought an Alsatian dog one day, where a prostitute used to come into the yard and sing a Dublin courtship song: '. . . And I tied up me sleeve to buckle her shoe.'

At Easter Rena and I were travelling again together. We had a camera and in Cork, outside Frank O'Connor's cottage, where a woman neighbour had chased an anti-Parnellite priest with a stick, we were photographed and little boys, many of them, arrived out of nowhere and posed behind us, cheering. It was as if they were cheering on my own stories. The roll of film was lost.

The previous Easter we'd stayed in a cottage one weekend in Ballinskelligs with a photograph of a young man in a zoot suit, kipper tie, wingtip shoes, on the wall.

The following weekend, Easter weekend, I returned to Kerry alone and swam in olive-drab underpants in the turquoise water at Clogher Strand.

In the summer we camped near a cliff-side barracks in Duncannon in County Wexford and mutually flirted with the soldiers.

Rena had gone to school in the west of Ireland in a school with a picture of a Penal Days' Mass on the wall, and bits of information from an erudite old nun there were always breaking through her conversation.

'Lord Cornwallis who suppressed the Rising of 1798 had previously lived in Yorktown—New York.'

Near Enniscorthy we picked up a boy in a tiger-stripe tank top and hipster jeans and he slept in the tent with us and after I'd made love to Rena my hand touched his chest.

Some weeks after our trip to Cork bombs went off in Dublin and shortly afterwards Rena went to California.

In October 1976 I went to California from Dublin to see her. In the evening at San Francisco airport her eyes were the blue of a bunch of chicory. She wore a long scarlet skirt surviving from Connemara days. I gave her an old edition of a book by Kate O'Brien. Inside was a motif of swans.

The following afternoon on a boat on San Francisco Bay she asked me about death, mortality. She'd joined a religious group.

We hitchhiked north together, staying in a motel in Mendocino. I'd been working with a street-theatre group in Dublin.

She wore a honeycombed swimsuit. The whales were going south, a *passegiata* on the horizon.

There was a great palm tree on the beach, maybe the last one north. The distant whales and the morning ultramarine of the Pacific were framed by rocks on either side of the beach as if it was a theatre scene.

She returned to Dublin the following May. The last time I made love to her easily there was an image of Mexican forests in my mind. At a party in Dublin, in front of everyone, a girl accused me of impotence and after that I couldn't make love to Rena anymore. Rena returned to California.

Years later in southern California a boy in a lumber jacket with mailbox pockets would explain the nature of schizophrenia to me —people say things or do things that have no connection with their emotions, with what they feel.

In the summer in southern Egypt, near where some of the Gnostic Gospels were found, Coptic priests in flowing black robes among the little white houses, iron Coptic crosses nearby in the desert, I swam in the Nile, despite the fact that I was warned that there were insects in it that could get into your blood. The Nile was an earthenware-jar cerulean.

I was feeling dead after the attack in Dublin. I walked out into the night in southern Egypt. There were great palm trees against the stars and distantly a man on a camel moved in the desert. In the desert night there were strange sounds, almost songs, half-chants by male voices. There was nothing to distinguish the scene from two thousand years ago. That night I decided to live.

Next morning I went for a swim in the Nile again. There were a few little boys paddling in nappy-like garments. No other swimmers.

On the way back north I visited an Irish poet on a Greek island whose address I'd been given in Dublin. On his hall stand was a Spanish hat.

There were dances on the island in a dance venue that was covered but with open sides. Young men in glove-fitting jeans and girls in white party dresses stood around. The instruments were shot gold and the band played the summoning mariache music of a village afternoon gala. Priests drank coffee by tables that were covered chequered red and white.

Sophisticated Americans, in bush shirts belted below the waist or cheesecloth peasant dresses, came to dinner one night and everyone dined on the patio. The Americans showed little interest in me.

When they were gone the poet said: 'Tomorrow you'll be gone and nothing I say will make any difference.'

On the wall there was a signed black-and-white photograph of Anna Akhmatova. He'd met her in Taormina in 1964 when she'd been awarded the Taormina Prize.

Before I left he gave me a book of her poems. I saw dolphins in the Aegean on my way back to the mainland.

In a café in Belgrade there was a bunch of marigolds beside a bottle of white wine in half-wicker.

Rena's voice returned with some information the old nun had given her.

'Emile Gravelet, "Blondin", stood upon his head, wheeled a man in a barrow blindfold and cooked an omelette on a stove on a tightrope across the Niagara Falls.'

A raven had lived near the convent and once stole one of the nuns' habits for its nest.

Did I know what ravens' eggs looked like, Rena asked me on a boat in San Francisco Bay. Remarkably small for the size of the bird, pale blue or pale green, dark-brown spots and ashy markings, but sometimes just pale blue.

It's like painting a bunch of marigolds, I thought, years later in southern California, to keep the light, to make something. It's to accept the gravity of the marigolds; marigolds on the station platform of a small town in County Galway; a bunch of marigolds on a shelf in a café in Belgrade on a Fall morning.

There are frontiers beyond which a person can't go, frontiers of shatterment. My friend vanished into a village of condominiums and caravans in northern California. Often in the British Library in London, placed in a book, I'd come across a card for the religious group she'd joined, an emblem of laminated pink rosebuds on what could have been the silver of an old man's hair.

Sweet Marjoram

Lowden, in black, pulled-down woollen cap and cream chinos, drives me to the ocean after class in his Malibu Chevrolet.

He is a Chinese boy, a karate champion, born in Toronto, his parents from Taiwan. They moved to the Bay Area when he was a child and later to southern California.

Lowden visited Taiwan recently when the pearl cherries were ripe, and despite the fact he speaks Chinese they asked who the American was.

He feels lost, lonely in the States, he says. And he adds: 'We live in an evil time.'

He's got to meet his American girlfriend who wears orange-brick lipstick and I say I'd like to stay on the beach and go for a swim.

He leaves and I swim.

A drunken man in an ox-blood lumber jacket, chaperoned by two young sons, one in bermudas with a pattern of golfing appendages, the other in bermudas with chickens on bicycles on them, looks on.

'You'll freeze your ass.'

'Dad, come on.' His children lead him away.

'Give peace in our time, O Lord,' goes a prayer in the Book of Common Prayer and, as a sandpiper flies against the biblical papaya of the sky, I think of Lady Tamar Strathnairn and how she tells of the time I live in.

I was sitting at a terrace table on Museum Street in the summer of 1977 when she approached me in a white shift dress and dark-cherry ballet slippers.

Her jaw-length hair was japanned-black and her skin ultra-white.

A Boadicea with a beehive was arranging vegetables at the British Museum side of the street as Lady Tamar spoke to me.

I'd just come back from southern Europe and I was wearing the knee-high boots I'd bought in an Ottoman alley in Hania.

In Marktplatz in Heidelberg on my way back I'd bumped into a friend from Cork who, in an Elizabethan Irishwoman's cloak, fastened with a fibula and falling in folds to the ground, was husking with her guitar, and I bottled for her in sea-cerulean dungarees.

The song she sang most frequently was 'Only Our Rivers Run Free.'

An American lady, with saffron-rinsed hair, in black trouser-suit and peep-toe cut-out sandals, wept.

My friend and I had an Italian meal beside Heidelberger Schloss with the proceeds.

'Let the dead bury the dead,' she whispered by candlelight so she looked like Correggio Zingarella's 'Gypsy Girl.'

I attended Lady Tamar's supper in a flat near the Russian embassy for which Lady Tamar wore a stretch-lamé tube dress with a caterpillar brooch on it, which had purple stone eyes.

Her other guest was a youth in an Orator Hunt red neckerchief and red Stuart tartan trousers.

He was an official in the Troops Out movement.

Her father was a high-ranking officer who moved between Ebrington Barracks, Derry; Gough Barracks, Armagh; Royal Inniskilling Fusiliers, Omagh.

Her mother worked for the administration of the Church of England.

Tamar had a job as a secretary in an art gallery in Mayfair.

On the wall was a reproduction of *Venus and Adonis* by Christiaen van Couwenbergh; Adonis with hippie-length hair, Venus with parure in her strawberry-blonde hair.

At the beginning of my travels in the summer I'd stopped at Plâs Newydd at Llangollen in Wales to visit the home of Lady Eleanor Butler, who'd run away with Sarah Ponsonby from the banks of the Nore in County Kilkenny in 1778, Eleanor aged thirty-nine, Sarah aged twenty-three; black-and-white marble-stoned floor, coloured oriel window, Gothic-crossed timber outside—where I met a boy in a multi-coloured woollen jersey.

'If you're a Taffy and wearing a pendant you're alright,' he said to me.

Lady Eleanor used to wear the Bourbon Croix de Saint-Louis around her neck.

A fat girl, who frequently wore a lady's horned medieval hat, and a thin boy who said he was from West Mercia—western midlands—were having a bath together on the street of squats I lived in, lit by a scented candle, to John McLaughlin's 'Swan on Irish Waters,' reading passages of George Borrow's *Lavengro* to one another, from a copy stolen from Wandsworth Library, when the ceiling fell down.

'There's a great sadness in you,' a fellow squatter, with a palmer's haircut, in Robin Hood hose stockings, said to me, by candlelight so he looked like Gerrit van Honthorst's *Christ Before the High Priest* I'd just seen at the National Gallery.

There were boys in the squat who played Little John and William Scathelock to this Robin Hood.

Some of them left the squat to go to a commune of screamers on an island off County Mayo—people who screamed for therapy.

Lady Tamar frequently visited me now that I was back in London, still in my knee-high boots from Crete.

I shared a room with a boy with a ruby-auburn cockscomb from County Kerry, whose father used to bathe him in the Smearla—blackberry—River, whose National School teacher used to give him the ass's bite—clench in the groin.

We slept on mattresses on the floor.

Late one night he told me about a friend.

A boy who was an electrician from Athlone, Correggio's shepherdboy, Ganymede, or Murillo's young St Thomas of Villanueva, who's distributing his clothes to poor boys, in hipster jeans and pip necklace.

On the way to Berlin from Ireland, he'd slept in a house of labourers in Dollis Hill. He had to share a bed with one of the labourers and he touched the labourer's penis. For him a sacrosanct gesture. But the labourer went around telling everyone:

'He touched my Seán Thomas.'

The basking shark and the porbeagle shark and the blue shark would draw in sight of my room-mate's part of Kerry in the autumn after shoals of herring.

'Can I sleep with you?' he asked one night, displaying his mouse's nest pubic area. He got into bed beside me.

In bed he told me this story:

Near his home in Kerry were sea caves.

During the Civil War a group of Irregulars hid in them. The Free Staters smoked them out by throwing down burning bales of hay. Subsequently they cut a rope and three of the Irregulars were drowned in the rising tide.

But a survivor turned out to be a young Englishman, a deserter from the British army.

Next morning Lady Tamar arrived in a black kaftan and top hat, with a pile of scarlet-rose blankets and Elizabeth Shaw Peppermint Creams.

When I was in Scotland in February, where I heard a cinnamon-haired boy in Barra sing 'The Gypsy Laddie,' she came looking for me and slept with my friend.

They drove around London in her chocolate-and-cream Sun Singer convertible and went to a church hall near the squat to see a boy from Hayling Island do a thaumaturgic dance, with bare chest, in Turkish trousers, watched by white witches from Rochester, Sandgate, Havant, Herne Bay.

Shortly afterwards the boy from Kerry went to live in Milwaukee where some of his fellow county people still speak Irish.

> She gave them the good wheat bread,
> And they gave her the ginger,
> But she gave them a far better thing,
> The gold ring off her finger.

In May, when I lived in a room near St Paul's, Hammersmith, Lady Tamar sat with me through the night before I took a plane to New York.

She asked me why I never made love to her, was I gay?

Under a postcard of Goya's *The Forge*, full of biceps and male décolletage, I told her I'd been in love with a girl with narcissus-coloured hair, that a woman had attacked me at a party in Dublin and accused me of impotence.

Sexual harmony was ruptured; the hose of a Japanese ballet dancer in Madrid as it pressed on his genitals.

Against a postcard of Renoirs Alexander Thurneyssen as a young shepherd—rag hat, sheepskin, flute—Lady Tamar confided to me that a few years before she'd been in and out of mental hospitals.

She got these attacks sometimes.

Something hit her.

She took to walking the streets in a trance, in her mother's flat Second World War hat tilted to one side, studying shop signs or the numbers and manufacturers' names on pavement lids.

She was much better now.

A small group of young men with yeminis—painted handkerchiefs— around their necks playing Jewish violins in Central Park; then a Greyhound bus down Roman roads in Wyoming.

In the Patio Café on Castro Street, San Francisco, which was frequented by a red-breasted American house finch, my friend from Dublin told me she was getting married to a man who wore a blue ombré headband.

I went to Yosemite National Park after she told me, and halfway up Tuolumne Meadows, in a grove of blossoming bear garlic, I repeated to myself a bit of Native American history:

'Black Elk returned to Wounded Knee to mourn the butchered women and children.'

Autumn that year was a bunch of marigolds on a cabinet table under the glowing and sidelong face of Rembrandt's *Nicolaes Bruyning*, 1652.

Black Elk put on his ghost shirt before the Battle of Wounded Knee and in the next few years in London a ghost shirt was necessary.

Lady Tamar occasionally sent me At Home cards.

At these gatherings, which resembled John Tenniel's Mad Hatter's Tea Party, were guests from the art gallery and its world—young men in collarless suits, young lords named Meriwether or Redvers or Egerton who addressed you as Lord Emsworth might his pig, the Empress of Blandings.

One of these young lords said that Tamar looked like a London marchesa who used to make herself up to look like a corpse.

I taught in a comprehensive in South Kensington.

I brought them to Hampton Court, children from the stucco villas of Holland Park and the faubourgs of White City. Sad, adult-faced boys with pommelled hairstyles who cycled junior bicycles on the walkways of White City; blond, troubador-haired boys with slightly stooped shoulders who smote your fists with their fingers.

A boy with kibbled hair called Elidore after a boy of Welsh legend told me how his mother, who was active in the Troops Out movement, living in a commune where she wore a floating evening gown patterned with double-humped camels, had disowned him, banging the door on him when he called to see her.

In early summer I brought them to Brighton beach and Tamar came too.

One of them—an Arab boy—wouldn't go into the water so I lifted him in his black silk shirt, napped black trousers, and dropped him into the sea, which that day was Medici blue.

She seemed to be forever going off on holidays to far-off places and she sent me postcards—flowering peach in Virginia; a bougainvillaea esplanade in Famagusta; a skiing slope in the Lebanon.

She even went to visit her father in Northern Ireland and sent me a postcard of William Conor's wax-crayon Belfast jaunting car; bowler-hatted jarvey, woman with deep-terracotta scarf holding a child wrapped in cinnabar red; little boy with girl-length hair, in army-green jersey, at the back, naked legs dangling.

Towns with no evangel but the Union Jack; a soldier who jogged every day by Lough Neagh with a backpack of bricks; Sunday service at Campbell College where William Conor, walking entirely in black through Belfast, was recalled; a young soldier doing a sailor's hornpipe in green hunting tartan; a swan on Irish waters.

Then she threw up her job in the art gallery and went to Cambridge as a late pupil for four years.

I visited her on a day trip.

As a student she had strangely become more conservative in her dress. She wore two-tone shoes, blue and cream, a deep-flared peplum jacket, divided skirt. There was a vintage rose in her cheeks.

In her flat in an isolated ivy-overgrown house by the River Cam she sat under a reproduction of Lucas Cranach's *The Virgin and Child Under an Apple Tree.*

Outside Cambridge station a man in Morris costume, bucket in hand, had been busking for the striking miners.

> O eat your cherries, Mary,
> O eat your cherries now,
> O eat your cherries, Mary,
> That grow upon the bough.

We had tea and almond-and-amaretto Madeira cake in a café near a cinema painted Reckitt's blue with posters for fifties British films in the foyer—*The Belles of St Trinian's, Carry on Sergeant, Dracula*—served by a waitress with pillar-box-red lipstick and afterwards in a church we listened to an Anglican canticle: 'There is no Health in Me.' In March 1985 the miner's strike ended.

After Cambridge she went to teach in a girls' public school near her family home in East Sussex, for which she donned half-moon rimless spectacles, and I was invited to her house for a weekend.

The baronial house with Tudor gables, dormer windows, had a lake beside it, a herringbone path leading there.

Dog wagons had once drawn wood from the nearby forest to this house and Gypsy children, with hair the colour of sunlit chestnuts, had come looking for partridge eggs in the hedgerows bordering the forest—olive and ochre, occasionally blueish-white, blotched with red ochre.

The white blossom of the wild service tree, the barren strawberry in spring; the blue pimpernel; the true fox sedge in summer; red berries of the butcher's broom in the forest in autumn—the Flora Annie Steel *Fairy Tales* of my childhood could have happened here.

I met Lady Tamar's mother.

Hair dressed away from her face, in vicuña slacks, mules.

With Bobbly, her cat, on her lap, seated on a scroll-ended sofa, Lady Tamar's mother, who was a winter swimmer—on winter weekdays she swam in the carpet of gold leaves in the Ladies' pond in Highgate with Jewish women who were survivors of Auschwitz, or in Leg of Mutton Pond in Hampstead—named feast days in her conversation to mark the year as a Russian might—St Lucy's Day, Ember Day, the Nativity of Saint John the Baptist, Midsummer's Day, when garlands of St John's wort are put on the door in East Sussex and you draw a circle around yourself with a rowan stick and poles of herbs are hoisted.

In the morning in the garden she showed me, beside the yellow calceolarias, a bed of sweet marjoram, and told me the story of Amaracus, a Greek youth at the court of the kings of Cyprus who, with a chaplet of vine leaves in his hair and in *all'antica* sandals, accidentally dropped a vessel containing perfume.

His terror on realizing the magnitude of his crime caused him to faint.

The gods, sparing him dire punishment, transformed him into a sweet-smelling plant named after him.

She plucked a bunch of burnt-orange chrysanthemums and gave them to me.

Shortly afterwards I was invited to the southern States.

In the southern States I lived in a carpenter's Gothic house, a weeping-fig tree outside it.

My first memory is of crossing water on a train. Yachts on the water. Was it somewhere near Bray, County Wicklow? Had it been a dream?

The only similar experience in my life, apart from the lagoon train to Venice, was the train that crosses the bridge over Lake Pontchartrain.

Strange the feeling of returning over that bridge in winter from New Orleans where troupes of boys in rubber shorts with the backs cut out did the cancan, where the Ursuline Sisters who delivered New Orleans by prayers to Our Lady of Prompt Succour during the Battle of New Orleans in 1815 still had the reward of free passage on the public transport system, to the winter Bible country—Covenanters' bungalows with dogtrots.

An Amaracus of a boy, with a Titus crop, in linted jeans, briefly told me his story.

He'd belonged to the wrong family. He'd travelled in a Ford

Ranger with the American flag in front on dirt roads, on fire roads, from California.

Now he was with the right family.

On my return, London no longer seemed home.

I spent a few years going back and forth between London and Berlin, from which I sent Lady Tamar Martin Schongauer's *Nativity*—Rhinemaiden Madonna, cow with elk-like antlers—and she and I didn't meet and when those transits ceased and we did meet she had a pug-royal look.

There was grey in front of her hair the way Lady Eleanor Butler had put powder in front of her hair, her lipstick rose of Lancaster red.

She was living in London again, teaching there.

She was getting bad attacks again, wandering the streets in a scarlet coat dress and unstructured hat with wide turned-back brim, studying the pagodas in a travel poster or standing on benches in churches to examine the plaques.

Aristocratic ancestors, she told me, by way of explanation, had the task of carrying news of their coming executions to fellow aristocrats.

Screech owls, bloodhounds . . .

In Berlin, just before I left, I saw a production of Schiller's *Mary Stuart*, in which Maria Stuart mounted the scaffold at the end:

'Constancy becomes all folks well, and none better than princes . . .'

A stone came through my French windows in south-east London, where I'd lived for twelve years, shattering the glass over a mosaic of postcards from The Hermitage in St Petersburg—Luca Giordano's beefcake *Forge of Vulcan*; Veronese's *Pietà* with a red-headed man taking Christ's hand; Correggio's *Portrait of a Lady*—black dress, jewel in her hair, brown scapular of a Franciscan tertiary on her bosom . . .

Portrait of a Lady . . .

Lady Tamar often visited me in my last six months in London, in a room overlooking a noisy throughfare in Hampstead, and, just as when I first arrived, she brought cheese from Paxton and Whitfield's and Elizabeth Shaw Peppermint Creams.

Sometimes we went to swim in Highgate ponds. She'd go to the Ladies' pond and I'd go to the Men's.

On Saturdays and Sundays there were three boy late swimmers—Dominic, Ben and Stephen—who liked to stand around naked after their swim.

'Safe Des.'

'When parents break up who gets the custody of the hamster? The mother gets hold of it on weekdays. And the father at weekends.'

Afterwards, Lady Tamar and I would sit on a bench just above the Men's pond, dedicated to the memory of a young man, she in a thistle-printed crêpe-de-Chine blouse or a knitted jersey with appliqué kingfishers.

Anglican bells for the dead occasionally rang from St Anne's Church whose grounds abounded in ladybird-infested pyracantha.

When Keats, whose house was nearby, had been at school, the teacher, Rev. Clarke, would bring his pupils into the courtyard to see the departure of the swallows.

> Be careful ere ye enter in, to fill your baskets high
> With fennel green . . .
> Cool parsley, basil sweet, and sunny thyme.

Lady Eleanor Butler—of one of the steadfast Catholic families of Ireland, whose cousin's house, Cill Chais in County Tipperary, was the subject of a poem learnt at National School, a lament for the great Catholic house by a young priest—had been devoted to a herb garden near the river Dee in Wales, which reminded her of the Nore in County Kilkenny, its wild privet banks, its yellow water-lily-covered water, its poppy-bordered river paths.

The tragic measure; Shakespeare was performed in the Kilkenny of Lady Eleanor Butler's girlhood.

My arm would go around Lady Tamar's shoulder for the affair we never had.

As autumn became late autumn an Amaracus in old-fashioned black bib swimming togs would walk out on the pier in the Men's pond to swim—just as boys do late in the year at the weir in Bishop's Meadows in Kilkenny with their distant view of St Canice's Cathedral—often against a late-afternoon sun that was as red-orange as Californian poppy.

The Hare's Purse

The old alchemists considered mercury the spirit, sulphur the soul, salt the body.

Sulphur united with mercury and salt for Seán South on the evening of January 1st 1957—when County Monaghan country people say there's a cock step more light—with the burst of a Bren gun.

Fergal O'Hanlon—Fergal Máire (Mary) Ó hAnnluain—aged twenty, from Park Street, Monaghan town; Seán South—Seán Sabhat—aged twenty-nine, from Henry Street, Limerick: killed in a raid on Brookeborough police station, County Fermanagh, five miles over the Northern Ireland border, with twelve other men, four of them injured, one critically.

A Christian Brother with embonpoint, who taught at the Abbey CBS in Tipperary town, had once told Seán South, in the Royal Hotel by the willowherb-choked Ara River, Tipperary town, the story written in Greek by Lucian of Samosata about a group of adventurers who, as they sail through the Strait of Gibraltar, are lifted by a giant waterspout and deposited on the moon.

There they witness the war between the king of the moon and the king of the sun over the colonization rights of Jupiter, involving armies of stalk-and-mushroom men, acorn-dogs, cloud-centaurs, with the moon men, hit in combat, dissolving into smoke.

The Slieve Beagh mountain march by the twelve survivors through the hilly, boggy countryside between Brookeborough and the border took five hours.

Lights and flares of search parties lit up the countryside.

The County Donegal golden eagle was an occasional visitor to this mountain.

Doing a roller-coaster on sighting a hare, soaring upward to a point, then tucking its wings to descend at a speed of up to two hundred miles per hour.

Golden to blonde feathers at the neck; thus the name.

Chrysos being the Greek word for golden, the Tipperary-town Christian Brother once having informed Seán South.

Atropos being the Greek goddess who determined life or death, he added the same evening.

Atropos had determined death for Seán South and Fergal O'Hanlon that night.

But for the survivors, with the lights and flares it was like the battle on the moon frequently related in Irish by Seán South.

The Cortolvin Bridge over the old Ulster Canal was lined with people in Monaghan town awaiting Fergal O'Hanlon's hearse.

Woodland blue, bluebell—*cloigín gorm*—eyes, cheeks red as the little cup of the yew tree, lips like Joe Louis, teeth that lost a gold crown, chased tweed jackets with shamrock, primrose or *fáinne*—ring-shaped badge of the Irish Language Association—in lapel.

A draughtsman in Monaghan courthouse.

Played for Senior Monaghan Harps in their white and blue. In the shower had a body like a bunch of the garden plant, lamb's cars.

Coached Minor Monaghan Harps.

Remembered sitting on the edge of Gavan Duffy Park, instructing young players.

Gavan Duffy, from Dublin Street, Monaghan town, the only Irish rebel knighted by Queen Victoria.

Chiefly remembered in Monaghan town for having had four children in his seventies.

Hearse passed Magnet Cinema on Glaslough Street—four-penny, eight-penny, shilling seats—where *Rebel Without a Cause* had very recently been shown.

James Dean in wine-coloured zip-up jacket and azure skinny jeans.

A blue-and-white long-distance coach having taken Dean from Chicago Greyhound Bus Station to southern California where he gained the confidence to shed his gawky Hoosier Indiana adolescence and emerge like this.

Fergal's coffin was taken off the hearse outside St Louis Convent, where exchanging manicure sets was then in vogue, and borne through Monaghan town by youths with shellacked cockscombs, farmhands' cockscombs, slicked-back hair like James Dean, or the Levee (the Panama)—back-sweep and crest, greased side-boards.

They'd all seen the colour-drenched chickie run in *Rebel Without a Cause*—car race towards cliff edge, jumping out at the last moment.

Bearers of the coffin halted in front of the O'Hanlon home in Park Street—his mother's name, Darby, linked her by a marriage to Tommy Donnelly, commandant of Fifth Northern Division, Old IRA—while a tricolour flew from a window.

Seán South, a clerk at MacMahon's timber firm in Limerick city— hair the ginger of the ginger daub at the top of a mushroom, with sidecombed crest and back-swept sides, eyes low-tide blue, earnest glasses.

He'd been compared for his very serious expression to Stewart Granger in *King Solomon's Mines*, based on Henry Rider Haggard's novel.

The hearse followed on O'Connell Street, Dublin, under Player's Please and Jacob's Chocolates advertisements, by Fianna Éireann— olive-green uniforms and cocked hats like the Ancient Order of Foresters who used to sing patriotic songs in nineteenth-century Dublin music halls.

It was raining heavily as the hearse arrived at the Old County Hospital, Dublin Road, Portlaoise, as part of its nine-and-a-half-hour journey from Dublin to Limerick city.

His widowed mother met the hearse in Roscrea.

Eleven thousand marched and eleven thousand lined the streets in Limerick city.

Twenty prominent religious leaders, city and county councillors, senators, a member of parliament, the Forty-Ninth Battalion of the FCA—Local Defence Force—bus- and garage-men, Gaelic football and hurling teams, Gaelic League, Old Irish Volunteers, Nationalist Women's Society, followed the hearse past Spillane's who made Garryowen Plug tobacco.

Curragower Falls on Shannon in torrent.

A busker heard to play 'Father Murphy of Old Kilcormac' and 'Don't Forget Your Dear Old Mother' on mouth organ.

Never known to sing or play a violin in Limerick city, Seán South had played a violin as a lady played on piano, and afterwards sang 'Eibhlín A Rún'—Eileen So Coy—in Monaghan town a few days prior to the attack on Brookeborough police station.

The IRA of the 1950s consisted of mavericks—carpenters or plumbers with artistic inclinations who'd launch into a ballad in the box snug of a pub with cartoons outside of an ostrich snatching a glass of Guinness from a Royal Irish Constabulary man in his rifle green, or Royal Irish Constabulary men in the same rifle green with their caps popping in the air as a pelican makes off with their Guinness bottles in his beak, or a tortoise transporting a pint of Guinness.

Dearg-ghráin—intense hatred—was the attitude to England.

Because of this *dearg-ghráin*, the brother of novelist Edith Somerville—white lisle dresses, bow ties, who'd seen the *Titanic* pass west Cork and the corpses washed in from the Lusitania as her gingham umbrella was raised—was murdered when he answered the door at The Point, Castletownsend, west Cork, on the evening of 24 March 1936, for writing references for farmers' sons with marigold and buttercup hair who wished to join the Royal Navy.

These IRA men—some of whom were known to dress in apricot jackets with triple wooden buttons at cuffs, ultramarine shirts, lizard-skin pumps—could recite the poem by north Leinster Séamus Dall Mac Cuarta about the King-Badger who loved not pleasure, or the poem by County Fermanagh Cathal Buí Mac Giolla Ghunna about the yellow bittern who, for all the vanity of its powder-down feather, died of thirst, laid out like the ruin of Troy, water voles at its wake, clearly showing the importance of being frequently drunk because there wouldn't be drink when you're dead!

The Irish language is an encyclopaedia of oppression.

Seán South, who grew a beard in his last month and swore he wouldn't shave it until the Six Counties were free, was forever quoting a line by Angus Mac Daighre Ó Dálaigh:

> Ag seilg troda ar fhéinn eachtrann
> Gá bhuil fearrann bhur sinnsear.
> (Urging fight against the foreign soldiery
> that holds your fatherland.)

Eachtrann being foreign.

Eachtraí being –
Storyteller. Traveller. Exile.

Storyteller. Traveller. Exile.

One song is built on the ruin of another the way the swallow builds its mud saucer on a spotted flycatcher's domed house.

A song was quickly written about puppy-faced Fergal to the air of 'The Merry Month of May':

> Was in the merry month of May
> When flowers were a blooming.

In another version of Barbara Allan:

> Since my love died for me today,
> I'll die for him tomorrow.

Fergal's song was made internationally famous by an American lady singer who wore headbands with patterns of snowshoe hares or lobster moths and by a scrannel-voiced American male singer with a gun-shot expression.

The songwriter was best man at the Brookeborough column commander's—Pearse column after the 1916 revolutionary—wedding and the song accompanied the songwriter to the grave because that Pearse column commander gave the oration at his graveside.

A song was also quickly written about Seán South to the air of 'Roddy McCorley':

> Young Roddy McCorley goes to die
> On the bridge at Toome today.

But that song, which was very often sung with 'The Boys of Bluehill,' only had an Irish audience.

> We are the boys who take delight
> In smashing Limerick lamps at night.

It was a Limerick song—'The Boys of Garryowen'—that General Custer's Seventh Cavalry Regiment sang as they left General Terry's column at Powder River.

Garryowen a district in Limerick city around St John's Cathedral and an affectionate name for Limerick city.

'The Boys of Garryowen' a Royal Irish Regiment marching song.

The Royal Irish Regiment celebrated for valour at the Battle of Namur in 1695 where one of William of Orange's lieutenants used Capuchin friars as spies.

Met, on the opposite side, some of their former comrades who'd opted to go with the Wild Geese—Irish soldiers who exiled themselves in Europe after the Treaty of Limerick, 1691—at the Battle of Malplaquet, 1709, during the War of Spanish Succession.

Custer heard a Royal Irish Regiment emigrant sing the song while drunk at Fort Riley, Kansas.

The United States had previously known the Royal Irish Regiment when they'd been garrisoned at the Illinois Country until they fought at Lexington, Concord and Bunker Hill during the American War of Independence.

The Royal Irish Regiment was present at Yorktown, Virginia, 1781, when the triumphant Americans played 'Yankee Doodle,' 'Redcoats' and 'The World Turned Upside Down,' a children's rhyme from the English Civil War:

> Derry down, down, hey derry down,
> I am come to make peace in this desperate fray.

Fergal O'Hanlon, born Candlemas Day—Candelmaesse—1936.

Candlelight processions to the altar to commemorate the purification of Mary and presentation of Christ at the Temple began 381–4 AD.

The following month German troops reoccupied the demilitarized Rhineland in violation of the Treaty of Versailles.

At the Christian Brothers' School, Monaghan town, he learnt that a Monaghan-town man, General Don Juan McKenna, was one of the founders of Chile.

A De La Salle brother from Limerick came and tried to take him to the De La Salle Brothers in Limerick when he was fourteen.

But his destiny was to excel at Latin at St Macartan's College.

Caesar Augustus forbade boys to run during the Lupercalia festival, who hadn't shaved off their first beards.

Boys without their first beards played football in the black-and-amber jerseys of St Macartan's College and in tube football togs—togs down to their knees met by black-and-amber calf socks.

By the Blackwater the lesser celandine—*grán arcáin* (piglet's grain)—grew.

In the summer the foxglove in profusion.

> Méirín puca.
> Méirín sí.
> Méirín dearg.
> (Hobgoblin finger.
> Fairy finger.
> Red finger.)

Boys whose first pubic hair was like the buff dust on the dark-brown wood argus butterfly's wing swam in the Blackwater at Patton's Mill.

There was a school day trip to see the tympanum of Portland stone in the Cathedral of Christ the King in Mullingar, where the canal ended; of Pope Plus XI; the Most Reverend Thomas Mulvany, Bishop of Meath; Cardinal MacRory, Primate of All Ireland.

Working for Monaghan County Council, Fergal would tie children's shoelaces on the street, lift children on his broad shoulder.

He trained with the FCA rifle practice.

Remembering nineteen-year-old IRA volunteer Thomas Williams hanged by the Northern Ireland government during the Second World War, despite the pleas of the lord mayor of Dublin, the Dublin Fire Brigade and the people of Achill Island, County Mayo.

Christmas 1955, Fergal inscribed in an autograph book a Horace epigram massively popular with the British Empire during the Boer War:

'Sweet and appropriate thing to die for one's country.'

Christmas 1956, wrote in his diary:

'Keep cool and pray. A good conscience is a continual Christmas.'

The song about him is about an IRA *Bildungsroman*—a young person's education.

He'd been a member of the IRA for two years before volunteering for column work. It was a secret in Monaghan town that he was in the IRA.

At parochial-hall dances he led girls to Teresa Brayton's 'The Old Bog Road.'

On his death a number of Monaghan-town girls left to be nuns in the Dominican Convent, Portstewart, County Derry, and with the Sisters of St Francis Xavier in Omagh, County Tyrone.

Seán South's home, 47 Henry Street, had been a synagogue when it was the home of a draper, Louis Goldberg, a blond Lithuanian who escaped conscription into the Russian army by taking a timber ship to Ireland where, after obtaining a pedlar's licence for ten shillings, he began by selling pictures of saints and popes.

Limerick Jews, mainly from the village of Akmijan, province of Kovna Gubernia, Lithuania, were a familiar sight, eating ginger butter cakes, poppyseed butter cakes, sugar pretzels under the walnut blossom, the kanzan cherry blossom, the ornamental red hawthorn, the sweet chestnut trees in Pery Square park.

Shortly after Chanukkah, feast of lights, early 1904, year of the canonization of Gerard Majella, a Jewish wedding for which the bride had a bouquet of white carnations and maidenhair fern, the bridesmaids' satin capes trimmed with swan's down, green marzipan and candied orange slices served at the feast, inspired the wrath of Father John Creagh, in a city where the lice of the poor were so large they caused Father Creagh's Redemptorists to vomit.

Father John Creagh—biretta, incised Limerick mouth, arched brows, melancholy dreaming eyes.

As director of the Archconfraternity of the Holy Family, from the pulpit Father Creagh accused the Jews of deicide.

April of the subsequent boycott, Jewish businesses were collapsing. Sophia Weinronk, out to get food, was attacked on Bowman Street, off Coloney Street—Jewish street of transoms and railings—her head beaten against the wall.

A poor herdsman's daughter in the hills of Shanagolden declared that only for Jews she would have no clothes or covering.

The parish priest of Kilcolman and Coolcappa made her return two blankets she'd just bought from a travelling Jewish draper, also from Henry Street.

Back in Limerick, Father Creagh claimed a Jew had tried to sell him a music-hall broadsheet with 'Squeeze Her Gently' on it.

Boherbuoy Brass and Reed Band led the superior general of Redemptorists from the station in July.

Confraternity salute was raised, right hand.

Papal blessing was given in three instalments—Monday, Tuesday to men, Wednesday to boys.

The pleas of Rabbi Elias Bere Levin from Tels, Lithuania, reached deaf ears.

Eighty Jews were driven from Limerick. Forty left.

Ginsbergs left. Jaffes left. Weinronks followed Greenfields to South Africa.

The Hebrew headstones survived in Kilmurry Cemetery, near Castleconnell.

'Why shouldst thou be as a stranger in the land and as a wayfaring man that turneth aside to tarry for a night?'

In Seán South's room in 47 Henry Street were bottles of Indian ink, paintbrushes, pens.

In the bookcase works by Charles Kickham, Canon Sheehan, Henry Rider Haggard, *Biggles* books, *The Little Prince* by the French aviator Antoine de Saint-Exupéry, with Sainte-Exupéry's drawing of the little prince in a jumpsuit with flared trousers and bow tie on the jacket.

A statue of the Sacred Heart wrapped in cellophane on top of it.

The Messenger of the Sacred Heart, Irish School Weekly.

A postcard of *The Race of the Gael* by Seán Keating—who'd painted a portrait of Bishop Edward Thomas O'Dwyer who settled a pork butcher's strike, a Mass said for him each year attended by pork butchers—two men staring with determination over a stone wall.

Gramophone records, Pat Roche's Harp and Shamrock Orchestra,

The Pride of Erin Orchestra, 'O Sole Mio' by Enrico Caruso.

Seán South was a member of numerous organizations.

He founded a Limerick branch of Maria Duce in 1949, an organization with an anti-Semitic past—originated in the 1940s by the Very Reverend Dr Denis Fahey of the Holy Ghost Fathers, now targeting Hollywood actors inclined towards communism.

Member of the Gaelic League—Friends of the Irish Language—campaigned to have Irish spoken again on the streets of Limerick.

Member of Pacemakers of Freedom—a nationalist organization.

Of An Réalt—the star—an organization dedicated to the Virgin Mary.

One of his drawings is of Mary of Perpetual Help. In the words of St Ambrose, Mary, the Temple of God.

Pope Pius IX had sent an ikon of Our Lady of Perpetual Help to the Limerick Redemptorists in 1866, when the first Redemptorists in Ireland were being brought to court for burning Protestant Bibles.

Seán South vehemently campaigned against the Jehovah's Witnesses, one out of four having lost their lives in the Germany of the Third Reich; through constant litigation in the USA causing the Fourth Amendment to be more clearly defined, thus safeguarding the rights of all.

He studied drawing by doing an English art-school postal course—'Which is the best way of demolishing a bridge?'—his last cartoon shows a beefcake IRA man guarding a classroom, an RUC man batoning the B-Special pupil beside him, another pupil in scanty mid-thigh shorts.

The drawings Antoine de Saint-Exupéry did to accompany *The Little Prince*, written in a rented house in New York in 1943, helped Seán South to develop his drawing style, such as Saint-Exupéry's one of the conceited man with auguste's nose.

At fifteen, in the year *The Little Prince* was written, Seán South enlisted in the Auxiliary Army Force, which supplemented the Irish army during the Second World War, having darker-than-ordinary uniforms.

Two-hour FCA session per week.

Became a sergeant in the FCA proper April 1946 and became skilful in archery.

Out of the FCA, IRA full-time in April 1955 just after the premiere of *East of Eden* in which, against Californian clapboard, James Dean wears a sleeveless jersey with collegiate diamond pattern, his hair brushed up, the still of which quickly reached Limerick.

But Seán South's favourite organization was Servants of Freedom—boys with their first patina of body hair, between ten and fourteen.

The boys would have iced buns with hundreds and thousands—sugar strands—on them, kitsch queen cakes with thick pink icing, viridian jellies buried in the icing or tiny stars on it or, at Christmas, glittering studs, and tea from rose-patterned cups in a room with chocolate-indulgence-patterned wallpaper and a picture of Romulus and Remus, two putti who founded Rome, being borne on a wolf's back, in gilt frame with beaded edge.

Football, hurling, handball.

Recitations such as Sigerson Clifford's 'The Ballad of the Tinker's Daughter.'

Cartoon strips by Seán South for them in their magazine—*The Servant*—featuring Conor Mac Neasa and Cúchullain with cross-gartered legs.

Cromwell's second-in-command, Ireton, came to Limerick in 1651.

A children's rhyme from the English Civil War:

> If ponies rode men and if grass ate the cows . . .
> If the mamas sold their babies
> To the Gypsies for half a crown . . .
> Derry down, down, hey derry down.

Seán South brought his boys on an outing to identify estuarine reeds near the castle of Gerald, Earl of Desmond, who survived on horse-flesh with sixty gallowglasses (Scottish mercenaries) during the Munster Rebellion in Elizabethan days until they tracked him down and beheaded him in a Kerry wood—the yellow bittern (*an bonnán buí*) of Cathal Buí Mac Giolla Ghunna's poem.

Ordinarily like a hen but it can make itself reed-like, by pointing its bill and body upward, as camouflage.

Voice of a cow who has lost her calf.

Dearg-ghráin.

Seán South told his boys that the favourite meal of Henry VIII of England was the innocent yellow bittern.

Seán South was renowned in Limerick for driving snogging couples from cinemas.

When *One Million BC* with a fur-clad Victor Mature was showing at Grand Central.

Cecil B. DeMille's *Samson and Delilah* at the Lyric with Hedy Lamarr's bellybutton inspiring epidemic snogging.

Demetrius and the Gladiators at the Savoy with Susan Hayward in peplum.

Athena with Dick DuBois in pristine white swimming trunks on the deck of a ship at the Thomond near Donkey Ford's Chipper. 'You'll end up in a Magdalene Laundry,' he was heard to say on that occasion to the girl in question, Magdalene Laundries being where unmarried pregnant girls were sent to labour.

But he brought his Servants of Freedom to *Lady and the Tramp* at the City Theatre.

Vegetables were scarce during the war, butter ration reduced, bacon limited.

The tasks of the volunteer soldiers in their forage caps and uniforms with chromium buttons were cattle-burying, turf-cutting.

Cut the turf in May with a slean—turf-spade—branch it, spread it.

In June the first footing. In July the second footing.

Then to Finner Camp in Donegal.

Michelangelos of young soldiers in the Atlantic; reddish-brown pubic hair in the showers, like the hare's coat; ice cream, swimming rings, toffee stands on Bundoran beach; Painted Lady butterflies with white marks on the black tips of the forewings on soldiers' black boots; tufted sedge, flat sedge, meadow foxtails, fuchsia reflected in young soldiers' torso tans, face freckles; ladybirds—scarabaeids—on young soldiers' forearms, in bronze hair.

Ladybird.

(*Bóin samhraidh.*

Cow of summer.)

French children tell the ladybird the Turks are coming to kill their children.

The Turks were coming then.

A man broadcast from Germany in Irish, continually reminding the Irish people that Germany had cooperated with the Shannon hydroelectric scheme near Limerick city in the late 1920s, the progress of which was painted by Seán Keating.

Before the war Glasgow prostitutes used to come to the environs of Finner Camp—thus it was known as the Scotch Fair.

But without the Glasgow prostitutes there was another kind of longing, like the hare's cry in the night.

Early August the volunteer soldiers would bring turf to towns and villages in County Limerick.

The Donie Collins Band toured County Limerick at harvest time during the war years, playing in dancehalls owned by farmers.

Packets of tea and cups were brought to them during an interval, in Jacob's biscuit tins.

The touring cinemas came then also—marquees in which films were shown—and stayed for a week.

Three Stooges films were particularly popular.

Canachán—hare's purse.

Working on the turf the volunteer soldiers slept under canvas.

Where hares grazed, checking the growth of grass, the large blue butterfly thrived—black spots on upper side of forewing—laying its eggs on wild thyme.

It had other secret, iridescent colours as its wings absorbed all the colours of the spectrum except blue.

The race of the Gael.

There were young soldiers' eyes like that.

The Arctic hare and the mountain hare of Europe turned white in winter.

But a young soldier, with bounty of chestnut hair and a metropolis of freckles on his face, from Lough Mask, County Mayo, where

Lord Haw Haw, to whom Hitler awarded the War Merit Cross First Class, was from, told Seán South that in Mayo there were albino hares—white year-round.

The colonization rights of Jupiter . . .

The IRA campaign of 1956 began in December with a failed attempt to blow up the statue of General Gough on his horse in the Phoenix Park, Dublin.

Newspapers announced that some IRA men had been arrested at the border and were being detained by gardaí.

Headquarters was phoned.

The garda in charge warranted no ammunition had been found on them.

Whereupon instructions were that the IRA men be released.

The IRA men refused to be released because they'd abandoned their vehicle.

The garda in charge immediately ordered taxis and they were brought to Dublin for Christmas.

A garda in Limerick found a dock labourer from St Ita's Street in a car on Christmas Eve clasping a stolen plum pudding, value five shillings, and a stolen shoe, value fifteen shillings.

'Pray for me,' were Seán South's last words before leaving Limerick, with a bottle of Lourdes water.

Storyteller. Traveller. Exile.

In Dublin he attended a pantomime—*geamaire*—in which Jimmy O'Dea and Harry O'Donovan played the dames.

In the Monte Carlo Chipper in Monaghan town was a photograph of Gene Vincent and his Blue Caps—after President Eisenhower's baby-blue golf cap.

Four Blue Caps, who included Jumpin' Jack Neal and Wee Willie Williams, in black shirts and white ties; Gene Vincent, who shot swans as a boy in the swamps of Virginia for food, in a letterman jacket.

Gene Vincent had been fined ten thousand dollars the previous May by Virginia State Court because of a phoenetic error.

'Hugging on his Woman Love,' because of all the moaning and panting, was mistaken for another word.

In keeping with the name of the chipper, Edith Piaf was playing on the jukebox—'Les Trois Cloches' (Three Bells. Little Jimmy Brown. In the valley the bells are ringing).

Outside the Magnet Cinema a Teddy boy with floral-design cuffs was combing his hair with a metal comb.

A Marlborough Street magistrate, sentencing three Teddy boys for assault, had recently declared that their drainpipe trousers were a pity, because it made them difficult to pull down and give the boys a hiding.

In Dublin Street, Monaghan town, Gavan Duffy had been inspired by James Clarence Mangan's translations from medieval Irish.

In famine-striken Ireland state prisoners of Kilmainham Gaol subscribed three shillings and ten pence to Mangan when he descended into destitution.

Swans in the swamps of Virginia.

There were many swans in Monaghan because of all the lakes. Each lake with a narrative. Even the Convent Lake in Monaghan town had a narrative because there was a crannóg in it—a man-made island, a lake dwelling.

In the Pearse column, in squaddie's denims, with blackened face, Seán South's every order was given in Irish, then translated by him on the way to Brookeborough in a stolen council truck with tipper, which Sten guns would not penetrate, through lake countryside, through Scots pine—*giúis Albanach*—countryside.

He'd visited Patrick Pearse's cottage in Connemara, August 1954, and in his last hours he proclaimed about establishing Northern Ireland—where people watched *Dixon of Dock Green* on television, X-certificate films in the cinema, and listened to *Mrs Dale's Diary* and *The Archers* on radio—as a gaeltacht (Irish-speaking region).

At Brookeborough police station out rushed the assailants with a mine. Juice turned on.

Nothing happened.

A second installed. Failed.

Attempt to lob hand grenades through the barracks windows.

The previous year Seán South had visited many RUC barracks along the border to assess armaments. In Brookeborough he'd seen only pistols and Sten guns in the RUC arsenal, which was on open display.

A Bren gun was kept in married quarters upstairs.

An RUC sergeant opened fire with this Bren.

Seán South stayed by the Pearse column Bren until they riddled him.

He'd emptied three magazines into the barracks.

Small Fergal, as the Pearse column called him—he was five-foot, six-inches—was shot in the back and thighs.

The RUC Bren burst through the right door, roof, floor of stolen council truck. Tipper kept rising.

Bullet caught driver's foot.

Lights of a police patrol car down the road on their left as they made a getaway.

When the police patrol car was one hundred yards from them it opened fire.

At Altwark Cross, between Brookeborough and Rosslea, they stopped at a farmhouse.

Two Pearse column men went to the door. Knocked.

No reply.

One got in through the back. In the kitchen was a picture of the Sacred Heart.

They brought Seán and Fergal to an outhouse where a light was on. Under the light an act of contrition was whispered in Seán's ear.

Wounded column commander volunteered to stay.

Second-in-command ordered him away.

Fergal, Seán, truck abandoned.

But people in a nearby farmhouse, where there were Stygian greyhounds, asked to get a priest and doctor.

Police and B-Specials shot up farmhouse and outhouse.

Fergal died in a last burst of fire. Bled to death from a wounded thigh.

Since my love died for me today,
    I'll die for him tomorrow.

Bren guns were mounted on the wall of Fermanagh County

Hospital, Enniskillen, where the inquest was told that Seán South's head was bruised and discoloured.

Six survivors carried four wounded across Slieve Beagh.

Frequently they were forced to lie down because of the lights and flares. A compass guided them.

The bittern laid out like the ruin of Troy; hair turned white that night like the Arctic hare or the mountain hare of Europe in winter.

CinemaScope—letterbox screen—launched with *The Robe* starring Victor Mature and Jean Simmons, distorted faces, squeezed them.

Panavision improved this.

That night was in Panavision.

The House of Mourning

A stored digital photograph on a mobile phone; boy, tall, in off-white tank top, hair newly dyed, olive-gold, against the Shannon estuary in north Kerry, sea rocks shaped like manatees on which occasional blue fulmars spray a foul and oily substance.

He stands like a young guillemot about to parachute from a cliff nest to the sea.

In the theatre of another mobile phone the same boy in pale-blue Samsung-mobile-phone Chelsea T-shirt, a silver pendant around his neck, which is a replica of a silver pendant found near the second-century Hadrian's Wall in the north of England.

Rihanna's—Barbados girl of Irish descent—'Unfaithful' plays for a few seconds on the same mobile phone.

'There was a mink on the Nun's Strand! I swear on my mother's life.'

Was the mink he saw Canadian or European? European minks had a white mark above the mouth. Both Canadian and European had a white mark below the mouth. Hard to see.

The mink would wait by the montbretia rushes for prey—rats, mice, shrews, rabbits.

The pawmarks of the mink on the sand—he wanted necklaces, bracelets like that.

He'd also have liked bracelets like the otter's pawmarks on the sand with webbing between five toes.

Eelgrass, after its crop in September and October, carpets the tide-edge on the black sands—like Haiti—alongside the Nun's Strand with deposits in November.

To walk on this your tackles—trainers—get slightly wet but the feeling is luxuriant.

The white-breasted black brent geese have heard of these deposits in the Canadian High Arctic and can be seen on the black sands, known as Rhenafoyle, alongside the Nun's Strand, in November, and heard calling to one another.

It was in November that Delvcaem was murdered.

Ropes hang from trees in Moyross, north Limerick city, so boys can swing from them.

Little girls play with pogo sticks.

A lemon sulky is drawn by a tittuping scarlet caparisoned, stockinged, snowy Irish draught horse, driven by a Traveller boy in Bronx 69 T-shirt, who's speaking on a mobile phone.

Another Traveller boy, in Sex Pistols T-shirt, rides a wild Arabian horse.

There's a jilted junior bicycle among the bulrushes, a discarded lady's slingback shoe with high, slender heel.

On the gateposts of one house are stone herons and in the garden of another a plastic, life-size horse.

In the garden of Delvcaem's house, the house of mourning, are scarlet mushrooms with white polka dots.

Primroses—*sabhaircíní*—are growing.

By the door a mother duck in bonnet, blue pinafore, child duck in blue apron carrying yellow roses.

Delvcaem's mother answers the door, still in her dressing gown, patterned with daisies among dill-like foliage.

Sapphire-blue eyes, cinereous mare's tall.

It is Delvcaem's nineteenth birthday.

The forget-me-not—*lus míonla* (gentle herb)—is returning to the Shannon banks.

In north Kerry they light the paschal fire on Cnoc an Óir—the hill of gold, the hill of autumn—to commemorate St Patrick, who outwitted the druids by lighting the paschal flame before the flame of Lá Bealtaine—May Day.

On Delvcaem's bedroom wall is a torso shot of Richey Edwards of Manic Street Preachers—scrolled rose tattoo on left arm—never seen since February 1995 when his Vauxhall Cavalier was found at a service station by the Severn estuary, which has the second highest tide in the world; Justin Timberlake in small-band denim cowboy hat; Shayne Ward with cobweb facial hair; Lee Otway with mouse-nest blond hair, bone necklace, white singlet with stardust; Boy George in Welsh lady's hat; Christina Aguilera of the Marlene Dietrich mouth in mid-thigh dress of Tyrian purple and fishnet stockings; Britney Spears and troupe of dancers in Catholic girls' school uniforms; Sugababes in décolleté sequinned black; the Garryowen Pipe and Drum Band in forage caps and white gaiters; Andy Lee of Southill, Limerick city, with his opponent, Alfredo Angulo López, at the 2004 Athens Olympics; grinning teenage Kildare boxing star, David Oliver Joyce, with boxing gloves poised at the camera.

On a rack are intersport jerseys—rugby, soccer, Gaelic—from Elverys Sports shop, won from a voucher on a Coca-Cola bottle.

Delvcaem was wearing a zippie jacket with the words *'El Club que Encajona'*—the club that fits together—black-and-cream shoes with winkle-picker toes, when he was murdered.

Beaten on the head with an iron bar outside an off-licence, knife through the temple.

Nedeen, Moss, Macla, Gobby were with him when he was attacked, all on the way home from a martial arts film, *Kung Fu Hustle*, at the Omniplex.

Delvcaem ran.

Attackers pursued him.

Gobby—Gobby Kissane—shaven head, face a medley of bruises, scars and bur-marigold coloured freckles, followed and held him before the ambulance arrived.

'I'm dying,' were Delvcaem's last words.

Gobby wore a viridian soccer jacket with orange zipper, words 'The Shamrock Luck.'

Christina Aguilera had just married Jordan with a reception held over three days among cherry-blossom trees in a Californian vineyard and two months previously Sean Preston Federline had been born to Britney Spears and dancer Kevin Federline.

Delvcaem, changing hair; sometimes black, sometimes honey-blonde.

Tattoos that came on and off.

Baseball cap sideways, armlet tattoo on left arm.

Which boy was it?

Who was it?

The question mark of a forelock surviving all the hair dyes.

I rifle through the faces at Parteen swimming hole on a Saturday the previous July.

A boy with guinea-gold Titus cut by a Shannon canal with tattoo tapestry on his body like Justin Timberlake, eyes the blue of a campus of bluebells.

The salmon were so plentiful here once they used to jump into boats.

People used to row up to Sunday Mass here, once, because Parteen Church kept summer time in winter and Mass was therefore an hour later in winter.

The boy surrounded by Moyross boys with faces like the underparts of the mistle thrush from intensity of freckles.

Fiend dog on his chest, Celtic cross on his back.

His body told a story the way the Ruthwell Cross in Scotland tells the story of the 'Dream of the Rood'—the dream of the tree hewn down at the wood's edge so that Christ could be crucified on it.

Classicizing tulip-white shorts.

Incipient posture to his body, like the feet of the whooper swan—lemon-and-ebony bill—who flourishes in the Shannon Callows (water meadows) a little to the north.

As if he was afraid of something.

But in spite of this, true to the alternative meaning of *eala*, the Irish word for swan—noble person.

Because it was a good summer the death's head hawkmoth—skull shape (eye sockets and jaws) on thorax—was sighted on a hawthorn bush.

One of the boys touched it and it issued a high-pitched squeak like a mobile phone announcing a text message has just arrived.

The word used for penis at this swimming hole is 'langur.'

Same word as the long-tailed Asian monkey.

After the Moyross boys had gone there were pages with photographs of ladies with blow-dry hair dos administering shiny, black dildos to their rears, all over the bank.

As a child in Moyross Delvcaem would collect ladybirds in

Cara—friend—matchboxes.

Ladybird, ladybird, fly away home
Your house is on fire, your children will burn.

At St Nessan's Community College he was later told that these words referred to the firing of hop fields in Kent after harvest.

He was also told in St Nessan's Community College about the Irish hop pickers swept away and drowned at Hartlake Bridge in Kent in 1853, a few years after the Great Famine.

He'd visited the Famine graveyard near Mitchelstown, County Cork, once with his parents when they were travelling to visit his grandmother who lived at Green's Bridge, Kilkenny town.

In St Nessan's Community College was a framed photograph of Tom Crean, Antarctic explorer from Annascaul, County Kerry, and companion of Robert Falcon Scott, in a sledge that had a flag on it with a harp in the centre.

Delvcaem was informed that Christmas Day was celebrated on 21 June in the Antarctic, and that Tom Crean had seal soup under a Christmas tree made of ski sticks, decorated with penguin feathers.

Delvcaem gave up fruit pastilles and cinder toffees—toffees that looked like ashes—for Lent.

For his Confirmation in Corpus Christi Church, Moyross, he got a white-gold neck chain from Argos.

He had a buff Airedale called Bisto who wore a scarlet dog collar with a pattern of white dog bones. Bisto's favourite food was Jonnie Onion Rings and Drifter bars.

In the summers he and his friends used to camp by Plassey Castle.

He'd go with his mother on Saturdays to admire the black-bordered blue speculum—wing colouring—of the mallard at Westfields' Bird Sanctuary, the mallard's glossy green head, purple-brown breast, and also the features of the red-breasted merganser.

He got his first detention sheet at St Nessan's Conununity College because he failed to bring an apple in a box to school for a science experiment.

Skinny-dipping with the Kilkenny boys in the Nore at Caney

Woods when he visited his grandmother.

He once brought a bunch of field roses from the edge of Caney Woods to his grandmother.

He boxed with Garra Beasley, sheep-coloured hair in a turf cut, at St Francis' Boxing Club, where Andy Lee learned to box, near Four Star Pizza, near Lidl's German supermarket with its sign of blue, yellow and Indian red.

Garra Beasley had no pubic hair until he was fourteen, then a handsel of blonde hair.

He moved from Moyross to live in a trailer in Southill, near Limerick jail.

Delvcaem would meet him then to stand on a table against the wall at Colbert Station, put there for the purpose, to watch soccer matches in adjoining Jackman Park.

Garra now always wore a baseball hat with the colours of the French flag; blue, white with red peak.

Delvcaem got four valentines one year.

Two the next.

Only one the year after that.

He went out with a girl called Becfola who in summer was always in a flamingo miniskirt with double-serrated hem, flamingo calf boots, tank top that, in the way of All Saints, displayed a bellybutton.

The Missus, Delvcaem called her.

She was from Garryowen, by St John's Cathedral, where a boy neighbour had recently been repeatedly hit in the face with a hurley in the small hours, by a boy neighbour of Delvcaem's, and lost the sight of both eyes.

'We'll break windows, we'll break doors,' the song 'Boys of Garryown' went.

She asked him to guess what colour underwear she wore.

He guessed rightly. Pink, of course.

She asked him did he wear underwear with tongs legs like her grandfather?

He said no. He wore boxers with the signs of the zodiac on them.

He'd put a dab of aftershave on both ears before seeing her.

Had a nought-and-scissors haircut then—nought at the sides, scissors on top.

Took her to Donkey Ford's Chipper in John's Street, and Freda's Takeaway in Killeely.

Took her to McDonald's near St Francis' Boxing Club where he bought her a McFlurry ice cream.

When the loosestrife was shedding its petals onto the Shannon she told him she didn't want to go out with him anymore but stole six cans of Bulmers Cider from the house in doing this.

Garra Beasley got married at sixteen in the Church of the Holy Family in Southill.

They played Dion DiMucci's 'A Teenager in Love' at the reception in the Shamrock Hotel, Bunratty, with cake from Ivan's.

Dion DiMucci was given an old Gibson guitar when he was ten and learning Hank Williams' songs.

Garra Beasley and his wife honeymooned in Amsterdam where they found they had to be twenty-one to get into sex shops.

Delvcaem's grandmother in Kilkenny sent him fifty euros and died.

He forgot to set his watch forward, one year, and arrived at Corpus Christi Church in Moyross one hour early for Mass.

When asked what he was doing for that hour, he said he was praying.

Aelred, his cousin, in Margate, Kent, with a tattoo bulldog with the words 'Proud to be British,' was killed in a quad accident at Studland beach near Bournemouth and someone sent a wreath of red roses in quad shape to the service at Long Melford Church, Suffolk.

Bobby Dazzler, he'd called Delvcaem on a visit to Limerick.

Spent his time with Mush, a Buffer—settled—Traveller friend after his dating Becfola.

'Cous' (cousin), Mush called him.

Mush—two curls like a cat's whiskers on his forehead, his hair dyed canary yellow, parted in the middle, flapper-style—had the habit of regaling compère Cilla Black of *Blind Date*, his chest bare, taking a few steps towards the television and shaking his fist at her.

Traveller boys, with diamonds or boxes hairstyles—step top, diamond- or box-pattern at the sides—would sit around afterwards drinking WKD (blue, yellow, green or red vodka), Stonehouse beer, Bavaria Crown lager, listening to music presented by DJ Tiësto, DJ Pulse, DJ Rankin, or Lisa Lashes of Tidy Trax Girls' fame, familiar to Aelred as regular DJ at Slinky's in Bournemouth.

Occasionally in the small hours Traveller boys would doff their shirts and bare-knuckle box for bets of two hundred euros.

Mush's car was torched and he moved to the cormorant coast of Galway.

Delvcaem also had a friend, Heapy, hair on the road between chestnut and nasturtium, a kick-boxer who had a tattoo 'KICK' on his buttock from a tattoo shop in Fermoy, County Cork, where Daubenton's bats hang upside down in cracks under the bridge all day, making wide circles very close to the water at dusk as they grab insects off the surface with their larger-than-usual hind feet.

Heapy joined the FCA—Local Defence Force—in Roscommon town.

The Shannon, the Shiven and the Suck were the rivers up there, glistening white with river-crowfoot blossom in summer.

Heapy would spend his time, when he wasn't training, standing around Goff Street with other young soldiers or in a pub whose sign said in Irish it was for the rakes—*réicí*.

Heapy told Delvcaem how Lieutenant Kevin Gleeson's Irish UN peacekeeping patrol was ambushed in Niemba, November 1960, by screaming tribesmen using poisoned arrows.

Lieutenant Gleeson, said Jambo, raising his left hand in a peaceful sign.

They sent an arrow through it.

Eight Irish soldiers were killed.

One died later from wounds.

There were two survivors.

A patrol under Commandant Hogan, Irish Battalion second-in-command, came across one of the two survivors, Private Thomas Kenny, with two arrows in him.

He saluted and said he was Private Kenny, Thomas.

Driven by Gobby Kissane, Delvcaem started going to north Kerry. Gobby would do doughnuts (handbrake turns) on the sand.

Gobby always wore a woollen cap with 'Prague' on it for these trips to the Atlantic.

Casinos where men of fifty, who have children up to twenty-five, merge with boys from Limerick in camouflage baseball caps or with Traveller couples on honeymoon—youth with a tattoo of a panther with wide-open rose mouth, horseshoe penetrated by a dagger, girl with mascara blue as the kingfisher's wing and fillet orange as the kingfisher's breast.

'Have you got euro? Have you got euro?' fellow Moyross boys importuned.

A boy in the casino who looked like a heron in jeans said of Midleton, County Cork, where he was from, that it had the highest suicide rate in Ireland.

A boy in the casino, with a laugh like a kookaburra, in a hoodie jacket, told Delvcaem his parents were alcoholics and he'd take the twenty euros they gave him for food and gamble it in the casinos, buying hashish or marijuana—weed—if he won.

The bouncer had two crucifixes upside down around his neck, the smaller hanging from a crown of thorns, a miniature rifle.

'I was deported from England in 1974 for fighting for my country,' he said under Britney Spears' 'From the Bottom of My Broken Heart.'

Summers then when seven-spot ladybirds came out like stars, ragwort grew up high as human beings, and the seagulls were your first cousins.

Bearded skewbald horses became attached to you and nearly followed the bus with Bus Éireann's logo—orange setter with legs gathered in—back to Limerick.

Snail shells of mahogany and sunflower colouring, smashed by a stone, indicated this was the anvil stone of a song thrush so he could eat the snails within.

The mistle thrush sang on a 'No Trespassers' sign and at Clancy's Strand, by meadows where nasturtiums that had run away from home lived, they threw greyhounds into the Atlantic, who could no longer run at Shelbourne Park, Dublin.

A scarecrow wore a T-shirt, 'Irish by birth, Munster by the grace of God.'

Delvcaem took a digital photograph on his mobile phone of a topaz-and-ebony she-goat, jet-black kid, two nougat-coloured kids, monarchial consort.

Hashish through horse tranquillizers to ecstasy, LSD, speed, cocaine, were used on Castle Green.

Delvcaem asked a toy boy with the features of a bottlenose dolphin in pursuit of mackerel why he had broken someone's nose.

The boy replied: 'Because I'm suffering from ADHD [Attention Deficit Hyperactivity Disorder].'

Strobe lights at the disco were like the garnet red of the burnet moth hovering over ragwort.

Delvcaem brought a girl, who looked like poultry stuffed into jeans, behind Buckley's Garage and made love to her.

Afterwards his body smelled like the urine the fox sprays to denote its territory trail.

Two stories he heard about the mink.

One, they'd been bought from Canada in the 1950s and escaped from primitive mink farms.

Two, they'd been brought from Sweden, Poland, Romania and Russia several years back and had been released by animal activists.

They were shooting mink in Galway because they raided farmyard fowl.

Old and unwanted greyhounds were flung into the Atlantic at Clancy's Strand.

Was Delvcaem victim of a ghetto kangaroo court or a tribal fight?

'If a Shankey sees a Cullivan and the Cullivan is just standing there the Shankey will go up and give him a clout.'

'Don't go over to where the Shankeys live whatever you do. You'd be found with the fishes in the morning.'

Plaster of Paris statues of Our Lady of Medjugorje were placed by a tree near the off-licence where Delvcaem was murdered.

Our Lady of Medjugorje had been appearing to a group of young adults of Delvcaem's age in the Croatian village of Medjugorje, Bosnia and Herzegovina, since June 1981, telling the visionaries that these were her final appearances on earth, and despite the subsequent war, hundreds of thousands of pilgrims were still making their way there.

Bunches of red carnations on the tree the way bunches of sea asters grow on the sea cliffs in north Kerry in autumn.

When women threw themselves off the Metal Bridge bunches of flowers would be left in the bushes at Thomondgate Dock.

Even the black Our Lady of Montserrat found her way into the tree by the off-licence.

Girls in shell-pink exercise suits, black leggings with their skirts, scarlet ankle boots, Playboy Bunny earrings, belts with Playboy Bunny buckles—diamanté bunnies with magenta eyes—silver kewpie dolls, with wine- or blue-coloured glass flowers on their pinafores, around their necks, studs in pierced cheeks, hoop earrings like Rihanna, kept vigil, carrying the flowers of autumn—Michaelmas daisies, asters, heliotrope, veronicas, clematis, knotweed.

'In Rama was there a voice heard . . .'

I walk away from the house of mourning.

'JCB' by Nizlopi plays from a car stereo.

Some boys are roller-blading.

Others are having a water-balloon fight.

In good summers you see the half mourner butterfly—after the black-and-white dress worn in the period following full mourning—on the buddleia that grows in abundance by the walls here.

Bobby Dazzler . . .

Delvcaem in his Confirmation jacket; Delvcaem in paisley-pattern neckerchief, Delvcaem in Ordinary Boys diamond-pattern sleeveless jersey; Delvcaem in pink-and-silver party styrofoam Stetson for his eighteenth birthday; Delvcaem with naked torso in hipster-level jeans, Le Coq Sportif boxers showing, naval-length chain, slight advertisement of pubic hair; Delvcaem with Adolf moustache; Delvcaem in space-age sunglasses and black boots with white laces; Delvcaem in

Liverpool jersey with Carragher on it.

The Severn estuary has the second-highest tide in the world.

There were packets of Embassy Regal cigarettes scattered in the back seat of small-town south Wales-boy Richey Edwards' car when it was found.

The Shannon is in spring flood and at Curragower Falls boys in wetsuits, where Delvcaem is not included, brave kayaks through the tide.

Essex Skipper

Traveller's joy on the hedges becomes old man's beard in the autumn.

When I was a boy my father gave me a collection of art books, loose reproductions going with them.

One of the reproductions was *The Drunkenness of Noah* by Michelangelo—a naked, wreathed youth, whose own genitals are showing, covering the nakedness of Noah who has a wine jug alongside him, the youth's head turned back to a naked young man who is gloating over Noah's embarrassment.

Men known as breeches-makers were employed by the Vatican, I tell the two boys who are visiting me—one of whom looks like a Cyclops or a myopic pine marten—to cover the nakedness of Michelangelo youths—*ignudi*—with ribbons, drapery, entire garments.

But this one escaped.

I tell them the story as they look at the painting:

As an old man Michelangelo was walking through the snow to the Coliseum when Cardinal Farnese accosted him and asked him why a man of his age was out in the snow.

'To learn something new,' was the famous reply.

Giovanni Bellini, from whose mastery of light the hour of the day can be deduced, gave a version of old age in those loose reproductions: Noah with beard of ermine and baby-nakedness.

The boys also look at Mary Cassatt's *Mother and Child*: naked American he-child who looks as if he's destined for a career in the navy.

Mary Cassatt took her influence from Correggio, I tell the boys.

In Chapter 14 of Mark, Christ is deserted by all except a boy wearing nothing but a linen cloth who follows Him as He's being taken away, gives Him the cloth and runs away naked.

Correggio painted this scene but the painting is lost.

There's a copy of it in Parma; boy with vermilion cloak on his shoulder being pursued by a soldier in an indigo cuirass.

The following Monday the guards investigate.

A young detective in black jobber—half-boots—pays attention to *The Rape of Ganymede*, thought to have been by Titian, by Damiano Mazza, in which the rapist eagle has a decurved beak and wings with ctenoid edges—like the teeth of a comb, Ganymede's buttocks resolved for penetration while coral-pink drapery liberates itself from his body.

François Boucher's *Cupid* with his love arrows in a gold-topped scarlet pouch is examined.

Even a child with golden hair and painted cheeks in biscuit (marble-like) unglazed porcelain by the eighteenth-century Düsseldorf sculptor Johann Peter Melchior is scrutinized.

Sent by the girlfriend of a boy dying of AIDS, I'd thought it for many years to have been a depiction of Melchior, one of the three wise men, his name meaning king of light.

An older detective seems unsettled by Franz von Lebach's *The Little Shepherd*: boy in scarlet waistcoat, short trousers like the ones Hugo von Hofmannsthal wore in his prodigious Viennese boyhood, lying among poppies.

The young detective picks up the Penguin edition of Alain-Fournier's *Le Grand Meaulnes* with a black-and-white photograph of a boy's naked torso on the cover, an *ignudo* shadowed by leaves.

Certain evidence of paedophilia and he consults with the clerkish older detective.

I had a copy of this book as a child with Sisley's *Small Meadows in Spring* on the cover . . .black-stockinged girl by poplars . . .blue ribbon around her hat . . .head dipped as if she's admiring a flower in her hand . . .Augustin Meaulnes used to gather the eggs of the red-headed moorhen in meadows such as these for his mother.

The great black-backed gull eats other gulls.

Earlier I was arrested on the strand by the young detective.

A file of five guards or detectives came into my chalet like Spanish inquisitors in their cone hats.

A stout, rugby-playing ban garda (woman garda) looks through my album with images from the Národní Gallery in Prague, the State Gallery in Stuttgart, collections in Arnhem, Cracow.

My shoes are confiscated and I am put in a cell with a ground latrine and the name Dinny scrawled on the wall.

Mudlarks with bumfluff moustaches and German shepherd dogs alongside them search for golf balls in the shallow river of this town.

I am interrogated under video camera.

I make no comments.

On my return to my chalet, despite the fact I'm next door to the garda station, I find the two windows broken.

A gang of boys approach the chalet four times, completely demolishing the back-lane window glass so people can climb through.

A heavy rock is thrown in at me.

'Come out here. But call the ambulance first.'

'That was only a crowd of young lads who did that,' a young ginger-haired guard, who arrives on the scene, tells me.

After four nights of terror I abandon the chalet in haste.

The curtains of the bedroom I move into in Tralee have been rubbed with faeces.

A drunken youth tries to break into my room one night, accusing me of stealing a Radiohead CD.

One of the house residents served with Global Strategy Mercenaries in Iraq, saw the North Gate of Baghdad, and when I try to ask him about his experiences he threatens me with the IRA.

'What do you want to know about that for?'

I stayed in the Salvation Army hostel in Edinburgh once and this is just like it.

There was a former professor from St Andrews University who'd made the hostel his home.

I swim near a lighthouse.

The ringed plover—*feadóg an fháinne*—lives in abundance here.

When threatened it drags its body along the ground, tail spread, one wing extended and flapping as if it was injured.

I recognize the black armpits of the grey plover—*feadóg ghlas*—which you can see in flight.

I move into a tiny room near the Lee River that flows into Trá Lí Mic Dedad (the beach of Lí, son of Dedad).

I frequently spot a heron by the river.

Cinder-sifter boys search for discarded carbonators by this river, which can be used for plumbing or heating.

Girls sit on the crossbars of boys' bicycles like visiting aristocracy in the howdah on an elephant's back.

'I thought someone just left it here,' a boy tells me as I stop him stealing my bicycle.

A crowd of school children bang on my back-lane window.

I look out.

'Queer,' one calls back.

A few evenings later, a Friday evening, there is a knock on the window.

It is the same boy. A tall gander-like boy. An adolescent gorilla.

His T-shirt says: 'I'm a workaholic. Every time I work I need a beer.'

He asks if he can come in.

'I want to stay the night with you,' he says.

I bring him to the beach and give him my spare swimming briefs, which he jogs in while I swim.

In a corner of the beach he towels himself naked.

Gooseberry-velutinous chest—soft, fine hairs; moustachial hairs under his navel; genitals the salmon red of the linnet's breast.

The geography of Essex with its many tidal rivers in its early body hair.

He is the young warrior who, after letting his beloved hawk fly into the Weald, advances towards his doom in battle with the Vikings as the causeway tide goes out.

Bricin—Bricin Pluckrose is his name.

His father is from the wastes of Essex near Chelmsford.

Bricin brings a childhood snapshot of himself in rag hat with butterfly on it—Essex skipper, orange with black rim.

He brings a photograph of his father standing against a Union Jack in olive-green polo shirt with red-rimmed collar, black braces, black laced-up boots.

His father used to sell fruit and vegetables in Chelmsford in scarlet work boots with white laces, jeans with rolled-up ends, scarlet braces and shaven head like William Pitt's niece and social hostess Lady Hester Stanhope, who used to beat her servants in Phoenicia with a mace and employed an ex-general of Napoleon as soothsayer there.

His father's sister—his nan—was a skinhead.

'No earring but a bald head. No jail record.'

She said then: 'I want to slow down and marry.'

She married a heavyweight boxer in Brentwood.

'He saved my bacon,' she said of him.

The boy who tells these stories has hair the black of the defensive liquid the ten-armed cuttlefish emits, pockmarks like the webbing between the sea otter's feet, Rudolph Valentino in mayhem good looks, mackerel-blue eyes.

Eyes that suddenly liquify into anguish at the remembrance of some insult or some uncertainty as to my expectations of him.

They are different expectations, new expectations.

Occasionally his eyes rivet dangerously.

Speech is frequently interrupted; a stammer, a caesura.

The Queen's father, George VI, had a stammer, I tell him.

His grandmother, who witnessed the Canvey Island disaster of February 1953, has a framed message from George VI on her incrusted line-patterned wallpaper.

'Help to make the world a better place and life a worthier thing.'

'She's with the fairies,' Bricin borrows an expression from his Irish mother who drinks an eggnog every night and occasionally a Club Dry Gin with it.

Bricin disappears from my life just as the Essex skipper vanishes from a musk thistle.

She is the fairies' midwife . . .
Her waggon-spokes made of long spinners' legs;
The cover, of the wings of grasshoppers . . .
Her chariot is an empty hazel-nut . . .

It is St Patrick's night and the shelter from which I swim is invaded.

A bin filled with glass from occasional winter drinkers has been emptied out.

A small English boy with a café-crème baseball cap and a jail-bird stride indicates he carries a flick knife.

A girl in a T-shirt with the words 'Oopsy Tipsy! One too Many' is walking around with jeans down to her knees.

A flamingo bottom like François Boucher's toiletting Venus.

In the Boucher painting putti-bearing chaplets administer to Venus.

Here the putti wear baseball caps.

I ask two of these putti—one with a T-shirt with the words: 'So wotcha say?'—to look after my bicycle while I'm swimming.

They throw it to the ground, smashing the lamp to smithereens.

A girl with 'Will try anything twice' flaunted on her T-shirt throws grit at me as I change.

I ask her to stop whereupon the putti who threw my bicycle to the ground approach to beat me up.

I manage to appease them and I make a getaway from this demonic theatre.

A boy with Fatty Arbuckle features, hair and freckle colouring of the red squirrel, eyes blue as hedge periwinkles, in tropical shirt and Dr Livingstone shorts reconciles me to Bricin.

He delivers him to me.

The following Friday as he eats a forest-berry Bavarian cream cake he tells me that his cousin Uinseann—Gaelic for Vincent— who has Adam Ant braids, eyes like the Japanese sika deer in Killarney National Park, and tennis-star sisters Venus and Serena Williams on his mobile phone, used to make love to him in the shower of his home.

Bricin is wearing a J. Nistlerooy, Manchester United, black away shirt.

Uinseann has a girlfriend now who has beet-red dye in her hair, wears Mickey Mouse knickers, and said to Bricin: 'If you were a product you'd be mustard.'

They went to a nightclub in Tralee together where the boys danced with the boys and the girls danced with the girls and a boy and a girl had oral sex on the floor.

When Bricin is distressed he can make his jaws look like the Aristotle's lantern—the spherical jaws of a sea urchin.

Alternatively, he diverts to his father's Essex Polari—a mixture of pig Latin, Romany, criminal argot.

Dosh, he calls money.

In the casinos, some boys sell themselves for sex for twenty euros.

My father, donor of Michelangelos and Bellinis—from the books he gave me I learnt that Leonardo wrote in mirror writing (reversed writing)—referred to my girlfriends as Mary Annes.

Also known as Mary Annes were the London telegraph boys of the 1880s in their light-blue uniforms and sideways caps, whom speculation said satisfied the desires of the heir presumptive with spiv's moustache and frogged Hussar's tunic, who, on his early death, was mourned each day by his mother, with fresh flowers laid on his deathbed.

One of those London Mary Annes was found to have connections with the Golden Lane Boy Brothel near the Liffey in Dublin, frequented by Dublin Fusiliers and Grenadier Guards, which the Home Rulers used as propaganda against the British rulers.

Sometimes Bricin comes into my place from the casinos like a ruffled young barn owl with its kitten head and protuberant eyes.

A man in a denim cowboy hat in the casino told him: 'I put ads in the paper and get couples. I only go with couples.'

His mouth is smeared with the Mississippi mud pie he's been eating.

Dalta—foster-child; Bricin in my life.

Late August he visits Essex with his father.

'I love this country,' his father declares when the Tube reaches Epping.

'In my childhood a mug cost a penny and very big ones too.'

They feast on jumbo sausages, curry, chips and gravy, and Memory

Lane Madeira cake in Colchester.

This is a conversation Bricin hears on a bus in Colchester:

'And the cat got into the fridge.'

'How did the cat get into the fridge?'

'Don't ask me. And it was so smelly.'

In a supermarket he witnesses a youth, accosted by store detectives, pulling down his trousers in front of the delicatessen, showing his Ginch Gonch underwear.

'I haven't got anything!'

His family knows the Roman roads of Essex, the ploughman's spikenard, same fragrance as the ointment Mary anointed the feet of Jesus with.

'Goodbye Bud,' his uncle, who wears a silver lurex shirt and who has a bull terrier called Daniela, says to him when he's leaving.

He has returned from Essex wearing a black-and-white baseball cap with rabbit ears and a belt with a monkey motif buckle—three monkey cameos.

There are male strippers in Galway, Bricin has heard. For hen parties; some of them appear in nothing but Stetsons from Euro-Saver shops.

Perhaps he'll go there, wear Union Jack kit, bill himself as the Essex stripper or British kit stripper.

In September he turns up in the shelter in the evenings while I'm swimming, as a black-headed gull—chocolate-brown head—drawn to sportsfields, does.

Body like a wounded gull.

Joins hands, prays for his dead Irish grandfather.

'If he was alive he'd give me fifty euros.'

Often he lights candles in church for his grandfather before coming to meet me.

Here he may spend a votive ten minutes.

His mother got a portrait tattoo of his grandfather in Limerick on her right arm.

His grandfather used to wear a hat with a scarlet cockade and pheasant feather on the brim.

I have to ban Bricin from my place. Coming too often, danger.

He bangs on my window for admittance, like the busty Caroline of Brunswick, in spite of her affair with Italian courtier Bartolomeo Pergami, banging on the doors of Westminster Abbey during the coronation of her husband George IV, the doors barred against her.

The Polish boy who fixes my bicycle is from Katowice, Henryk Górecki's town, composer of *Symphony of Sorrowful Songs*, a tape lost in my flight.

The bicycle man with handlebar moustache frequently passes me in a Toyota truck and honks at me.

I arrived on the first of November, a Friday—Samhain—to have my bicycle chain fixed.

He was in jail for not paying his taxes, an old lady, who reprimanded me for wearing shorts in November, told me.

I called at the buff bungalow of a boy, who wore a lemon baseball cap with the words 'The Doctor,' who'd pledged to help me if I was in trouble with my bicycle.

He ambushed a girl with tricolour hair—hazel in front, fuschia on top, ebony ponytail—on a madder rose junior bicycle, which featured the bobbed-haired Dora the Explorer in lemon ankle socks, and forcibly took a link from her chain.

She threatened the Demon Man on him.

The link didn't fit.

I was led to a greensward where boys in a flea market of baseball caps stood around a Samhain bonfire.

Between the first of November and the first of May the *filí*—poets—would tell a story for each night.

A Raleigh racing bicycle, which wobbled like jelly, was produced from a shed.

I was asked twenty-five euros for it.

I only had twenty-two euros.

I was given it for that and I walked the two bicycles the ten miles back against the night traffic and met a man with greyhounds, pink and white electric-fence twine attached to them.

The hermit crab crawls into the mollusc abandoned by the mussel or the oyster.

A nosegay of snowdrops—*pluíríní sneachta*—comes to my door. A child is a graph; he measures the year.

I see him again in a scarlet-and-navy-banded blue-striped Tommy Hilfiger jersey and pointy shoes, eyes the blue of the hyacinths the rubbish-dump-frequenting herring guff decorates its nest with; white polo shirt with vertically blue-striped torso, listening to Rihanna's 'Good Girl Gone Bad' on his mobile phone; I see him crunching a Malteser—small round chocolate with honeycombed centre—sucking a strawberry Fun Gum or biting on a raspberry and pineapple Fruit Salad bar; I see his eyes again, blue as the blue pimpernel flower of Essex.

There was a honey-haired and honey-browed young drug dealer who ultimately used to reside in the shelter in the evenings.

His mother's people were from The Island in Limerick, where swans colonize the turloughs (winter lakes) with a view of council houses beyond.

On his motorbike, with yellow backpack, he'd travel over rivers like the Oolagh and the Allaghaun, to places like Rooskagh, to sell marijuana and hashish to boys waiting on summer evenings in diamond-pattern shorts.

The Lueneburg Manuscript of the middle of the fifteenth century tells how in the year 1284, on the twenty-sixth of June, Feast of Saints John and Paul, one hundred and thirty children from Hamelin, Germany, were led from the town by a piper dressed in diverse colours to a place of execution behind the hills. A stained-glass window in Marktkirche, Hamelin, depicted the colours. Jacob Ludwig Carl and William Carl Grimm, known to embellish, retold the story.

Were the children drowned in the Weser?

Did they depart on a Children's Crusade?

Were they murdered in the forest by the piper?

Did they anticipate Theresienstadt where children were allowed to paint in diverse colours before being gassed?

Did they anticipate the children pulled out from the rubble in Dresden, on a night a Vermeer was burned, in Harlequin and Pierrot

costumes because the bombing of Dresden took place at Fasching—
Shrovetide carnival?

Divers colours: the paintings of Michelangelo, Leonardo, Giovanni Bellini, Damiano Mazza—two boys look at them and then, like
the two children of Hamelin who didn't follow the piper, debouch to
the garda station to report this montage of pornography.

Old Swords

Luke Wadding, seventeenth-century Waterford friar in Rome, who sent the sword of the Earl of Tyrone—buried in the Franciscan Convent of San Pietro in Montorio—back to Cromwellian-overrun Ireland, did most of his writing between sunset and midnight, we were told at National School . . .

On her fern- and ivy-collecting visit to County Kerry in the late summer of 1861, shortly before her husband's death from shock over his son's affair with an actress, Queen Victoria was presented with a davenport writing desk, lions and unicorns rampant on it, made by three Killarney carpenters, the surviving brother of the Liberator Daniel O'Connell coming to meet her in the home of the Herberts, who were catapulted into bankruptcy by the expenses Queen Victoria incurred for them.

The stories come back like the lesser celandine blossoms by the sea in early spring: stories from history, stories from your life . . .

The parents of Iarla Corduff, whose hair was the pale red-bronze of the grouse when affiliated to heather, eyes the green of the County Clare Burren moth, were married in Baltimore, Maryland, where they were emigrants.

Iarla's father worked as a fisherman and his mother was pregnant when they were summoned to the church hurriedly. Iarla's father wore his fisherman's wellingtons at the wedding.

The grouping for photographs taken at a reception at which the reel 'Salute to Baltimore' was played on an Excelsior accordion—but not any of the photographs Iarla's mother subsequently framed on the parlour flock wallpaper—wallpaper with pattern made by powdered wool: a beaming lady with clubbed hair and roll fringe, in zebra-stripe dress, holding out a tender yellow-and-faded-scarlet rectangular box of Kodak film.

Back in a *breac-ghaeltacht*—mixed Irish- and English-speaking district—she had a miscarriage picking seaweed.

Herrings between July and February, mackerel between April and July. New potatoes after July, basil near the carrots in summer, turnips September–October, the pig killed in autumn, winter cabbage, a knife on the cement for the goose near Christmas.

A finger was put to the back of the goose when it was killed so the blood went to the neck. After six hours in water the feathers fell off. Women bathed their feet in the water corpses had been washed in because they thought it was holy water.

Uisce coisricthe.

In the parlour of their bungalow on a *tóchar*—causeway—was a picture of *The Irish Brigade before Battle*—their ancient tricolour sent back from France to the new Irish Free State and blessed anew by Father Pigott on St Patrick's Day in Cork.

The ruin of Daniel O'Connell's parents' house was near, though he himself was born in an emergency in a neighbour's cottage.

They'd kept a print of the Pretender James III there. When wives were sought for him in Europe, one was rejected because she was a dwarf.

O'Connell was fostered to his uncle Hunting Cap, who made a fortune smuggling silks and brandy.

He sent O'Connell's cousins to France to join the Irish Brigade and O'Connell himself to France to study Condillac and Helvétius, where François Boucher had shortly before painted John the Baptist in a Turkish delight-red cloak as if he'd got a loan or endowment from a king and Marie Antoinette had requested Philip Astley and his son John—the English rose—to bring the circus that Philip had introduced to England at Halfpenny Hatch, Lambeth Fields in 1768, to France.

Iarla's family had a book in their parlour beside the Pye wireless with the name Athlone on it, about O'Connell, published in Ave Maria Lane, London.

O'Connell with hair en brosse in front beside the stream where his father used to put out salt pans—vessels for getting salt by evaporation.

Iarla's mother had lovely American clothes when he was a child.

Her proudest possession a paisley shawl, the kind Pier Angeli wore, victim of a broken engagement to Kirk Douglas.

But one night she came upon two battling rats in her room and they turned on her.

She defended herself with a lighted candle and her clothes horse went on fire, her American clothes, including her paisley shawl.

However, a Charlie Chaplin brooch from Baltimore survived, which was appropriate as Charlie Chaplin, his wife Oona O'Neill and their *passeggiata* of children frequently holidayed in the area.

Ties of maple red, ties the red of a bull's rosette, ties the red of the red grouse's wattle, ties the red of the chough's legs—Iarla wore these as a child for occasions like Confirmation—*faoi láimh eaispaig* (under the Bishop's hand)—Morning of the Assumption.

The National School teacher would keep a heavy girl, who excelled at making diamond-pattern bed covers, behind in the afternoons to feel inside her skirt.

She'd tell her parents she'd been kept behind for misbehaviour and they'd beat her.

In the town, under a red sandstone mountain called the Giant's Arse because it was shaped like buttocks, was a butcher, Mr O'Muirgheasa, who marched by himself down the street with a red flag every May Day.

He'd met and conversed with General de Gaulle when he'd visited the town.

Mr O'Muirgheasa claimed he'd never gone to Mass since he was a child, when the County Mayo librarian, Letitia Dunbar-Harrison, was boycotted because she was a Protestant.

Despite his irreligiosity there was a statue in his butcher shop; no one could make out whether it was Mary or a figure from Celtic mythology: a woman in white tunic, blue veil, a severed male hand on her left shoulder.

A leatherback turtle had crawled up the main street as far as the azure Player's Please sign the year Dr Gilmartin, Archbishop of Tuam, had congratulated the County Mayo commissioners responsible for the boycott of Miss Dunbar-Harrison.

Iarla shared a room with his brother, Brecan, a year older than him.

Over Iarla's bed was a colour photograph of Kirk Douglas showing his legs to Tony Curtis in *The Vikings*.

With Brecan he'd walk to the grave of Scota—daughter of the Pharaoh of Egypt, wife of Miliseus of Spain, killed at the Battle of Slieve Mis.

From there they could see Banna Strand where Sir Roger Casement landed in a German U-boat, Easter 1916, and was marched by the English to Tralee where the Royal Irish Constabulary man's wife cooked him a steak.

Casement left his pocket watch as appreciation before being moved on to his execution in Pentonville Prison.

The story, told by a Christian Brother catechism examiner, who'd felt Iarla's neonate ginger-auburn hair inside his swain's short trousers, was recorded in an exercise book with fleurons on the cover.

It was Brecan, who had a haircut like Brian Poole of the Tremeloes, who'd returned to his family's butcher business, who'd first made love to him.

Brecan slept in the Kerry colours—green and dust-gold.

There was an amorist in town, originally from Dublin, with a horseshoe beard like Yul Brynner in *Solomon and Sheba*, who swam in winter and won best actor award at the amateur drama finals in Scarriff, County Clare.

The adjudicator at Scarriff later drove his car off Corrib Bridge by Fisheries' Field in Galway and drowned.

St Swithin of Winchester requested to be buried in the cathedral yard so his grave would be rained on, and St Swithin's Day, 15 July, determined the weather, rain or shine, for the next forty days.

It was on St Swithin's Day the Dublin man seduced Iarla in a copse behind a flank of mountain ashes after Iarla had swum in a stream.

Looking at Iarla standing naked in the stream one day, the man said he reminded him of Tom, the dirty little chimney sweep in Charles Kingsley's *The Water-Babies*, who came down his friend Ellie's chimney uninvited and subsequently, like the boys in Henry Scott Tuke's paintings, had to purify himself—Tom, the dirty little chimney sweep, immediately put on the Vatican's *Index*

Librorum Prohibitorum.

Iarla was by his side in a hotel in a neighbouring town after a performance one night.

On the wall was a colour photograph of the Rose Garden, Bangor, County Down.

A taciturn-faced boy with Fräulein-blonde facial hair, eyes chestnut-fringed, green rugby player's chest, in a V-neck vermilion jersey, sat on the floor.

There was a feeling of expectancy. Was someone going to sing a song?

And then indeed the boy in the vermilion jersey did sing a song:

> I sold my rock
> I sold my reel
> When my flax was gone
> I sold my wheel
> To buy my love a sword of steel.

In the town, the drama group would meet in an Augustan pub called The White Causeway, a sign without that featured an undertaker celebrating with a glass of wine and a picture within of a bottle of wine beside a wine glass, with the words: 'Salina Helena, Napa Valley Reserve, 1917.'

The grey seals were born in autumn as white-coated pups on the Góilín—inlet—a coral strand made up of calcerous algae washed in by the winter tides.

They remained on the strand for three weeks, after which the mothers abandoned them and hunger forced them to sea.

'Most people say you're turning into a right old poufter. Other people say you're sound,' a youth in a whipcord jacket and goffered shirt said to Iarla at a dance one night when Big Tom and the Mainliners were playing.

When a poster for a parish-hall showing of *The Swordsman of Siena*—Stewart Granger in full Sienese garb waving a sword, a trembling décolleté Sylva Koscina with droplet earrings and a fearless

Christine Kaufmann in a tam by his side—turned up in town, Iarla went to study in Dublin, dancing on Saturday nights in an Aran cardigan with wooden buttons at The Television Club.

He had his tarot read by a girl who sat beside him on a chaise lounge in South King Street.

He threw up his studies after a year and a half and went off to England.

'The swan would die of pride if it hadn't black feet,' his mother said to him.

Her Pier Angeli had died of a barbiturates overdose.

In London he lived on pans of onions, which he fried wearing a sheepskin coat, and drank tea from a mug with Gainsborough's shepherd girl on it.

He regularly went to a pub near St Martin-in-the-Fields to hear a woman from the Donegal gaeltacht, her photograph in an Abbey Theatre programme once, recite poems she never wrote down, her bedsit in Tufnell Park a legend of cats.

She'd upbraided George Bernard Shaw when he was considering her for a major part and subsequently descended to menial work.

The death of one of her dogs in a street accident occasioned a nervous breakdown.

Iarla heard her tell an audience of Irish boys in cloaks, green-and-red half boots, Irish girls in Queen Nefertiti or Queen Nitocris shift dresses, that her poems were millions of years old.

Old as Queen Scota maybe.

A line from one of her poems about walking holding someone's hand in Ireland decided him to return to Kerry.

In early spring, by the stream, he saw again the hart's tongue fern and the lords and ladies fern and the buttercup leaves and the celandine leaves and later the hemlock and the ramsons—the wild garlic—and the alexanders and the eyebright and the goosegrass and the chickweed.

There is a red rim to the chickweed flower and he often saw that red in the whites of his eyes. It wasn't that he cried. But he was always near tears.

Near a *ráth*—an earthen ring fort—he found the small feathers of a singing thrush, which told him that a merlin had plucked its prey here, and he thought of the punitive, sometimes Augean places he'd lived in London, Thin Lizzy's album *Shades of a Blue Orphanage* borne to each of them.

Brecan managed the local Spar supermarket now, which had advertisements for Ardfert Retreat Centre.

He married a Galway girl, his mother wearing a toque of lopped coins with a cobweb veil hanging from it for the wedding, pancake make-up on her face and angel-hair eyelashes like Joan Collins' in *Esther and the King*.

After a few years in Kerry, working around the bungalow, walking to the Góilín on days when the sky looked as if it was going to kick a ball at you, time of the cuckoo's sostenuto, Iarla went to New York.

'Slán go fóill [goodbye for the moment],' said his lover friend of early adolescence, 'I hope New York does you justice.'

In Tralee before getting the bus for the onward journey he saw the Christian Brother catechism examiner of childhood hanging around the lavatory in Bill Booley's Lane.

'I went to Carthage where I found myself in the midst of a hissing cauldron of lust.'

His friend would quote St Augustine to describe a sojourn in North Africa. 'All naked boys had to wear the horn of a gazelle when they reached puberty.'

In a steam room in New York a young black soldier with a silver-dollar crew cut said: 'Balls are the nature of man. When they're big, man's nature is big. Yours are big as an infant's head.'

He worked in Irish bars in New York, mostly one on the East River whose owner was from Cois Fharraige (beside the south Connemara Atlantic).

'At sixteen I lived on the Holloway Road with just Gaelic.

'Up at six. On the road for an hour.

'We had to get it ready for the chippies. They did the slabbing and we put the plaster on it.

'One hour getting back.

'Then to the pubs.

'Madison and Fifth Avenue was a two-way system when I arrived, with gold traffic signals with small statues of Mercury, messenger of the gods, on them.

'We knew nothing about sex in Connemara.

'The priest called the shots.

'On South Boston men's beach, in a sauna, the peanut whistle going outside, we found out.'

Iarla had had a young lover friend in Dublin who was an electrician from Athlone where groups of boys hang out on the Shannon Bridge near the redstone, green-panelled Dillon Shoes building.

There were fathers in the Athlone area, that boy had told Iarla, who let their friends make love to their teenage sons and watched while they were doing it.

With a Sagittarius stone—turquoise—this boy had gone to live in Berlin.

After a year in New York, Iarla went to Toronto, Canada, country of Leonard Cohen whom he heard singing 'Kevin Barry' in a 1960s *Weltanschauung* version at a concert in Dublin.

'Just a lad of eighteen summers . . .'

He lived in a house with shiplap siding in a run-down district.

There were stories about gay people thrown at night into Toronto harbour.

Occasionally he saw the Italian word *froci*—queers—written on the walls.

He sent his Dublin friend a postcard of Vuillard's *Toulouse-Lautrec*—mushroom hat, poppy shirt, baggy lemon trousers.

'Are you in the land of the living?'

The reply was an ancient John Hinde colour postcard of the town under the Giant's Arse mountain.

Shortly after Iarla got this card his mother died of cancer in Marymount Hospice in Cork, with a Norah Lofts book by her bed.

In Kerry he found her love letters to his father in a yellow, royal-blue and scarlet Weetabix cereal tin she'd sent away for with coupons she'd collected.

'I looked after old people for a penny a day when I was a girl,' she'd told Iarla once, 'put turf and bog gale under their beds.'

Iarla left Toronto shortly after returning from Kerry and went back to New York, to pubs run by Irishmen with TV-cop moustaches.

Early one winter, thrush in the mouth turned into pneumonia and he spent a winter in bed.

He thought about his friend in Berlin and then a card drifted through from him, belatedly condoling him on his mother's death: Jerg Ratgeb's *Crucifixion*; the tongue of the thief on Christ's right side hanging out, a woman in shrimp-pink gown thrusting herself at the foot of the Cross and crows pecking around the Cross in oblivion.

Big Tom and the Mainliners played in New York, attracting an audience of heroin addicts by mistake because mainlining is an American term for injecting into the main vein, and Iarla returned to Ireland for a short sojourn, going via London.

The Irish streets in London didn't seem changed; the posters in the windows, the names of singers with what were either the titles of their songs or maxims, after their names.

Dominic Kirwin: 'Always.' Scan O'Farrell: 'Today.' Joe Dolan: 'Come Early.'

An omnipresent poster: 'Brendan Shine Live.'

A black woman stood at a bus stop in embroidered lapis-lazuli garb, in blue headdress, series of filigree pendants in her ears. On the bus was the ubiquitous Irish story:

'Do you know "The Lonely Woods of Upton?" You don't know it,' the man was looking at Iarla's black leather matador jacket, 'because you've never been there.

'My mother and father didn't care about me. They gave me to an orphanage there in Ireland when I was three. She's married to another man in Scotland now. He's dead.

'I have three bairns in Scotland. People don't know how hard it is. I've got to come here and support them. And I drink. I'm nobody's child. You're nobody's child but your own.'

And then he started singing:

Those men who died for Ireland
In the lonely woods of Upton for Sinn Féin.

Iarla could see the contrast between the Irish in England, his
London years, and New York. He'd that experience in his life, that
vicissitude.

In the Postcard Gallery on Neal Street he bought a card for his Dublin
friend who'd returned to his city: Alfred Eisenstaedt's *Dutch Woman
and Boy Looking At Rembrandt's Nightwatchmen*, the woman with a
mole on her face, shadows filling the eyes and the curious, serious
mouth of the boy, her grandson, the woman's right hand clenched in
threads of light.

A barred feather, which fell in his path in Kerry, told him that a spar-
rowhawk was close by, seeking prey.

Glebe, this place was called—earth.

A ruined castle reminded Iarla that County Kerry was known as
the Kingdom.

In the small park in the town, a man in his Sunday suit played 'A
Nation Once Again' on bagpipes under a statue of Kerry Antarctic
explorer Tom Crean with ski sticks—who'd been seen off on one of
his voyages by the Dowager Empress Marie Feodorovna, mother of
Tzar Nicholas II, who, with his wife Princess Alix of Hesse, Queen
Victoria's granddaughter, and his children, was murdered in a blood
-stained cellar in Ekaterinburg in 1918—two women with reticules
seated on a stone bench watching the performance, the older with
pumps with almond-shaped toes, the younger with French pleat at
the back of her hair.

A Denny van drew up during the recital, with four lonely-looking
sausages on the van.

Iarla thought his experience of the west of Ireland was the experience of a missing face, like the face of a boy, chestnut-fringed green
eyes, in a V-neck vermilion Jersey, he'd seen at a party in a hotel after
a play once, a woman belting out Isabel Leslie's 'The Thorn Tree' that

night as she played on a piano with a red silk front.

'But if your heart's an Irish heart you'll never fear the thorn tree.'

The green-headed mallard, who mates with our farmyard geese, stays for summer, but I must go.

Before flying back to New York, where he found the helper, suppressor cells were quickly vanishing from his body, Iarla met a man with a turf cut, in suede shoes with a metallic sheen, above Clancy's Strand in Limerick.

'You wouldn't think I'd want to have my hair short,' he said, 'I was in the army for so long. I was out in the Lebanon. I saw a man choke his own daughter. She was handicapped and showed her panties. You wouldn't think I'd miss the Lebanon. But I do.'

'Old friends, like old swords, still are trusted best . . .'

Iarla's friend told him about his own swim and the winter swim in Dublin; of the chute at Blackrock Baths; of bathing places with graffiti urging assignations; of jetties into the Irish Sea, which people wandered as if seeking revelations; of two villas called Milano and La Scala adjacent to the sea near his home; of going to *Song of Norway* performed at a theatre with organ-pipe pillars on either side of the stage—the women in dirndls (Alpine costumes); of an attempt at being a seminarist; then the profligacy of men's swimming places—cormorants flying low over the gnashing and discontented sea at swimming coves, academic-looking seals coursing by you while in England a peer sent to jail for alleged sexual assault on two Boy Scouts in a beach hut and the police raiding men's houses and examining their photograph albums; of bran-faced young FCA men fresh from army summers at Finner Camp offering themselves for fellation at urinals with the word 'FIR' (men) outside, the experience of serving in the Belgian Congo where gonorrhoea being rampant greatly increased the numbers of soldiers in urinals; of the ship that brought him past the swimming places of Dublin Bay, the cerulean mountains that virtually formed letters of the alphabet, the nimbused valleys, to the minarets of North Africa; of how earlier in the century Mr Carson approached the Forty Foot in winter with a lantern, would swim to Bullock Harbour in Dalkey and back, was prosecuted and

fined two and sixpence for swimming naked in 1906; of Dr Oliver St
John Gogarty who was taken captive during the Civil War in January
1923 by men who entered his house using a woman, later to become
a nun in Rathmines, as a decoy, was taken to a house near Salmon
Pool on Island Bridge to be shot, twice claimed he had to urinate
outside because of nervousness, second time threw himself into the
Liffey and swam, was swept along by the current, came to a house
where he was given brandy by a garda doctor. In 1924 he presented
two swans, which were sent from Lady Leconfield's lake in Sussex, to
the goddess of the Liffey as thanksgiving. The swans wouldn't get out
of the crate so W.B. Yeats, who was presiding over the ceremony, had
to give the crate a good kick.

Cicero—as the pupils of Green's CBS in Tralee in their blue-grey jerseys know—told the story:
   The young courtier Damocles in the city of Syracuse was heard to
envy his lord Dionysius whereupon Dionysius proposed he sit on his
throne for one day and the feasting Damocles noticed a sharp sword
hanging over him by a thread, the price of power!
   Iarla had Richard Westall's paintings from the Postcard Gallery,
Neal Street, London—a Neronic young man not unlike the neo-
classical rugby youths in the showers of O'Dowd Park, Tralee.

Wasn't there the story too, passed down from a drama adjudicator
who'd drowned himself, of Georges d'Anthe, white horseguards' uniform, wavy blonde hair—perhaps like the youth in the hotel—the
adopted son of the Dutch ambassador of St Petersburg and reputedly
his pathic, who fell in love with Alexander Pushkin's wife, a 'Raphael
hour,' and slew Pushkin, whose winter coat was missing a button, in
a duel?

In the National Portrait Gallery in London, Iarla had seen the portrait of Robert Devereux, Second Earl of Essex, after Marcus Gheer-
aerts the Younger, with chin-frizz beard, whose face Elizabeth I had
slapped after he'd turned his back on her.
   In Essex Birhtnoth's beautiful and ornamented sword was coveted
and Birhtnoth slain by the causeway—*tóchar*.

Then would he wish to see my Sword, and feel
The quickness of the edge, and in his hand
Weigh it . . .

Perhaps he picked up the HIV virus from a youth from Red
Wing, Missouri, with a Joe Dallesandro headband.

There'd been a priest, a Raphael hour, eyes the blue of the chicory
that grew at the béguinage gates at home, he'd made love to in an
apartment full of street jewellery in New York, he wasn't sure of.

Between waking and sleeping in a Brooklyn hospital, after listening
to a broadcast of Jessye Norman singing in Central Park to commemorate Princess Diana, Iarla dreams of Dr Oliver St John Gogarty, a story from his adolescence, a fellow Irish exile in New York.

Dr Gogarty survived.

He turned up at tea parties in Lady Cunards in New York during
the Second World War.

The former Maud Burke of California, relative of Robert Emmet,
sung about by Count John McCormack of Athlone.

Alone in New York: Gogarty a bohemian, an autumn leaf.

He is an autumnal person.

And always there's the sea, the radiance of the sea at the Forty
Foot, which he made his own and where he used to swim with
tempestuous regularity in his youth. And there's the bitter cold of
the Liffey, the Liffey into which he jumped one winter and swam to
save his life, the bitter cold of the Irish emotions that had tried to
murder him.

*They'd burned his library in north Connemara where the panelling
had been made of the wood of shipwrecks . . .Condillac, Helvétius . . .*

With the crow's feet of his temples, the raised, almost halter-like
enclosure of hair around his temples, he drops in for an hour or so at
a tea party in New York—Worcester tea service and Derby Botanical
dessert service—and then he walks off, a winter swimmer remembering Dublin, the way light hit the warm-gold lettering of a pub mirror, the way radiance hit a certain joker's pub anecdote.

And somewhere in him, in these late-autumn days, is a naked

young swimmer's buttocks, bruised together like the face of a young Byronesque-featured wit at a Catholic public school that had the acrid smell of shoe polish.

Yes, in these days of Fall, he remembers his brother-poet Catullus: 'What human form is there which I have not had? A woman, man, youth, boy . . .'

And though it's Fall there's the urge for a swim, Coney Island maybe, the peanut whistle sounding, past the monuments to Garibaldi and to the Unknown Soldier, the Stars and Stripes fluttering over a few gentlemen swimmers who still wear the old-fashioned, black, bib top, swimming suits so that we are presented with epochs that eddy together—like the autumn and Atlantic-caressed flag.

Wooden Horse

'Took me into the gaff. Shot me in both arms. Three weeks in Tallaght hospital. Three weeks at home recovering.'

Fifteen-year-old youth, whose body looks like a suburb of Baghdad. Sunflower-yellow hair, head shaped like one of the horses' heads in the production of *Equus* I saw, a play about a teenager who is sexually attracted to horses.

Eyes, an emerald that has been wronged, green as the horse trampled Scheme greensward.

Septic scar on his chin.

One of the eyes of the man who shot Horsey swollen so that part of his face looked like a rancid onion.

'What happened to him?'

'He's dead.'

Horsey has a horse and saddle ring given to him by Joker Jewin.

Joker Jewin was born between Epsom and Croydon. Worked on the roads at Grove Park Kent with forty-six Irishmen. He was the only Englishman.

Became interested in the Republican movement.

Tattoo on his back of crossed Republican rifles, which he got in Croydon. Horse and saddle tattoo on his right arm.

Two bottles smashed in his face in a hotel in Croydon by an Orangeman. 'A nice scar for life.' Thus the name Joker as Joker in *Batman* who has a scar.

Rides around Tallaght in a daffodil-coloured Philip Jowett dray drawn by a monkey-coloured pony with a white square on its forehead.

Knows how to make gin-traps for rabbits and mesh traps with perch swing for crows and magpies who steal chickens' eggs or eat the young of other birds.

They have made me feel like a crow or a magpie who's been eating the blue eggs of the song thrush.

'Lie down with the dogs, wake up with fleas,' says Figroll, in a primrose-coloured hoodie jacket, 'Lie down with the pigeons and you'll wake up tumbling.'

Horsey deals drugs, often owes money.

Figroll has lonely, lonely lapis lazuli eyes. Blue of the classroom orb of planet Earth when I was a child. In his hoodie cuirass has a head like a popping peanut.

A field mouse who has run in from the fields, a grey squirrel clasping an acorn in the Phoenix Park. The grey squirrels have reached the Grand Canal from the Phoenix Park but they who eliminated the red squirrels are in turn being coerced by escaped chipmunks.

'There's a bed and a television there,' Figroll informs me, looking at the Grand Canal. 'You could lie on the bed and watch the television.'

At fourteen or fifteen they go to the Phoenix Park at night, join the Rumanian, the Polish, the Chinese boys among ilex trees, among chestnut trees and Scotch pines, among blackberry and hawthorn bushes, raise a flickering lighter. Those trackie bottoms come down. Their buttocks manifest. White ammunition.

Fifty euros each time.

Money for horses. Money for drugs.

The rabbits nibbling and the stags rutting.

'It's been going on for hundreds of years. Got stage fright at first,' says Ryaner, aged fourteen, hair the colour of New England in autumn, skin white as a squall of gulls. In an Afghan hat face like a cuckoo that comes out of a cuckoo clock.

Sometimes the guards shine magnetic cling headlights at them and they scatter into a grove of evergreen oaks.

'They go to the Phoenix Park not just for money. They want that experience.'

I'm talking to a man in a hat, T-shirt with a tropical scene—sea, sunset, palm trees—the Grand Canal.

'Where are you from?'

'You know, where the horse hair is held.'

'Peace and love.'

241

Young desperado Scythians. Scythians one of the earliest people to master the art of riding. Every Scythian had at least one personal mount. They owned large herds of Mongolian ponies. Some of these sacrificed with wife, children, servants on the owner's death. Mathias, the thirteenth apostle, was saved from being eaten by them by the Apostle Andrew who'd crossed the Black Sea by express boat.

Some of the boys smoke finely rolled joints—like the cigarette sweets Rosaleen Keane in my town sold when I was a child—as they rode horses.

Palomino is a colour they say. There's a dead palomino in the fields. An abandoned piebald—all ribs.

When the horses are confiscated they're just ordinary kids, asking you to buy them smokes, asking you to buy them wine, asking you to buy them score bags—heroin, pulling up an Iron Maiden T-shirt which has a face with skeleton's teeth, one of the teeth a miniature skull, to show you bullet wounds in their arms they got for not paying for drugs.

When the horses are gone the girls lead the boys along the canal as if they were horses.

Girls with elaborate bouffants like cross dressers—toffee-coloured, Danny La Rue blonde, wing quiffs brushed in flamingo.

In the case of one of the boys, Eak, who has a Sicilian lemon blond turf-cut, eyes the blue of a pet parrot someone has abandoned to an Irish wilderness, a horse had previously been the girlfriend. A chestnut and white foal with chestnut measles on the white patch who would try to nuzzle his pubes the colour of carrot cake.

'Ride a cock horse to Coventry Cross
  To see a fine lady on a white horse . . .'
Lady Godiva rode naked through Coventry once and Peeping Tom was struck blind for looking at her when all menfolk were supposed to be indoors.

Kil, youth with butter-bath body, eyes the blue of Homer's seas, in boxers patterned with Hell flames, rides a grey Australian pony—'a filly with a willy,' he calls her—into the Square Pond

'You could put that six pack in the fridge,' Figroll comments.

Three or four year old newts returned to the Square Pond in early

autumn. Crabs, lobsters here. Pike. 'Pike will bite your toes.'
Otters by the Scheme Bridge.
Otters are born blind, I tell Kil.
'No way.'
'Kil rode his bird in the canal once,' Figroll announces.

'I'm fishing for little, small roach,' Denone, half Traveller, half Costa
Rican, his mother's mother from North West Guanacaste region—
Spanish, Indian, Blacks brought to raise bananas.
    A bit like a Dundee cake himself—knobs of hair, nuts of
freckles.
    Denone caught an otter while fishing for pike. Snapped the line.
Otters have strong teeth.
    Pike here—freshwater shark, perch, roach, hybrids—roach and
bream mate. Tench only feed in summer. Go underwater in winter.
    Denone lived for a while at Pegham Copse near Colchester where
his father Pittir got a job welding gates and boxed with Three Finger
Jack White at Dummers Clump in Hampshire where that Ferguson
who went to Buckingham is from.
    Denone learns to box at Matthew's Boxing Club in Ballyfermot
and on his wall he has an advertisement for Brutal Nutrition, bare
breasted, putty-breasted ladies intermingled with boxers and the cap-
tion: 'The bad part was yesterday.'

    They have a game—tea bags.
    Older ones pin the younger ones on the ground and take their
genitals in their mouths.
    Young boys like the three puppies—mutts he called them—Tyr-
ian purple and an icense rising inside his vertically blue and white
striped hoodie jacket, which Figroll saved from being drowned in the
Grand Canal.
    'Do you want to buy one?'
    Some of the genitals are too small, the older boys complain.
    Genitals like beetroot leaf, like sweet pea, like the catkins of the
hazel tree.
    Female catkins of the alder tree are hard and cone-like in autumn
and maybe the small boys' penises are like that in the mouths of the

older boys.

Their grandfathers used to go bird-nesting—seek the buff eggs of the golden plover, the brown eggs of the lapwing, the whitish ones of the kestrel—pocaire gaoithe, windfucker—and perhaps the small boys' genitals were like these eggs in the mouth.

Figroll's grandfather Bomber Sheehan was in Artane Industrial School for joyriding at thirteen and he told Figroll about Dirty Hairy Sixpence who used to visit the school and get the boys to retrieve sixpences from down his trousers as if they were the Cleeve's toffees or Sweet Afton cigarettes thrown towards Artane boys in Croke Park.

'Sing a Song of Sixpence
A bag full of rye
Four and twenty naughty boys,
Bak'd in a pye . . .'

A small boy who looks like a garden gnome in tracksuit, puts his hands down his tracksuit bottoms, showing a Jacob's Coconut Cream-white belly.

Big Lips, silken blond turf with tramlines he gets in the barber's own home on Sundays, eyes the blue of a Bible picture Nile, after his breakfast of Weetabix Chocolate Chip Minis, rides Sweet Feet, his Lucozade-coloured mare to school, tethers it to the railings, then rides it home to a lunch of a potato, a scone, a Mr Kipling Chocolate Whirl.

In the evening by the Square Pond he makes sure Sweet Feet eats white cabbage and chopped carrots as a Victorian mother would make her children eat their porridge.

'The kids think they're Tony Montana in *Scarface.*

'In this country, you got to make the money first. Then when you make the money, you get the power. Then when you get the power, then you get the women.'

Angel Lips has blonde hair in Tyrolese pigtails, heavy doll eye make-up, green nail varnish, white plimsolls with billiard-green laces.

'You look like the fellow who robs gaffs in *Home Alone.* I love black babies. I'd love to have one. Black boys have big willies. I love

Akon. He's blacker than Soulja Boy.'

Risha, aged seventeen, margarine or jaundice colour running through her hair, zebra stripe boots, has her three-year-old son Lenzo's name in pillar tattoo on her wrist.

Lace, aged nineteen, Beaujolais Nouveau-coloured hair, has her six-year-old son Ezy's name in pillar tattoo on her neck.

The government is farming out the population.

She and Ezy are going to live on Holly Estate in Tralee.

'I give him the peanut butter with jelly in it.'

Bo, aged fifteen, features that look as if they'd been fastened together by safety pins, navy leggings with a pattern of rocking horses, is pregnant by Horsey and is going to live in Limerick. Mayross she calls Moyross for beautification.

'What do you work at?'

'Bits and pieces.'

'Bits and bobs. Are you on the buildings?'

'Are you on the scratcher?' Figroll cuts in, boxers with a pattern of Santa Claus hats showing above his trackie bottoms.

'Do you want that?' Boo asks. She offers me the butt of a cigarette.

Kissy, banana-blonde hair, who wears a yellow, red, blue, green rosary around her neck, found Cleo in Palmerston Woods. A Shetland pony with a ginger mane which made him look like a Billy boy. Sores all over her body from being whipped. Suffering from bog burn—hairs falling off from the mud. Took him to Figroll who has had horses all his life.

'Sold fifteen horses this week. In the fields and upland. Turned over fifteen grand.'

Figroll bought a Clydesdale from his father. Bred near the M1, North London. 'A Clydesdale out of England.' Sold it back to him.

'Have you ever been to the Appleby Fair?' I ask Figroll.

'I heard people get raped at Appleby. Boys and girls. On the hill where they camp.

If all the money was in England and there were no euros in Ireland, I wouldn't go to England.'

If you go into Palmerston Woods bring a stick in case a badger attacks you. If he attacks break the stick because he'll think that's a bone breaking. The badger will attack you until a bone in the ankle breaks.

Figroll was camping by Blessington Lakes once. There was an American pit bull on a leash there. A badger attacked Figroll. He threw a stick at it.

A miniature Jack Russell will shake a rat and break its neck if he catches it. But the badger will kill a Jack Russell.

Smelly John from Edmonton, a tomato-coloured laceration under his right eye, has half a black Border collie called Loo, blind in one eye, and a Santa Claus Pomeranian called Judge, who can combat badgers.

Twelve badgers live in Palmerston Woods and have built tunnels of escape there. I feel like them.

'You'd be better off in jail,' says Smelly John from Edmonton looking towards Wheatfield Prison where he spent time for staging American pit bull fights, 'Three square meals a day. Television. Snooker. Training courses. They treat you well if you belong to an illegal organisation. Catholic or Protestant. There are Orangemen in the South. There are Orangemen all over the South.

'There was a fellow there with the Orange lily and 1690 on his leg.'

'How's your love life?'

In winter twilight, a cilium of very yellow reed canary grass by the canal, Figroll suddenly pulls down his trackie bottoms.

'Is there a bruise on me arse?'

Donkey Lips, a jack rabbit in a scarlet Éire-Ireland T-shirt 2011, lights up the intense orifice with the light of his mobile phone, buttocks like the pronunciations on the heron's neck.

Dirck van Baburen couldn't have done better.

On a May evening when purple lilac is mixed with the hawthorn blossom, Figroll suddenly demonstrates his penis as if it was a machine.

His hair Easter chick yellow and barley, but an arc of a penis above eclipsed water-rat coloured pubes.

'Doesn't Figroll have a very big prick?' asks Tooler admiringly, eyes blue as Croagh Patrick, protean, early adolescent features, changed since autumn when his hair looked like a wren's nest stomped on his head, and he wore a wild bear colour anorak.

A baby bear escaped from Dublin zoo sixteen years ago and came to the Square Pond.

Figroll looks like one of the sons of Laocoön in the sculptural group which influenced Michelangelo, constrictor sea serpent from the Greek camp on the Island of Tenedos wound about date cluster genitals.

Laocoön was a priest of Troy who broke his vow of celibacy by begetting Antiphates and Thymbraeus and was punished for both.

Wooden horse built by Epeius, the master carpenter, so the Greeks could gain access to Troy.

Smithfield—cattle, hay market since 1664. Horses sold here since late 1800s. Everything sold here—ferrets, rats.

I'd seen the turnover in horses, the sudden rejection of paramour horses, the sallying to Smithfield Square which had been lined with farmyards until recently, to buy a new horse or exchange a horse with fifty euro in the difference.

'He doesn't sleep with his Mum and Dad. He's got a girlfriend. He fancies me. But he fancies you the same.'

Three Romany girls near me at Smithfield Market early March.

One in poinsettia red mini dress.

One with miniature melon picture hat as hair ornament.

One in denim hot pants with bib, and reflector yellow high heels.

One of the girl's fathers comes from England to sell rope harnesses here but his mother has settled in Kilmacthomas in County Waterford.

The girl's bodies have creosote oil on them used for railway sleepers, used for the wooden engine of the Bouncy Castle Rodeo Bull, the young, city centre based manager I'm talking to, horse at side, cartoon cowboy on it, which he brought to Appleby Fair, which he brought to the Horse Fair in the town I'm from, when the left arm of a youth—a koala bear, a brindled boxer dog, a tortoise shell butterfly in a black, white fur trimmed hoodie jacket—is slashed with a machete nearby.

'Sliced like an orange by a sword,' Tooler, whom I meet shortly afterwards, describes it.

Shots are fired from a makeshift gun, causing mayhem—lost purses, stolen horses—and a horse stampede, which looks like one of Michael Cimino's panoramas of the Wyoming Johnson War of the 1890s.

'Doesn't he have big balls?'

Tooler's older brother Fluffy, eyes the blue of a cornflower that has run away from home, in a jacket with a Native American horse at the back of it, pulls back the tail of a chestnut New Forest pony bought at Smithfield and walked home along the Grand Canal that Sunday when blows were rained with tyre irons.

'Indiana Jones,' he cries, riding away on the New Forest pony, recalling Indiana Jones riding a rhinoceros while chasing a truck in Africa.

'Did you sell any horses in Smithfield?' I ask Baz, a boy whose hair in autumn was chick feather light dun. Now it's turtle coloured. It grows on his head like a clump of chives from an old teapot. But his eyes are still the eyes of babyhood.

'No, I sold donkeys.'

The Jerusalem two-stroke Figroll calls a donkey.

Baz has a little donkey, Amy, from County Mayo, who looks as if snow has fallen on her and some of it turned to slush.

'You could get Channel Four on those ears,' extols Figroll.

In 1600 Cheapside vintner William Banks' bay gelding Marocco, shoed in silver, known to Shakespeare, Ben Jonson, Sir Walter Raleigh, Dekker, Rowley, Middleton, climbed to the top of Saint Paul's Cathedral, to the applause of braying donkeys.

Donkey Lips' eyes are a piñata—a children's party he doesn't want me to come to. When I ask the colour of his eyes and try to look at them he scrunches up his face like a scrolled baby's napkin.

'That's a weird question for these parts. Would you ask the Limerick boys what's the colour of their eyes?'

'I had to stop Donkey Lips from knifing you for asking the colour of his eyes,' Figroll warns me later.

Limerick boys . . .

When you've lived in a place for thirteen years, and you're suddenly driven out—the riverine haw, the sloes, the rosehips you miss, the riverside and companionable Travellers' horses.

The piebald horses had snowdrop white patches. Snowdrops the comfrey that came to the Shannon meadows in May was called.

The loss of a child is a terrible thing; the loss of children (plural) is even more terrible. The loss of a community of children is devastating.

In exile though you remember your friends, their faces . . .

Remembering them, their kindness, remembering the river, gives you fortitude and resolve . . .

Laocoön and Cassandra, priest and priestess of Troy gave their oracles and were not believed.

Laocoön tried to set the wooden horse on fire.

He threw a spear at it.

A few days after that Sunday at Smithfield someone comes to the Square Pond and shoots Big Lips' mare Sweet Feet in the head just as she is about to have a foal. Foal comes out anyway and Big Lips starts hand-feeding it.

It is like the story of Jane Seymour and Edward VI.

'King Henry, King Henry, I know you to be:
Pray cut my side open and find my baby.'

Then the Pound, in apparent retaliation for the violence of a Traveller family who got to a Traveller family they were feuding with, in a wooden horse, swoops.

Eighteen horses and four donkeys driven down fields to field owned by NAMA. National Asset Management Agency.

Horsey's stallion Flash hides in the osiers and escapes.

Five days to claim them. They are kept twenty-eight days. 'Pound said it all cost thirty-eight grand.'

Figroll, Horsey, Kil, Fluffy, Tooler, Big Lips, Donkey Lips, Denone, Eak go to the Council Offices in Tallaght to plead, led by

Skaf, a youth in his twenties, woollen hat making his eyes look troglodyte, buried. But it's like chasing the tooth fairy. Figroll's mother, whose medication for migraine is wearing the calcium on her teeth, rings up. The horses and donkeys are dead.

Figroll tells me that the horses from the Traveller Site at Fonthill Road—where a Traveller man with hair dyed the red of Danny Kaye had asked me one day: 'Did you get married yet?'—were brought to Kinnegad, County Westmeath, put down, burned in the cement factory.

'They give horse meat to feed tigers in the zoo, to dog food factories, they give the dead horses to glue factories.'

Two youths from Ballymun sit on the edge of the almost deserted Smithfield Plaza towards the end of the fair, like herons waiting in unison by the Grand Canal. Horses are confiscated at Smithfield now, that don't have a horse passport or don't have a microchip, so there is a samizdat horse fair on the top of Chapelizod Hill.

'I'll give you a thousand euros now and the rest in Coolock.'

Someone rings up the Joe Duffy show to say the Scheme boys were cruel to horses and deserved the horses and donkeys being taken. The boys are convinced it was me. Identical voice.

'Didn't you ring up the Joe Duffy show and say we were cruelty to horses?' Figroll accuses.

'Two English people went to Coolock and asked to see the horses. Then the Pound came.'

Surrounded by boys, some like the wolf of Gubbio with a stud in its ear, some with a caduceus—staff of Mercury—by a torched Go-Kart, I am made to feel like Gypo Nolan in John Ford's film, who is taunted by a prostitute during the War of Independence because he doesn't have the fare to the USA, accepts a British award leading to the arrest of his friend Frankie McPhillip, revealing Frankie's whereabouts, seeks expiation in Dublin's churches, tried in secret by his former comrades, shot.

It was no use denying I'd rung up the Joe Duffy show. I had to accept it though it wasn't true, and go through a period of vilification.

'Paedo. Faggot. Rat. You egg. You fuel. You did the monkey.

What's the colour of your eyes? I'll buy you a pair of socks.'

Figroll gets a replacement horse, a skewbald from the Leitrim mountains with white fur like a goose's feathers.
'A psycho horse.'
'He's a spirit. Mad as a brush. Mad as a fork. Mad as a spoon.'
I feel like that horse, on the ground by the Square Pond, head tethered by many ropes held by the youths, beaten on the face with a fleecey butter-green poplar bough by Figroll until the blood runs from his face and mouth, thought to have expired, rising, standing, anticipating further blows.

Banger, a Chihuahua of a boy, hair as black as the black of a chess board, eyebrows like black sickle moons, cherry cordial lips, cheekbones scalloped like a holy water font, runs excitedly in the middle of this entertainment as a moorhen hobbles in the fields.

Banger has two bracelets of miniature ikons, one large, one smaller, dominant ikon in large one that of a Christ who looks like Tony Montana in *Scarface*.
'Where did you get the bracelet?'
'In Lourdes.'
'When were you in Lourdes?'
'I wasn't. My nanny was. Where's yours?'
Figroll has two similar bracelets. One a Gypsy woman had given him in town. 'She only gives them to special people.' One the Leitrim owner of the skewbald had given him for luck.

In identical magenta tracksuits, two girls smoke cigarettes on the gate, but with the look of Martha and Abby Brewster, the two spinster aunts in *Arsenic and Old Lace*, before they poison one of their gentlemen victims with elderberry wine laced with arsenic, strychnine, cyanide.

Suddenly one of them screams.
'He did a shit.'
Horsey emerges from behind the hawthorn bushes, carrying a stick with excrement at the end, and goes in the direction of the girls. Excrement gets on the white jackets he's carrying. He looks to the Grand Canal for a solution.

The Pound strike again, confiscating the Leitrim skewbald, and that is the finish for me. 'You were a spy from the SPCA.'

Fluffy in a hoodie jacket patterned with skulls tries to tether my bicycle to an elder tree. Figroll simultaneously tries to wrest the bicycle from me.

'I was fond of you,' I plead.

I want to say you and the other boys came into my life in a wooden horse.

I wanted to say I'd known a wooden horse since childhood. The Horse Fair in my town was a wooden horse in which people who were different came.

Thomas Omer started building the Grand Canal in 1757. One of his houses is by the twelfth lock with Deadly Nightshade on the other side of the canal. The twelfth lock was built too narrow on the Dublin side. It had to be widened. The mares and foals among the ragwort by the twelfth lock know not to eat it because of its poisonous juices.

The Grand Canal was built with gunpowder, picks, shovels, candles.

Horses used to draw barges by the canal. That's why the boys claimed in Tallaght Council Offices they had a right to own horses.

'Have you ever heard the expression "Keep on the straight and the narrow"?' Kil asked me one day, in Bermudas patterned with Brazil nuts, 'It comes from the Grand Canal. The long barges were pulled by a horse on a straight and narrow path. The path had to be straight and narrow to keep the tension of the barge.'

Getting across the Bog of Allen took five years.

They got to Daingean—Philipstown after Queen Mary's Spanish husband ('My marriage is my own affair.')—where there was another reformatory school. I knew someone who was turned barefoot out of it.

Then the canal extended to Shannon Harbour. An extension beyond the Shannon to the town I'm from.

There was a Guinness depot there. Coffee Bradley, a Somme veteran, came down the Grand Canal in a Guinness barge, as King of the Horse Fair, like Elizabeth I sailing down the River Effra to visit Sir Walter Raleigh at Raleigh Hall, who mentioned Banks' horse Marocca in his History of the World.

Redser Lardon's mother used to walk an armada of cocker spaniels, Chinese pug dogs, Welsh corgis around town. She usually wore an olive and beige scarf at her neck. They lived in a Regency town house with moss coloured door, lead lights over door, foot scraper by door.

He suffered from Down syndrome.

When I used to be hitchhiking outside town, close to the Church of Our Lady of Lourdes, he'd stop and talk. Always wore a belted great coat. Strawey cockscomb. Would shuffle and snort with laughter. Sometimes carried *Eagle* and *Beano* comics and would engage you in conversation about Dan Dare or Walter the Softy. Inference was that I was a bit of a Walter the Softy.

'What goes around, comes around,' he'd say.

When his mother died he drowned himself in the Grand Canal.

'I liked you too,' Figroll says—he's in a squirrel-coloured hoodie jacket, 'but I think there's something weird about you.

'What makes you wet the bed? Are you a steamer? Will you steam with me? I'm fast on bald men. I went with Baldy Paddy Beatley.'

Baldy Paddy Beatley let four dogs go wild in the fields.

A lurcher (greyhound/deerhound), face of a patterdale.

Whippy—cross Labrador, Staffordshire terrier, with carrion skin.

Greyhound/Irish deerhound/Saluki (Arab hunting dog), bit of Bedlington.

A dog he called a lurcher but with its fur looked like soaked breadcrumbs.

'If they attack you you put your finger up their arse,' Tooler had advised me.

'He was bareback.'

Naked, Baldy Paddy Beatley had crow-coloured hairs all over his body, his body looked like a potato field covered with crows.

'Baldy Paddy Beatley used to box. His favourite punch was backhand. I was a whippet he said. I'm not eighteen anymore. I've no fucking teeth.

He said he boxed with two Knackers from Mullingar who went on to the Olympic Games. The Knackers in Mullingar stand fifty feet apart from one another and throw things at one another he said.'

Figroll flings an empty Perlenbacher bottle at me.

'Baldy Paddy Beatley has his woolly hat pulled over his eyes. Like a real paedo. Why don't you pull your hat over your eyes?'

'It's either in you or it isn't. It's a tradition. The horses are more like dogs. Come to the door in this weather.' The snowmen in the Scheme look more like crazy banshees than snowmen. 'They come home. The scatter-brained ones won't.'

Sometimes when I wake up at night or can't sleep it's as if a horse comes to the door. A horse that's been put down. A youth's face like one of the ghosts of horses on the walls of Trois Frères. An asymmetrical henna-coloured horse like one of the horses on the walls of Lascaux. The prehistoric white horse carved on top of the Berkshire Downs at Uffington. The horse presented as gift by King Oswin that Saint Aidan of Lindisfarne—whose bones were brought back to Galway by his successor Colman—immediately gave to a poor man.

Near Lindisfarne in Northumberland there's a poppy field.

An autobiography-writing horse like the disabled Anna Sewell's Black Beauty.

'Boys you see think a horse is like a steam engine or a thrashing machine, and can go as long and as fast as they please; they never think that a pony can get tired, or have feelings.'

William Banks' gelding Marocco who was possibly burned by the Inquisition with his master in Rome or Lisbon.

The kissing and counting mare Samuel Pepys saw at Bartholomew Fair on a September day on which he was later invited by a wench to her room in Shoe Lane.

The horse on which the actor Edmund Keane, as a boy, dressed as a monkey, used to do somersaults on at Bartholomew Fair and fell off, damaging both legs.

Begun in the early Middle Ages Bartholomew Fair in West Smithfield in London—Ruffians Hall—where men fought with sword and buckler for twelve pence, was suppressed by the Victorians on the grounds of debauchery.

'. . . it causeth swearing, it causeth swaggering, it causeth snuffling and snarling, and now and then a hurt . . . Hide, and be hidden; ride and be ridden, says the vapour of experience . . .'

When Ben Jonson's work failed elsewhere he turned to the expensive, private theatres where only young boys acted.

A wooden horse comes to my door—a youth in a hoodie jacket with hair over his mouth the colour of Biblical dates who turned into a wooden horse.

Wreathes by the Grand Canal change from white to electric blue, from poly-colours to white and scarlet, scarlet of blood, scarlet of poinsettia wreathes of New Orleans.

A girl with geyser hair-style, crimson on top, cerulean cord around her hair, kneels by the Grand Canal and weeps for her brother as the sun sets.

I take her hand.

'It was just a stupid accident.'

'I've suffered too,' I tell her. 'I know what it's like.'

'There are no cash machines in graveyards,' says Mad Mickey Teeling, 'Spend what you have now.'

Mad Mickey Teeling wears a cap covered in badges—Martin Doherty killed Ardoyne Belfast, James Larkin, James Connolly, Che Guevara, nine Hunger Strikers ('one missing,' he apologizes), the Irish colours and also a 1960 halfpenny on it.

He has a Central Asian shepherd dog called Eric.

'You get ten years for robbing a shop,' he complains, 'but paedophiles only get two. The priest who baptised me and married my parents molested children.'

The horses were their imagination, the horses were narratives, the horses were anthropoid like Dumbo the flying elephant and his one friend Timothy Mouse, or like Anna Sewell's Black Beauty, Ginger, Merrylegs.

'Can you remember Black Beauty's friend's name?' Figroll asked me one day.

He hadn't read the book but he'd seen the film where Black Beauty narrated his story voice-over.

'Ginger? Merrylegs?'

Hash dipped in acid, hash with melted down glass dipped in diesel, Kepplers cider, house music.

Monksfield after ten when the off-licences close, the guards coming looking for them.

Dumbo was taunted by the other elephants because he had big ears. Mrs Jumbo, his mother, was locked up as a mad woman for defending her child. Dumbo was forced to be a circus clown who has to fall into a vat of pie filling. With the help of his friend Timothy Mouse and some crows Dumbo discovered his ability to fly because of his big ears and he became a circus celebrity.

There was a circus in the field opposite the Jensen Hotel and Shell garage.

They wanted Mad Mickey Teeling's Central Asian shepherd dog when he brought it to the circus grounds.

'He can be a cunt. You'd want to see the hiding I gave him,' he told them to put them off.

A man with a belly like a plum pudding with cream on top, asked the boys to distribute circus leaflets with the motorbike globe of death on them, and when their task was done, as the circus lights turned from yellow to red to aquamarine to purple, as the jungle drums beat within the tent, had sex with some of them.

Figroll smoked three joints one morning, took twenty-four-hour pills, drank a bottle of Huzzar vodka, stole a scarlet, white and yellow Honda CO 21.

'A horse must have jumped on it.'

Set it on fire in Brennan's Field.

'I was on a buzz. I pissed on my mobile. You could see the piss on the screen.'

In Ireland in the nineteenth century it was believed that the song thrush built its nest cup of leaves and twigs, lined with mud, low in trees and bushes so the fairies in their houses in the grass could enjoy their music. But this did not prevent Figroll from telling a song thrush in Brennan's Field, 'Shut your fucking mouth.'

'Someone snitched on me. I was crying when I got to the police station. It takes a big man to say sorry and Figroll says sorry.'

Pinocchio's nose grew longer when he lied. The moustaches or lip growth on boys in Oberstown Boys Centre where Figroll was sent told you they'd committed a crime. Figroll joined the boys with faces pale as mousetrap cheese, youths you would formerly see at Smithfield Horse Fair; anxious to sell horses, with a half-starved look, knifed cheeks.

'Now farewell to the Faire . . .'

City of exile, city of loneliness.

I live in a world without stories. Without friends.

Diogenes of Greece walked the street with a lighted candle looking for a human being.

I feel like him.

Seven doomed horses and a donkey from Mayo sequestering themselves under the trees, at different angles from one another, nosing one another.

There's something very human about horses.

They tried to stop my heart the way they stop horses' hearts, giving them an injection.

'Love is boat that swim for most,' says Bo, in a leopard spot top with bare midriff, before she leaves for Moyross, Limerick, holding a baby like a marshmallow hedgehog in a fluffy jacket.

'What leave ye to your father, King Henry, my son?
The keys of old Ireland, and all that's therein . . .'

DESMOND HOGAN was born in Ballinasloe, Ireland. He has published five novels as well as several books of stories and a collection of selected travel and review pieces. In 1971 he won the Hennessy Award, and in 1977 the Rooney Prize for Literature. He won the John Llewellyn Rhys Memorial Prize in 1980 and was awarded a DAAD Fellowship in Berlin in 1991.

MICHAL AJVAZ, *The Golden Age.*
  The Other City.
PIERRE ALBERT-BIROT, *Grabinoulor.*
YUZ ALESHKOVSKY, *Kangaroo.*
FELIPE ALFAU, *Chromos.*
  Locos.
IVAN ÂNGELO, *The Celebration.*
  The Tower of Glass.
ANTÓNIO LOBO ANTUNES, *Knowledge of Hell.*
  The Splendor of Portugal.
ALAIN ARIAS-MISSON, *Theatre of Incest.*
JOHN ASHBERY AND JAMES SCHUYLER,
  A Nest of Ninnies.
ROBERT ASHLEY, *Perfect Lives.*
GABRIELA AVIGUR-ROTEM, *Heatwave*
  and Crazy Birds.
DJUNA BARNES, *Ladies Almanack.*
  Ryder.
JOHN BARTH, *LETTERS.*
  Sabbatical.
DONALD BARTHELME, *The King.*
  Paradise.
SVETISLAV BASARA, *Chinese Letter.*
MIQUEL BAUÇA, *The Siege in the Room.*
RENÉ BELLETTO, *Dying.*
MAREK BIEŃCZYK, *Transparency.*
ANDREI BITOV, *Pushkin House.*
ANDREJ BLATNIK, *You Do Understand.*
LOUIS PAUL BOON, *Chapel Road.*
  My Little War.
  Summer in Termuren.
ROGER BOYLAN, *Killoyle.*
IGNÁCIO DE LOYOLA BRANDÃO,
  Anonymous Celebrity.
  Zero.
BONNIE BREMSER, *Troia: Mexican Memoirs.*
CHRISTINE BROOKE-ROSE, *Amalgamemnon.*
BRIGID BROPHY, *In Transit.*
GERALD L. BRUNS, *Modern Poetry and*
  the Idea of Language.
GABRIELLE BURTON, *Heartbreak Hotel.*
MICHEL BUTOR, *Degrees.*
  Mobile.
G. CABRERA INFANTE, *Infante's Inferno.*
  Three Trapped Tigers.
JULIETA CAMPOS,
  The Fear of Losing Eurydice.
ANNE CARSON, *Eros the Bittersweet.*
ORLY CASTEL-BLOOM, *Dolly City.*
LOUIS-FERDINAND CÉLINE, *Castle to Castle.*
  Conversations with Professor Y.
  London Bridge.
  Normance.
  North.
  Rigadoon.
MARIE CHAIX, *The Laurels of Lake Constance.*
HUGO CHARTERIS, *The Tide Is Right.*
ERIC CHEVILLARD, *Demolishing Nisard.*
MARC CHOLODENKO, *Mordechai Schamz.*
JOSHUA COHEN, *Witz.*
EMILY HOLMES COLEMAN, *The Shutter*
  of Snow.
ROBERT COOVER, *A Night at the Movies.*
STANLEY CRAWFORD, *Log of the S.S. The*
  Mrs Unguentine.
  Some Instructions to My Wife.
RENÉ CREVEL, *Putting My Foot in It.*
RALPH CUSACK, *Cadenza.*
NICHOLAS DELBANCO, *The Count of Concord.*
  Sherbrookes.
NIGEL DENNIS, *Cards of Identity.*

PETER DIMOCK, *A Short Rhetoric for*
  Leaving the Family.
ARIEL DORFMAN, *Konfidenz.*
COLEMAN DOWELL,
  Island People.
  Too Much Flesh and Jabez.
ARKADII DRAGOMOSHCHENKO, *Dust.*
RIKKI DUCORNET, *The Complete*
  Butcher's Tales.
  The Fountains of Neptune.
  The Jade Cabinet.
  Phosphor in Dreamland.
WILLIAM EASTLAKE, *The Bamboo Bed.*
  Castle Keep.
  Lyric of the Circle Heart.
JEAN ECHENOZ, *Chopin's Move.*
STANLEY ELKIN, *A Bad Man.*
  Criers and Kibitzers, Kibitzers
  and Criers.
  The Dick Gibson Show.
  The Franchiser.
  The Living End.
  Mrs. Ted Bliss.
FRANÇOIS EMMANUEL, *Invitation to a*
  Voyage.
SALVADOR ESPRIU, *Ariadne in the*
  Grotesque Labyrinth.
LESLIE A. FIEDLER, *Love and Death in*
  the American Novel.
JUAN FILLOY, *Op Oloop.*
ANDY FITCH, *Pop Poetics.*
GUSTAVE FLAUBERT, *Bouvard and Pécuchet.*
KASS FLEISHER, *Talking out of School.*
FORD MADOX FORD,
  The March of Literature.
JON FOSSE, *Aliss at the Fire.*
  Melancholy.
MAX FRISCH, *I'm Not Stiller.*
  Man in the Holocene.
CARLOS FUENTES, *Christopher Unborn.*
  Distant Relations.
  Terra Nostra.
  Where the Air Is Clear.
TAKEHIKO FUKUNAGA, *Flowers of Grass.*
WILLIAM GADDIS, *J R.*
  The Recognitions.
JANICE GALLOWAY, *Foreign Parts.*
  The Trick Is to Keep Breathing.
WILLIAM H. GASS, *Cartesian Sonata*
  and Other Novellas.
  Finding a Form.
  A Temple of Texts.
  The Tunnel.
  Willie Masters' Lonesome Wife.
GÉRARD GAVARRY, *Hoppla! 1 2 3.*
ETIENNE GILSON,
  The Arts of the Beautiful.
  Forms and Substances in the Arts.
C. S. GISCOMBE, *Giscome Road.*
  Here.
DOUGLAS GLOVER, *Bad News of the Heart.*
WITOLD GOMBROWICZ,
  A Kind of Testament.
PAULO EMÍLIO SALES GOMES, *P's Three*
  Women.
GEORGI GOSPODINOV, *Natural Novel.*
JUAN GOYTISOLO, *Count Julian.*
  Juan the Landless.
  Makbara.
  Marks of Identity.

HENRY GREEN, *Back.*
Blindness.
Concluding.
Doting.
Nothing.
JACK GREEN, *Fire the Bastards!*
JIŘÍ GRUŠA, *The Questionnaire.*
MELA HARTWIG, *Am I a Redundant
   Human Being?*
JOHN HAWKES, *The Passion Artist.*
Whistlejacket.
ELIZABETH HEIGHWAY, ED., *Contemporary
   Georgian Fiction.*
ALEKSANDAR HEMON, ED.,
   Best European Fiction.
AIDAN HIGGINS, *Balcony of Europe.*
Blind Man's Bluff
Bornholm Night-Ferry.
Flotsam and Jetsam.
Langrishe, Go Down.
Scenes from a Receding Past.
KEIZO HINO, *Isle of Dreams.*
KAZUSHI HOSAKA, *Plainsong.*
ALDOUS HUXLEY, *Antic Hay.*
Crome Yellow.
Point Counter Point.
Those Barren Leaves.
Time Must Have a Stop.
NAOYUKI II, *The Shadow of a Blue Cat.*
GERT JONKE, *The Distant Sound.*
Geometric Regional Novel.
Homage to Czerny.
The System of Vienna.
JACQUES JOUET, *Mountain R.*
Savage.
Upstaged.
MIEKO KANAI, *The Word Book.*
YORAM KANIUK, *Life on Sandpaper.*
HUGH KENNER, *Flaubert.*
Joyce and Beckett: The Stoic Comedians.
Joyce's Voices.
DANILO KIŠ, *The Attic.*
Garden, Ashes.
The Lute and the Scars
Psalm 44.
A Tomb for Boris Davidovich.
ANITA KONKKA, *A Fool's Paradise.*
GEORGE KONRÁD, *The City Builder.*
TADEUSZ KONWICKI, *A Minor Apocalypse.*
The Polish Complex.
MENIS KOUMANDAREAS, *Koula.*
ELAINE KRAF, *The Princess of 72nd Street.*
JIM KRUSOE, *Iceland.*
AYŞE KULIN, *Farewell: A Mansion in
   Occupied Istanbul.*
EMILIO LASCANO TEGUI, *On Elegance
   While Sleeping.*
ERIC LAURRENT, *Do Not Touch.*
VIOLETTE LEDUC, *La Bâtarde.*
EDOUARD LEVÉ, *Autoportrait.*
Suicide.
MARIO LEVI, *Istanbul Was a Fairy Tale.*
DEBORAH LEVY, *Billy and Girl.*
JOSÉ LEZAMA LIMA, *Paradiso.*
ROSA LIKSOM, *Dark Paradise.*
OSMAN LINS, *Avalovara.*
The Queen of the Prisons of Greece.
ALF MAC LOCHLAINN,
The Corpus in the Library.
Out of Focus.
RON LOEWINSOHN, *Magnetic Field(s).*
MINA LOY, *Stories and Essays of Mina Loy.*

D. KEITH MANO, *Take Five.*
MICHELINE AHARONIAN MARCOM,
The Mirror in the Well.
BEN MARCUS,
The Age of Wire and String.
WALLACE MARKFIELD,
Teitlebaum's Window.
To an Early Grave.
DAVID MARKSON, *Reader's Block.*
Wittgenstein's Mistress.
CAROLE MASO, *AVA.*
LADISLAV MATEJKA AND KRYSTYNA
   POMORSKA, EDS.,
*Readings in Russian Poetics:
   Formalist and Structuralist Views.*
HARRY MATHEWS, *Cigarettes.*
The Conversions.
*The Human Country: New and
   Collected Stories.*
The Journalist.
My Life in CIA.
Singular Pleasures.
*The Sinking of the Odradek
   Stadium.*
Tlooth.
JOSEPH MCELROY,
Night Soul and Other Stories.
ABDELWAHAB MEDDEB, *Talismano.*
GERHARD MEIER, *Isle of the Dead.*
HERMAN MELVILLE, *The Confidence-Man.*
AMANDA MICHALOPOULOU, *I'd Like.*
STEVEN MILLHAUSER, *The Barnum Museum.*
In the Penny Arcade.
RALPH J. MILLS, JR., *Essays on Poetry.*
MOMUS, *The Book of Jokes.*
CHRISTINE MONTALBETTI, *The Origin of Man.*
Western.
OLIVE MOORE, *Spleen.*
NICHOLAS MOSLEY, *Accident.*
Assassins.
Catastrophe Practice.
Experience and Religion.
A Garden of Trees.
Hopeful Monsters.
Imago Bird.
Impossible Object.
Inventing God.
Judith.
Look at the Dark.
Natalie Natalia.
Serpent.
Time at War.
WARREN MOTTE,
*Fables of the Novel: French Fiction
   since 1990.*
*Fiction Now: The French Novel in
   the 21st Century.*
*Oulipo: A Primer of Potential
   Literature.*
GERALD MURNANE, *Barley Patch.*
Inland.
YVES NAVARRE, *Our Share of Time.*
Sweet Tooth.
DOROTHY NELSON, *In Night's City.*
Tar and Feathers.
ESHKOL NEVO, *Homesick.*
WILFRIDO D. NOLLEDO, *But for the Lovers.*
FLANN O'BRIEN, *At Swim-Two-Birds.*
The Best of Myles.
The Dalkey Archive.
The Hard Life.
The Poor Mouth.

FOR A FULL LIST OF PUBLICATIONS, VISIT:
www.dalkeyarchive.com

The Third Policeman.
CLAUDE OLLIER, *The Mise-en-Scène.*
Wert and the Life Without End.
GIOVANNI ORELLI, *Walaschek's Dream.*
PATRIK OUŘEDNÍK, *Europeana.*
The Opportune Moment, 1855.
BORIS PAHOR, *Necropolis.*
FERNANDO DEL PASO, *News from the Empire.*
Palinuro of Mexico.
ROBERT PINGET, *The Inquisitory.*
Mahu or The Material.
Trio.
MANUEL PUIG, *Betrayed by Rita Hayworth.*
The Buenos Aires Affair.
Heartbreak Tango.
RAYMOND QUENEAU, *The Last Days.*
Odile.
Pierrot Mon Ami.
Saint Glinglin.
ANN QUIN, *Berg.*
Passages.
Three.
Tripticks.
ISHMAEL REED, *The Free-Lance Pallbearers.*
The Last Days of Louisiana Red.
Ishmael Reed: The Plays.
Juice!
Reckless Eyeballing.
The Terrible Threes.
The Terrible Twos.
Yellow Back Radio Broke-Down.
JASIA REICHARDT, *15 Journeys Warsaw*
to London.
NOËLLE REVAZ, *With the Animals.*
JOÃO UBALDO RIBEIRO, *House of the*
Fortunate Buddhas.
JEAN RICARDOU, *Place Names.*
RAINER MARIA RILKE, *The Notebooks of*
Malte Laurids Brigge.
JULIÁN RÍOS, *The House of Ulysses.*
Larva: A Midsummer Night's Babel.
Poundemonium.
Procession of Shadows.
AUGUSTO ROA BASTOS, *I the Supreme.*
DANIËL ROBBERECHTS, *Arriving in Avignon.*
JEAN ROLIN, *The Explosion of the*
Radiator Hose.
OLIVIER ROLIN, *Hotel Crystal.*
ALIX CLEO ROUBAUD, *Alix's Journal.*
JACQUES ROUBAUD, *The Form of a*
City Changes Faster, Alas, Than
the Human Heart.
The Great Fire of London.
Hortense in Exile.
Hortense Is Abducted.
The Loop.
Mathematics:
The Plurality of Worlds of Lewis.
The Princess Hoppy.
Some Thing Black.
RAYMOND ROUSSEL, *Impressions of Africa.*
VEDRANA RUDAN, *Night.*
STIG SÆTERBAKKEN, *Siamese.*
Self Control.
LYDIE SALVAYRE, *The Company of Ghosts.*
The Lecture.
The Power of Flies.
LUIS RAFAEL SÁNCHEZ,
Macho Camacho's Beat.
SEVERO SARDUY, *Cobra* & *Maitreya.*

NATHALIE SARRAUTE,
Do You Hear Them?
Martereau.
The Planetarium.
ARNO SCHMIDT, *Collected Novellas.*
Collected Stories.
Nobodaddy's Children.
Two Novels.
ASAF SCHURR, *Motti.*
GAIL SCOTT, *My Paris.*
DAMION SEARLS, *What We Were Doing*
and Where We Were Going.
JUNE AKERS SEESE,
Is This What Other Women Feel Too?
What Waiting Really Means.
BERNARD SHARE, *Inish.*
Transit.
VIKTOR SHKLOVSKY, *Bowstring.*
Knight's Move.
A Sentimental Journey:
Memoirs 1917–1922.
Energy of Delusion: A Book on Plot.
Literature and Cinematography.
Theory of Prose.
Third Factory.
Zoo, or Letters Not about Love.
PIERRE SINIAC, *The Collaborators.*
KJERSTI A. SKOMSVOLD, *The Faster I Walk,*
the Smaller I Am.
JOSEF ŠKVORECKÝ, *The Engineer of*
Human Souls.
GILBERT SORRENTINO,
Aberration of Starlight.
Blue Pastoral.
Crystal Vision.
Imaginative Qualities of Actual
Things.
Mulligan Stew.
Pack of Lies.
Red the Fiend.
The Sky Changes.
Something Said.
Splendide-Hôtel.
Steelwork.
Under the Shadow.
W. M. SPACKMAN, *The Complete Fiction.*
ANDRZEJ STASIUK, *Dukla.*
Fado.
GERTRUDE STEIN, *The Making of Americans.*
A Novel of Thank You.
LARS SVENDSEN, *A Philosophy of Evil.*
PIOTR SZEWC, *Annihilation.*
GONÇALO M. TAVARES, *Jerusalem.*
Joseph Walser's Machine.
Learning to Pray in the Age of
Technique.
LUCIAN DAN TEODOROVICI,
Our Circus Presents . . .
NIKANOR TERATOLOGEN, *Assisted Living.*
STEFAN THEMERSON, *Hobson's Island.*
The Mystery of the Sardine.
Tom Harris.
TAEKO TOMIOKA, *Building Waves.*
JOHN TOOMEY, *Sleepwalker.*
JEAN-PHILIPPE TOUSSAINT, *The Bathroom.*
Camera.
Monsieur.
Reticence.
Running Away.
Self-Portrait Abroad.
Television.
The Truth about Marie.